JUSTICE FOR HIRE

THE PRIVATE EYE WRITERS OF AMERICA
ANTHOLOGIES

JUSTICE FOR HIRE

The FOURTH PRIVATE eye WRITERS of AMERICA ANTHOLOGY

Edited by

ROBERT J. RANDISI

THE MYSTERIOUS PRESS

New York • London

Tokyo • Sweden • Milan

Contents

JUSTICE FOR HIRE

Introduction

Collecting stories for and editing an anthology can be tedious. Ask the anthology masters—Edward D. Hoch, Martin H. Greenberg, Bill Pronzini—and they will tell you it is so in most cases.

Not for me, though. My formula is simple. Deal with the very best writers in the business, and ask for brand-new stories. Each of the PWA anthologies has been a collection of original stories. Some of the names are the same—Max Allan Collins, Loren D. Estleman, John Lutz, and Bill Pronzini have been in all four books. Some are familiar— Lawrence Block, Michael Collins, Marcia Muller, Wayne D. Dundee, and Dick Stodghill appear for a second time. And invariably, I manage to convince someone who has never contributed to give us a try—like Jeremiah Healy, Julie Smith, James Ellroy, and W. R. Philbrick. From time to time I'm even able to persuade writers who have never tried the short story form before to give it a shot; this class is represented here by Michael Allegretto and Paul Engleman.

The result—as with the previous three PWA anthologies—is a fine mix of writers with different styles, lending their own special brand of talent and their own fresh outlook to the P.I. story.

1

With every PWA anthology, some—if not all—of the contributors manage to stretch the form to some degree. That can't be done with reprint anthologies. Let me clearly state that I am not denigrating reprint anthologies; let's face it, *most* anthologies are reprint. But it's the degree of originality inherent in writing a *new* story *specifically* for a private eye collection that makes these PWA anthologies special to read, and a pleasure to edit.

The P.I. story is alive and well, prospering in the typewriters and computers of some of the best writers in the world.

Just take a look.

Bob Randisi
Brooklyn, N.Y.
November 1989

Denver-based P.I. Jacob Lomax has appeared in three novels to date, the first of which, Death on the Rocks, *won Michael Allegretto the Shamus Award that year for best first novel. We are proud to say that "The Bookie's Daughter" is Lomax's first short story appearance. Although it appears here after the publication of the third Lomax novel,* The Dead of Winter, *it was the basis for that book.*

The Bookie's Daughter

by Michael Allegretto

M y daughter's been . . . kidnapped," the woman said, struggling with her words.

Her name was Angela Dardano. She was an attractive woman, about forty, with black hair streaked with gray and hardly any makeup. She'd unbuttoned her coat and removed her gloves before she'd sat in the visitors' chair. Her hands were in her lap, clinging to each other.

"Have you been to the police?" I asked.

"No."

"You know, private eyes deal with runaway kids, not kidnapped kids."

"I can't go to the police."

"Why not?"

"Please . . . don't you want to hear about my daughter?"

I started to answer, but the radiator banged loud enough to interrupt me. It was the last day of November, and Denver was in the hard, icy grip of winter. My office was warm, but the pipes sometimes drowned out conversation and usually leaked enough to fog the windows.

3

"Sorry," I said, meaning the pipes. "When was your daughter taken?"

"The day before yesterday. Gloria goes—that's her name, Gloria; it was my grandmother's name—Gloria goes to college at Auraria. She's a freshman, and she's a real good student, she . . ." Mrs. Dardano sucked in her breath and looked away, fighting back the tears.

"Would you like some coffee?" I asked. "Or maybe something stronger?"

She shook her head no. Her eyes were moist and her bottom lip trembled, but she refused to cry.

"Gloria takes the bus to and from school," she said, her voice quavering. "She always gets home by three or four in the afternoon. When she didn't come home the day before yesterday, Joseph and I called the school, and then her friends, and everyone else we could think of."

"Except the police."

She nodded.

"You know," I said, trying not to sound too blasé, "sometimes kids take off just for the hell of it and don't bother to tell anyone, not even their parents."

Mrs. Dardano fumbled in her purse. She came out with a folded sheet of ruled notepaper, opened it, and handed it across my desk. Printed in pencil in block letters, all caps, was the message:

IF YOU WANT TO SEE GLORIA AGAIN DONT TESTIFY. NO COPS EITHER OR SHES DEAD.

"That was in our mailbox yesterday morning," she said.

"I see. And what does this mean, 'don't testify'?"

"That's meant for Joseph."

I handed her back the note, which she tucked in her purse as carefully as if it were a letter from the old country.

"My husband was arrested last week, Mr. Lomax," she said. "For bookmaking. He's had the same barbershop for almost thirty years, and he's run a little book out of there for almost as long. But it's mostly for friends, you know? Friends and customers. It doesn't hurt anybody. It's just to help pay the bills. Anyhow, he's one of the ones that got raided last week."

I'd been reading about the city's current "sweep of illegal gambling." It was a joint operation of local and federal authorities, and it happened every ten years or so, whenever some civic group got up on its hind legs and demanded that the city be rid of gambling, never mind that the sports pages of both local papers listed the point-spread for every baseball, basketball, and football game in the country, pro *and* college. The cops had rounded up twenty or so bookies, most of whom also operated legitimate businesses, and were going to parade them in front of a grand jury starting next week. It was more show than substance, and no one expected the bookies to get more than small fines and slaps on their wrists.

"Joseph's been out on bond since the arrest," Mrs. Dardano said, "but if he refuses to testify next week, he'll go right back to jail, and after that they'll . . . they'll send him to prison."

She was probably right. The Feds would not take kindly to those refusing to testify. They'd consider them to be hard cases, and the Feds hated hard cases. It made *them* look soft. And it made them act hard. It had nothing to do with the law; it had to do with human nature.

"Joseph doesn't know I'm here," she said. "I got your name through a friend." She told me who. He was also a bookie. *My* bookie, in fact, and he still owed me a hundred and a half. "Joseph's prepared to go to jail to save Gloria," Mrs. Dardano continued. "But how can you trust people like this?" She touched her purse to indicate the note. "I could lose . . . I could lose them both."

Apparently, she was at the end of her rope.

"You still haven't told me why you can't take this to the police," I said.

"Because the man who's got her would find out and then he'd kill her."

"But the police are very careful about . . ."

"He's probably got informants with the police."

"You sound like you know who kidnapped your daughter."

She nodded gravely. "Anthony Costanza."

"Costanza? Are you sure?"

"Yesterday afternoon one of Joseph's regular customers came into the shop for a haircut. He said to Joseph, 'Mr. Costanza wants to know if you got your mail all right this morning.'"

"What was the customer's name?"

"Eddy Eames."

"Tell me something, Mrs. Dardano, is your husband connected?"

"Connected?"

"Is he tied in any way to Anthony Costanza?"

"Of course not," she said emphatically. "Joseph isn't a *criminal*. Please, Mr. Lomax, will you help me?"

I let her write me a check.

I spent the rest of the morning on the phone, and most of the afternoon on the streets.

I already knew a little about both Costanza and Eames, none of it good, and I was trying to find out more.

Anthony "Fat Tony" Costanza had been busted in the illegal gambling sweep along with Joseph Dardano and a score of others. Fat Tony, though, played in a different league. He was not only into bookmaking but also loan sharking, prostitution, and dope. The word on the streets was that he was the big fish the Feds were trying to net. The little fish had been scooped up incidentally. No one was going to worry too much about them if they eventually slipped away, so long as they cooperated at the hearing.

Eddy Eames I'd met. He was a weasel. The word was that he worked for Costanza. Worked, that is, if you considered "flunky" to be a job description.

Eames, I was told, spent a lot of time in a joint called Morrisey's out on East Colfax. So that's where I found myself at seven that night, my backside planted firmly on a barstool, my hand wrapped around a cold bottle of Coors.

The clientele at Morrisey's was a mix of blue-collar workers, frayed-white-collar workers, and guys who didn't work but acted like they had more money than the workers. This last group wore zircon rings, laughed at their own jokes, and smelled heavily of Binaca.

Eddy "the Foot" Eames belonged to the last group, and he finally walked in around nine. Limped, actually. He wore a lime-green suit, an open yellow shirt, and pointy-toed high-heeled boots. He had a woman on each arm, one black, one white, both hookers, both about six feet tall in heels, which put them a few inches taller than Eddy the Foot even in *his* heels.

He hobbled up and down the bar, showed off his toys for the night—the black one really wasn't too bad-looking—and ordered a bottle of champagne. Then he took his bottle and his whores to a table in the back, limping all the way.

Eddy the Foot limped because he didn't have any toes on his right foot. His explanation for the missing digits depended on whom he was trying to impress. "I was wounded in Nam," he'd say, "rescuing a bunch of guys from a POW camp." Or, "I was in a shoot-out with some stinking Feds down in Miami, while I was unloading a boatload of coke." Or, "I was saving some drowning little beaners down in Acapulco when a shark took it off. At least the kids got out okay."

The truth wasn't quite as exciting, but then it usually isn't. When Eddy was a juvenile delinquent he got caught shoplifting at J. C. Penney's. The store dick gave him a scolding and let him go. Eddy went right outside and decided to show the cop who he'd been messing with. He kicked in the huge, heavy front window. The bottom part of the glass caved in and the top part immediately slid down in its frame like a guillotine, slicing off the end of Eddy's foot.

I took my beer over to his table. He and the ladies were laughing it up. Eddy frowned when he saw me. The ladies kept smiling. Of course, they were getting paid for it.

"Hi, Eddy."

"Do I know you?"

"Jacob Lomax."

"Sorry, pal, doesn't ring a bell," he said, but he squinted one eye at me. "And this is a private party, so beat it."

"Let me refresh your memory," I said. "The last time we met I was arresting you."

He gave me a sour look. It had been six years ago, but he remembered all right.

I'd been in uniform then, and my partner and I had a warrant to pick up Eames on a charge of extortion. When we'd shown up at his apartment, he'd pulled a knife. I'd taken it away from him, but somehow his arm had gotten broken in the process. Plus a couple of ribs and most of his front teeth.

"What the hell do you want?" Eddy the Foot asked me, his capped teeth not much better-looking than the originals.

"Just being neighborly," I said, and put my beer on the table and sat down.

"He's kind of cute," the white girl said to the black girl. She had bleached blond hair, blood-red lipstick, and false eyelashes long enough to knock the ash off my cigar, if I'd been smoking one.

"Shut up," Eddy told her.

She pouted.

"Take it easy, Eddy," I told him. "Have some champagne." I picked up the bottle and poured some in his glass. "Looks like you're in the chips these days."

"He will be soon," the blond hooker said, and Eddy reminded her to shut up.

"No kidding," I said to Blondie. "When?"

"Soon as he starts his oper—"

"I told you to shut up!" Eddy yelled at her.

"You should learn to control that temper, Eddy," I said. "Fat Tony might not like it, now that you're working for him."

He squinted one eye at me. "You got a problem with that?"

"Costanza's the one with the problem. Kidnapping is a Class A felony."

"Kidnapping," Eddy said warily. "Who's he supposed to have kidnapped?"

"A young lady named Gloria Dardano."

"Who told you that? Are the cops involved?"

"No cops," I said. "Just me."

Eddy seemed to relax. He smirked, anyway.

"I'm working for the girl's mother," I told him. "She wants proof that her daughter's all right."

"So what's that to me?" He sat back and put his arms around his whores, letting his coat fall open to show me the gun in his shoulder holster. I resisted the urge to take it away from him and smack him with it.

"Maybe I should turn you over to the cops right now," I said.

"Assuming you could, which you can't," he said, "what would you tell them? I don't know nothing about no kidnapping."

"You know enough to deliver a message from Costanza to Joseph Dardano about his mail."

"Fine. But that's *all* I know."

I guess I believed him. Costanza wouldn't tell a gofer like Eames any more than was necessary. Eames might be able to guess what Costanza had done, but he wouldn't know where the girl was being held.

"And if the cops want to talk to Mr. Costanza," Eames said, "that's fine, too. 'Course if that happens, I wouldn't be too surprised if Gloria Dardano was never seen again."

That's what I was most afraid of.

But what was Costanza afraid of? Why would he go to such lengths to protect himself against a small operator like Dardano?

I asked Eames.

He gave me another smirk. He was so good at it I figured he must practice at home in front of the mirror.

"You're not too smart, are you, Lomax?" he said. "It's *Costanza* the Feds are gunning for, and he's going to make sure they have as little ammunition as possible. He doesn't want *anybody* testifying against him."

Then he leaned forward on his elbow and pointed his finger at me. "And you'd better not even think about messing with Costanza. Guys who do don't live to brag about it."

* * *

What Eddy said about Costanza was true. Fat Tony was like a big bear at a mountain resort. If you left him alone, he'd just roll around in the garbage pile and never even show you his teeth or his claws. But if you kicked him in the side, he'd eat you alive.

So what was I doing standing by the garbage cans at two-thirty in the morning? Maybe I had a special hatred for kidnappers. It had to do with my wife—my dead wife—but that's another story.

I waited in the shadows near the rear entrance of Pasquali's Italian Restaurant, shuffling my feet and rubbing my hands together and trying to keep from freezing to death.

The parking lot was empty except for one car—a shiny new black Cadillac.

I'd learned that the restaurant closed at ten and the poker game started at ten-thirty and usually finished by two, by which time Fat Tony and his cronies had tired of shuffling cards, sipping Strega, and smoking cigars. When I'd arrived here an hour ago, there'd been six cars in the lot. Now it was down to one: Tony's Caddy.

Suddenly the back door opened. Two large men wearing overcoats stepped out. The shorter of the two, who was as wide as a dump truck, wore a hat.

"Jesus, Mary, and Joseph, it's cold," he said.

"You wanna go back inside, Mr. Costanza? I'll warm up the car."

"Naw, the hell with it, Vinny, I'm already out here."

They moved toward the Cadillac, and I quickly and quietly moved up behind Costanza. I grabbed his left shoulder from behind and poked the muzzle of the .357 magnum under the brim of his hat.

"What the f—"

"Just hold still, Tony."

Vinny had turned and was already grabbing for the piece under his coat. I kept Fat Tony between us.

"Tell him not to do anything stupid, Tony, or I'll get his coat dirty with your brains."

"You son-of-a-bitch, you let him go," Vinny said. The look on his face could've scared a pit bull away from his favorite bone. I wondered how many of us would get out of this alive.

"Take it easy, Vinny," Fat Tony said calmly. "This cheapie only wants my money, ain't that right, cheapie?"

"I don't want your money," I told him. "Get in the car."

"What for?"

"Move it."

"I could take him, Mr. Costanza," Vinny said.

"Not *here*, Vinny. You're forgetting something, right?"

Vinny paused. "Oh, yeah, right."

"Right," Fat Tony said.

They were sharing some little secret, and it made me more nervous than I'd been to begin with, if such a thing were possible. I moved them around to the driver's side of the car. Vinny got in behind the wheel and Fat Tony lumbered into the back seat with me hanging onto his coat.

"Both hands on the wheel, Vinny," I said. "Try anything and your boss dies."

"Now, Mr. Costanza?"

"Not yet. Let's hear what the cheapie has to say."

"Start the car," I told Vinny. "We're going to drive around to keep you busy."

"Okay, Mr. Costanza?"

"Sure, why not."

Vinny turned the key and the motor purred itself awake.

"Take the freeway," Fat Tony said, and settled himself in the back seat as if he were the mayor of Naples out for a Sunday drive. He had a wide face and a small nose, which had probably made him look angelic when he was a chubby little kid. Now he was a jowly, sixty-year-old man, who'd been suspected of a lot more crimes than he'd ever been charged with, and charged with a lot more than he'd ever been convicted of. As far as I knew, he'd never set foot in a prison.

Vinny pulled out onto Thirty-eighth Avenue and turned east. There was very little traffic at this hour. I saw a cop car go by in the other direction and I instinctively lowered the gun; then I realized no one could see us in here, not with the dark-tinted windows.

"So," Fat Tony said, "we're in the car. Nice, huh? My wife picked it out. Now what the hell do you want?"

"Gloria Dardano."

"Huh?"

"Don't play dumb. She's the daughter of Joseph Dardano, one of the bookies who got busted last week. And you snatched her two days ago so he wouldn't testify against you."

"You gotta be nuts."

We dipped down under the railroad bridge, then Vinny swung the Caddy around the on-ramp and headed south on I-25. He kept our speed at a rock-solid fifty miles an hour, and the few cars that were out this late flew by us as if we were parked.

"For one thing," Costanza said, "I never even *heard* of this guy Dardano."

"You're lying," I said, but I wasn't too sure.

"You hear that, Vinny? He called me a liar."

"I heard him, Mr. Costanza. Now?"

"Not yet, Vinny."

"Not ever, Vinny," I said, not knowing what he was talking about, but not liking it just the same. "If either one of your hands comes off the wheel, I'll turn your boss's head into lasagna."

"Just say the word, Mr. Costanza," Vinny said, not paying much attention to me.

"You're not too smart, are you, cheapie?" Costanza said to me. "For one thing, there's nothing anybody can say to the grand jury that can hurt me. I already *know* they're gonna indict me, and I've got lawyers who can handle things after that. For another thing, I *like* kids, I don't snatch them. I'm a family man. And why would I risk a kidnapping charge, which is a very serious offense, to avoid a bookmaking charge, which is nothing? You wanna answer me that?"

I did, but I couldn't come up with much.

"If Dardano doesn't testify, he goes to prison," I said. "Maybe that's what you want."

"Why the hell would I want that?"

Then it occurred to me. "When he's gone, you can add his bookmaking operation to yours."

"What operation, for chrissake? I never heard of the guy, which means he probably don't take in more than forty, fifty grand a year."

"Fifty grand sounds like serious money," I said.

"Maybe to a two-bit cheapie like you."

As bold as he was talking, you'd think I was pointing a hot dog at him, not a handgun. Okay, so next time I'd bring a rifle.

"Are you denying you sent Eddy Eames to Dardano with—"

"Eames? That little *stronzo* hasn't worked for me in how long, Vinny, a year?"

"I think a year, Mr. Costanza."

Fat Tony looked at me and said, "I think maybe you made a big mistake, cheapie. See, I don't give a damn whether Dardano testifies or not. But I'll tell you something. If somebody kidnapped the man's daughter like you say, I'd personally like to get my hands on whoever did it. I've got daughters of my own. Now, why don't you put away the piece and I won't tell Vinny to kill you."

He showed me his bear's teeth. I put away the gun.

"Now, Mr. Costanza?"

"Relax, Vinny. What's your name, anyway, cheapie?"

"Jacob Lomax."

"Lomax. What the hell kind of name is that?"

"A last name."

"You hear that, Vinny? A comedian."

"I heard, Mr. Costanza."

"Well, one thing, Mr. Jacob Lomax, you got guts. Maybe you'd like to work for me. You look like you need a job."

"I've got a job. Finding Gloria Dardano."

"Whatever. Vinny, turn us around."

We drove back to Pasquali's.

"After tonight," I asked, "should I be looking over my shoulder for Vinny?"

Fat Tony laughed. "Who can say for sure?"

"Can I ask you something else? What's the secret you and Vinny have been keeping from me?"

They both laughed at that.

"Promise not to tell?" Fat Tony asked, grinning from ear to ear like a naughty, chubby little boy. "See, there's some, whaddaya call 'em, security devices installed behind the rear seats, a couple on each side. Spring-loaded bayonets with needle points and razor-sharp blades."

I instinctively jerked away from the seat, which made Fat Tony chuckle.

"If Vinny pushed a button with his foot," he said, "the correct button, for my sake, you woulda got a very large surprise in your back. I had 'em installed when I bought the car. Pretty neat, huh?"

"Yeah, neat," I said, and tried to grin and swallow at the same time.

"I'd show you how they work, but it messes up the fine Corinthian leather, you know?"

Vinny laughed, as if he'd seen it happen. I climbed out and started down the alley to where I'd left my car.

"Hey, Lomax."

I turned around. Vinny and Fat Tony both had their windows down. They were both pointing guns at me and grinning like playground bullies. I held perfectly still.

"You ever get cute like that again, Mr. Jacob Lomax," Fat Tony said with a chuckle, "and you're gonna be looking up at the world with six feet of dirt in your eyes. *Capisce?*"

I did. They drove away.

Eddy Eames lived in a small rented frame house on the west side. I got there just before dawn, picked the back door lock without too much trouble, and moved quietly through the dark, smelly kitchen to the bedroom.

Eddy was lying on his back under the covers and snoring loudly. I waited for him to inhale, then pressed the muzzle of the magnum against his right nostril. He jerked awake, then tried to pull back, his eyes wide enough to glow in the dark. I kept his head pinned to the pillow with the gun and clicked on the light.

"Lomax, wha—"

"I risked getting eaten by a bear tonight because of you."

"What are you—"

"Shut up and listen. I know why you kidnapped Gloria Dardano. You figured you could scare her father into not testifying, and when the Feds sent him to prison, you'd take over his bookmaking operation. The fifty grand a year would be worth the risk to a cheapie like you." Okay, so I'd learned a new word tonight. "You were a regular customer of Dardano and you'd seen his operation up close, so you figured no sweat. You also figured that if you tossed around the name of Fat Tony Costanza that nobody would help Dardano."

"I don't know wha—"

"I'm not going to kill you, Eddy. I'm not even going to torture you. But if you don't tell me where Gloria is, I'm going to turn you over to Fat Tony."

Eddy didn't say a word. His face was whiter than the pillowcase.

"Where is she?" I asked.

"In the basement."

I yanked out the lamp cord and used it to tie Eddy's hands behind him. After I'd tied his feet with the pillow case, I went downstairs.

Gloria Dardano was lying on a bare mattress under a thin blanket. She was naked and bruised. Her wrists and ankles were bound with duct tape. There were two more strips wrapped around her head—one over her eyes, one over her mouth. It looked like Eddy had had some fun with her during the past few days.

Gloria heard me coming, and she shrank away from the sound.

As gently as possible, I removed the tape. She was too weak to walk, so I carried her up the stairs and through the kitchen.

"Hey, what about me?" Eddy yelled from the bedroom floor.

"Don't worry," I said. "You'll be taken care of."

I drove Gloria to St. Anthony's Hospital. After a nurse and an intern took over, I made two phone calls. The first to Angela Dardano, the second to Fat Tony Costanza.

* * *

The grand jury hearing took a week and a half. When it was over, the only bookie indicted was Costanza. He didn't seem too worried about it.

The Dardano family went to Arizona for the Christmas holidays, and from what I hear, Gloria has just about fully recovered. She even sent me a Christmas card. So did her parents, who included some extra holiday cheer: a check for five grand.

And Eddy "the Foot" Eames? Well, I haven't seen Eddy around at all, and neither has anyone else.

*Lawrence Block's Matt Scudder story "By Dawn's Early Light,"
published in the first PWA anthology* The Eyes Have It *in
1984, won both the MWA Edgar Award and the PWA Shamus
award for best short story. His Scudder novel* Eight Million
Ways to Die *won the Shamus for best P.I. novel of 1982. His
most recent Matt Scudder novel is* Out on the Cutting Edge.
This is Block's second appearance in a PWA anthology.

Batman's Helpers

by Lawrence Block

Reliable's offices are in the
Flatiron Building, at Broadway and Twenty-third. The
receptionist, an elegant black girl with high cheekbones
and processed hair, gave me a nod and a smile, and I went
on down the hall to Wally Witt's office.

He was at his desk, a short stocky man with a bulldog jaw
and gray hair cropped close to his head. Without rising he
said, "Matt, good to see you, you're right on time. You
know these guys? Matt Scudder, Jimmy diSalvo, Lee
Trombauer." We shook hands all around. "We're waiting
on Eddie Rankin. Then we can go out there and protect
the integrity of the American merchandising system."

"Can't do that without Eddie," Jimmy diSalvo said.

"No, we need him," Wally said. "He's our pit bull. He's
attack trained, Eddie is."

He came through the door a few minutes later and I saw
what they meant. Without looking alike, Jimmy and Wally
and Lee all looked like ex-cops—as, I suppose, do I. Eddie
Rankin looked like the kind of guy we used to have to
bring in on a bad Saturday night. He was a big man, broad

17

in the shoulders, narrow in the waist. His hair was blond, almost white, and he wore it short at the sides but long in back. It lay on his neck like a mane. He had a broad forehead and a pug nose. His complexion was very fair and his full lips were intensely red, almost artificially so. He looked like a roughneck, and you sensed that his response to any sort of stress was likely to be physical, and abrupt.

Wally Witt introduced him to me. The others already knew him. Eddie Rankin shook my hand, and his left hand fastened on my shoulder and gave a squeeze. "Hey, Matt," he said. "Pleased to meetcha. Whattaya say, guys, we ready to come to the aid of the Caped Crusader?"

Jimmy diSalvo started whistling the theme from "Batman," the old television show. Wally said, "Okay, who's packing? Is everybody packing?"

Lee Trombauer drew back his suit jacket to show a revolver in a shoulder rig. Eddie Rankin took out a large automatic and laid it on Wally's desk. "Batman's gun," he announced.

"Batman don't carry a gun," Jimmy told him.

"Then he better stay outta New York," Eddie said. "Or he'll get his ass shot off. Those revolvers, I wouldn't carry one of them on a bet."

"This shoots as straight as what you got," Lee said. "And it won't jam."

"This baby don't jam," Eddie said. He picked up the automatic and held it out for display. "You got a revolver," he said, "a .38, whatever you got—"

"A .38."

"—and a guy takes it away from you, all he's gotta do is point it and shoot it. Even if he never saw a gun before, he knows how to do that much. This monster, though"—and he demonstrated, flicking the safety, working the slide—"all this shit you gotta go through, before he can figure it out I got the gun away from him and I'm making him eat it."

"Nobody's taking my gun away from me," Lee said.

"What everybody says, but look at all the times it

happens. Cop gets shot with his own gun, nine times out of ten it's a revolver."

"That's because that's all they carry," Lee said.

"Well, there you go."

Jimmy and I weren't carrying guns. Wally offered to equip us but we both declined. "Not that anybody's likely to have to show a piece, let alone use one, God forbid," Wally said. "But it can get nasty out there, and it helps to have the feeling of authority. Well, let's go get 'em, huh? The Batmobile's waiting at the curb."

We rode down in the elevator, five grown men, three of us armed with handguns. Eddie Rankin had on a plaid sport jacket and khaki trousers. The rest of us wore suits and ties. We went out the Fifth Avenue exit and followed Wally to his car, a five-year-old Fleetwood Cadillac parked next to a hydrant. There were no tickets on the windshield; a PBA courtesy card had kept the traffic cops at bay.

Wally drove and Eddie Rankin sat in front with him. The rest of us rode in back. We cruised up to Fifty-fourth Street and turned right, and Wally parked next to a hydrant a few doors from Fifth. We walked together to the corner of Fifth and turned downtown. Near the middle of the block a trio of black men had set up shop as sidewalk vendors. One had a display of women's handbags and silk scarves, all arranged neatly on top of a folding card table. The other two were offering tee-shirts and cassette tapes.

In an undertone Wally said, "Here we go. These three were here yesterday. Matt, why don't you and Lee check down the block, make sure those two down at the corner don't have what we're looking for. Then double back and we'll take these dudes off. Meanwhile I'll let the man sell me a shirt."

Lee and I walked down to the corner. The two vendors in question were selling books. We established this and headed back. "Real police work," I said.

"Be grateful we don't have to fill out a report, list the titles of the books."

"The alleged books."

When we rejoined the others Wally was holding an

oversize tee-shirt to his chest, modeling it for us. "What do you say?" he demanded. "Is it me? Do you think it's me?"

"I think it's the Joker," Jimmy diSalvo said.

"That's what I think," Wally said. He looked at the two Africans, who were smiling uncertainly. "I think it's a violation, is what I think. I think we got to confiscate all the Batman stuff. It's unauthorized, it's an illegal violation of copyright protection, it's unlicensed, and we got to take it in."

The two vendors had stopped smiling, but they didn't seem to have a very clear idea of what was going on. Off to the side, the third man, the fellow with the scarves and purses, was looking wary.

"You speak English?" Wally asked them.

"They speak numbers," Jimmy said. "'Fi' dollah, ten dollah, please, t'ank you.' That's what they speak."

"Where you from?" Wally demanded. "Senegal, right? Dakar. You from Dakar?"

They nodded, brightening at words they recognized. "Dakar," one of them echoed. Both of them were wearing western clothes, but they looked faintly foreign—loose-fitting long-sleeved shirts with long pointed collars and a glossy finish, baggy pleated pants. Loafers with leather mesh tops.

"What do you speak?" Wally asked. "You speak French? Parley-voo Français?" The one who'd spoken before replied now in a torrent of French; Wally backed away from him and shook his head. "I don't know why the hell I asked," he said. "Parley-voo's all I know of the fucking language." To the Africans he said, "Police. You parley-voo that? Police. *Policia*. You capeesh?" He opened his wallet and showed them some sort of badge. "No sell Batman," he said, waving one of the shirts at them. "Batman no good. It's unauthorized, it's not made under a licensing agreement, and you can't sell it."

"No Batman," one of them said.

"Jesus, don't tell me I'm getting through to them. Right, no Batman. No, put your money away, I can't take a bribe, I'm not with the Department no more. All I want's the Batman stuff. You can keep the rest."

All but a handful of their tee-shirts were unauthorized Batman items. The rest showed Walt Disney characters, almost certainly as unauthorized as the Batman merchandise, but Disney wasn't Reliable's client today so it was none of our concern. While we loaded up with Batman and the Joker, Eddie Rankin looked through the cassettes, then pawed through the silk scarves the third vendor had on display. He let the man keep the scarves, but he took a purse, snakeskin by the look of it. "No good," he told the man, who nodded, expressionless.

We trooped back to the Fleetwood and Wally popped the trunk. We deposited the confiscated tees between the spare tire and some loose fishing tackle. "Don't worry if the shit gets dirty," Wally said. "It's all gonna be destroyed anyway. Eddie, you start carrying a purse, people are gonna say things."

"Woman I know," he said. "She'll like this." He wrapped the purse in a Batman tee-shirt and placed it in the trunk.

"Okay," Wally said. "That went real smooth. What we'll do now, Lee, you and Matt take the east side of Fifth, and the rest of us'll stay on this side and we'll work our way down to Forty-second. I don't know if we'll get much, because even if they can't speak English they can sure get the word around fast, but we'll make sure there's no unlicensed Batcrap on the Avenue before we move on. We'll maintain eye contact back and forth across the street, and if you hit anything give the high sign and we'll converge and take 'em down. Everybody got it?"

Everybody seemed to. We left the car with its trunkful of contraband and returned to Fifth Avenue. The two tee-shirt vendors from Dakar had packed up and disappeared; they'd have to find something else to sell and someplace else to sell it. The man with the scarves and purses was still doing business. He froze when he caught sight of us.

"No Batman," Wally told him.

"No Batman," he echoed.

"I'll be a son-of-a-bitch," Wally said. "The guy's learning English."

Lee and I crossed the street and worked our way

downtown. There were vendors all over the place, offering clothing and tapes and small appliances and books and fast food. Most of them didn't have the peddler's license the law required, and periodically the city would sweep the streets, especially the main commercial avenues, rounding them up and fining them and confiscating their stock. Then after a week or so the cops would stop trying to enforce a basically unenforceable law, and the peddlers would be back in business again.

It was an apparently endless cycle, but the booksellers were exempt from it. The courts had decided that the First Amendment embodied in its protection of freedom of the press the right of anyone to sell printed matter on the street, so if you had books for sale you never got hassled. As a result, a lot of scholarly antiquarian booksellers offered their wares on the city streets. So did any number of illiterates hawking remaindered art books and stolen bestsellers, along with homeless street people who rescued old magazines from people's garbage cans and spread them out on the pavement, living in hope that someone would want to buy them.

In front of St. Patrick's Cathedral we found a Pakistani with tee-shirts and sweatshirts. I asked him if he had any Batman merchandise and he went right through the piles himself and pulled out half a dozen items. We didn't bother signaling the Cavalry across the street. Lee just showed the man a badge—Special Officer, it said—and I explained that we had to confiscate Batman items.

"He is the big seller, Batman," the man said. "I get Batman, I sell him fast as I can."

"Well, you better not sell him anymore," I said, "because it's against the law."

"Excuse, please," he said. "What is law? Why is Batman against law? Is my understanding Batman is *for* law. He is good guy, is it not so?"

I explained about copyright and trademarks and licensing agreements. It was a little like explaining the internal combustion engine to a field mouse. He kept nodding his head, but I don't know how much of it he got. He understood the main point—that we were walking off with his stock and he was stuck for whatever it cost him. He didn't like that part, but there wasn't much he could do about it.

Lee tucked the shirts under his arm and we kept going. At Forty-seventh Street we crossed over in response to a signal from Wally. They'd found another pair of Senegalese with a big spread of Batman items—tees and sweatshirts and gimme caps and sun visors, some a direct knockoff of the copyrighted Bat signal, others a variation on the theme, but none of it authorized and all of it subject to confiscation. The two men—they looked like brothers and were dressed identically in baggy beige trousers and sky-blue nylon shirts—couldn't understand what was wrong with their merchandise and couldn't believe we intended to haul it all away with us. But there were five of us, and we were large intimidating white men with an authoritarian manner, and what could they do about it?

"I'll get the car," Wally said. "No way we're gonna shlep this crap seven blocks in this heat."

With the trunk almost full, we drove to Thirty-fourth and broke for lunch at a place Wally liked. We sat at a large round table. Ornate beer steins hung from the beams overhead. We had a round of drinks, then ordered sandwiches and fries and half-liter steins of dark beer. I had a Coke to start, another Coke with the food, and coffee afterward.

"You're not drinking," Lee Trombauer said.

"Not today."

"Not on duty," Jimmy said, and everybody laughed.

"What I want to know," Eddie Rankin said, "is why everybody wants a fucking Batman shirt in the first place."

"Not just shirts," somebody said.

"Shirts, sweaters, caps, lunch boxes—if you could print it on Tampax they'd be shoving 'em up their twats. Why Batman, for Christ's sake?"

"It's hot," Wally said.

"'It's hot.' What the fuck does that mean?"

"It means it's hot. That's what it means. It's hot means it's hot. Everybody wants it because everybody else wants it, and that means it's hot."

"I seen the movie," Eddie said. "You see it?"

Two of us had, two of us hadn't.

"It's okay," he said. "Basically, I'd say it's a kid's movie, but it's okay."

"So?"

"So how many tee-shirts in extra large do you sell to kids? Everybody's buying this shit, and all you can tell me is it's hot because it's hot. I don't get it."

"You don't have to," Wally said. "It's the same as the niggers. You want to try explaining to them why they can't sell Batman unless there's a little copyright notice printed under the design? While you're at it, you can explain to me why the assholes counterfeiting the crap don't counterfeit the copyright notice while they're at it. The thing is, nobody has to do any explaining because nobody has to understand. The only message they have to get on the street is 'Batman no good, no sell Batman.' If they learn that much we're doing our job right."

Wally paid for everybody's lunch. We stopped at the Flatiron Building long enough to empty the trunk and carry everything upstairs, then drove down to the Village and worked the sidewalk market on Sixth Avenue below Eighth Street. We made a few confiscations without incident. Then, near the subway entrance at West Third, we were taking a dozen shirts and about as many visors from a West Indian when another vendor decided to get into the act. He was wearing a dashiki and had his hair in Rastafarian dreadlocks, and he said, "You can't take the brother's wares, man. You can't do that."

"It's unlicensed merchandise produced in contravention of international copyright protection," Wally told him.

"Maybe so," the man said, "but that don't empower you to seize it. Where's your due process? Where's your authority? You aren't police." Poe-lease, he said, bearing down on the first syllable. "You can't come into a man's store, seize his wares."

"Store?" Eddie Rankin moved toward him, his hands

hovering at his sides. "You see a store here? All I see's a lot of fucking shit in the middle of a fucking blanket."

"This is the man's store. This is the man's place of business."

"And what's this?" Eddie demanded. He walked over to the right, where the man with the dreadlocks had stick incense displayed for sale on a pair of upended orange crates. "This your store?"

"That's right. It's my store."

"You know what it looks like to me? It looks like you're selling drug paraphernalia. That's what it looks like."

"It's incense," the Rasta said. "For bad smells."

"Bad smells," Eddie said. One of the sticks of incense was smoldering, and Eddie picked it up and sniffed at it. "Whew," he said. "That's a bad smell, I'll give you that. Smells like the catbox caught on fire."

The Rasta snatched the incense from him. "It's a good smell," he said. "Smells like your mama."

Eddie smiled at him, his red lips parting to show stained teeth. He looked happy, and very dangerous. "Say I kick your store into the middle of the street," he said, "and you with it. How's that sound to you?"

Smoothly, easily, Wally Witt moved between them. "Eddie," he said softly, and Eddie backed off and let the smile fade on his lips. To the incense seller Wally said, "Look, you and I got no quarrel with each other. I got a job to do and you got your own business to run."

"The brother here's got a business to run, too."

"Well, he's gonna have to run it without Batman, because that's how the law reads. But if you want to *be* Batman, playing the dozens with my man here and pushing into what doesn't concern you, then I got no choice. You follow me?"

"All I'm saying, I'm saying you want to confiscate the man's merchandise, you need you a policeman and a court order, something to make it official."

"Fine," Wally said. "You're saying it and I hear you saying it, but what I'm saying is all I need to do it is to do it, official or not. Now if you want to get a cop to stop me, fine, go ahead and do it, but as soon as you do I'm going to press charges for selling drug paraphernalia and operating without a peddler's license—"

"This here ain't drug paraphernalia, man. We both know that."

"We both know you're just trying to be a hard-on, and we both know what it'll get you. That what you want?"

The incense seller stood there for a moment, then dropped his eyes. "Don't matter what I want," he said.

"Well, you got that right," Wally told him. "It don't matter what you want."

We tossed the shirts and visors into the trunk and got out of there. On the way over to Astor Place Eddie said, "You didn't have to jump in there. I wasn't about to lose it."

"Never said you were."

"That mama stuff doesn't bother me. It's just nigger talk, they all talk that shit."

"I know."

"They'd talk about their fathers, but they don't know who the fuck they are, so they're stuck with their mothers. Bad smells—I shoulda stuck that shit up his ass, get right where the bad smells are. I hate a guy sticks his nose in like that."

"Your basic sidewalk lawyer."

"Basic asshole's what he is. Maybe I'll go back, talk with him later."

"On your own time."

"On my own time is right."

Astor Place hosts a more freewheeling street market, with a lot of Bowery types offering a mix of salvaged trash and stolen goods. There was something especially curious about our role as we passed over hot radios and typewriters and jewelry and sought only merchandise that had been legitimately purchased, albeit from illegitimate manufacturers. We didn't find much Batman ware on display, although a lot of people, buyers and sellers alike, were wearing the Caped Crusader. We weren't about to strip the shirt off anybody's person, nor did we look too hard for contraband merchandise; the place was teeming with crackheads and crazies, and it was no time to push our luck.

"Let's get out of here," Wally said. "I hate to leave the car in this neighborhood. We already gave the client his money's worth."

By four we were in Wally's office and his desk was heaped high with the fruits of our labors. "Look at all this shit," he said. "Today's trash and tomorrow's treasures. Twenty years and they'll be auctioning this crap at Christie's. Not this particular crap, because I'll messenger it over to the client and he'll chuck it in the incinerator. Gentlemen, you did a good day's work." He took out his wallet and gave each of the four of us a hundred-dollar bill. He said, "Same time tomorrow? Except I think we'll make lunch Chinese tomorrow. Eddie, don't forget your purse."

"Don't worry."

"Thing is, you don't want to carry it if you go back to see your Rastafarian friend. He might get the wrong idea."

"Fuck him," Eddie said. "I got no time for him. He wants that incense up his ass, he's gonna have to stick it there himself."

Lee and Jimmy and Eddie went out, laughing, joking, slapping backs. I started out after them, then doubled back and asked Wally if he had a minute.

"Sure," he said. "Jesus, I don't believe that. Look."

"It's a Batman shirt."

"No shit, Sherlock. And look what's printed right under the Bat signal."

"The copyright notice."

"Right, which makes it a legal shirt. We got any more of these? No, no, no, no. Wait a minute, here's one. Here's another. Jesus, this is amazing. There any more? I don't see any others, do you?"

We went through the pile without finding more of the shirts with the copyright notice.

"Three," he said. "Well, that's not so bad. A mere fraction." He balled up the three shirts, dropped them back on the pile. "You want one of these? It's legit; you can wear it without fear of confiscation."

"I don't think so."

"You got kids? Take something home for your kids."

"One's in college and the other's in the service. I don't think they'd be interested."

"Probably not." He stepped out from behind his desk. "Well, it went all right out there, don't you think? We had a good crew, worked well together."

"I guess."

"What's the matter, Matt?"

"Nothing, really. But I don't think I can make it tomorrow."

"No? Why's that?"

"Well, for openers, I've got a dentist appointment."

"Oh yeah? What time?"

"Nine-fifteen."

"So how long can that take? Half an hour, an hour tops? Meet us here ten-thirty, that's good enough. The client doesn't have to know what time we hit the street."

"It's not just the dentist appointment, Wally."

"Oh?"

"I don't think I want to do this stuff anymore."

"What stuff? Copyright and trademark protection?"

"Yeah."

"What's the matter? It's beneath you? Doesn't make full use of your talents as a detective?"

"It's not that."

"Because it's not a bad deal for the money, seems to me. Hundred bucks for a short day, ten to four, hour and a half off for lunch with the lunch all paid for. You're a cheap lunch date—you don't drink—but even so. Call it a ten-dollar lunch, that's a hundred and ten dollars for what, four and a half hours' work?" He punched numbers on a desktop calculator. "That's twenty-four forty-four an hour. That's not bad wages. You want to take home better than that, you need either burglar's tools or a law degree, seems to me."

"The money's fine, Wally."

"Then what's the problem?"

I shook my head. "I just haven't got the heart for it," I said. "Hassling people who don't even speak the language, taking their goods from them because we're stronger than they are and there's nothing they can do about it."

"They can quit selling contraband, that's what they can do."

"How? They don't even know what's contraband."

"Well, that's where we come in. We're giving them an education. How they gonna learn if nobody teaches 'em?"

I'd loosened my tie earlier. Now I took it off, folded it, put it in my pocket.

He said, "Company owns a copyright, they got a right to control who uses it. Somebody else enters into a licensing agreement, pays money for the right to produce a particular item, they got a right to the exclusivity they paid for."

"I don't have a problem with that."

"So?"

"They don't even speak the language," I said.

He stood up straight. "Then who told 'em to come here?" he wanted to know. "Who fucking invited them? You can't walk a block in midtown without tripping over another super salesman from Senegal. They swarm off that Air Afrique flight from Dakar, and first thing you know they got an open-air store on world-famous Fifth Avenue. They don't pay rent, they don't pay taxes, they just spread a blanket on the concrete and rake in the dollars."

"They didn't look as though they were getting rich."

"They must do all right. Pay two bucks for a scarf and sell it for ten, they must come out okay. They stay at hotels like the Bryant, pack together like sardines, six or eight to the room. Sleep in shifts, cook their food on hotplates. Two, three months of that and it's back to fucking Dakar. They drop off the money, take a few minutes to get another baby started, then they're winging back to JFK to start all over again. You think we need that? Haven't we got enough spades of our own can't make a living, we got to fly in more of them?"

I sifted through the pile on his desk, picked up a sun visor with the Joker depicted on it. I wondered why anybody would want something like that. I said, "What do you figure it adds up to, the stuff we confiscated? A couple of hundred?"

"Jesus, I don't know. Figure ten for a tee-shirt, and we got what, thirty or forty of them? Add in the sweatshirts, the rest of the shit, I bet it comes close to a grand. Why?"

"I was just thinking. You paid us a hundred a man, plus whatever lunch came to."

"Eighty with the tip. What's the point?"

"You must have billed us to the client at what, fifty dollars an hour?"

"I haven't billed anything to anybody yet—I just walked in the door—but yes, that's the rate."

"How will you figure it, four men at eight hours a man?"

"Seven hours. We don't bill for lunch time."

Seven hours seemed ample, considering that we'd worked four and a half. I said, "Seven times fifty times four of us is what? Fourteen hundred dollars? Plus your own time, of course, and you must bill yourself at more than regular operative's rates. A hundred an hour?"

"Seventy-five."

"For seven hours is what, five hundred?"

"Five and a quarter," he said evenly.

"Plus fourteen hundred is nineteen and a quarter. Call it two thousand dollars to the client. Is that about right?"

"What are you saying, Matt? The client pays too much or you're not getting a big enough piece of the pie?"

"Neither. But if he wants to load up on this garbage"—I waved a hand at the heap on the desk—"wouldn't he be better off buying retail? Get a lot more bang for the buck, wouldn't he?"

He just stared at me for a long moment. Then abruptly, his hard face cracked and he started to laugh. I was laughing, too, and it took all the tension out of the air. "Jesus, you're right," he said. "Guy's paying way too much."

"I mean, if you wanted to handle it for him, you wouldn't need to hire me and the other guys."

"I could just go around and pay cash."

"Right."

"I could even pass up the street guys altogether, go straight to the wholesaler."

"Save a dollar that way."

"I love it," he said. "You know what it sounds like? Sounds like something the federal government would do, get cocaine off the streets by buying it straight from the Colombians. Wait a minute, didn't they actually do something like that once?"

"I think so, but I don't think it was cocaine."

"No, it was opium. It was some years ago—they bought the entire Turkish opium crop because it was supposed to be the cheapest way to keep it out of the country. Bought it and burned it, and that, boys and girls, that was the end of heroin addiction in America."

"Worked like a charm, didn't it?"

"Nothing works," he said. "First principle of modern law enforcement. Nothing ever works. Funny thing is, in this case the client's not getting a bad deal. You own a copyright or a trademark, you got to defend it. Otherwise you risk losing it. You got to be able to say on such and such a date you paid so many dollars to defend your interests and investigators acting as your agents confiscated so many items from so many merchants. And it's worth what you budget for it. Believe me, these big companies, they wouldn't spend the money year in and year out if they didn't figure it was worth it."

"I believe it," I said. "Anyway, I wouldn't lose a whole lot of sleep over the client getting screwed a little."

"You just don't like the work."

"I'm afraid not."

He shrugged. "I don't blame you. It's chickenshit. But Jesus, Matt, most P.I. work is chickenshit. Was it that different in the Department? Or on any police force? Most of what we did was chickenshit."

"And paperwork."

"And paperwork—you're absolutely right. Do some chickenshit and then write it up. And make copies."

"I can put up with a certain amount of chickenshit," I

said. "But I honestly don't have the heart for what we did today. I felt like a bully."

"Listen, I'd rather be kicking in doors, taking down bad guys. That what you want?"

"Not really."

"Be Batman, tooling around Gotham City, righting wrongs. Do the whole thing not even carrying a gun. You know what they didn't have in the movie?"

"I haven't seen it yet."

"Robin, they didn't have Robin. Robin the Boy Wonder. He's not in the comic book anymore, either. Somebody told me they took a poll, had their readers call a 900 number and vote, should they keep Robin or should they kill him. Like in ancient Rome, those fighters, what do you call them?"

"Gladiators."

"Right. Thumbs up or thumbs down, and Robin got thumbs down, so they killed him. Can you believe that?"

"I can believe anything."

"Yeah, you and me both. I always thought they were fags." I looked at him. "Batman and Robin, I mean. His *ward*, for Christ's sake. Playing dress-up, flying around, costumes, I figured it's gotta be some kind of fag S-and-M thing. Isn't that what you figured?"

"I never thought about it."

"Well, I never stayed up nights over it myself, but what else would it be? Anyway, he's dead now, Robin is. Died of AIDS, I suppose, but the family's denying it, like what's-his-name. You know who I mean."

I didn't, but I nodded.

"You gotta make a living, you know. Gotta turn a buck, whether it's hassling Africans or squatting out there on a blanket your own self, selling tapes and scarves. Fi' dollah, ten dollah." He looked at me. "No good, huh?"

"I don't think so, Wally."

"Don't want to be one of Batman's helpers. Well, you can't do what you can't do. What the fuck do I know about it, anyway? You don't drink. I don't have a problem with it myself. But if I couldn't put my feet up at the end of the day, have a few pops, who knows? Maybe I couldn't do it either. Matt, you're a good man. If you change your mind—"

"I know. Thanks, Wally."

"Hey," he said. "Don't mention it. We gotta look out for each other, you know what I mean? Here in Gotham City."

Max Collins is one of four people who has been a staple in every PWA anthology, for which we are very grateful. All of his appearances have been stories featuring his historical P.I. Nathan Heller. Once again, with "Private Consultation," Collins expertly blends fact with fiction—a talent for which he won a Shamus Award for best novel with True Detective, *the first Nathan Heller novel.*

Private Consultation
A Nathan Heller short story

by Max Allan Collins

I grabbed the Lake Street El and got off at Garfield Park; it was a short walk from there to the "Death Clinic" at 3406 West Monroe Street. That's what the papers, some of them anyway, were calling the Wynekoop mansion. To me it was just another big old stone building on the West Side, one of many, though of a burnt-reddish stone rather than typical Chicago gray. And, I'll grant you, the three-story structure was planted on a much wealthier residential stretch than the one I'd grown up on twelve blocks south.

Still, this was the West Side and more or less my old stomping grounds, and that was no doubt part of why I'd been asked to drop by the Wynekoop place this sunny Saturday afternoon. The family had most likely asked around, heard about the ex-cop from nearby Douglas Park who now had a little private agency in the Loop. And my reputation on the West Side—and in the Loop—was of being just honest enough, and just crooked enough, to get most jobs done.

But part of why I'd been called, I would guess, was Earle Wynekoop himself. I knew Earle a little, from a distance. We'd both worked at the World's Fair down on the lakefront last summer and fall. I was working pickpocket duty, and Earle was in the front office, doing whatever front-office people do. We were both about the same age—I was twenty-seven—but he seemed like a kid to me.

Earle mostly chased skirts, except at the Streets of Paris exhibition, where the girls didn't wear skirts. Tall, handsome, wavy-haired Earle, with his white teeth and pencil-line mustache, had pursued the fan dancers with the eagerness of a plucked bird trying to get its feathers back.

Funny thing was, nobody—including me—knew Earle was a married man till November, when the papers were full of his wife. His wife's murder, that is.

Now it was a sunny, almost warm afternoon in December, and I had been in business just under a year. And like most small businessmen, I'd had a less than prosperous 1933. A retainer from a family with the Wynekoops' dough would be a nice way to ring out the old and ring in the new.

Right now, I was ringing the doorbell. I was up at the top of the first-floor landing; Dr. Alice Wynekoop's office in an English basement below. I was expecting a maid or butler to answer, considering the size of this place. But Earle is what I got.

His white smile flickered nervously. He adjusted his bowtie with one hand and offered the other for me to shake, which I did. His grip was weak and moist, like his dark eyes.

"Mr. Heller," he said. "Thank you for stopping by."

"My pleasure," I said, stepping into the vestibule, hat in hand.

Earle, snappily dressed in a pinstripe worsted, took my topcoat and hung it on a hall tree.

"Perhaps you don't remember me," he said. "I worked in the front office at the fair this summer."

"Sure I remember you, Mr. Wynekoop."

"Why don't you call me Earle."

"Fine, Earle," I said. "And my friends call me Nate."

He grinned nervously and said, "Step into the library, Nate, if you would."

"Is your mother here?"

"No. She's in jail."

"Why haven't you sprung her?" Surely these folks could afford to make bail. On the phone, Earle had quickly agreed to my rate of fifteen bucks a day and a one-hundred-dollar nonrefundable retainer. And that was the top of my sliding scale.

An eyebrow arched in disgust on a high, unwrinkled brow. "Mother is ill, thanks to these barbarians. We've decided to let the state pay for her illness, considering they've provoked it."

He tried to sound indignant through all that, but only managed petulance.

The interior of the house was on the gloomy side; a lot of dark, expensive, well-wrought woodwork, and heavy plush furnishings that dated back to the turn of the century, when the house was built. There were hints that the Wynekoops might not be as well fixed as the rest of us thought: Ornate antiquated light fixtures, worn Oriental carpets, and a layer of dust indicated yesterday's wealth, not today's.

I sat on a dark horsehair couch; two of the walls were bookcases, filled with leather-bound volumes, and the others were hung with somber landscapes. The first thing Earle did was give me an envelope with one hundred dollars in tens in it. Now Earle was getting himself some sherry off a liquor cart.

"Can I get you something?" Earle asked. His hands were shaking as he poured himself sherry.

"This will do nicely," I said, counting the money.

"Don't be a wet blanket, Nate."

I put the money-clipped bills away. "Rum, then. No ice."

He gave me a glass and sat beside me. I'd rather he had sat across from me; it was awkward, looking sideways at him. But he seemed to crave the intimacy.

"Mother's not guilty, you know."

"Really."

"I confessed, but they didn't believe me. I confessed five times."

"Cops figured you were trying to clear your mama."

"Yes. I'm afraid so. I rather botched it, as a liar."

It was good rum. "Then you didn't kill your wife?"

"Kill Rheta! Don't be silly. I loved her, once. Just because our marriage had gone . . . well, anyway, I didn't do it, and mother didn't do it, either."

"Who did, then?"

He smirked humorlessly. "I think some fool did it. Looking for narcotics and money. That's why I called you, Nate. The police aren't looking for the killer. They think they have their man in mother."

"What does your mother's attorney think?"

"He thinks hiring an investigator is a splendid idea."

"Doesn't he have his own man?"

"Yes, but I wanted you. I remembered you from the fair . . . and I asked around."

What did I tell you? Am I a detective?

"I can't promise I can clear her," I said. "She confessed, after all—and the cops took her one confession more seriously than your five."

"They gave her the third degree. A sixty-three-year-old woman! Respected in the community! Can you imagine?"

"Who was the cop in charge?"

Earle pursed his lips in disgust. "Captain Stege himself, the bastard."

"Is this *his* case? Damn."

"Yes, it's Stege's case. Didn't you read about all this in the papers?"

"Sure I did. But I didn't read it like I thought I was going to be involved. I probably did read Stege was in charge, but when you called this morning, I didn't recall . . ."

"Why, Nate? Is this a problem?"

"No," I lied.

I let it go at that, as I needed the work, but the truth was, Stege hated my guts. I'd testified against a couple of cops, which Stege—even though he was honest and those two

38 • JUSTICE FOR HIRE

cops were bent even by Chicago standards—took as a betrayal of the police brotherhood.

Earle was up pouring himself another sherry. Already. "Mother is a sensitive, frail woman, with a heart condition, and she was ruthlessly, mercilessly questioned for a period of over twenty-four hours."

"I see."

"I'm afraid . . ." And Earle sipped his sherry greedily. Swallowed. Continued: "I'm afraid I may have made the situation even worse."

"How?"

He sat again, sighed, shrugged. "As you probably know, I was out of town when Rheta was . . . slain."

That was an odd choice of words; "slain" was something nobody said—a word in the newspapers, not real life.

"I went straight to the Fillmore police station, when I returned from Kansas City. I had a moment with mother. I said . . ." He slumped, shook his head.

"Go on, Earle."

"I said . . . God help me, I said, 'For God's sake, mother, if you did this on account of me, go ahead and confess.'" He touched his fingertips to his eyes.

"What did she say to you?"

"She . . . she said, 'Earle, I did not kill Rheta.' But then she went in for another round with Captain Stege, and . . ."

"And made that cockamamie confession she later retracted."

"Yes."

"Why did you think your mother might have killed your wife for you, Earle?"

"Because . . . because mother loves me very much."

Dr. Alice Lindsay Wynekoop had been one of Chicago's most esteemed female physicians for almost four decades. She had met her late husband, Frank, in medical college, and with him continued the Wynekoop tradition of care for the ill and disabled. Her charity work in hospitals and clinics was well known; a prominent clubwoman, humanitarian, a leader in the woman's suffrage movement, Dr. Wynekoop was an unlikely candidate for a murder charge.

But she had indeed been charged: with the murder of her daughter-in-law, in the basement consultation office in this very house.

Earle led me there, down a narrow stairway off the dining room. In the central basement hallway were two facing doors: Dr. Wynekoop's office at left, and at right, an examination room. The door was open. Earle motioned for me to go in, which I did, but he stayed in the doorway.

The room was narrow and wide and cold; the steam heat was off. The dominant fixture was an old-fashioned, brown-leather-covered examination table. A chair under a large stained-glass window, whose ledge was lined with medical books, sat next to a weigh-and-measure scale. In one corner was a medicine and instrument cabinet.

"The police wouldn't let us clean up properly," Earle said.

The leather exam table was blood-stained.

"They said they might take the whole damn table in," Earle said. "And use it in court, for evidence."

I nodded. "What about your mother's office? She claimed burglary."

"Well, yes . . . some drugs were taken from the cabinet, in here. And six dollars from a drawer . . ."

He led me across the hall to an orderly office area with a big rolltop desk, which he pointed to.

"And," Earle said, pulling open a middle drawer, "there was the gun, of course. Taken from here."

"The cops found it across the hall, though. By the body."

"Yes," Earle said, quietly.

"Tell me about her, Earle."

"Mother?"

"Rheta."

"She . . . she was a lovely girl. A beautiful redhead. Gifted musician . . . violinist. But she was . . . sick."

"Sick how?"

He tapped his head. "She was a hypochondriac. Imagining she had this disease, and that one. Her mother died of tuberculosis . . . in an insane asylum, no less. Rheta came to imagine she had t.b., like her mother. What they did have in common, I'm afraid, was being mentally deranged."

"You said you loved her, Earle."

"I did. Once. The marriage was a failure. I . . . I had to seek affection elsewhere." A wicked smile flickered under the pencil mustache. "I've never had trouble finding women, Nate. I have a little black book with fifty girl friends in it."

It occurred to me that a real man could get by on a considerably shorter list, but I keep opinions like that to myself when given a hundred-buck retainer.

"What did the little woman think about all these girl friends? A crowd like that is hard to hide."

He shrugged. "We never talked about it."

"No talk of a divorce?"

He licked his lips, avoided my eyes. "I wanted one, Nate. She wouldn't give it to me. A good Catholic girl."

Four of the most frightening words in the English language—to any healthy male, anyway.

"The two of you lived here, with your mother?"

"Yes . . . I can't really afford to live elsewhere. Times are hard, you know."

"So I hear. Who else lives here? Isn't there a roomer?"

"Yes. Miss Shaunesey. She's a high school teacher."

"Is she here now?"

"Yes. I asked if she'd talk to you, and she is more than willing. Anything to help mother."

Back in the library, I sat and spoke with Miss Enid Shaunesey, a prim, slim woman of about fifty. Earle lurked in the background, helping himself to more sherry.

"What happened that day, Miss Shaunesey?"

November 21, 1933.

"I probably arose at about a quarter to seven," she said with a little shrug, adjusting her wire-frame glasses. "I had breakfast in the house with Dr. Alice. I don't remember whether Rheta had breakfast with us or not . . . I don't really remember speaking to Rheta at all that morning."

"Then you went on to school?"

"Yes," she said. "I teach at Marshall High. I completed my teaching duties and signed out about three-fifteen. I went to the Loop and shopped until a little after five and went home."

"What, at about six?"

"Or a little after. When I came home, Dr. Alice was in the kitchen, preparing dinner. She fried some pork chops. Made a nice salad, cabbage, potatoes, peaches. It was just the two of us. We're good friends."

"Earle was out of town, of course, but what about Rheta?"

"She was supposed to dine with us, but she was late. We went ahead without her. I didn't think much of it. The girl had a mind of her own; she frequently went here and there—music lessons, shopping." There was a faint note of disapproval, though the conduct she was describing mirrored her own after-school activities of that same day.

"Did Dr. Wynekoop seem to get along with Rheta?"

"They had their tiffs, but Dr. Alice loved the girl. She was family. That evening, during dinner, she spoke of Rheta, in fact."

"What did she say?"

"She was worried about the girl."

"Because she hadn't shown up for supper?"

"Yes, and after the meal she telephoned a neighbor or two, to see if they'd seen Rheta. But she also expressed a more general concern—Rheta was fretting about her health, you see. As I said, Rheta frequently stayed out. We knew she'd probably gone into the Loop to shop and, as she often did, she probably went to a motion picture. That was what we thought."

"I see."

Miss Shaunesey sat up, her expression suddenly thoughtful. "Of course, I'd noticed Rheta's coat and hat on the table here in the library, but Dr. Alice said that she'd probably worn her good coat and hat to the Loop. Anyway, after dinner we talked, and then I went to the drugstore for Dr. Alice, to have a prescription refilled."

"When did you get back?"

"Well, you see, the drugstore is situated at Madison and Kedzie. That store did not have as many tablets as Dr.

Alice wanted, so I walked to the drugstore at Homan and Madison and got a full bottle."

"So it took a while," I said, trying not to get irritated with her fussy old-maid-school-teacher thoroughness. It beat the hell out of an uncooperative, unobservant witness, though. I guessed.

"I was home by half past seven, I should judge. Then we sat down in the library and talked for about an hour. We discussed two books—*Strange Interlude* was one and the other was *The Forsyte Saga*."

"Did Dr. Wynekoop seem relaxed, or was she in any way preoccupied?"

"The former," Miss Shaunesey said with certainty. "Any concern about Rheta's absence was strictly routine."

"At what point did Dr. Wynekoop go downstairs to her consultation room?"

"Well, I was complaining of my hyperacidity. Dr. Alice said she had something in her office that she thought I could use for that. It was in a glass case in her consulting room. Of course, she never got that medicine for me."

Dr. Wynekoop had been interrupted in her errand by the discovery of the body of her daughter-in-law, Rheta. The corpse was face-down on the examination table, the head up on a white pillow. Naked, the body was wrapped in a sheet and a blanket snugged in around the feet and pulled up over the shoulders, like a child lovingly tucked into bed. Rheta had been shot—once, in the back. Her lips were scorched as if by acid. A wet towel was under her mouth, indicating perhaps that chloroform had been administered. A half-empty bottle of chloroform was found on the washstand. And a gauze-wrapped .32 Smith and Wesson rested on the pillow above the girl's head.

"Dr. Wynekoop did not call the police?" I asked, knowing the answer. This much I remembered from the papers.

"No."

"Or an undertaker, or the coroner's office?"

"No. She called her daughter, Catherine."

Earle looked up from his sherry long enough to interject: "Catherine is a doctor, too. She's a resident at the Children's Department at Cook County Hospital."

And that was my logical first stop. I took the El over to the hospital, a block-square graystone at Harrison and Ogden. This job was strictly a West Side affair.

Dr. Catherine Wynekoop was a beautiful woman. Her dark hair was pulled back from her pale, pretty face; in her doctor's whites, she sat in the hospital cafeteria stirring her coffee as we spoke.

"I was on duty here when mother called," she said. "She said, 'Something terrible has happened at home . . . it's Rheta . . . she's dead . . . she has been shot.'"

"How did she sound? Hysterical? Calm?"

"Calm, but a shocked sort of calm." She sighed. "I went home immediately. Mother seemed all right, but I noticed her gait was a little unsteady. Her hands were trembling, her face was flushed. I helped her to a chair in the dining room and rushed out to the kitchen for stimuli. I put a teaspoonful of aromatic spirits of ammonia in water and had her drink it."

"She hadn't called anyone but you as yet?"

"No. She said she'd just groped her way up the stairs, that on the way everything went black, she felt dizzy, that the next thing she knew she was at the telephone calling me."

"Did you take charge then?"

A half-smile twitched at her cheek. "I guess I did. I called Mr. Ahearn."

"Mr. Ahearn?"

"The undertaker. And I called Dr. Berger, our family physician."

"You really should have called the coroner."

"Mother later said that she'd asked me to, on the phone, but I didn't hear that or understand her or something. We were upset. Once Dr. Berger and Mr. Ahearn arrived, the coroner's office was called."

She kept stirring her coffee, staring into it.

"How did you and Rheta get along?"

She lifted her eyebrows in a shrug. "We weren't close. We had little in common. But there was no animosity."

She seemed goddamn guarded to me; I decided to try and knock her wall down, or at least jar some stones loose.

I said, "Do you think your mother killed Rheta?"

Her dark eyes rose to mine and flashed. "Of course not. I never heard my mother speak an unkind word to or about Rheta." She searched her mind for an example, and came up with one: "Why, whenever mother bought me a dress, she bought one for Rheta also."

She returned her gaze to the coffee, which she stirred methodically.

Then she continued: "She was worried about Rheta, actually. Worried about the way Earle was treating her. Worried about all the . . . well, about the crowd he started to run around with down at the World's Fair. Mother asked me to talk to him about it."

"About what, exactly?"

"His conduct."

"You mean, his girl friends."

She looked at me sharply. "Mr. Heller, my understanding is that you are in our family's employ. Some of these questions of yours seem uncalled for."

I gave her my most charming smile. "Miss Wynekoop . . . doctor . . . I'm like you. Sometimes I have to ask unpleasant questions, if I'm going to make the proper diagnosis."

She considered that a moment, then smiled. It was a honey of a smile, making mine look like the shabby sham it was.

"I understand, Mr. Heller." She rose. She'd never touched the coffee once. "I'm afraid I have afternoon rounds to make."

She extended her hand; it was delicate, but her grasp had strength and she had dignity. Hard to believe she was Earle's sister.

I had my own rounds to make, and at a different hospital; it took a couple of streetcars to do the job. The county jail was a grim, low-slung graystone lurking behind the Criminal Courts Building. This complex of city buildings was just south of a West Side residential area, just eight blocks south of Douglas Park. Old home week for me.

Alice Wynekoop was sitting up in bed, reading a medical journal, when I was led to her by a matron. She was in the corner and had much of the ward to herself; the beds on either side were empty.

She was of average size, but frail-looking; she appeared much older than her sixty-three years, her flesh freckled with liver spots, her neck creped. The skin of her face had a wilted look, with dark patches under the eyes, saggy jowls.

But her eyes were dark and sharp. And her mouth was a stern line.

"Are you a policeman?" she asked. Her tone was neutral.

I had my hat in hand. "I'm Nathan Heller," I said. "I'm the private investigator your son hired."

She smiled in a businesslike way, extended her hand for me to shake, which I did. Surprisingly strong for such a weak-looking woman.

"Pull up a chair, Mr. Heller," she said. Her voice was clear and crisp. Someone very different from the woman she outwardly appeared to be lived inside that worn-out body.

I sat. "I'm going to be asking around about some things . . . inquire about burglaries in your neighborhood and such."

She nodded, twice, very businesslike. "I'm certain the thief was after narcotics. In fact, some narcotics were taken, but I keep precious few in my surgery."

"Yes. I see. What about the gun?"

"It was my husband's. We've had it for years. I've never fired it in my life."

I took out my small spiral notebook. "I know you're tired of telling it, but I need to hear your story. Before I go poking around the edges of this case, I need to understand the center of it."

She nodded and smiled. "What would you like to know exactly?"

"When did you last see your daughter-in-law?"

"About three P.M. that Tuesday. She said she was going for a walk with Mrs. Donovan . . . ."

"Who?"

"A neighbor of ours who was a good friend to the child. Verna Donovan. She's a divorcee; they were quite close."

I wrote the name down. "Go on."

"Anyway, Rheta said something about going for a walk with Mrs. Donovan. She also said she might go downtown and get some sheet music. I urged her to go out in the air, as it was a fine day, and gave her money for the music. After she left, I went for a walk myself, through the neighborhood. It was an unusually beautiful day for November, pleasantly warm."

"How long were you gone?"

"I returned at about four-forty-five P.M. I came in the front door. Miss Shaunesey arrived from school about six o'clock. I wasn't worried then about Rheta's absence, because I expected her along at any minute. I prepared dinner for the three of us—Miss Shaunesey, Rheta, and myself—and set the table. Finally, Miss Shaunesey and I sat down to eat, both wondering where Rheta was but, again, not terribly worried."

"It wasn't unusual for her to stay out without calling to say she'd miss supper?"

"Not in the least. She was quiet, but rather . . . self-absorbed. If she walked by a motion-picture marquee that caught her eye, she might just wander on in, without a thought about anyone who might be waiting for her."

"She sounds inconsiderate."

Alice Wynekoop smiled tightly, revealing a strained patience. "She was a strange, quiet girl. Rather moody, I'm afraid. She had definite feelings of inferiority, particularly in regards to my daughter, Catherine, who is, after all, a physician. But I digress. At about a quarter to seven, I telephoned Mrs. Donovan and asked her if she had been with Rheta. She said she hadn't seen her since three o'clock, but urged me not to worry."

"Were you worried?"

"Not terribly. At any rate, at about seven o'clock I asked Miss Shaunesey to go and get a prescription filled for me. She left the house and I remained there. She returned about an hour later and was surprised that Rheta had not yet returned. At this point, I admit I was getting worried about the girl."

"Tell me about finding the body."

She nodded, her eyes fixed. "Miss Shaunesey and I sat and talked in the library. Then about eight-thirty she asked me to get her some medicine for an upset stomach. I went downstairs to the examination room to get the medicine from the cabinet." She placed a finger against one cheek thoughtfully. "I recall now that I thought it odd to find the door of the examination room closed, as it was usually kept open. I turned the knob and slipped my hand inside to find the electric switch."

"And you found her."

She shuddered, but it seemed a gesture, not an involuntary response. "It is impossible for me to describe my feelings when I saw Rheta lying there under that flood of light! I felt as if I were somewhere else. I cannot find words to express my feelings."

"What did you do?"

"Well, I knew something had to be done at once, and I called my daughter, Catherine, at the county hospital. I told her Rheta was dead. She was terribly shocked, of course. I . . . I thought I had asked Catherine to notify the coroner and to hurry right over. It seemed ages till she got there. When she did arrive, I had her call Dr. Berger and Mr. Ahearn. It wasn't until some time after they arrived that I realized Catherine had not called the coroner as I thought I'd instructed her. Mr. Ahearn then called the authorities."

I nodded. "All right. You're doing fine, doctor. Now tell me about your son and his wife."

"What do you mean?"

"It wasn't a happy union, was it?"

Her smile was a sad crease in her wrinkled face. "At one time it was. Earle went with me to a medical convention in Indianapolis in . . . must have been '29. Rheta played the violin as part of the entertainment there. They began to correspond. A year later they were wed."

"And came to live with you."

"Earle didn't have a job—you know, he's taken up

photography of late, and has had several assignments; I'm really very proud—and, well . . . anyway. The girl was barely nineteen when they married. I redecorated and refurnished a suite of rooms on the second floor for my newlyweds. She was a lovely child, beautiful red hair. And, of course, Earle . . . he's as handsome a boy as ever walked this earth."

"But Rheta was moody . . . ?"

"Very much so. And obsessed with her health. Perhaps that's why she married into the Wynekoop family. She was fearful of tuberculosis, but there were no indications of it at all. In the last month of her life, she was rather melancholy, of a somewhat morbid disposition. I discussed with her about going out into the open and taking exercise. We discussed that often."

"You did not kill your daughter-in-law."

"No! Mr. Heller, I'm a doctor. My profession, my life, is devoted to healing."

I rose. Slipped the notebook in my pocket. "Well, thank you, Dr. Wynekoop. I may have a few more questions at a later date."

She smiled again, a warm, friendly smile, coming from so controlled a woman. "I'd be pleased to have your company. And I appreciate your help. I'm very worried about the effect this is having on Earle."

"Dr. Wynekoop, with all due respect . . . my major concern is the effect this is going to have on you, if I can't find the real killer."

Her smile disappeared and she nodded sagely. She extended her hand for a final handshake, and I left her there.

I used a pay phone in the visitors' area to call Sergeant Lou Sapperstein at Central Headquarters in the Loop. Lou had been my boss on the pickpocket detail. I asked him to check for me to see what officer in the Fillmore district had caught the call the night of the Wynekoop homicide.

"That's Stege's case," Lou said. Sapperstein was a hard-nosed, fair-minded, balding cop of about forty-five seasoned years. "You shouldn't mess in Stege's business. He doesn't like you."

"God, you're a great detective, picking up on a detail like that. Can you get me the name?"

"Five minutes. Stay where you are."

I gave him the pay phone number and he called back in a little over three minutes.

"Officer Raymond March, detailed with Squad Fifteen," he said.

I checked my watch; it was after four.

"He's on duty now," I said. "Do me another favor."

"Why don't you get a goddamn secretary?"

"You're a public servant, aren't you? So serve, already."

"So tell me what you want, already."

"Get somebody you trust at Fillmore to tell Officer March to meet me at the drugstore on the corner of Madison and Kedzie. Between six and seven."

"What's in it for Officer March?"

"Supper and a fin."

"Why not?" Lou said, a shrug in his voice.

He called me back in five or six minutes and said the message would be passed.

I hit the streetcars again and was back on Monroe Street by a quarter to five. It was getting dark already, and colder.

Mrs. Verna Donovan lived in the second-floor two-flat of a graystone three doors down from the Wynekoop mansion. The smell of corned beef and cabbage cooking seeped from under the door.

I knocked.

It took a while, but a slender, attractive woman of perhaps thirty in a floral dress and a white apron opened the door wide.

"Oh!" she said. Her face was oblong, her eyes a luminous brown, her hair another agreeable shade of brown, cut in a bob that was perhaps too young for her.

"Didn't mean to startle you, ma'am. Are you Mrs. Donovan?"

"Yes, I am." She smiled shyly. "Sorry for my reaction—I

was expecting my son. We'll be eating in about half an hour . . ."

"I know this is a bad time to come calling. Perhaps I could arrange another time . . ."

"What is your business here?"

I gave her one of my A-1 Detective Agency cards. "I'm working for the Wynekoops. Nathan Heller, president of the A-1 agency. I'm hoping to find Rheta's killer."

Her eyes sparkled. "Well, come in! If you don't mind sitting in the kitchen while I get dinner ready . . ."

"Not at all," I said, following her through a nicely but not lavishly furnished living room, overseen by an elaborate print of the Virgin Mary, and back to a good-size blue and white kitchen.

She stood at the counter making coleslaw while I sat at the kitchen table nearby.

"We were very good friends, Rheta and I. She was a lovely girl, talented, very funny."

"Funny? I get the impression she was a somber girl."

"Around the Wynekoops she was. They're about as much fun as falling down the stairs. Do you think the old girl killed her?"

"What do you think?"

"I could believe it of Earle. Dr. Alice herself, well . . . I mean, she's a doctor. She's aloof, and she and Rheta were anything but close, of course. But kill her?"

"I'm hearing that the doctor gave Rheta gifts, treated her like a family member."

Verna Donovan shrugged, putting some muscle into her slaw-making efforts. "There was no love lost between them. You're aware that Earle ran around on her?"

"Yes."

"Well, that sort of thing is hard on a girl's self-esteem. I helped her get over it as much as I could."

"How?"

She smiled shyly over her shoulders. "I'm a divorcee, Mr. Heller. And divorcees know how to have a good time. Care for a taste?"

She was offering me a forkful of slaw.

"That's nice," I said, savoring it. "Nice bite to it. So, you and Rheta went out together? Was she seeing other men, then?"

"Of course she was. Why shouldn't she?"

"Anyone in particular?"

"Her music teacher. Violin instructor. Older man, very charming. But he died of a heart attack four months ago. It hit her hard."

"How did she handle it?"

"Well, she didn't shoot herself in the back over it, if that's what you're thinking! She was morose for about a month . . . then she just started to date all of a sudden. I encouraged her, and she came back to life again."

"Why didn't she just divorce Earle?"

"Why, Mr. Heller . . . she was a good Catholic girl."

She asked me to stay for supper but I declined, despite the tempting aroma of her corned beef and cabbage and the tang of her slaw. I had another engagement, at a drugstore at Madison and Kedzie.

While I waited for Officer March to show up, I questioned the pharmacist behind the back counter.

"Sure I remember Miss Shaunesey stopping by that night," he said. "But I don't understand why she did."

"Why is that?"

"Well, Dr. Wynekoop herself stopped in a week before, to fill a similar prescription, and I told her our stock was low."

"She probably figured you'd've got some in by then," I said.

"The doctor knows we only get a shipment in once a month."

I was mulling that over at the lunch counter when Officer March arrived. He was in his late twenties and blond and much too fresh-faced for a Chicago cop.

"Nate Heller," he said, with a grin. "I've heard about you."

We shook hands.

"Don't believe everything Captain Stege tells you," I said.

He took the stool next to me, took off his cap. "I know Stege thinks you're poison. But that's 'cause he's an old-timer. Me, I'm glad you helped expose those two crooked bastards."

"Let's not get carried away, Officer March. What's the point of being a cop in this town if you can't take home a little graft now and then?"

"Sure," March said. "But those guys were killers. West Side bootleggers."

"I'm a West Side boy myself," I said.

"So I understand. So what's your interest in the Wynekoop case?"

"The family hired me to help clear the old gal. Do you think she did it?"

He made a clicking sound in his cheek. "Hard one to call. She seemed pretty shook up at the scene."

"Shook up like a grieved family member, or a murderer?"

"I couldn't read it."

"Order yourself a sandwich and then tell me about it."

He did. The call had come in at nine-fifty-nine over the police radio, about five blocks away from where he and his partner were patrolling.

"The girl's body was lying on that table," March said. "She was resting on her left front side with her left arm under her, with the right forearm extending upward so that her hand was about on a level with her chin, with her head on a white pillow. Her face was almost out of sight, but I could see that her mouth and nose were resting on a wet, crumpled towel. She'd been bleeding from the mouth."

"She was covered up, I understand," I said.

"Yes. I drew the covers down carefully, and saw that she'd been shot through the left side of the back. Body was cold. Dead about six hours, I'd guess."

"But that's just a guess."

"Yeah. The coroner can't nail it all that exact. It can be a few hours either direction, you know."

"No signs of a struggle."

"None. That girl laid down on that table herself—maybe at gun point, but whatever the case, she did it herself. Her clothes were lying about the floor at the foot of the examination table, dropped, not thrown, just as though she'd undressed in a leisurely fashion."

"What about the acid burns on the girl's face?"

"She was apparently chloroformed before she was shot. You know, that confession Stege got out of Dr. Wynekoop—that's how she said she did it."

The counterman brought us coffee.

"I'll be frank, officer," I said, sipping the steaming java. "I just came on this job. I haven't had a chance to go down to a newspaper morgue and read the text of that confession."

He shrugged. "Well, it's easily enough summed up. She said her daughter-in-law was always wanting physical examinations. That afternoon she went downstairs with the doctor for an exam and, first off, stripped to weigh herself. She had a sudden pain in her side and Dr. Wynekoop suggested a whiff of choloroform as an anesthetic. The doc said she massaged the girl's side for about fifteen minutes, and . . ."

"I'm remembering this from the papers," I said, nodding. "She claimed the girl 'passed away' on the examining table, and she panicked. Figured her career would be ruined if it came out she'd accidentally killed her own daughter-in-law with an overdose of chloroform."

"Right. And then she remembered the old revolver in the desk, and fired a shot into the girl and tried to make it look like a robbery."

The counterman came and refilled our coffee cups.

"So," I said, "what do you make of the confession?"

"I think it's bullshit any way you look at it. Hell, she was grilled for almost three days, Heller—you know how valid *that* kind of confession is."

I sipped my coffee. "She may have thought her son was guilty, and was covering up for him."

"Well, her confession was certainly a self-serving one. After all, if she was telling the truth—or even if her confession was made up outta whole cloth but got taken at face value—it'd make her guilty of nothing more than involuntary manslaughter."

I nodded. "Shooting a corpse isn't a felony."

"But she *had* to know her son didn't do it."

"Why?"

March smirked. "He sent her a telegram; he was in Peoria, a hundred and ninety miles away."

"Telegram? When did she receive this telegram?"

"Late afternoon. Funny thing, though."

"Oh?"

"Initially, Dr. Wynekoop said she'd seen Earle last on November twelfth, when he left on a trip to the Grand Canyon to take some photographs. But Earle came back to Chicago on the nineteenth, two days before the murder."

I damn near spilled my coffee. "*What?*"

March nodded emphatically. "He and his mother met at a restaurant, miles from home. They were seen sitting in a back booth."

"But you said Earle was in Peoria when his wife was killed . . ."

"He was. He left Chicago, quietly, the next day—drove to Peoria. And from Peoria he went to Kansas City."

"Do his alibis hold up? Peoria isn't Mars; he could've established an alibi and made a round trip . . ."

"I thought you were working for the family?"

"I am. But if I proved Earle did it, they'd spring his mother."

March laughed hollowly. "She'd be pissed off at you, partner."

"I know. But I already got their retainer. So. Tell me. What did you hold back from the papers?"

It was standard practice to keep back a few details in a murder case; that helped clear up confessions from crazy people.

"I shouldn't," he said.

I handed him a folded fin.

He slipped it in the breast pocket of his uniform blouse.

"Hope for you yet," I said.

"Two items of interest," March said softly. "There were three bullets fired from that gun."

"Three? But Rheta was shot only once . . ."

"Right."

"Were the other bullets found?"

"No. We took that examining room apart. Then we took the house apart. Nothing."

"What do you make of that?"

"I don't know. You'd have to ask Stege . . . if you got nerve enough."

"You said two things."

March swallowed slowly. "This may not even come out at the trial. It's not necessarily good for the prosecution."

"Spill."

"The coroner's physician picked up on something of interest, even before the autopsy."

"What?"

"Rheta had syphilis."

"Jesus. You're kidding!"

"A very bad dose."

I sat and pondered that.

"We asked Earle to submit to a physical," March said, "and he consented."

"And?"

"And he's in perfect health."

I took the El back to the Loop and got off at Van Buren and Plymouth, where I had an office on the second floor of the corner building. I lived there, since I kept an eye on the building in lieu of paying rent. Before I went up, I drank in the bar downstairs for half an hour or so, chatting with bartender Buddy Gold, who was a friend. I asked him if he was following the Wynekoop case in the papers.

"That old broad is innocent," the lumpy-faced ex-boxer said. "It's a crime what they're doin' to her."

"What are they doing to her?"

"I saw her picture in the paper, in that jailhouse hospital bed. Damn shame, nice woman like that, with her charities and all."

"What about the dead girl? Maybe she was 'nice.'"

"Yeah, but some dope fiend did it. Why don't they find him and put him in jail?"

I said that was a good idea and had another beer. Then I went up to my office and pulled down the Murphy bed and flopped. It had been a long, weird day. I'd earned my fifteen bucks.

The phone woke me. When I opened my eyes, it was morning but the light filtering in around the drawn shades was gray. It would be a cold one. I picked up the receiver on the fifth ring.

"A-1 Detective Agency," I said.

"Nathan Heller?" a gravelly male voice demanded.

I sat on the edge of the desk, rubbing my eyes. "Speaking."

"This is Captain John Stege."

I slid off the desk. "What can I do for you?"

"Steer clear of my case, you son-of-a-bitch."

"What case is that, Captain?"

Stege was a white-haired fireplug with dark-rimmed glasses, a meek-looking individual who could scare the hell out of you when he felt like it. He felt like it now.

"You stay out of the goddamn Wynekoop case. I won't have you mucking it up."

How did he even know I was on the case? Had Officer March told him?

"I was hired by the family to try to help clear Dr. Wynekoop. It's hardly uncommon for a defendant in a murder case to hire an investigator."

"Dr. Alice Lindsay Wynekoop murdered her daughter-in-law! It couldn't be any other way."

"Captain, it could be a lot of other ways. It could be one of her boyfriends; it could be one of her husband's girl friends. It could be a break-in artist looking for drugs. It could be—"

"Are you telling me how to do my job?"

"Well, you're telling me how not to do mine."

There was a long pause.

Then Stege said, "I don't like you, Heller. You stay out of my way. You go manufacturing evidence and I'll introduce you to every rubber hose in this town . . . and I know plenty of 'em."

"You have the wrong idea about me, Captain," I said. "And you may have the wrong idea about Alice Wyne-koop."

PRIVATE CONSULTATION • 57

"Bull! She insured young Rheta for five grand fewer than thirty days before the girl's death. With double indemnity, the policy pays ten thousand smackers."

I hadn't heard about this.

"The Wynekoops *have* money," I said. "A murder-for-insurance-money scheme makes no sense for a well-to-do family like that."

"Dr. Wynekoop owes almost five thousand dollars back taxes and has over twenty thousand dollars in overdue bank notes. She's prominent, but she's not wealthy. She got hit in the Crash."

"Well . . ."

"She killed her daughter-in-law to make her son happy and to collect the insurance money. If you were worth two cents as a detective, you'd know that."

"Speaking of detective work, Captain, how did you know I was on this case?"

"Don't you read the papers?"

The papers had me in them, all right. A small story, but well placed, on several front pages in fact; under a picture of Earle seated at his mother's side in the jail hospital, the *News* told how the Wynekoops had hired a local private investigator, one Nathan Heller, to help prove Dr. Alice's innocence.

I called Earle Wynekoop and asked him to meet me at the county jail hospital wing. I wanted to talk to both of my clients.

On the El, I thought about how I had intended to pursue this case. Having done the basic groundwork with the family and witnesses, I would begin searching for the faceless break-in artist whose burglary had got out of hand, leading to the death of Rheta Wynekoop. Never mind that it made no sense for a thief to take a gun from a rolltop desk, make his victim undress, shoot her in the back, tuck her in like a child at bedtime, and leave the gun behind. Criminals did crazy things, after all. I would spend three or four days sniffing around the West Side pawn shops and resale shops, and the Maxwell Street market, looking for a lead on any petty crook whose drug addic-

tion might lead to violence. I would comb the flophouses
and bars hopheads were known to frequent, and . . .

But I had changed my mind, at least for the moment.

Earle was at his mother's bedside when the matron left
me there. Dr. Alice smiled in her tight, businesslike
manner and offered me a hand to shake; I took it. Earle
stood and nodded and smiled nervously at me. I nodded
to him, and he sat again.

But I stayed on my feet.

"I'm off this case," I said.

"What?" Earle said, eyes wide.

Dr. Alice remained calm. Her appraising eyes were as
cold as the weather.

"Captain Stege suggested it," I said.

"That isn't legal!" Earle said.

"Quiet, Earle," his mother said, sternly but with gentle-
ness.

"That's not why I'm quitting," I said. "And I'm keeping
the retainer, too, by the way."

"Now, that *isn't* legal!" Earle said, standing.

"Shut up," I said to him. To her I said, "You two used
me. I'm strictly a publicity gimmick. To help make you
look sincere, to help you keep up a good front . . . just
like staying in the jail's hospital ward so you can pose for
pitiful newspaper pics."

Dr. Alice blinked and smiled thinly. "You're revealing an
obnoxious side, Mr. Heller, that is unbecoming."

"You killed your daughter-in-law, Dr. Wynekoop. For
sonny boy here."

Earle's face clenched like a fist, and he clenched his fists,
too, while he was at it. "I ought to . . ."

I looked at him hard. "I wish to hell you would."

His eyes flickered at me, then he glanced at his mother.
She nodded and motioned for him to sit again, and he did.

"Mr. Heller," she said, "I assure you, I am innocent. I
don't know what you've been told that gave you this very
false impression, but—"

"Save it. I know what happened, and why. You discovered, in one of your frequent on-the-house examinations

of your hypochondriac daughter-in-law, that she really *was* ill. Specifically, she had a social disease."

Anger flared in the doctor's eyes.

"You could forgive Earle all his philandering . . . even though you didn't approve. You did ask your daughter to talk to him about his excesses of drink and dames. But those were just misdemeanors. For your husband's wife to run around, to get a nasty disease that she might just pass along to your boy should their marriage ever heat up again . . . well, that was a crime. And it deserved punishment."

"Mr. Heller, why don't you go. You may keep your retainer, if you keep your silence."

"Oh, hitting a little close to home, am I? Well, let me finish. You paid for this. I don't think it was your idea to kill Rheta, despite the dose of syph she was carrying. I think it was Earle's idea. She wouldn't give him a divorce, good Catholic girl that she was, and Earle's a good Catholic, too, after all. It'd be hell to get excommunicated, right, Earle? Right, mom?"

Earle was shaking, his hands clasped prayerfully. Dr. Wynekoop's wrinkled face was a stern mask.

"Here's what happened," I said cheerfully. "Earle came to you and asked you to put the little woman to sleep—she was a tortured girl, after all; if it were done painlessly, why, it would be a merciful act. But you refused—you're a doctor, a healer. It wouldn't be right."

Earle's eyes were shifting from side to side in confirmation of my theory.

I forged ahead: "But Earle came to you again and said, 'Mother dear, if you don't do it, I will. I've found father's old .32, and I've tried it—fired two test rounds. It works, and I know how to work it. I'm going to kill Rheta myself.'"

Earle's eyes were wide, as was his mouth. I must have come very, very close, even perhaps repeated his very language. Dr. Alice continued to maintain a poker face.

"So, mom, you decided to take matters in hand. When Earle came back early from his Grand Canyon photo trip, the two of you rendezvoused away from home—though you were seen, unfortunately—and came up with a plan. Earle would resume his trip, only go no farther than Peoria, where he would establish an alibi."

Earle's face contorted as he took in every damning word.

"On the day of the murder," I told her, "you had a final private consultation with your daughter-in-law . . . you overdosed her with chloroform, or smothered her."

"Mr. Heller," Dr. Alice said icily, looking away from me, "this fantasy of yours holds no interest whatsoever for me."

"Well, maybe so . . . but Earle's all perked up. Anyway, you left the body downstairs, closing the examining room door, locking it probably, and went on about the business of business as usual—cooking supper for your roomer, spending a quiet evening with her . . . knowing that Earle would be back after dark, to quietly slip in and . . . what? Dispose of the body somehow. That was the plan, wasn't it? The unhappy bride would just disappear. Or perhaps turn up dead in a ditch, or . . . whatever. Only it didn't happen that way. Because sonny boy chickened out."

And now Dr. Alice broke form momentarily, her eyes turning on Earle for just an instant, giving him one nasty glance, the only time I ever saw her look at the louse with anything but devotion.

"He sent you a telegram in the afternoon, letting you know that he was still in Peoria. And that he was going to stay in Peoria. And you, with a corpse in the basement. Imagine."

"You have a strange sense of humor, Mr. Heller."

"You have a strange way of practicing medicine, Dr. Wynekoop. You sent your roomer, Miss Shaunesey, on a fool's errand—sending her to a drugstore where you knew the prescription couldn't be filled. And you knew conscientious Miss Shaunesey would try another drugstore, buying you time."

"Really," Dr. Alice said dryly.

"Really. That's when you concocted the burglary story. You're too frail physically to go hauling a corpse anywhere. But you remembered that gun, across the hall. So you shot your dead daughter-in-law, adding insult to injury, and faked the robbery—badly, but it was impromptu, after all."

"I don't have to listen to this!" Earle said.

"Then don't," I said. "What you didn't remember, Dr. Wynekoop, is that two bullets had already been fired from that weapon, when Earle tested it. And that little anomaly bothered me."

"Did it?" she said flatly.

"It did. Your daughter-in-law's syphilis, the two missing bullets, and the hour you spent alone in the house while the roomer was away and Rheta was dead in your examining room. Those three factors added up to one thing: your guilt, and your son's complicity."

"Are you going to tell your story to anyone?" she asked blandly.

"No," I said. "You're my client."

"How much?" Earle said, with a nasty, nervous little sneer.

I held my hands up, palms out. "No more. I'm keeping my retainer. I earned it."

I turned my back on them and began to walk away.

From behind me, I heard her say, with no irony whatsoever, "Thank you, Mr. Heller."

I turned and looked at her and laughed. "Hey, you're going to jail, lady. The cops and the D.A. won't need me to get it done, and all the good publicity you cook up won't change a thing. I have only one regret."

I made them ask. Earle took the honors.

"What's that?" Earle asked, as he stood there trembling; his mother reached her hand out and patted his nearest hand, soothing him.

I smiled at him—the nastiest smile I could muster. "That you won't be going to jail with her, you son of a bitch."

And go to jail she did.

But it took a while. A most frail-looking Dr. Alice was carried into the courtroom on the opening day of the trial—still playing for sympathy in the press, I figured.

Then, after eight days of evidence, Dr. Alice had an apparent heart seizure when the prosecution hauled the blood-stained examination table into court. A mistrial was declared. When she recovered, though, she got a brand-new one. The press milked the case for all its worth; public opinion polls in the papers indicated half of Chicago considered Dr. Alice guilty, the other half thought her innocent. The jury, however, was unanimous—it took them only fifteen minutes to find her guilty and two hours to set the sentence at twenty-five years.

Earle didn't attend the trial. They say that just as Dr. Alice was being ushered in the front gate at the Woman's Reformatory at Dwight, Illinois, an unshaven, disheveled figure darted from the nearby bushes. Earle kissed his mother good-bye and she brushed away his tears. As usual.

She served thirteen years, denying her guilt all the way; she was released with time off for good behavior. She died on July 4, 1955, in a nursing home, under an assumed name.

Earle changed his name, too. What became of him, I can't say. There were rumors, of course. One was that he had found work as a garage mechanic. Another was that he had finally remarried—a beautiful redhead.

Dr. Catherine Wynekoop did not change her name, and went on to a distinguished medical career.

And the house at 3406 West Monroe, the Death Clinic, was torn down in 1947. The year Dr. Alice was released.

AUTHOR'S NOTE: I wish to acknowledge several true-crime articles: "The Wynekoop Case" by Craig Rice, 1947, as reprinted in *The Chicago Crime Book*, 1967; "Who Killed Rheta Wynekoop?" by Harry Read, *Real Detective Magazine*, April 1934; and a 1987 *New York Daily News* column, "The Justice Story," by Joseph McNamara. Most names in the preceding fact-based story have been changed or altered (exceptions include Captain Stege, Rheta Wynekoop, Alice Lindsay Wynekoop, and Earle Wynekoop); fact, speculation, and fiction are freely mixed therein.

Michael Collins' one-armed detective, Dan Fortune, has been appearing in novels and short stories since 1967, when Act of Fear *won the Edgar Award for best first novel. In 1988 Michael Collins—in his true guise as Dennis Lynds—won a Life Achievement Award from PWA. Here, Fortune makes his first short story appearance since moving from New York to California.*

The Chair

---

by Michael Collins

Thin. That was the first thing you saw about him: the scrawny, almost delicate body. The face of a shy young girl on a body not developed enough to be a girl, or anything else.

Most of them were thin. With hollow cheeks and bony Indian faces and deep-set dark eyes. One was short and squat like a pre-Columbian Aztec stone statue. One was tall by the standards of the homeland to the south most of them had never seen. But only Molina had the delicate, almost girlish face with the smooth brown skin as the six boys stood sullen before the judge.

"His name's Pascual Molina," the deputy public defender had told me. "I have to have something to work with, Dan. It's wrong, I feel it, but I've got nothing I can use."

"You think he's innocent?"

Defense lawyers think all their clients are innocent. Or say they do. That's our system. Thieves, killers, and psychos go back on the streets, and that's the risk we take to be sure no innocent man is found guilty. It doesn't always save the innocent or convict the guilty, but it's the best system so far.

"He looks guilty. All six of them do."

He got my attention. A lawyer who said what he really thought.

"But something's missing, and Molina won't talk. He's not like the rest. They're street kids, gang tough. Molina goes to City College at night. He's got a job. His parents are hardworking people who own their home. Our chief investigator says Molina has no police record at all. The rest have sheets as long as their hair."

"Why don't your investigators follow up on it?"

"We've got six in the killing, and it's not our only case. I need special work on Molina."

It's one way a private detective lives. "Okay. Give me names, addresses, everything you know."

Now, in court for the reading of the information, I studied Pascual Molina. If he was different, he was trying hard not to show it. He was as surly and defiant as the rest as they stood in front of the judge, who seemed to see them and not see them as he read papers on his high bench and supposedly listened.

Behind the six boys on the hard seats of the courtroom in the fine old Moorish courthouse, the older people sat wrapped in bright colors and black hair and quick Spanish words. The constant whispering and touching of frightened people who understand little of what they are seeing and hearing, but who know that what they are seeing and hearing is important to them. So they shift and pluck at each other and talk, because they can only wait for someone to tell them what has happened, if it is a time to laugh or a time to cry.

". . . on the night of March tenth, about the hour of ten P.M., did commit homicide in the first degree. The victim of said homicide being one Walter Biggs, male Caucasian, aged sixteen years. Said homicide did take place in the public park . . ." The droning voice told in thick legal language how Raul Gonzales, Pascual Molina, Edgardo Montez, Pepe Santos, José Villareal, and José Gonzales, no relation to Raul, did murder one Walter Biggs.

"How do they plead?"

Each, nudged by the deputy P.D., mumbled his "not guilty."

The tall one, the oldest, Raul Gonzales, aged nineteen, said, "Hey, they gonna lay the gas on us, lawyer man?"

"Keep your clients quiet, counselor."

Six surly boys remanded to county jail to await trial. The date set. No bail. And loud Spanish wailing went slowly up the aisle of the courtroom and down the polished stone corridors into the city that was named in one language and owned in another.

Hands so small and delicate it was hard to imagine them holding a broom handle. Impossible to imagine the smooth brown skin with blood on it, the thin arm feeling the shock of bone as the club struck another human in the gloom of a park.

"They want Murder One," the lawyer said in the cell. "They say you were laying for white guys. You all planned it and Biggs got killed. Only I don't believe you planned a damn thing. I don't believe you knew what was really going down."

Ankles in the prison pant legs not much bigger than the lawyer's wrists. Chicken legs, a scrawny neck even I could break with my one arm, and a girl's hands. But a club, a knife, a gun are wondrous magic that make a man out of a thin boy, cut giants down to size, grow a delicate kid ten feet tall. A kid who looked at both of us with blank black eyes and said nothing.

Detective Sergeant Gus Chavalas is short and dark and everyone thinks he's Latino. He's actually Greek, but if being Latino gives him an edge in the *barrio,* it's fine with him.

"Molina's got no known gang connection until now, and his family's two hundred percent straight arrow," Chavalas said. "So what, Fortune? He's in a gang now, and we got three witnesses say he was right there laying it on Biggs with a broom handle."

"Witnesses?"

The surprise must have shown on my face. Chavalas laughed.

"The P.D. didn't tell you, huh? We got a transient sleeping under the bandstand, and a smoochy couple with their pants down in the bushes. It was dark, but they saw enough."

"What did they see?"

"Our six Latino guerrillas came into the park looking for trouble. Knocked over signs and benches, ripped up bushes, stomped flower beds. They wanted someone to kick butt on, and Walter Biggs showed up. Not that he didn't feed the fire by being a big-mouth asshole who figured he could handle ten beaners for breakfast. Turns out he was no angel himself—had a record of fights and drunks and drug busts longer than theirs."

"He provoked them?"

"He didn't turn the other cheek," Chavalas said. "But that didn't give them the right to gang him, Fortune. They killed him, and they'll pay for it."

"Molina's studying at City College. He's got a regular job, a steady girl."

"Jack the Ripper was a medical student. Jesse James had a steady girl." Chavalas shrugged. "He went bad. The work was too much for too little bread. School got too tough. How do I know? All we know is Molina was there and in it up to his mustache."

"He hasn't got a mustache," I said. "He can't grow one yet."

They were lined up on the flowered couch. The three women and the small boy, stiff and prim, hands in their laps. The father sat apart in a high-backed carved wood chair. No taller than his jailed son but twice as thick, a graying mustache under his straw sombrero, his black eyes outraged.

"My son is good boy. He work hard, has respect. He does not do what they say. No way."

The small boy was a miniature of his father and his brother. Thin and delicate, wearing a sombrero. The father traditional in the ways of an old country he had probably never seen but claimed as his own because everyone has to claim somewhere.

"Pascual he go to college," the older woman said. "Study, know all about America."

The women were somewhere between the country of their language and the country where they had been born and where they lived. The older woman, the mother, wore a loose print dress proper for a Mexican matron, but American, too. The youngest, the sister, sat in a pink party dress with a big bow for company. The third, Molina's girl friend, was young and slender in a white sheath and low heels, her dark hair short. American clothes and hair, but in the father's house she wore a dress.

A dress and scared eyes. "Pascual couldn't have done what they say, Mr. Fortune. He couldn't hurt anyone."

"What was he doing there that night, Miss . . . ?"

"Rita Cardenas." She was nervous and very young, and she didn't look at me. "I don't know what he was doing there."

"He is not where they say," the mother said. "He has good job, goes to college. He is American."

The father jumped up, his thick mustache bristling. "That is why he is in trouble! He listen to both of you. You make him want to be *gringo*. You see what is happen?"

There was confusion in the Molina household. To stay apart in your own world—not of the country you were born in, not in the country you are part of—or to cross over into the bigger world? Which one, and what will it do to you?

"When did you see Pascual last before Saturday, Rita?"

"Not for a week . . ."

"They go movie Friday . . ."

More than one kind of confusion. The two women looked scared as they spoke in unison and said different things.

"Well, what was it?" I said. "A week or the Friday before?"

"We went to the movies," Rita Cardenas said. "I forgot."

"Did something happen at the movies?"

"No."

I looked at all of them. They were scared; that was normal. But they were holding something back, too.

"None of you can tell me why Pascual was with that gang?"

"He not there," the mother said.

"I don't know," Rita Cardenas said.

"My son does not do what they say," the father said. I left them sitting stiff and proper and afraid in their small, neat living room.

"The professor says go on in, Mr. Fortune."

I'd met him at political rallies and militant parties. Officially, he's a Democrat, but he's a lot more radical than that. The FBI keeps an eye on him. He uses his FOIA rights to get their file on him. It's a chess game. They both enjoy it.

"Sit down, Dan. What can I help you with?"

His mustache is as thick as Molina's father's. He looks like Emiliano Zapata. He knows that. His eyes are as black as Molina's, and they flashed at me in his nice, comfortable office.

"You don't know what Molina was doing there, Dan?"

He looks a lot more like a Zapatista than a full professor of history and head of the Chicano Studies Department at a major university in the California system.

"He wasn't a gang member, Luis. He goes to college. He has no record. His father and mother are solid, honest people."

"That's the kind it happens to the hardest. The lawyer is right. Something happened. Something that made him see what he'd always really known."

"What had he always known?"

"That the wretched of the earth are that way because the Europeans made them that way. That our society institutionalizes injustice and corrupts human potential to keep itself in power."

"I don't think Molina's read Fanon or Marcuse," I said.

"You never know," he grinned, "but I agree with you. For Molina it was something more immediate, personal. His job is probably bottom menial. At City College he

walks around feeling invisible. And something happened
to trigger the explosion inside. Like Saul on the road to
Damascus. It would have to be some naked trauma. I'd
look for a personal kick in the balls."

He has a way with words.

"Thanks."

He smiled. *"De nada."*

It's not as hard as a meet with a Mafia don or Lieutenant
Colonel North when he ran our Latin American policy—
Santa Barbara isn't New York or L.A.—but it's hard
enough. You have to pass word you want to meet, and
maybe you get an answer, maybe you don't. As it does in
everything, it depends on what's in it for him.

"You tell the man we don' make this here noise. Raul 'n
all of 'em was on they own."

We were at a table in the back of a cantina off Milpas. I'd
gotten lucky. The attack in the park had been a private
rumble, unauthorized, and he wanted everyone to know
that.

"I'll tell them," I said. "How about Pascual Molina? He's
not one of your people."

"What you think, man?"

He was another skinny one, but a long way from girlish
or delicate. Scars and beard stubble and hard leather. The
same hot black eyes, but cold, too, with intensity at the
edge of sanity. He wore black jeans, a black sateen shirt
open to the silver cross in his chest hair, and a black leather
jacket like his troops, but he was an easy twenty-two,
probably older.

"When did he join?"

"Like, we don' give out that information, right?"

"Why did he join?"

He was half lost in the shadows of the cantina. "Hey, you
seen those old movies? Foreign Legion an' all? We don' ask
no questions, don' even got to give right name."

"It's a high-profile killing," I said. "The good citizens
take a bad view of gang kills in their parks, especially
outside the *barrio*. Biggs was an Anglo. That's a race riot."

I didn't have to draw pictures for him. He wanted to

divert the heat from the killing of Walter Biggs away from the gang. He wanted my voice, I wanted his. *Quid pro quo.*

In the shadows, he tilted back against the wall. "He come aroun' Saturday mornin'. Raul knows him, he says okay."

"You mean he joined the same day Biggs was killed?"

He shrugged. "José work same place. Molina come aroun' José an' Raul's pad early, say he want to be in gang."

"In the park," I said. "Raul was testing him?"

"No way, man!" His chair legs hit the floor. He leaned across the table. "Raul an' them was high, okay? They go out on they own. Just havin' some fun, you know? This Anglo got a gang, too; they starts on Raul an' the guys. Raul don' wanna fight, them Anglos make 'em. The one guy takes a fall, the others they runs. Cops show, say the bad *cholos* beat up the poor Anglo."

He was stating his official position. A communique from the White House, 10 Downing Street, the Kremlin. The explanation of a regrettable but unavoidable incident.

"I'll tell the cops," I said. "You tell me why Pascual Molina came around that Saturday morning?"

"Maybe he just wised up. How do I know? Go talk to Raul."

"Raul would have talked to you," I said.

He stared at me, then tilted back again. "Raul says the kid got in a hassle Friday night. He don' know what, on'y it made the kid wise up, Fortune. He got the real score."

"Yeah," I said. "Look what it did for him."

They came out of the high school in twos and threes, to hurry across the wide street deeper into the *barrio. Chicanas* with their eyes on the ground or watching the older boys who lounged in pickups and low-riders waiting for their girls.

Rita Cardenas came out alone. A few of the lounging Latino lotharios called to her but she ignored them, walked on looking straight ahead. I caught up with her halfway down the block.

"What happened that Friday night, Rita?"

She kept on walking. "Nothing happened."

"The lawyer's helping Pascual. I'm helping the lawyer."

She walked on.

"Those studs outside the school don't think he's coming back," I said. "They figure you're a target chicken now."

She started to cry.

"Is what happened that bad?"

She cried harder as she walked, her head down now. Whatever she knew, she didn't think it was gong to help Pascual Molina. She thought it would dig him in even deeper, and she cried all the way to her house. A man came out and watched me. I left.

I walked to Pascual Molina's house. The small boy and the young sister played in the neat fenced yard. The boy vanished somewhere around the house, but the girl stayed to stare at my missing arm. She was older; she remembered me coming earlier.

"Do you know what Pascual and Rita did on Friday night?"

"Go to the movies."

"What movies?"

"Plaza del Sol."

"How come you remember?"

"'Cause they walk."

"Walk?"

She nodded. "They walk 'cause Pascual only got ten bucks and that's what the movie cost."

"They walked from here to one of the Plaza Del Sol movies, then had to walk back? They must have come home awful late."

"Nope. They don't see the movie. Rita was crying. Pascual was mad."

"When did they get home? You remember that?"

She shook her head. "I was in bed. Maybe ten."

"What time did they go?"

"Maybe six-thirty."

Over a five-mile round-trip. Two hours to walk there for a nine-o'clock show. Two hours back. If they never got as far as the theater, they got close.

"What's your name, honey?"

"Margarita."

"Margarita, did they say anything when they got back? You were in bed, but you listened. Right?"

She giggled. "Rita cried 'cause she didn't see the movie. Rita said Pascual was crazy for a stupid chair. He got real mad. He said Rita should go home if he was so crazy. So she went home. I went to sleep."

"Chair?" I said. "What chair?"

"I don't know."

Stupid chair. The only way was to go out to the Plaza Del Sol and backtrack toward the barrio.

There was only one route from the Plaza Del Sol theaters to the distant *barrio*. A quarter of a mile from the theaters, I saw the furniture out in front of a second-hand shop. There were tables, lamps, sideboards, even a hat rack and an old refrigerator on the sidewalk. There were no chairs.

A bell jangled as I went in.

"Yeah?"

He was a narrow man in a frayed sweater, worn white shirt with a tie knotted so small it had to have been tied in the same place a thousand times, wool trousers, and bedroom slippers. His left forearm was in a cast and sling.

"I was looking for some chairs."

"I got chairs all over, mister." He waved his good arm at the cluttered store and turned away. "You got bad eyes."

"I didn't see any chairs outside."

He turned back and stared at me, suspicion all over his narrow face. "What's that supposed to mean?"

"It made me wonder if you had any chairs."

He turned away again, grumbling to himself.

"How'd you hurt the arm?"

Now he whirled and snarled. "What the fuck you want here? You some kinda cop? Checking up on me? I got nothin' to hide. I told the hospital and the cop just like it happened."

"Tell me."

Later he could accuse me of impersonating a police officer. But if Pascual Molina had broken his arm, I figured he wouldn't think about it. He'd be too anxious to testify against Molina.

He glared, but he wanted to be sure everyone knew his side of it. "Okay. I'm inside, see, working on some silver. I look up, and there's this goddamn punk Mexican and his *señorita* out there sitting on two of my chairs. I go out and tell them the chairs ain't there for people to wait for the bus. The little *chiquita* gets up, but the punk is snotty. He asks me how much for the chairs, you know? I tell him ten bucks. The girl starts crying, but the *cholo* gives me ten bucks, tells the girl to sit down and then sits down himself and sneers at me, right?"

He looked at me for approval. I said nothing. He growled to himself, went on. "I tell the goddamned beaner the chairs is ten dollars each. He bought one chair. He wants to sit with his bimbo he owes me ten more bucks." Now he laughed. "He ain't got another ten bucks, right? So he says he bought both chairs, I'm a liar. Then I really got mad, told him to get the hell off my chair. I told him to take his fucking chair and get the hell away from my store. Told him I'm going to call the police if he don't take the chair he bought and get away from my store."

He relived his rage like a movie in his mind, his eyes looking right through me. "That's when he hit me. Knocked me down. When I tried to get up, he hit me with the chair and broke my arm. I start yelling for the police. The punk greaser and the bimbo run. My wife took me to the emergency. They fixed the arm, and I told them and the patrolman just what I'm telling you."

I didn't tell him who I was, or what I was doing. He'd be happy soon enough when he knew the trouble Molina was in.

Thin and undeveloped even close on the narrow cell bunk, the girlish shoulders bent, the weak light dim on his black hair.

"I talked to Rita about that Friday," I said. "I talked to the store owner. You broke his arm."

"That guy'll find out soon what's happened," the lawyer said. "He'll tell his story in court."

"It's why you joined the gang," I said, "why you were in the park that night."

He didn't look up. "My old man, he got a big mustache, you know. He's a little guy, but he got this big mustache. Down in Mexico a man always got a big mustache, right? He's real macho, my old man, a big shot in the *barrio*. Only he works all his life digging holes for the white man."

When he did look up at us, the black eyes were anything but soft. "I never been to Mexico. Maybe I go sometime. Sit on the beaches. Not the good beaches, they're for the rich *gringos*. Go to the mountains and eat bananas. My aunt she goes once. She don' like it so good. She's got a white boyfriend, right? I mean, he's a dago an' no whiter than me."

His tongue lived in three worlds. Whole sentences from the high school where all boys are created equal. Words from the *barrio* slums where no one is equal. And the accent of *salsa* and *mariachis* and the past of Castilian cavaliers and slaughtered Indians and silent slaves both black and brown.

"Molina," the lawyer said, "you joined the gang only that morning. You should never have been in that park. Give me something I can use. What happened that Friday?"

The black eyes that were neither thin nor like the eyes of a girl studied us. "You got a girl, lawyer? I got a girl. Young, but real nice. She likes movies. All those rich white girls, you know? I got a job all day, an' I go to college three nights, so we don' got a lot of time to go to the movies. There's this real good movie she wants to see. It's out by Plaza Del Sol. Okay, I say. Friday we eat at McDonald's, an' take the bus to that movie. I promise my girl."

Someone was crying in another cell. I always feel buried in a jail or prison, stifled, crushed by the walls.

"Thursday I have a bad day pushing my stinking broom on the job, do lousy at school, get into a crap game late. All I got Friday is fifteen bucks. My girl says 'Okay, we eat cheap and we walk to the movie.' All the way to Plaza Del Sol! She says it's a nice day, we start early. So why not, you know? I walked that far before. Only she ain't walked that far, and she got to stop and look in all the stores. I think we never gonna get to the movie—she looks in all those stores." He looked at the lawyer, then at me. "Why the chicks got to do that, you know? It makes a guy feel like hell when he ain't got the money to buy all the stuff in them stores."

Somewhere a man whistled the same song over and over, flat and off-key. Voices in the silence of the jail told him to shut up.

"We walk and she's thirsty. I tell her we just got bread for the movie. She gets hot an' tired. I see this store with chairs out in front. Old wood chairs all beat up. My girl she looks at them chairs, and I say, 'Go ahead, sit down, honey. We're almost there, we got time.' So we sit and, man, it feels good. All the people walk by and look at us, but we don' care, you know? We sit maybe ten minutes. Then this guy comes out of the store yellin' like all hell. I mean, he's yelling like he's crazy. 'Hey! You *cholos* get outta those chairs! Get the hell out of those chairs! What the Christ you dumb beaners think you're doing?' Like that, you know, and all the people on the streets lookin' at us. 'You fucking greasers think you own the city? Lazy fucking bums! Get out of my chairs!'"

Two roaches scuttled across the jail floor. Molina's foot moved suddenly, crushed one. The other wobbled in fear across the concrete and out of sight.

"'You gonna pay me? You gonna buy those chairs, *pachuco*? Who buys them they see you beaners in them? No white man's gonna buy them, *cholo!*'" The polyglot jargon of a boy with the streets of the *barrio* under the smooth skin of his unmarked face.

"They all looks at us, you know? My girl she jumps up, she's gonna run away. She's scared, and they're all laughin'. I grab her. I say, 'Sit down, baby.' She starts cryin'. I say to that son of a bitch store guy, 'We just restin', mister. *Un momento por favor!*' Jesus, I'm talkin' Mex! The guy laughs, looks at the crowd. They're all laughin'. So I say, 'How much? For the chairs? How much?' My girl she's cryin', she wants to run. The big-mouth bastard's laughin', my girl's cryin', so I say, 'How much you want for the fucking chairs?'"

Down the corridor the man still whistled. Flat and off-key and no one shouted now. As if they knew it was really useless to try to stop a man who had to whistle in his jail cell.

"The guy stops laughin', says, 'Ten bucks. For you, *señor*, ten dollar American. Special. You got ten dollar, *señor*?' So I take the ten bucks for the movie and buy the goddamned chairs. I make my girl sit down again, and I sit, too. All the people look and they don't laugh no more. The guy he says, 'The chairs're ten dollars each, *cholo*. Ten more bucks.' I tell him he sold both fucking chairs, he's a fucking liar. He grabs me, yells get out of his goddamned chair and get the hell away from his store. He's gonna call the cops. He's gonna charge me with trespassing and trying to steal a chair. So I hit him. When he gets up I hit him with the chair and knock him down again and he starts yellin' 'Thief' and 'Robber' and 'Police' and me and Rita run. We walk all the way back to my house and she cries all the way and we fight and she goes home. Next day I go find José and Raul and tell 'em I want to join the gang and go get fucking Anglos!"

In the silence of the cell, his voice echoed away. His black eyes watched us with the question in them. I didn't have an answer. The lawyer put his papers into his briefcase. The cell smelled of sweat and urine. Molina looked at us, and his thin shoulders moved. A delicate, almost imperceptible shrug, the black eyes flat and empty, the girlish face expressionless.

"They can't get Murder One," the lawyer said. "I'll plead you guilty to involuntary manslaughter. They probably won't buy that, but maybe they'll go for voluntary."

I said, "We'll bring in that store owner, put him on the stand. We'll put Rita up there. I'll get the right people to testify you were never in a gang. We'll bring in your parents."

Molina's black eyes had no expression at all.

"*Gracias*," he said.

Wayne D. Dundee's first appearance in a PWA anthology with P.I. Joe Hannibal earned him nominations across the board—for a Shamus, an Edgar, and an Anthony Award. Dundee's first Hannibal novel, The Burning Season, *was published in 1988 to rave reviews. His second novel,* The Skin Tight Shroud, *was published in 1989. There are two more Hannibal novels forthcoming.*

Naughty, Naughty
A Joe Hannibal story

---

by Wayne D. Dundee

1

"You have to remember, Mr. Hannibal," Corrie Belsen was saying, "that the whole thing started on a dare. I mean, it's not like we're a couple of exhibitionists or anything."

"That's right," her sister chimed in. "Posing for Tommy and then letting him run that ad was all supposed to be a big joke—you know, a put-on. We never dreamed the ad would get the kind of response it did. After all, who could have known there were so many lonely, horny old guys out there?"

Corrie and Kellie Belsen were both quite young and both quite lovely. Lovely enough—especially in stereo—to keep my male engine revved; young enough—nineteen and eighteen, respectively—to make me feel somewhat guilty about the way they made me feel. Kellie's reference to "horny old guys" caused me to shift uneasily in my chair.

We were seated in the living room of the Belsen home, a sprawling ranch-style located in one of Rockford's higher-priced subdivisions. I'd been summoned there via phone, and it was only upon arrival that I discovered I was dealing with a sister act, and one of such tender years to boot. After overcoming some initial reservations about that, I'd agreed to hear them out with a promise of confidentiality but no guarantees as to whether or not I would take their case. They were in the process now of explaining to me exactly what their problem was, and what they hoped I could do about it.

"Who is this Tommy?" I wanted to know.

"Tommy Jessup," Kellie replied. She gave a little shrug and her long dark hair rippled like silk. "I guess you'd call him my boyfriend. We're not a real heavy item, but we've been dating and doing stuff together for about a year now."

I gestured toward the newspaper that lay on the coffee table between us. It wasn't the kind of paper that is carrier-delivered to your door or available outside your favorite coffee shop in a convenient vending machine. It was a weekly tabloid called *Grind*, the kind of rag that is euphemistically referred to as an "underground" newspaper and purchasable primarily in adult bookstores and less discriminating newsstands.

The copy of *Grind* had been folded open to the Personals, and one ad in particular was an attention grabber, made even more so by the circumstances. The Belsen sisters were pictured in provocative poses near the center of the page, Corrie wearing a cobwebby, see-through affair and Kellie clad in a garter belt and leopardskin bra and panties. "Naughty! Naughty!" proclaimed bold letters above the grainily reproduced photos. And then: "Hey, mister, wanna see what a couple of naughty sisters are willing to do just for you? We'll pose to please . . . and we *do* mean please!" Below the pictures there was a Rockford P.O. box address and instructions to send five dollars for sample photos and a personal letter.

"And Tommy's the one who took these pictures?" I asked.

Kellie nodded.

"Of course, those aren't the original snaps he took,"

Corrie said. "The first, well, photo session I guess you'd call it, took place one afternoon late last summer. Kell and I were out by the pool when Tommy came by to show off his new camera. He'd gotten really excited about photography that spring and worked and saved all summer to afford one of those thirty-five-millimeter jobs with all sorts of lenses and attachments."

"The whole thing actually started the night before," Kellie said. "That's when a copy of that stupid newspaper first turned up. There was this party, see—a going-away party for one of our friends who moved to California. We were all there—Tommy and me, and Corrie, too. Well, a couple of the guys showed up with a copy of *Grind* they'd bought somewhere and got to passing it around. We were all pretty well buzzed by then and starting to get a little rowdy anyway, so we began reading out loud from it and holding up some of the pictures, trying to out-gross each other. The personal ad section and some of the things they promised there got a lot of attention."

I was able to connect the dots. "And when Tommy came over to show off his brand-new camera the next day and found you two poolside, not exactly overdressed I'd guess, the subject of racy pictures could hardly help but come up."

"A dare, like Corrie said."

"A whole series of dares," Corrie amended. "And crazy acceptances. It all seemed so exciting at first—you know, outrageous. And when the money from the ad started rolling in, it was pretty amazing. It made it easier to overlook the sleaziness. And we kept telling ourselves we could end it any time we wanted. But then it got out of hand."

I regarded my two would-be clients. I suppose I should have been shocked to some degree by what they were involved in, but in my line of work you get shockproof real fast or you get out. I've overheard twelve-year-olds of both sexes offering to give head for the price of a movie ticket. After something like that, the thought of these cool young beauties posing for a few naughty snapshots didn't seem particularly mind-boggling.

I said, "How did it get out of hand? What went wrong?"

Kellie Belsen reached down into a cardboard shoebox on the floor beside her chair and withdrew a handful of envelopes bound by a red rubber band. She tossed them onto the coffee table with a dramatic flair and the bundle rolled lumpily toward me. "Those," she said, "are what went wrong."

I removed the rubber band and shuffled the envelopes. There were about twenty in all, each addressed to the P.O. box mentioned in the ad and each carrying a return address for an M. Strom, Cincinnati, Ohio. The postmarks confirmed Cincinnati, and the dates ranged from November of last year through mid-July, a couple weeks ago.

"You'll probably want to take them and read them," Corrie said. "They're from a guy named Myron Strom in Ohio. After the first couple orders he zeroed in on me for some reason and started requesting poses and letters from me alone. We didn't think much of it in the beginning because there had been a few others like that. I think most of them get off on the letters as much as the pictures. Actually, our photos are pretty tame. We promise a lot more than we deliver. The shots you see there in the ad are about as raunchy as we get. Mostly they want us posing together because they get two bods for the price of one, and I suppose the fact that we're sisters adds a kind of kinky bonus. But there are a few who single out just one or the other of us so, like I said, when Strom went that route we didn't think anything of it."

"Only *this* character turned out to be something else," Kellie said, rolling her eyes. "It wasn't long before he started writing stuff like he could see in Corrie's eyes that she wanted him—"

"'Hungered' for him," Corrie injected disdainfully.

"Yeah, 'hungered' for him as much as he did for her. And that their love deserved a better fate than to be spent merely on pieces of paper. He actually asked for directions to our house so he could come up and see her—to 'consummate' their love. We didn't agree, naturally, but that didn't slow him down any."

Corrie nodded solemnly. "I should have ended it right there."

"It was probably already too late," her younger sister said.

"Maybe. But I should have realized what a fruitcake he was and told him to fuck off, if not for my sake, then at least for yours. Let's face it, I was greedy. He was writing two, sometimes three letters a month, each one with a fat money order for more pictures. Only it was a lot more than just pictures he wanted."

Kellie turned back to me. "A week and a half ago, right after his last letter, he *did* show up here at the house. He must have staked out the post office and watched for one of us to get the mail from our box, then followed us home. God, when I answered the door and saw him standing there I almost crapped my pants!"

"How were you able to recognize him?" I asked.

She gestured toward the envelopes I still held. "In there. He sent Corrie a picture of himself along with one of his letters. It's, uh, a pretty explicit pose and we got a big laugh out of it when it arrived. But even with clothes on, there was no mistaking who was standing there on our front steps. I managed to convince him that Corrie wasn't at home but that our father was, and got him to leave. Ever since then, our life has been a nightmare."

"He's been back?"

Both girls nodded. Corrie said, "He's shown up at the house, he's called on the phone, he's followed us when we've gone out. I guess we should explain that our mother passed away earlier this year, after an illness, and our father has sort of buried himself in his work. He's a troubleshooting engineer for the micro-circuitry division of ROC-LEC, and dealing with their accounts takes him all over the country. Of course, he cut back on his travel when Mother was so sick, but now that she's gone he seems to *want* to be away. He's somewhere in Arizona right now— won't be back until the weekend, or possibly later. We never could have kept this Strom thing from him if he hadn't been away so much. Obviously, we'd like to have it cleared up before he returns. After what happened last night, it can only get uglier."

I skipped any inane expressions of sympathy over the loss of their mother and said, "What was it that happened last night?"

They exchanged glances. After a minute, Corrie said, "We came up with an idea for getting rid of this creep. It involved Tommy Jessup, partly because he already knew about the ads and stuff and partly because he's a high school jock and a pretty husky guy. The way it was supposed to work was that instead of hanging up on Strom when he called, I'd pretend to give in, encourage him to come on over and . . . well, Tommy would be waiting and would beat him up. We figured that would scare Strom away, make him leave us alone."

It was pretty obvious things hadn't worked out that way. "What went wrong?"

"Tommy was the one who got beat up," Kellie replied. "Got beat up bad. We had to take him to the emergency room and make up this story about him getting mugged outside a video arcade. We had to give statements to the police and everything. There was even a little piece about it in this morning's paper. God, what a screwed up mess it's all gotten to be!"

"What about Strom?" I asked. "Have you heard from him since the beating?"

Corrie shook her head. "No. And somehow that's more frightening than if we had."

Nobody said anything for a while. The house's central air unit whispered around us, keeping the heat of the August afternoon at bay. In another room, a radio was playing. On the coffee table, the pulpy pages of *Grind* rustled in a draft from the air conditioning.

"Well," Corrie said, "you can see our predicament. We're in over our heads. Strom is dangerous. We can't handle this ourselves, and we can't go to the police without admitting to the pictures and the letters and everything and causing a great deal of embarrassment for our father and Tommy's family. We have cash money to cover your fee, Mr. Hannibal. Will you help us?"

I looked from her to her sister, then back again. Slender faces framed by long dark hair, imploring eyes, supple young bodies poised on the edges of their seats. Modern damsels in uniquely modern distress. And yeah, I was willing to be their hired knight. But only a fool would attach the word "chivalry" to any of it.

My initial plan was pretty basic—actually, just a variation on what had already been tried. I would simply confront Myron Strom the next time he showed up and threaten him with legal action if he didn't stay away from Corrie and Kellie Belsen. As a private detective, of course, I have about as much legal clout as a door-to-door salesman. But I was banking that someone in Strom's position might view me as being not so far removed from a real cop. On the other hand, if he decided to try and get physical the way he had with Tommy Jessup, well, that would suit me all right, too. Since I have a state-issued license to consider, I can hardly offer strong-arm services as part of the package, but any time I get a chance to bust the gourd of a sleazeball like Strom I take it as a fringe benefit.

In the meantime, I had some preparations to make. I left the Belsen home around two, with the promise to return by evening. I made sure they had both my office and home phone numbers so they could reach me instantly in case Strom made contact before I got back.

Thirty seconds in my un-air-conditioned Plymouth and I was drenched with sweat. The sun was a hazy white glare scorching a cloudless sky, and some guy on the car radio informed me that the temperature and the humidity were running a race to see which one would hit the hundred mark first. There wasn't a hint of a breeze, and the air that poured through my vents as I drove was like steam off a boiling kettle.

I entered my second-floor Broadway office, snapped on the window air conditioner, and dialed it to high. I listened to it wheeze and clank and rattle the glass for a full five minutes before it started coughing out any cool air. I dug a can of Bud from the mini-fridge in the closet and drank from it while I checked my answering machine for messages. There were none that amounted to anything. By the time I settled behind the desk—with a second can of Bud—and started going through Myron Strom's letters, the office had begun to cool and the sweat patches on the back of my shirt pressed cold against my skin.

I started with the envelope that contained Strom's picture. It was, as Kellie Belsen had said, quite explicit. The black and white Polaroid showed a balding, pudgy guy in his late forties or early fifties standing naked in front of an unlit fireplace. The only thing that appeared very formidable about him was the size of his erection; otherwise he barely looked capable of unscrewing the cork from the wine bottle on the mantle, let alone beating up a husky high school jock. Maybe he held up his pants—when he wore any—with a karate master's black belt.

The content of the letters was pretty much the same. Lots of flowery passages about Corrie Belsen's alabaster skin and the smoldering promise in her eyes, and then graphic descriptions of how Strom would "make love" to her if only given the chance. Crud like that. Nor was there much variety in the poses he requested. He seemed to have a thing for black lace and exposed inner thighs.

I'd pored through the letters hoping I might learn something more about Myron Strom than his sexual fantasies, something that would give me some extra leverage in case he didn't run from my chest-thumping and hollow threats. Having come away empty, I decided to try another route. Since I didn't know any P.I.s in the Cincinnati area first-hand, I let my fingers do the walking and dialed the first agency listed. I gave them Strom's name and address and told them I needed everything they could dig up on him as soon as possible. We made arrangements for payment and they promised to get back to me within forty-eight hours.

It was five o'clock when I snapped off the office AC and headed home for a quick shower and change of clothes. I checked with the Belsen girls before leaving, made sure there'd been no sign of Strom, told them I'd be by shortly. Outside, the sun was less brutal and the temperature had leveled off, but the humid air still clung to everything like the sticky side of a giant Band-Aid.

It stormed that night. That's all that happened. Myron Strom made no attempt to contact Corrie Belsen or her sister. I spent eight hours in the cramped confines of my car, parked just down the street from the Belsen house, watching, waiting, smoking cigarettes, munching takeout chicken from a grease-stained bucket and washing it down with cans of Bud dug from an ice chest in the back seat. Stewing in my own sweat for the first half dozen hours until the cooling wind and rain came.

At three A.M. I decided to pack it in. Drove back home, flopped across the bed, fell asleep without removing my wet socks.

I was back on watch again the next evening. Me, my ice chest of Bud, and a jumbo garbage pizza I'd sworn I was going to nurse along but which was already half gone. If Strom didn't show pretty soon, I was going to end up as portly as he was. Hell, maybe he was a private dick back in Cincinnati who'd spent too much time on stakeouts eating starchy junk food.

Corrie and Kellie's aunt had driven down from Beloit that morning, and the three of them had spent the day shopping. Since I felt it was unlikely Strom would make a serious move in any of Rockford's busy malls, I'd spared myself the boredom and wasted shoe leather of tagging along.

Instead, I'd paid a visit to Tommy Jessup. I was still hoping to gain some insight into Myron Strom before I confronted him, and while I didn't really expect that he had shared any deep inner feelings with Tommy as he pounded hell out of him, you never can tell what a person might let slip under adverse conditions, or what another person might pick up on.

Jessup was indeed a big kid. A couple inches taller than my six-one, almost as broad across the shoulders if not the gut, with unruly reddish hair and a toothy grin that he managed to flash once or twice despite the bruises around his mouth. I'd found him hobbling back and forth in the front yard of his parents' home, using a Weedeater to trim along the sidewalk.

After I'd introduced myself, I asked him to recount his clash with Strom.

He'd shaken his shaggy head and said, "Man, that's something I want to forget as soon as I can. He looked like such a chubby wimp in the picture, you know? Even with his yard-long dong. But when he came up the sidewalk that night he sure didn't look like no wimp. Same bald head and little Ben Franklin glasses, only like somebody was holding a magnifying glass up to him or something. When I jumped out from behind the hedge and threw a headlock on him it was like clamping my arm around a lamppost. He spun around, his glasses went flying, I went flying, and the next thing I knew he was all over me like ugly on ape. He pinned me against the side of the house and pounded on my face for what seemed like a couple hours, and when I finally got my arms up to protect my head he went downstairs and broke four of my ribs. That's why I'm shuffling around like somebody's grandpop—they got an elastic bandage wrapped around me tighter'n Tallulah's tush."

I'd grinned. "That tight, huh?"

"Hey, I'm really glad Kellie and Corrie brought you in on this. They're a couple of pretty swell chicks, you know? They don't deserve to get dragged through the mud. I mean, just because they showed some skin for a few pictures don't go thinking they're tramps or anything. I'm the one who prodded them into that and got us all in this mess."

"I hired on to help, kid, not pass judgment."

"Yeah, I've read about you in the papers. That asshole tries to pin you up against a wall, he'll be in for a surprise. You get the chance, you give him a couple shots for me, you hear?"

"I'll do that. But first I've got to flush him out of whatever sewer he's crawled into. Think back to that night, Tom. Did he say anything, or did you notice anything that might be of some help to me?"

Another shake of the head. "No, he didn't say a word. And all I was seeing were stars. Stars and that damn tattoo coming at me."

"Tattoo?"

"Yeah, he had a tattoo on the back of one hand—his right hand. When he had me up against the wall slapping the shit out of me, a couple times he reared back and came around with a big sweeping backhand. When he drew back for it he'd lean out into the light for a second or two and I could see the tattoo. Then it would be coming at me, but there wasn't a damn thing I could do to get out of the way."

"What was it a tattoo of?"

"I'm not sure. I never really saw it that good. It looked like a cross—a crucifix, with a snake or something wrapped around it. Does that help?"

I'd shrugged. "Maybe, maybe not. But it's something I didn't know five minutes ago."

Reflecting back on it now, seated in my heap outside the Belsen house with darkness descending around me, I decided it really didn't amount to much. About the only thing my conversation with Tommy Jessup *had* accomplished was to intensify my desire to meet up with Strom. Tormenting young women, caving in the ribs of a high school boy . . . Yeah, more and more I wanted to get my hands on the fucker.

It was full dark by nine. I was feeling restless, edgy. Waiting for somebody else to make the first move has never been my favorite thing. On top of that, my clients had split up on me. Corrie was in the house where she belonged, but Kellie was a dozen or so blocks away, babysitting for some young couple named Mulvaney, and wouldn't be back until around midnight. I'd tried to talk her into canceling, but she protested that that would put the Mulvaneys in a last minute bind and, besides, since Corrie was the one Strom was interested in, all I had to do was stick close to her and what was the big deal? I'd gone along with it, but I wasn't too crazy about the idea.

At least the weather was more cooperative. The oppressive heat and humidity had been chased off by the previous night's storm. The air was still plenty warm, but there was a nice breeze pushing it around. Overhead, there were a zillion stars in the sky.

At ten o'clock, a pair of headlights swung onto the Belsens' street and moved slowly in my direction. A tingle of anticipation ran through me. The Belsen house was located near the inner boundaries of the subdivision and thus got very little through traffic by it. During the night and a half I'd been on watch so far, only three other vehicles had turned down this way. Maybe it was only wishful thinking on my part, but I had a strong hunch the game was afoot.

I scrunched low in my seat and a few seconds later, when the car got closer, I saw that, sure enough, it was a light-colored VW bug—the description of the vehicle Corrie and Kellie had seen Strom driving on the occasions he'd followed them. I couldn't get a good look at either license plate from my angle, but a dome-topped profile and the glimmer of eyeglasses on the shadowy face of the driver removed any uncertainties I had left—it was Strom. He rolled slowly past where my Plymouth was curbed and drifted to a stop directly in front of the Belsen house. The only lights on inside were a soft yellow glow from the kitchen area and the flickering bluish eye of the television visible through the drawn drapes of the living room window. Strom sat for what seemed like a long time. I could *feel* him watching and it made my skin crawl. I wondered if Corrie, the object of his hungry stare, sensed it, too. I gripped and ungripped the steering wheel several times, priming myself for the moment when I would drag the sick son-of-a-bitch from his car and—

Abruptly, the bug hopped forward and began pulling away. Not recklessly fast, but considerably faster than it had approached to begin with. It appeared as if something had spooked Strom but, scanning the street in either direction, and the housefronts that lined it, I could see nothing that should have caused that. Nevertheless, by the time he reached the other end of the street, where it came to a T, he made a quick, choppy turn that reinforced my impression he was fleeing from something. A wild thought crossed my mind: Maybe he felt *me* watching *him*. I drummed my fingers on the steering wheel. Whatever had brought it about, I felt certain Strom was rabbiting, not just circling the block for another look. And I damn sure didn't want to wait around another two or three days for him to show up again.

I twisted the key in the ignition, dropped the Plymouth into gear, and took out after him.

I made the T turn on two wheels, followed the outer drive of the subdivision around, and caught sight of the bug's taillights just as it exited onto Perryvile and turned south. I made the same turn a few seconds later, then eased off on the gas a little and gave my quarry plenty of room. It was a clear night, traffic was light, and I had every reason to believe I knew the lay of the land better than he did. And no matter how hard he tried, he wasn't going to outrun me in a bug—not even considering the dilapidated condition of my Plymouth.

Strom made the sweep around Cherryvale Mall, cut back on Harrison, then picked up Bypass 20 and took it south and west, skirting the lower edge of the city. He hurried his stops and turns, but on the straightaways he kept his speed right on the double nickels. I couldn't tell if he knew I was tailing him or not. Not that it mattered much one way or the other anymore. I intended to run him to ground, and before I was through with him he was going to know exactly who I was and where I was coming from.

We put Rockford behind us as the bypass merged with the business route of U.S. 20. We continued due west toward Freeport. Wherever Strom was headed, he seemed bent on eating up a sizable chunk of northern Illinois real estate. It occurred to me that the only way he could outdistance me was to run me out of gas. But before I let that happen, I'd put him and his damn pregnant roller skate in a ditch somewhere.

It was just short of eleven when we reached the Freeport city limits. I still wasn't sure whether or not Strom realized he had a tail. We'd been the only two vehicles on the road most of the time, meaning he'd have to be awfully preoccupied not to have taken some notice of me. Yet he was making no evasive moves. Less familiar with the Freeport turf and uncertain of what he might be up to, however, I decided to narrow the gap between us. I'd no sooner done this than the bug made one of its quick, darting turns into a gaudily lighted motel.

The place was a fairly large setup called the East Side Rest. There was a narrow frontage road to cross after turning off 20, and then a black-topped drive, flanked by twin metal signs announcing NO OUTLET, that led onto the motel grounds. Strom drove right between the signs. Watching, I grinned like a shark. From all appearances he was getting ready to settle in for the night, blissfully unaware of my presence.

The drive angled to the right, crossing in front of the registration office, then cut back between the buildings with parking slots branching off on either side. I eased my Plymouth around the corner of the office. There was no sign of Strom's bug nor any glow of taillights ahead of me. So he'd already parked. I rolled on, scanning the slotted vehicles to my right and left. By the time I'd reached the turnaround at the far end of the drive, I'd counted three Volkswagens: one bright red Superbeetle, two Rabbit station wagons. But no sign of Strom's bug. I sat in the middle of the turnaround, engine idling, craning my neck in all directions. What the hell?

And then I saw what he'd done.

The motel's two single-storied, multi-unit rectangles were set in the shape of a V, with the drive/parking area in the middle and the turnaround at the inner point. Directly ahead of me, cutting across the strip of dew-beaded grass that rimmed the turnaround, was a set of tire tracks. Up over the sidewalk they went, then across another strip of grass, then disappearing through the slight gap that separated the ends of the two buildings—a gap barely wide enough for the bug and definitely too narrow for my full-sized sedan to ever fit through.

Son-of-a-bitch!

He'd known I was behind him all the time, and the sneaky bastard had led me on a wild goose chase before ditching me like a Sunday morning whore. Through that gap and across a lawn or two there would be a street, and then another street and another until he had a hundred different ways he could go.

I pounded the dashboard and turned the air blue with a string of curses. Then, out of breath, rubbing my sore hand on my thigh, I swung the Plymouth around and headed back toward Rockford and Corrie Belsen. I couldn't wait to tell her and Kellie what a swell job their hired knight had done on his first encounter with the dragon.

The Belsen house looked exactly as I had left it. Light on in the kitchen, TV flickering behind living room drapes. It was just short of midnight, and the absence of more lights indicated Kellie probably wasn't home yet from her babysitting gig. I parked in the driveway, went up to the front door, and thumbed the bell button. When there was no answer, I remembered belatedly that on my previous visits the doorbell hadn't been working. I knocked. Still no answer.

There was no reason to think Strom would return here tonight and, even if he had, he couldn't have beaten me back by more than a couple minutes. I knocked again. Again no answer.

Growing alarmed, I stepped off the stoop and walked over toward the wide living room window. But a thick, coarse hedge grew all along the front of the house and I couldn't get close enough to peer in. I continued on around the end of the house. The living room also had a window in the back and, if I remembered right, no hedge on that side.

Before rounding the back corner, I paused, reached down, pulled the derringer from its spring holster inside my right boot. It's a two-shot .22 magnum, not worth a damn for any distance, but a handy close-quarters emergency piece and one I'm never without. Maybe I was overreacting, but I'd been careless once already that night, I didn't want to be again. This Strom was shaping up to be a lot tougher and slicker than anyone had figured him for in the beginning.

I moved along the back side of the house with the derringer at my side. The stars were out in full force, bathing everything in soft silver light. Off to my left, the water in the swimming pool sparkled behind a chain link fence. But my attention was caught and held by something else, a lumpy shape on the ground directly ahead of me, half in and half out of the shadow cast by the house. As I moved closer, I saw that it, too, had points of sparkle.

And then I was standing over it and my heart was thudding and I was squeezing the derringer so hard it made cuts in my palm. The lumpy shape was a man—a dead man. He lay in line with the living room window, which was broken. The points of sparkle that covered him were shards of glass. Tendrils of still wet blood, splayed across his face and chest, also caught and reflected the starlight.

I looked over at the shattered window. I knew instinctively what lay on the other side. Corrie Belsen would be somewhere in there, probably crouched in the dimness outside the flickering light from the television, probably still clutching the gun, certainly in a state of shock. Not too long ago she had shot and killed what she believed to be an intruder—in her mind, Myron Strom.

I looked down at the dead man. I was able to recognize him from the numerous photographs I'd seen inside the Belsen house.

I felt sick.

The dead man at my feet wasn't Myron Strom. It was the girls' father.

The police reconstruction of the events leading up to and resulting in the death of Aaron Belsen went like this:

On the night in question, Corrie Belsen was at home alone. Exhausted from a day-long shopping spree as well as from the strain she'd been under due to Myron Strom's harassment (the whole business about the pictures and the letters and ensuing developments had had to come out), she fell asleep watching television. Her last recollection of the time was nine-thirty P.M.

At approximately eleven, Aaron Belsen, Corrie's father,

returned home unexpectedly from an out-of-state business trip. When last he spoke to his daughters, he had indicated he anticipated being away through the weekend; but it was not unusual for such trips to be of indeterminate length. There was no way of knowing whether or not Belsen had tried to contact the girls when he realized he would be returning sooner. He was often absentminded about such things and, even if he had tried to call, they would have been unreachable throughout most of the day because of the shopping trip.

At any rate, upon arriving home, Belsen parked in the attached garage (which explained why I didn't see his car when I got back from my wild goose chase) and tried to enter the house from there. What he had no way of knowing was that his daughters had installed additional locks—dead bolts—as a safeguard against Strom, thereby rendering his house key useless. Unable to gain entry from the garage, Belsen went around to the front door and tried there. When his keys failed to work again, he undoubtedly tried punching the broken doorbell. He would have been able to see the light from the TV, just as I had, and would have drawn the conclusion that whoever was watching it had fallen asleep in front of the set. Getting no response from the doorbell, he tried knocking and calling out. When that, too, failed to roust anyone, he walked around to the back of the house in apparent hopes of having better luck there.

Meanwhile, inside the house, Corrie had been awakened by the fumbling at the garage entry door. She immediately went to the window, and when she looked out and saw that my car was gone, the first wave of panic hit. When someone began fumbling at the front door, she had time only to make out the shape of a man before jumping back from the window. Her panic growing now, she went to the phone and tried to call her sister at the Mulvaneys. The line was busy. The man at the front door began pounding and calling her name. Raised voices aren't easily distinguishable, especially when the receiving mind is clouded by terror. Corrie failed to recognize her father's shouts and her mind went racing with the worst possible scenario she could imagine: Strom had somehow managed to overpower me, driven my car away, probably to be abandoned with my corpse left inside the trunk, and now had returned for her. From the drawer of the phone stand, she pulled the .32 caliber pistol—the one she had taken from her father's bedroom and placed there several days before, after Strom had first shown up. Outside, she could hear him walking across the lawn, moving around to the back of the house. Desperately, she dialed the Mulvaneys' number a second time, and again she got a busy signal (it would later be determined that, most likely as a result of one of the kids fooling around, the kitchen phone at the Mulvaneys had not been properly cradled, thus leaving the circuit open). The intruder was at the back of the house now, approaching the window. Trembling, holding the pistol in the two-handed grip she had seen Cagney and Lacey use so often on TV, Corrie raised the weapon, and when the shape appeared on the other side of the glass she began pulling the trigger.

They buried Aaron Belsen on a Monday, four days after the shooting. I gave it a good deal of thought before finally deciding to attend the funeral. While the news media was extremely sympathetic toward Corrie, glossing over the details of her and Kellie's model-by-mail enterprise practically to the point of making it sound like a pen pal service for lonely shut-ins, a couple of editorials saw fit to rake me over the coals. "By seizing the opportunity to line his pockets with money from those distraught, confused young women rather than encourage them to seek guidance and assistance from the proper authorities," one claimed, "Mr. Hannibal might well have been as lethal a factor in the tragic outcome as one of the bullets in the gun." County Sheriff Dar Schmidt, whose office handled the investigation, since the shooting had taken place outside Rockford's city limits, put it more succinctly: "You fucked up, Hannibal. You should have come to me. I would have booked that Strom pervert on every charge from farting in a grocery store to planting Jimmy Hoffa in the Rock River. Aaron Belsen would still be alive, and that little girl wouldn't have to spend the rest of her life knowing she killed her own father."

In the end, it was because of "that little girl"—and her sister—that I went to the funeral. I wanted to show them that I cared, that I was sorry for the way things had turned out. And I guess I wanted to show everybody else that I didn't give a fuck what *they* thought.

During the service, I found myself admiring the way Corrie and Kellie were holding up. Not that I had any right, but in a sort of paternal way (the flip side of the lecherousness they had initially inspired in me) I actually felt proud of them. Corrie, naturally, took it the hardest, and Kellie—who, under the circumstances, might have been forgiven some feelings of recrimination—instead served as her big sister's primary source of comfort and reassurance.

Afterward, I spoke with them briefly, mumbling my condolences. They were gracious enough not only to accept but to express their regret for the way I'd been treated by the press. I left then and went home, feeling sad and tired and ancient, sick of sudden death and teary-eyed mourners and of always being a survivor.

2

I spent the next several days trying to put the Belsen fiasco behind me. If the lousy press had any effect businesswise, it seemed to be strictly for the good. I suddenly had a steady stream of customers. Unfortunately, the jobs they brought with them were pretty standard, nothing to occupy my mind or my time as completely as I needed. At odd moments I'd catch myself replaying scenes from the Belsen case: the way Corrie and Kellie had looked at me that first day while waiting for me to answer whether or not I'd try to help them; their provocative poses reproduced on that pulpy page from *Grind*; Tommy Jessup grimacing as he recounted his beating at the hands of Myron Strom; the way Kellie's hair rippled when she shook her head. Most of all, I kept seeing Aaron Belsen with his blood glistening wetly in the moonlight and then remembering the stricken expression on Corrie's face when I found her crouching in the shadows of the living room.

By the second week I started snapping out of it. This was in no small part due to a jarring lecture I received one night from my buddy, Bomber Brannigan, after I'd swung into a surly mood with too much booze in me and tried to start a fight in his State Street bar, the Bomb Shelter.

"Get the fuck over it, man," he snarled, slamming his face close to mine as he held me pinned against the edge of the bar while the guy I'd tried to take a poke at scurried out the side door. "That chip you're carrying around on your shoulder is getting real heavy for the rest of us to hold up. So you had a lousy break, so what? You want everybody to feel sorry for you? Well, maybe they would if you weren't doing such a bang-up job of it all by yourself and not leaving anybody else any room."

He was right, of course. I went away and pouted, smarting from the words. But he was right—that's what it kept coming back to and that's what I had to deal with.

My mood lifted considerably after that. Hell, I was feeling almost chipper on the morning, a couple days later, when an attractive though somewhat stout middle-aged woman showed up at my office and introduced herself as Helen Gorcey.

"I expect you know who I am," she concluded.

I studied her over a thoughtful frown while I rolled the name back and forth through my memory a couple times. In the end, I had to shake my head. "Afraid I'm drawing a blank."

She studied me back, at least twice as long as I had her. "You're either a damned good actor," she said finally, "or you're on the level. Almost everyone I've talked to assures me it's the latter. I checked you out quite thoroughly."

"Should have come to me to begin with. Checking people out is one of my specialties. I could have told you right away what a sterling character I possess."

"If that's the case, then you were played for a sucker—along with everybody else."

NAUGHTY, NAUGHTY • 97

"I've been played for a sucker more times than I care to remember. But never by the same person more than once. Mind telling me just what it is you're talking about?"

"I'm talking about the murder of Aaron Belsen. Please note I said *murder*—his death was no accident."

I gave another shake of my head. "You're mistaken, Ms. Gorcey. I was there. It was an accident."

"*Mrs.* Gorcey, if you please. I'm a widow. In a manner of speaking, I guess you could say I've been widowed twice. You see, Aaron and I were to be married."

She paused, gave me time to digest what she apparently felt was something of a bombshell. When I made no response, she went on. "I was one of the nurses attending his wife during the final months of her illness. I'd lost my own husband to the same lingering, merciless disease, so it only seemed natural for Aaron to turn to me in his despair, begin to confide his deepest fears and feelings to me. In retrospect, I guess the attraction that developed between us was almost inevitable. It was never consummated, never put into words while his wife was still alive, but we both knew what was happening. Shortly after Iris passed away, Aaron came to see me and we did put it into words and we did consummate it. We both realized we had to wait a proper length of time before announcing our plans to wed, but he insisted we tell the kids right away. He had his daughters; I have two children of my own—a boy and a girl, both preteens."

Again a pause and again I didn't know what to say. She continued, this time with a scornfully arched brow. "But of course you had no way of knowing any of that, did you? When sweet little Corrie and Kellie unburdened all their troubles on you, they didn't bother mentioning that their father intended to remarry, did they? Nor did they tell you how, when he made those intentions known to them, they flew into a selfish, jealous, vicious rage. And they certainly wouldn't have told you how Corrie came to my home one day, called me an opportunist and a slut among other choice names, and then, in the coldest human voice I have ever heard, vowed she would see her father *dead* before she'd see him married to me!"

It was obvious there was a lot of bitterness built up in the woman. And it was becoming obvious, despite her initially calm demeanor, that she was also packing around a hell of a load of tension and might be close to cracking. I didn't want to be the one to trigger that.

Choosing my words carefully, I said, "Even if all that's true, Mrs. Gorcey, it certainly doesn't prove that Corrie Belsen purposely killed her own father. I'd venture to say that *most* teenagers would react badly to the news that a surviving parent was planning to remarry after only a short amount of time had passed since the death of the other parent. And as for anything that might have been said in anger—well, most of us have sounded off under those circumstances and usually regretted it later, right?"

The Gorcey woman shook her head slowly, as if in pity. "You're just like the county sheriff and all the others. You're blinded by their youth and their beauty. You refuse to see the evil that lurks inside them, just under those pretty exteriors. What's worse, you refuse to even accept the possibility that such evil could exist."

She annoyed me beyond my concern for her stress. "Jesus Christ, lady," I growled, "you expect me to believe that those two teenaged girls planned and carried out the murder of their own father just because they didn't approve of *you*?"

She came right back. "For God's sake, pick up a newspaper, watch the evening news—are you telling me things like that don't happen every day of the week? Besides, when you consider Aaron's life insurance policy—payable at double indemnity—then they gained considerably more than just preventing our marriage, didn't they? To give the devils their due, I'm sure they would *rather* have killed me if they somehow could have made out as well financially."

I shoved myself away from the desk and stood up. "Sorry, I'm not buying what you came here to sell, and I think I've listened to about enough of your sales pitch. I *know* these girls, remember? I was there."

"You keep saying that. But no, you *weren't* there—not while Corrie lay in wait like a stalking tigress, not while she pumped bullet after bullet into the face and chest of her own father!"

"All right, the reason I wasn't there at that precise moment was that I was chasing the creep who had been harassing the Belsen girls. Are you saying Myron Strom was some sort of accomplice? That doesn't wash, Mrs. Gorcey. I read his letters, I saw the postmarks. There was no hint of complicity in those letters and they dated back to November of last year. Yet by your own admission Belsen didn't tell his daughters about his plans to marry you until approximately March of *this* year. How do you make all of that fit into this pile of garbage you're trying to feed me?"

Helen Gorcey appeared flustered and for a moment I was afraid I'd pushed back too hard. But she quickly regrouped her emotions and channeled them into a kind of self-righteous anger. With flaring nostrils, she said, "I don't have all the answers, Mr. Hannibal. If I did, I wouldn't continue throwing myself against one brick wall after another. What I have are questions—questions the rest of you are too damn thick-headed to be asking. I was hoping at least you—the poor sucker they *used*, the credibility shield they hid behind even while you were getting your guts ripped out by the media—would see some glimmer of light, would be willing to help me uncover the *truth* about what happened."

The woman's intensity was exhausting. I sighed. "I'm sorry for your grief, Mrs. Gorcey. I truly am. But as far as I'm concerned, the truth has already been uncovered, has been there all along. Aaron Belsen died in a tragic accident—tragic for him, tragic for his daughters, tragic for you."

She stood abruptly. "You're a stubborn fool. You deserve everything they've done to you."

She turned and strode away, her heels rapping loudly off the worn linoleum that covered my office floor. Halfway out the door, she paused and, without looking back, said, "Sometime soon I want you to ask yourself this question: If the Belsen sisters were homely and unappealing, perhaps not so young, would you be as firm in your refusal to question their motives? Think long and hard about the answer. You'll have to live with it the rest of your life."

That night I dreamed I was chasing Myron Strom again. Only instead of the highways and byways of northern Illinois, our route was the dirt oval of a stock car racetrack. Round and round we went. I couldn't get past him and I couldn't pull even with him. The shiny dome of his bald head gleamed above the back of his car seat like a taunting beacon. And then, as we neared the start/finish line for the completion of yet another lap, Helen Gorcey suddenly appeared, frantically waving a yellow flag. "Caution! Caution!" she shouted as I went by. "You're on the wrong track! You're on the wrong track!"

I awoke the next morning with the dream vivid in my mind. The Gorcey woman's visit had obviously disturbed me more than I'd realized. After she was gone, I'd smoothed out the knot she left in my stomach with a couple extra beers over lunch and figured that was that. Now she was back, inside my head in the middle of the night. But why? She was clearly just overreacting to grief, right? Her accusations were absurd.

When I got to my office later, I phoned the county sheriff's department and was transferred three times before they finally caught up with Dar Schmidt.

"Hannibal here," I said. "You running laps around the building or what?"

"No, just going fourteen different directions at once, that's all. Nothing out of the ordinary. What's on your mind?"

"The Belsen thing."

"Oh? Figured you'd want to get past that as quick as possible and try to forget about it."

"That was the plan. Only I got my memory jogged yesterday by a visitor named Helen Gorcey."

Schmidt chuckled. "She finally got around to you, huh? That woman like to drove me nuts for about six days running last week. She wanted the Belsen girls arrested on everything from premeditated murder to kiddie porn, and she wanted everybody who'd ever spent more than five minutes with them to be hauled in as accomplices. You were her number one choice in the last category. Matter of fact, for a while there, as I recall, she had you pegged as maybe being the mastermind of the whole thing."

"Yeah, well, she's apparently since decided I look more like an innocent dupe than a mastermind. So what's the story on her? She just another slice of fruitcake that fell off the plate?"

"Way I get it—and I haven't exactly piled up the man hours on this, mind you—she and Belsen *were* sniffing around each other some after Mrs. Belsen kicked. Far as any marriage talk, well, nobody else seems to know anything about that. Maybe there was, maybe there wasn't. But *she* sure seems convinced it was headed that way. So I got her down in my book as a heart-broke middle-aged gal who can't accept what a lousy deal Fate dished out and is looking for somebody to blame. On the other hand, she could be just another cold-hearted bitch with dollar signs in her eyes trying to figure a way to get her hands on some of that insurance money."

"So Belsen *was* heavily insured, then?"

"Oh, that he was, that he was. To the tune of about half a million bucks when all is said and done. Not mentioning the value of the house and property."

"With Corrie and Kellie as beneficiaries."

"Yep. Hey, is that a hint of suspicion I detect in your voice? Don't tell me the Gorcey dame got to you."

"No. Fuck no. I was there, remember? The insurance bit is just something I hadn't thought of. Actually, I'm glad for those kids—at least they won't be in any kind of financial bind on top of everything else they've gone through. But you know what really sticks in my craw about the whole thing?"

"No, what?"

"That creep Strom. He just walks away from it all. Oh, he got his name muddied a little bit in the newspapers. Big deal. So did I, and I'm supposed to be one of the good guys. I only wish I could have gotten my hands on that asshole—just once."

"Yeah, I hear you. He still hasn't surfaced anywhere, you know."

"I know. I been keeping tabs."

"Not that it would make much difference. Wherever and whenever he does turn up, ain't a blessed thing I can do to him."

"Gee, aren't you the same guy who would have locked him up and thrown away the key if only the Belsen sisters had gone to you instead of me?"

"Yeah, well, you say things in the heat of the moment sometimes. I'd still like to think the situation might have turned out better if they *had* come to me . . . but who knows, right?"

"Couldn't have turned out much worse. I guess we know that much."

"Water over the dam, Hannibal. One thing, though."

"What's that?"

"If Strom should happen to show up around here again, I don't want you doing anything stupid, you hear? Let me handle it. I may not be able to put him behind bars, but I can damn sure make him feel unwelcome."

"We'd have to see," I said. "I got what you might call my own personal interest in making this particular douchebag feel unwelcome."

"Yeah, and I got what you might call a personal interest in not letting things like that go on in my county. Let's hope it don't come down to finding out whose feelings run deepest."

The second loose thread came in the form of a dead guy lying face-up in room number eight of the Masthead Inn, a cheap northside motel. He was sprawled just inside the door, his legs, rump, and lower back on a heavy plastic runner that stretched a couple yards into the room; his head, shoulders, and outflung arms on mustard-yellow carpeting. The guy had been a brawny six-footer in his middle thirties, and not even death could completely diminish the impressiveness of his rugged physique. He was clad in shiny cowboy boots, jeans, and a cream-colored cowboy shirt with maroon piping. There was a bullet hole just under his Adam's apple, and three more grouped in a loose triangle around the tip of his sternum. The front of his shirt had been messily recolored by blood from the wounds. More blood, congealing now, was puddled on the ribbed plastic between his legs.

"The way it reads," Ed Terry was saying, "he opened the door to somebody, they popped him four times, he fell straight back and was probably dead before he hit the floor. The shooter shut the door and left. Must have used a silencer. We rousted the whole place, but nobody heard anything that sounded like gun shots. No telling how long the victim might have lain there undiscovered if it hadn't been for the blood pooling up on that plastic and running out underneath the door. The manager got a call shortly after midnight to go quiet some rowdies in number twelve and saw the mess as he was coming down the corridor."

Terry is *Lieutenant* Ed Terry, Rockford Police Detective Squad. He's a fireplug with thick arms and legs and piercing cop eyes glaring out from below Spanish moss eyebrows. We're not exactly what you'd call friends, but our paths have crossed often enough so that we're sort of used to each other. At the moment, those cop eyes of his were red-rimmed from lack of sleep, as were the eyes of practically everybody in the cramped room. Except the dead guy's.

"Is that why you got me out of bed and had me hauled over here at two-fucking-thirty in the morning?" I wanted to know. "To explain to me how some drugstore cowboy bought the ranch?"

"This drugstore cowboy," Terry said, inclining his head. "You know him?"

"Never saw him before in my life."

"Well, he knew you. Or at least knew *of* you. We found this on him."

He held out a rectangle of off-white pasteboard with flat blue lettering. There were rust-colored splotches along one side that, after a moment, I realized were blood stains.

"Recognize it?" Terry asked.

"Of course I recognize it. It's one of my business cards. I've got them scattered all over town."

"But you never personally handed one to this guy?"

"Like I said, I never saw him before."

The lieutenant sighed. "All right, if the face isn't familiar let's try the name—Jack Crandell. Ring any bells?"

"Strike two," I answered. "Look, Ed, you have any idea how many people will pick up a card like that, thinking they might someday need whatever service is advertised, and then end up never even looking at it again? It gets buried in the other scraps of paper in their wallet and they'll carry it around for months before they finally dig it out and toss it."

"That was in his shirt pocket, Joe, and the shirt was brand-new. I'd say that's a pretty good indication he hadn't been packing it around for months."

"Okay, so he picked it up recently. Too recently to have had a chance to contact me. Maybe whatever trouble he thought he might need a private eye for is what caught up with him and killed him. Know anything about the guy?"

"Yeah, the computer at headquarters knew him real well. Rockford born and bred, in and out of trouble since his early teens, served time both as a juvie and as an adult. Been involved in everything from dope dealing to pimping to strong-arming to burglary, and back again."

"In other words, not exactly the kind of guy you're surprised to see end up full of bullet holes."

"No. But also not the kind of guy I'd picture hiring a private eye—leastways, not a legitimate one like you."

"Aw, you big flatterer, you."

"Don't let it go to your head. I damn sure don't have you listed under the heading of 'saint,' either. Every time I look around, you're up to your eyeballs in some kind of shit you shouldn't be messing with. That's why I couldn't afford to take any chances when that card turned up."

Henderson, one of the detectives Terry had sent to fetch me, disgorged himself from the background pack and walked over. "'Scuse me, Lieutenant, but now that Hannibal's had his look, the coroner's men would like to bag the body and get it out of here. And the lab boys are about ready to close up shop, too . . . unless you got anything else."

While they discussed wrapping up the crime scene, I knelt down and took another look at the dead guy. I didn't spend any more time on his facial features, as I'd already studied and dismissed them. But the corpse had some sort of bizarre haircut that rated more than passing interest. It appeared as if the crown of his head had been cleanly shaven until sometime recently, with the hair around his ears and high across the back of his neck left full. The shaved part had started growing back in and was covered with what looked like about two weeks' growth of dark whiskers. The overall effect was pretty striking, in a weird kind of way.

Terry had wandered over to talk with the lab men. Henderson, still hovering close by, seemed to read my thoughts. He said, "I can't decide if the poor fuck was trying for a punk hairstyle or if he maybe had a scalp disease of some kind he had to shave his head for."

"Who knows?" I said noncommittally. But I thought to myself, punkers hardly make a habit of decking out in cowboy shirts.

My eyes continued to scan. Lying the way he was, with his arms outflung and his palms up, I almost missed the tattoo. But I managed to catch a glimpse, and when I reached to roll his wrist for a better look, there it was. Across the back of his right hand—a wickedly pointed dagger with a slavering serpent coiled around it. It took a couple seconds for me to make the connection, but when I did Tommy Jessup's words tumbled through my mind in a rush. He had described the man who had beaten him up that night at the Belsens as having a tattoo on the back of his right hand that looked "like a cross—a crucifix, with a snake or something wrapped around it." Similar enough to be confused during a beating in semidarkness? The next question came automatically. And could the husky Crandell then, with the top of his head shaved and wearing the proper kind of glasses, be mistaken for wimpy Myron Strom, "only like somebody was holding a magnifying glass up to him"?

I straightened up, my brain whirling with further questions and a mad tangle of possibilities.

"What's the matter?" Henderson said.

"Nothing," I told him. "Nothing at all." I dug out a cigarette and got it going. "Look, I've really enjoyed the dog and pony show, and it might come as a big surprise considering my natural good looks and everything, but all of this is interrupting some much needed beauty sleep. If your boss is done with me, how about finding somebody to take me back home?"

It was past four when the black-and-white unit dropped me back at my apartment.

Despite the hour, sleep was out of the question. The inside of my head was churning like a summer sky just ahead of a thunderstorm. I plugged in the coffee pot, showered, and pulled on clean undershorts and a tee-shirt while the coffee was brewing, then sat down at the kitchen table with a steaming cup and a note pad in front of me. By the time I'd transferred most of the contents of the coffee pot into my stomach and filled a handful of pages with scribbling, I had it pretty much boiled down to three possibilities. They went like this:

(A) I was letting my imagination run away with me, making connections where none really existed, and arriving at some dangerously erroneous conclusions. I'm not often given to flights of fantasy, but for some reason the Gorcey woman had gotten to me and, as witnessed by my crazy dream the other night, had put some strange ideas in my head. Add to that my desire to see the Belsen sisters again and the fact I was still smarting from the whipping I'd taken at the hands of the press, and it wouldn't be impossible to surmise that maybe on some subconscious level I was wishing so hard for the case *not* to be over—in order to have a chance to make it turn out better than it had the first time around—that I was willing to grasp at straws I normally wouldn't touch. Yeah, maybe. But that still didn't explain Crandell's bizarre haircut, and tattoos on the back of the hand aren't that damn common.

(B) There was some truth in Helen Gorcey's wild accusations and Jack Crandell was part of an elaborate scheme to murder Aaron Belsen and make it look like an accident.

I wasn't ready to buy Corrie and Kellie as willing players in such a thing, but there was no denying they had gained monetarily from what had happened, and one of the oldest rules of thumb in my racket is: When in doubt, follow the money. Only that route had plenty of gaping holes. Foremost among them was the Cincinnati-postmarked letters I'd read. What had become of Myron Strom, and how did he fit in a conspiracy plot in the first place?

(C) Strom had indeed come to Rockford to consummate his "love" for Corrie Belsen, but for some reason grew suspicious of the assignation that was set up and hired Crandell, a local strong-armer, to go in his place. What might have transpired between the two after that I could only guess, but if you accepted the premise to begin with, then it was pretty hard to accept Crandell's death as something unconnected.

I found myself favoring possibility C, at least as a starting point. Pursuing A or B would mean admitting certain things about myself and/or my clients that I wasn't anxious to deal with. I'd go down those paths if I had to, but only if I ran into a stone wall the other way.

At half past six I pulled on some clothes, drove downtown, and began hitting the breakfast-special joints. Word was already on the streets about Crandell's killing. In the third place I stopped, I found a couple guys who had known him and were willing to talk to me. They didn't have much to offer, but I did learn that Crandell had been living with a woman named Betty Kittridge, a short order cook at a greasy spoon over on Kishwaukee. I paid for the two guys' breakfast, then headed for my Broadway office.

If the police hadn't already turned up Betty Kittridge's name, they would soon enough. I had to give them time to do their thing before I made my move on her. If Terry caught me sniffing around the edges of the Crandell kill after last night, he'd have me hanged from the nearest telephone pole. I figured I'd better steer clear of the Kittridge woman until later in the day.

I got to the office with three hours' worth of coffee

building pressure in my bladder and my nerves humming on a caffeine high. After making a beeline to the john, I did some digging through my files until I unearthed the packet the Cincinnati detective agency had put together on Myron Strom. By the time it had arrived, of course, it seemed a moot issue, and I'd paid it very little attention. I sat down with it now and went over it more thoroughly. Nowhere did it mention anything about Strom having any kind of tattoo. I went back to the phone number listed for Strom's residence, a rooming house, and decided I'd carry it a step further just to be sure.

When I had the landlord, one Peter Peltner, on the line, I said, "Mr. Peltner, my name is Joe Hannibal. I'm a detective calling long distance from Rockford, Illinois."

"Oh Christ, is this more to do with Myron Strom? Haven't you found him yet?"

"No, I'm afraid not yet."

He sighed. "Then this is just more 'routine' questions, right?"

"Well, basically only one."

"After all the questions you guys and the cops down here have already asked me, I'm surprised you can think of even one more. I'm only Strom's landlord, you know, not his friggin' father or something. But go ahead, ask away."

"What I need to know, Mr. Peltner, is if Strom had a tattoo?"

"A tattoo? Hell, no. A tattoo of what? Where?"

"The tattoo I'm interested in would have been on the back of his right hand."

"No way. Didn't have one. I couldn't have missed it there. That's the hand he signed his rent checks with."

I killed the rest of the morning half-heartedly working on some overdue paperwork. I walked up the street to Dan's Dog House and had a couple kraut dogs for lunch, spent a while shooting the breeze with the owner, Dan Modesto, and his beautiful wife, Sunshine. When I returned to the office, I decided I'd allowed the cops enough time to get finished with Betty Kittridge.

After receiving no answer at the number listed in the phone book, I tried the greasy spoon and was somewhat surprised to find she was at work. I ascertained that the cops had indeed come and gone, introduced myself and briefly explained my interest in Crandell's murder, arranged to meet with her during her two o'clock break.

The greasy spoon was called Nick & Maxine's and was located a long ways out on Kishwaukee. I got there early and one of the waitresses, a black girl with pinkish orange hair, motioned me into a corner booth and told me Betty would be out shortly. Betty Kittridge was a tall, big-boned woman in her late thirties. She had wilted red hair framing a rectangular face with a prominent nose and faded blue eyes in which all the sparkle had been replaced by a hard brittleness. She moved in that listless, plodding way that a lot of big women have, and it wouldn't require much imagination to picture her in a tenement doorway with a kid on her hip and two or three more peeking around from behind her skirt.

She slid into the booth opposite me, lit a cigarette, exhaled the smoke through her nostrils.

I said, "I appreciate you sparing me this time."

She shrugged. "You said you'd make it worth my while, right?"

"Right. I realize you've already gone through this with the police earlier, and I apologize for putting you through it again so soon after Jack's death, but—"

She cut me off with a wave of her hand. "Let's get something straight, Hannibal. Jack Crandell helped pay the bills and he was a good lay. But we'd been together less than six months, and the way it was headed it wasn't going to last another six. I'm sorry he's dead, I'm sorry if he suffered. But life goes on—like a big ball of shit rolling down a hill. You stop to feel sorry for yourself and the ball will squash you flat for sure. So take the funeral parlor hush out of your voice and ask what you came here to ask. I'm a big girl, I can handle it."

I looked into her brittle eyes. Each minute of her thirty-odd years showed in those eyes, and it hadn't been an easy trip. They were eyes that told me her tough talk was more than just an act to hide her grief. I guessed every relationship she'd ever had had been something measured in the span of a few months. Death was just another way for one to end. And that big ball of shit keeps on rolling.

"Do you have any idea why Crandell was at that motel last night?" I asked.

"When he left the apartment, he said he was going to meet somebody. Said he wouldn't be back until late."

"Did he often meet with people in motel rooms late at night?"

"I don't know. Jack was involved in . . . a lot of different things. I guess I don't have to tell you that some of them weren't exactly on the up and up. I imagine he met people in all sorts of places."

"Did he ever mention a man named Myron Strom?"

"No. No, he never talked much about what he was involved in or who was involved in it with him."

The denial seemed a shade too quick. I sensed she was lying, but I didn't push it for the time being. "It appeared," I said, "as if Jack's hair was starting to grow back in from some sort of strange haircut. Do you know what that was all about?"

She rolled her eyes. "Some crazy-ass job he took on. Said he had to look like a baldy—it paid a bonus or something. He made me shave the top of his head like that one night. Afterwards I told him he'd better wear a hat or a wig if he expected me to go out in public with him. He laughed and said not to worry, it only had to stay that way for a day or so and there was only a few days' difference between a good haircut and a bad one anyway." For just an instant the brittleness in her eyes seemed to soften, as if there might be some real feeling behind it. But that passed quickly.

"Do you recall exactly when that was, when he had you shave his head?"

"Uh, a couple weeks ago I guess. Not any longer than that. I remember it was in the middle of the week. Afterwards, he was flashing a wad of bills and feeling pretty cocky. He said the only hard thing about the job was parting with his hair."

"As I explained over the phone," I said, "after Jack was shot last night, the police found one of my business cards on him. Do you have any idea why? Had he mentioned my name recently or expressed any interest in hiring a private detective?"

"No. It's pretty hard to imagine Jack wanting to hire a private eye."

Again the too-quick denial, again the feeling on my part that she wasn't leveling with me. I tapped out a cigarette, made a production of lighting it, added to the smoke she already had billowing between us. I said, "Miss Kittridge, are you interested in seeing Jack's killer caught and punished?"

She gave me a look. "What kind of asshole question is that?"

"If you're holding out on me, then you damn sure held out on the cops."

"You calling me a liar?"

"Actually, I'm trying pretty hard *not* to call you a liar. But I don't think you're being entirely truthful, either. Tell me, how much time and effort do you really think the cops are going to spend on the death of a small-time no-good like Jack Crandell? They're going through the motions today because the bloodstains are still damp at the Masthead Inn and the story's on TV and in all the papers, and if they happen to stumble across a lead they'll be more than happy to bust somebody for it. But by the time Jack goes in the ground, his file will have started to gather dust—shoved aside for something hotter, bigger, more important. And no damn body is going to lay awake at night worrying about it after that."

"So what are you saying?"

"I'm saying if you know something that might help, then spill it. Tell the cops, tell me—tell somebody. Right now I figure I'm a couple steps ahead of the cops on this because I've spotted a link between Jack and the Strom guy I mentioned. Him I've got a personal beef with. I want him bad. I have reason to believe he was the one who hired Jack for that shaved head job, and I think last night they must have had a falling out over it and he ended up killing your man. Now, do you want to revise anything you've told me?"

She slowly ground out her cigarette in the ashtray between us. The charred tobacco made a soft, gritty sound against the pebbled glass blackened by a thousand previous butts. "All right," she said. "I lied when I said I never heard Jack mention Strom. I didn't want to get into names because . . . well, I didn't want anybody coming after me, you know?"

"What did he say about Strom?"

"Not much, really. Nothing that made any sense, anyway. He just said Strom's name—and yours."

"Mine?"

"I lied about that, too. It was last night, just a little before he went out, before he told me he'd be late and stuff. Whatever he was up to, it had him really wired all day yesterday. He kept saying it was going to be one of the best deals he ever pulled off, and after last night we could take a nice long ride on Easy Street."

"So how did Strom and me come into it?"

"I'm trying to remember his exact words. It was something like, let's see, the way he put it was, 'You can bet your sweet ass Strom and Hannibal cut themselves a fat piece of the pie; now it's my turn.'"

"Fat piece of what pie?"

"I don't know. Honest. Like I said, Jack never talked much about things he was involved in. Yesterday was kind of an exception, but even then he was pretty vague about it all."

To hell with it. It didn't matter right then. What mattered was that she'd confirmed for me that Crandell and Strom were indeed connected. Adrenaline pumped through me, making me feel like I was in motion sitting still. Strom was somewhere near, I could feel it. The son-of-a-bitch wouldn't get away from me again. I'd sort out all the little details once I had his neck between my hands . . .

"I don't know," Tommy Jessup said thoughtfully. "I guess it's possible. I mean, I was *expecting* it to be

Strom . . . I guess about any bald guy with glasses would have looked right."

Reciting from the profile the Cincinnati agency had put together for me, I said, "Myron Strom stands five-eleven, weighs somewhere in excess of two hundred pounds with a forty-inch-and-growing waistline."

"No way. Whoever I tangled with that night outside Kellie's house was at least as tall as me, and I'm almost six-four. And this guy was *hard*, you know? There wasn't that much puppy fat around his belly or anywhere else."

"I don't have any exact statistics on Crandell," I said, "but I'd put him in the six-four range and I'd guess his weight around two and a quarter. Most of that was in his shoulders and arms. He'd either pumped some iron or done some pretty heavy physical labor in his time. Maybe both. And he'd hired out for strong-arm work in the past, so he knew how to handle himself."

Tommy took a sip of his Coke and absently rubbed his side with his free hand, as if recalling just how well Crandell had been able to handle himself. We were seated on a grassy knoll overlooking the mini-putt range where Jessup worked as an attendant. I'd caught him on his evening break and had popped for a couple cans of soda out of the vending machine before guiding him over here where we could have some privacy while we talked.

"How about the tattoo?" I said. "Could it have been the dagger and serpent design I described?"

"Well . . . yeah, I suppose so. Like I told you, I never got to see it real good."

Tommy turned his head to look at me. The warm evening breeze that was blowing stirred his hair, pushing up a long cowlick. It made him look even more boyish.

"So what does it all mean, Mr. Hannibal?" he wanted to know.

I rolled my own can of Coke back and forth between my palms. "I'm not certain," I said. "I can only tell you what it could mean, what I'm afraid it might mean."

I laid it out for him then. Told him the rest of it about Crandell, about his murder, about the link I'd established between him and Strom. The only thing I omitted was the visit from Helen Gorcey. Whatever relevance that had to anything, it meant zilch as far as what I sought from young Jessup.

When I was through, he said, "You think Kellie and Corrie might be in danger, don't you?"

"That's a possibility I'm concerned about, yeah," I admitted. "If Crandell flushed Strom out of whatever rodent hole he's been hiding in and made him feel desperate enough to resort to murder, then it's hard to tell what state of mind that left him in. His obsession for Corrie had already manifested in some pretty extreme behavior, but the shooting of her father and the publicity apparently was enough to make him back off. Now, however, with this new killing, I'd say there's a chance he could have become unhinged to the point of making another try for her."

"Then hadn't we better call the police or something?"

"I think that's a decision that should be left up to Corrie and Kellie. You have to remember that I could be way the hell off beam. I don't want to alarm anybody unnecessarily, and I'm damn sure in no hurry to stir up another swarm of reporters."

"So what *are* we going to do?"

That was a good question. "I think you should go talk to the girls," I said. "I'm not sure they're ready to hear from me. Tell them what I've learned, what I suspect. If Strom really is on the prowl again, maybe they've already spotted or sensed something. I'll keep after it, if they want. Or maybe they'll just want to blow it all off, label me as paranoid. I'll go along with whatever they decide. At the very least, they'll have been alerted and will be more on their guard."

In an effort to soothe my gnawing doubts, I'd hunted up an out-of-the-way little bar where I wasn't likely to run into anybody I knew, and sat alone for a couple hours pouring down booze until the edginess grew sodden and controllable. Then home, a frozen dinner in front of the tube, sleep before the ten o'clock news was barely under way.

I was still sprawled in my easy chair, feet up, foil tray balanced precariously on my lap, when the phone went off. David Letterman and Paul Shaffer were exchanging smug, rodentlike grins on the TV screen, laughing at me as I clawed for the skidding tray with one hand and reached for the jangling phone with the other.

Corrie Belsen's voice rushed into my ear. "Mr. Hannibal? Thank God, I caught you at home."

I surged to my feet, sweeping away the tray, letting it clatter to the floor. "Corrie," I said. "Where are you? What's wrong?"

"It's Strom. He's shown up again . . . He followed us here!"

"Where? Where is 'here'?"

"Do you know where the Harlem Triplex is—just off Alpine?"

"I know it."

"Kellie and I came for the late show, a double feature. A few minutes ago, as we were letting out, I spotted Strom in the lobby. I'm calling now from the pay phone in the restroom lounge. He's out there waiting for us. You have to come, Mr. Hannibal. You have to help us!"

"I'm on my way. You stay put. Don't leave there under any circumstances."

I broke the connection and went out the door on a dead run. The night air was heavy with humidity, the threat of rain. Tufts of mist swirled grayish yellow in my headlight beams. Heat lightning flashed close in the sky.

I maneuvered recklessly from my southside apartment, cutting over to Alpine then hurtling northward toward the Harlem intersection. Mist hung heavier in the low reaches of my route. Traffic was sparse. As I drove, my mind boiled with thoughts.

I considered Sheriff Dar Schmidt's warning to lay off Strom in the event he showed up in this area. But nuts to that. I'd waited too long, endured too much. I also considered the possibility I might be driving into a trap. If I'd misread my former clients that badly, I decided, then I deserved it. Mainly what I sensed was this whole thing coming to a head, and I was eager for that no matter what it entailed.

When I swung into the Triplex parking lot, there were

only a handful of cars left. Strom's VW bug wasn't among them, but I had no trouble spotting the sleek Camaro that belonged to the Belsen sisters. I braked to a halt beside it. Before I had a chance to cut the engine, Corrie and Kellie emerged from the theater front's bank of glass doors and came trotting across the parking lot. Rain had begun to fall, widely spaced fat drops that thumped on the hood and roof of the Plymouth like small fists knocking to get in. The girls sprinted through this sudden shower and piled into the car—Corrie in the seat beside me, Kellie in the back—smelling of damp hairspray and perfume.

"I thought I told you to stay put," I growled by way of greeting.

"The theater manager was having a cow, wanting us to get out of there so he could close up," Kellie explained somewhat breathlessly.

"Besides," Corrie added, "Strom is long gone. He must have figured out we spotted him."

"Swell," I muttered. "Now we can go back to waiting and wondering when he'll try something again."

Corrie gave a somber shake of her head. "I don't think so. I have a bad feeling we won't have to wait very long at all. When I saw him tonight he was . . . well, different. More frightening than any of the other times. He looked sort of wild-eyed and crazy—like somebody who's really flipped out, you know?"

That seemed in keeping with my theory on Strom's possible mental state. I said, "Didn't Tommy Jessup get in touch with either of you earlier?"

Kellie nodded. "Yeah, he did. He told us about the talk you and he had, about your concerns." One side of her mouth turned down ruefully. "We decided you were probably overreacting. I guess it was wishful thinking on our parts . . . wanting so hard to believe that awful jerk was out of our lives once and for all."

I felt my own mouth pull into a hard, tight line. "I think Corrie may have nailed it. I've got the feeling, too, that this is finally going to be over one way or another real soon."

Corrie put a hand on my arm. "God, I hope you're right."

I looked down at where she was touching me, then glanced up to meet her eyes. She was watching me with the same imploring gaze she had used on me that first day. But was there something more there?

It turned out there was, all right. But damn sure none of the things I'd ever figured on.

Fiery hot pain stabbed suddenly into the big lat muscle running from the base of my neck across to my right shoulder. I jerked reflexively, twisting with surprise and agony, crying out. I fell against the car door, my face slapping cool glass, teeth biting the chrome frame. My throat seemed to be constricting and I felt all buttery-muscled and fuzzy. For an alarming instant I thought I'd been shot. But there had been no sound, no breaking of glass, no blood. I clawed at the steering wheel for support. The horn blared a protest. Everything was spinning, shape outlines melting before my rapidly blinking eyes. Corrie sat rigidly across from me, watching, her gaze curious now, expectant, but not at all concerned. I tried to say something to her, but my tongue wouldn't work. I rolled my head to look into the back seat, searching for Kellie. Everything spinning faster. Crazy, color-filled kaleidoscopic images. Kellie's face illuminated by a splash of dashboard light. Evil green smile. Ruby eyes. Turquoise-silver highlights glinting off the huge hypodermic needle in her hand . . .

I came to slowly, oozing out of unconsciousness like a slab of frozen meat thawing from a crust of ice. I gradually realized my face was lying in a puddle of puke. My own. My first instinct was to recoil from it. But a stronger instinct—survival—cautioned me not to move.

I was in a car, still my Plymouth by the feel and sound of it. The vehicle was in motion. I was sprawled with my chest and head on the passenger seat, my rump on the floor, my left arm pinned. My right arm hung limply down across my hip, my legs bent uncomfortably against the transmission housing. I was cramped and aching. My brain sloshed in and out of a fog bank, my stomach threatened to void more of its contents. I wanted to take some deep breaths, suck in great mouthfuls of soothing oxygen. But I squeezed my eyes tightly shut and fought to keep my breathing even.

My brain floated clear of the fog and began screaming questions: How long had I been out? Where were we going and how far had we traveled? What the fuck was going on—what had Kellie injected me with? And why? The fog rolled back before I finished formulating questions, let alone any of the answers.

Then voices. Above and beside me. So close they startled me.

Kellie said, "He makes me nervous, just lying there like that. I wish we'd brought along something to tie him up with."

"Relax, for crying out loud," Corrie replied. "The only thing we have to worry about from him is the stink of his vomit. We tripled the dosage Doc Traynor taught us to give Mother. You saw how it used to work on her. He isn't going any damn where for a long time."

"Oh, he's going somewhere all right. He's going straight to the bottom of that gravel pit along with Strom. The sooner the better. That's what we should have done with that Crandell asshole, too, and none of this would have been necessary."

"No, Crandell wasn't as big a sap as ol' Myron or Hannibal here. He had us figured out and never would have given us a chance to get cute. A couple quick bullets was the only way to take care of him."

"Maybe we should have stuck with that routine then."

"I can do without the noise and the mess for once, thank you. As long as we had the choice, this is much tidier."

So there it was. Incredibly, sickeningly, yet undeniably. I wanted to groan out loud. Corrie and Kellie had killed both Strom and Jack Crandell. And they currently seemed bent on taking *me* for a one-way ride. Which could only mean that the shooting of their father had been premeditated as well. Helen Gorcey's warning echoed hauntingly through my mind. Everything she'd claimed had been true. I'd been a sucker all right. A goddamned fool. Even when I finally had gotten around to having a few doubts, I'd ignored them and walked straight into a trap. Maybe I

did deserve what was in store for me. I felt the urge to
throw up again, and this time it had nothing to do with any
side effect from whatever had been pumped into me.

"Slow down, our turn-off's coming up before long. You
can't see shit in this rain."

The words caused my body to go tense. Adrenaline
coursed through me, swirling away the fog, clearing my
mind. No, damn it all, I *didn't* deserve to die. I didn't *want*
to die. I wasn't ready to spend eternity sharing a watery
grave with Myron Strom.

I'd determined from their exchanges that it was Corrie
behind the wheel. When she slowed to make the turn, I'd
take my shot.

I wondered if my legs would work. Jammed and
cramped like they were, I couldn't be sure. There was no
way I could test them unnoticed. I knew my left arm, its
circulation pinched off, was out of commission. I tried my
right, slowly rolling the wrist first one way then the other.
It was okay. God, I hoped my legs would be. Feet, don't fail
me now . . .

I listened to the whine of tires through the seat, strain-
ing to catch the lower pitch that would signal diminishing
speed. Change of direction isn't easy to determine when
you're lying more or less horizontal with your eyes closed.
I felt shifting inertia tug at my body bulk. The tire whine
lowered to a dull buzz. I heard the crunch of loose gravel.

Now.

If I didn't split my skull or break my back on impact, I
just might have a chance. And if I did, well, hell, better to
go out fighting. Last-second doubts rocketed through my
brain, though: Had Kellie reloaded the hypodermic? Was
one of the girls packing the gun they'd killed Crandell
with? Was it crazy to depend on my drugged condition to
carry me through an escape attempt? But being too
careful can get you killed just as dead as being too rash.
Fuck it.

I jerked my head up, twisted around, punched the door
handle. The door flew open. Rush of air, hiss of rain, cool
mist. I kicked against the transmission housing. My legs
came unbent painfully, but did their job, propelling me

out into the night. I heard one of the girls swear. Hunching my shoulders and wrapping my right arm around my head for as much protection as possible, I hit the ground skidding. Cloth ripped, gravel chewed exposed flesh. Breath *whoofed* out of me as my feet and legs whipped around in an awkward, flopping backward somersault. And then came the welcome slap of grass, followed by the soggy cushioning of high, wet weeds as I rolled to a stop in the pocket of a ditch.

I wanted to just lay there, sucking air, reveling in the damp softness. But that, of course, was a luxury I couldn't afford. Even as I thought it, I was aware of the screech of tires that signaled the car braking to a halt. The Belsens weren't about to give up easily.

I pushed to a low crouch, wiped rain from my eyes. The ditch I was in ran alongside a narrow black-topped road. Lightning flashes showed a grove of trees—an orchard of some kind—behind me across a sagging wire fence.

The Plymouth's taillights were visible a couple hundred yards down the road. I heard the sounds of doors opening and closing, frantic feet on pavement, words being tossed back and forth between Corrie and Kellie. Circles of light bounced on, began bouncing about. Beams of pale yellow stabbed in my direction, searching.

I lunged for the fence, dragged myself up and over. Gnashing barbs tore at my hands and legs, but I didn't have time for the pain. I toppled heavily to the other side. Rolled and struggled to my feet. Tried to run. All the exertion triggered an abrupt second-wave reaction to the drug I'd been given. My head reeled, my legs turned to rubber bands. I fell back down. I lay there, gasping, feeling dangerously exposed by the staccato bursts of lightning that licked the sky.

I scooped handfuls of water from the long grass, vigorously rubbed my face and hair and the back of my neck. The spinning inside my head began to slow. I couldn't be sure why the drug had failed to have the completely immobilizing effect it was expected to have. Maybe it was too old, had lost some of its potency; maybe my size and/or metabolism were sufficient to counter the dose. For whatever reason, I'd managed to handle it okay so far, and I told myself that now was no damn time to let it get the best of me.

On bloodied hands and knees, I crawled for the protection of the nearest tree. Behind me, the flashlight beams were poking through the ditch, nearing the approximate spot where I'd gone over the fence.

I got in back of a rain-slick trunk and collapsed against it, breathing hard. My poor fog-edged brain was trying desperately to cope, to sort and analyze and plan for everything that was coming down. Corrie and Kellie Belsen—killers. Jesus Christ.

The circles of light were inside the fence now. I pulled myself to my feet and moved deeper into the orchard. I had to assume the girls were armed in some way or it didn't seem likely they would be pursuing me as boldly as they were. Inasmuch as they'd had the foresight to strip me of my weapons during the time I'd lain unconscious in the car, I knew they weren't lacking for artillery even if they hadn't brought any of their own.

Corrie and Kellie Belsen—armed killers. Jesus Christ.

Ripped and battered and semidrugged as I was, I had to face the fact that I didn't have the endurance to continue trying to make a run for it. My head seemed reasonably clear at the moment, my legs felt strong, I even had my left arm working after a fashion. I decided to pick a spot and make a stand before I was overcome by another attack of the woozies. Killers they might be, but that didn't make them trained stalkers.

A thick, thorny berry bush appeared to offer the concealment I required while at the same time affording a fairly clear view of my lightning-strobed surroundings. I edged carefully into this cover, aware that behind me the flashlight beams had fanned out and were sweeping the orchard in a circling pattern.

It took several minutes—which seemed like several hours—before one of the flashlight-wielders moved within striking distance. Intermittent overhead bursts revealed it to be Kellie, shiny two-cell gripped in one hand, short-snouted weapon (my own boot derringer) protruding from the other. Corrie's dancing beam was a dozen yards away, off to my right.

I sprang from the bush, chopping down at the wrist of Kellie's gun hand. The derringer pinwheeled away. She emitted a cry and lashed out with the other hand, trying to brain me with the flashlight. I blocked the blow and attempted to grab her wrist. But the effort was made with my not-fully-functioning left hand and I was unable to maintain my grip. She swung at me again, cursing, her eyes and teeth flashing. I blocked a second time, punching my right fist into the inside of her elbow. The flashlight clattered to the ground and went dead. We clinched, struggling.

"Kellie!" Corrie shouted, having heard her sister's cries. The glowing orb of her light bounded toward us.

I twisted Kellie around so that she was facing away from me. I slammed my left forearm across her throat, locked it there with the crook of my right elbow, cupped the back of her head in my palm. It was a hold designed to produce— with sudden pressure in opposite directions—a cleanly broken neck. Kellie seemed to recognize its potential and her struggles became minimal.

"Hold it right fucking there, Corrie!"

My command halted the approach of the bobbing light.

"Point the light away."

She hesitated, then angled the beam slightly off to one side.

"I've got a gun, Hannibal, and I know how to use it."

"With this hold, I can snap your sister's neck in a fraction of a second."

"I'd still get you."

"Maybe. It's dark. It's storming. Maybe I'm willing to bet you aren't that good."

Silence. Except for the rain and an occasional low rumble of thunder.

"Of course, we all know you're perfectly capable of killing, don't we?" I said. "You and sis here have demonstrated that beyond any shadow of doubt. But for the love of God *why*—why murder your own father?"

"Because we were sick and tired of being deprived, of making sacrifices, that's why."

"*You?* What the hell do *you* know about being deprived?"

"You try going through your teenage years with a terminally ill parent. I had to delay starting college, Kellie couldn't even begin to make any plans along those lines. We didn't complain, because we loved our mother. We spent endless hours nursing her, being there for her. We watched her die. But then, when it was finally over, when we should have been able to get on with our lives, our father announced that he planned to remarry. A scheming bitch with dollar signs in her eyes and two whining brats on her apron strings. Aside from the slap to Mother's memory, that would have meant a whole new series of sacrifices."

"So just like that, you murdered him."

"Not 'just like that,' no. We didn't hate our father—don't ever think it was easy. But in the final analysis that's what it came down to."

"And where did Strom fit in?"

"Everything we told you about the mail order photos and Strom was true. Except we left out the simple little fact that he came here only after I encouraged him to. Once we'd decided what we had to do, we recognized that he'd make a perfect scapegoat."

"Along with me."

"You, Tommy—whoever else we had to use. You would have come out of it all right—alive anyway—if you hadn't insisted on sticking your nose back in. You men are all such pathetic fools. I saw the way you looked at us, how your eyes followed me. There's not that much difference between you and the Stroms of the world. Believe it."

"So how did you get him to lead me on that wild goose chase the night your father was killed?"

"Strom was already out of the way by then. That was Kellie—wearing a bald cap and glasses and driving his car—you followed to Freeport. The Mulvaney kids always sleep like rocks once they've been tucked in, and their parents are never home before one or two in the morning. It was no risk for her to bump the phone off the hook and slip away. And while it was true that Daddy Dear had a history of absentmindedness when it came to notifying us about his return plans, we went to great pains to determine almost to the minute when he would be arriving home on this particular occasion."

"That only leaves the question of Crandell."

"We paid him to shave his head and pretend to be Strom and beat the snot out of Tommy so we'd have justification for hiring you. You were important to our credibility. Crandell was a little smarter than we figured, though. When everything started hitting the papers, he was able to put two and two together. He tried blackmailing us. We knew if we paid him the first time he'd bleed us dry. We had to show we couldn't be fucked with."

I shook my head, marvelling at her calmly delivered explanations. They sketched a plot that was stunning in its complexity and cold-bloodedness, made even more so by the fact it had been concocted and carried out by two teenaged girls.

I said, "Which brings us to the here and now. I suppose you've got another car stashed at the gravel pit, where you already deep-sixed Strom and his VW when you were through with it, and planned to sink me and my Plymouth along with them."

"That's close enough."

I shook my head. "It was a good try, kid, but it fell a little short. If a couple quirky things hadn't dropped just a certain way, you might actually have pulled it off. But not now. Even if you manage to kill me, I've raised too many questions, started too many wheels turning. You'll never get away with it."

More silence. In my arms, Kellie was starting to breathe more rapidly, anticipating the situation reaching a climax. I wished I could see Corrie's face better, see what impact my words might be having.

Before I had time to wonder too long, her gun made a flat cracking sound and spewed dull orange flame. The bullet hit Kellie solid, thudding her back against me. For a crazy instant, I believed Corrie must be trying to shoot *around* my prisoner, trying to get at me. But when the flashlight beam targeted us clearly and a second slug punched into the girl in my grasp, I saw the action for what it was.

Corrie Belsen was purposely killing her own sister (an additional sacrifice she *was* willing to make), stripping away my shield, eliminating my bargaining chip, telling me in no uncertain terms that she'd seen through my bluff and still meant to take me out. God only knew what story she had in mind to explain away Kellie's death, but it was a point of damn little concern to me right at the moment.

As I felt Kellie sag in my arms, the life draining out of her, soiling the front of me, something inside snapped. All the anger and frustration and pain and humiliation I'd experienced during my association with the Belsen sisters fused to an uncontrollable pressure point and erupted in a face-stretching, eye-bulging, saliva-spraying roar of pure rage. Red mist sizzled before my eyes. Every muscle, every fiber was taut and strong and inflamed with self-righteous fury. No fear, only rage.

Seizing the limp, dead form that had once been Kellie Belsen by its waistband and the hair, I held it at arm's length in front of me and began running as hard as I could straight toward my would-be executioner. More shots rang out. The sack of meat in my grip jerked with the impact of the bullets. The glare of the flashlight loomed closer, stinging my eyes. A slug ripped the edge of my thigh. My bellowing roar continued, like a crazed aria.

In the instant before I rammed Corrie, a burst of lightning showed me her face clearly. It was a vision I would see repeated in bad dreams for months.

The collision came with bone-jarring, teeth-cracking force. The string of obscenities Corrie had been screaming stopped abruptly. Something hard and unyielding drilled into my solar plexus. I fell to one side, losing both my balance and my grip on Kellie. Fiery pain streaked the length of my leg, adrenaline-delayed reaction to the bullet wound. Breath pounded out of me and my stomach muscles convulsed.

I lay in wracking spasms for I don't know how long, a tiny corner of my brain clinging to awareness, anticipating the sound of a trigger snick and then the exploding shell that would signal my doom.

It never came.

The pulverizing waves of cramping nausea eventually subsided.

I pushed myself to a sitting position.

Kellie lay a foot or two from where I'd fallen.

Corrie stood over her.

At least that's the way it appeared. My breath caught at the sight and all motion on my part froze.

It was only after several moments of wide-eyed study that I realized there was something wrong with the picture. Corrie's stance was awkward, unnatural. Her head lolled forward on her chest, her arms hung limply at her sides, her legs were buckled in a strange, unsupportive way.

I let out my breath cautiously and pushed the rest of the way to my feet.

I took a step, reached out to touch her.

She suddenly moved forward and I heard the cracking sound of her gun.

I leaped back, bleating like a frightened child.

But instead of continuing her attack, Corrie immediately collapsed and fell in a heap across her sister's legs.

I remained at a respectable distance for several beats, my heart hammering, my fists clenching and unclenching, my eyes glued to the two motionless forms.

When my curiosity had shored up my courage once more, I limped over to where Corrie's flashlight lay blazing in the grass. Scooping it up, I turned and slowly swept its beam over the scene.

My charge had driven Corrie back against one of the trees. A low branch had bent and sheared away under the crunch of bodies, leaving a wicked foot-long stub that had impaled Corrie through vital organs. She'd hung suspended on it until my touch had shifted her weight sufficiently to break off another portion—the cracking sound I'd heard—allowing her to slip free.

I played the light over the bodies again.

Looking down at them, I felt as cold and remorseless as the rain that pelted me.

For some bizarre reason, the sisters' death sprawls made me think of the poses they'd struck for the pages of *Grind*. "Naughty! Naughty!" their ad had proclaimed. "See what a couple naughty sisters are willing to do just for you!"

Yeah, these bitches had been willing to do plenty. Only strictly for themselves.

Patricide . . . fratricide . . . plain old murder . . .

It doesn't get much naughtier than that.

While best known for such huge cop novels as L.A. Confidential, The Big Nowhere, *and* The Black Dahlia, *James Ellroy
began his crime-writing career with Los Angeles private eye and
Beethoven buff Fritz Brown* (Brown's Requiem, *1982*).

*Ellroy's "Torch Number" is set in his beloved hometown of L.A.,
circa 1942, and introduces the laudanum-tippling investigator
Spade Hearns. It's also Ellroy's first contribution to a PWA
anthology.*

Torch Number

by James Ellroy

Before Pearl Harbor and the
Jap scare, my living room window offered a great night view:
Hollywood Boulevard lit with neon, dark hillsides, movie
spots crisscrossing the sky announcing the latest opening at
Grauman's and the Pantages. Now, three months after the
day of infamy—blackouts in effect and squadrons of Jap
Zeros half expected any moment—all I could see were
building shapes and the cherry lamps of occasional prowl
cars. The ten P.M. curfew kept night divorce work off my
plate, and blowing my last assignment with Bill Malloy of the
D.A.'s Bureau made a special deputy's curfew waiver out of
the question. Work was down, bills were up, and my botched
surveillance of Maggie Cordova had me thinking of Lorna all
the time, wearing the grooves on her recording of "Prison of
Love" down to sandpaper.

> *Prison of Love.*
> *Sky above.*
> *I feel your body like a velvet glove. . . .*

I mixed another rye and soda and started the record over. Through a part in the curtains, I eyeballed the street; I thought of Lorna and Maggie Cordova until their stories melded.

Lorna Kafesjian.

Second-rate bistro chanteuse—first-rate lungs, third-rate club gigs because she insisted on performing her own tunes. I met her when she hired me to rebuff the persistent passes of a rich bull dagger who'd been voyeur perving on her out at Malibu Beach—Lorna with her swimsuit stripped to the waist, chest exposed for a deep cleavage tan to offset the white gowns she always wore on stage. The dyke was sending Lor a hundred long-stemmed red roses a day, along with mash notes bearing her *nom de plume d'amour*: "Your Tongue of Fire." I kiboshed the pursuit quicksville, glomming the tongue's Vice jacket, shooting the dope to Louella Parsons—a socially connected, prominently married carpet muncher with a yen for nightclub canaries was prime meat for the four-star *Herald*. I told Louella: She desists, you don't publish; she persists, you do. The Tongue and I had a little chat; I strong-armed her nigger bodyguard when *he* got persistent. Lorna was grateful, wrote me the torch number to torch all torch numbers—and *I* got persistent.

The flame burned both ways for about four months—from January to May of '38 I was Mr. Ringside Swain as Lorna gigged the Katydid Klub, Bido Lito's, Malloy's Nest, and a host of dives on the edge of jigtown. Two A.M. closers, then back to her place; long mornings and afternoons in bed, my business neglected, clients left dangling while I lived the title of a Duke Ellington number: "I Got It Bad, and That Ain't Good." Lorna came out of the spell first; she saw that I was willing to trash my life to be with her. That scared her; she pushed me away; I played stage door Johnny until I got disgusted with myself and she blew town for fuck knows where, leaving me a legacy of soft contralto warbles on hot black wax.

Lorna.

Lorna to Maggie.

Maggie happened this way:

Two weeks ago Malloy co-opted me to the D.A.'s Bureau—the aftermath of the bank job was running helter-skelter, he needed a man good at rolling stakeouts, and a citizens committee had posted extra reward gelt. The B of A on North Broadway and Alpine got knocked off; two shitbirds—caucasians, one with *outré* facial scars—snuffed three armed guards and got away clean. A score of eyeball witnesses gave descriptions of the robbers, then—blam!—the next day a witness, a seventy-three-year-old Jap granny set for internment pickup, got plugged—double blam!—as she was walking her pooch to the corner market. LAPD Ballistics compared the slugs to the pills extracted from the stiffs at the bank scene: match-up, straight across.

Malloy was called in. He developed a theory: One of the eyewitnesses was in on the robbery; the heisters glommed the addresses of the other witnesses and decided to bump them to camouflage their guy. Malloy threw a net around the three remaining witnesses; two square johns named Dan Doherty and Bob Roscomere—working stiffs with no known criminal associates—and Maggie Cordova—a nightclub singer who'd taken two falls for possession and sale of marijuana.

Maggie C. loomed as the prime suspect: She toked big H and maryjane, was rumored to have financed her way through music school by pulling gang bangs, and played it hardcase during her two-year jolt at Tehachapi. Doherty and Roscomere were put out as bait, not warned of the danger they were in, carrying D.A.'s Bureau tails wherever they went. Malloy figured my still-simmering torch for Lorna K. gave me added insight into the ways of errant songbirds and sent me out to keep loose track of Maggie, hoping she'd draw unfriendly fire if she wasn't the finger woman or lead me to the heisters if she was.

I found Maggie pronto—a call to a booking agent who owed me—and an hour later I was sipping rye and soda in the lounge of a Gardena pokerino parlor. The woman was a dumpy ash blonde in a spangly gown, long-sleeved, probably to hide her needle tracks. She looked vaguely familiar, like a stag film actress you were hard for in your youth. Her eyes were flat and droopy and her microphone gestures were spastic. She looked like a hophead who'd spent her best years on cloud nine and would never adjust to life on earth.

I listened to Maggie butcher "I Can't Get Started," "The Way You Look Tonight," and "Blue Moon"; she bumped the mike stand with her crotch and nobody whistled. She sang "Serenade in Blue" off-key and a clown a couple of tables over threw a handful of martini olives at her. She flipped the audience the finger, got a round of applause, and belted the beginning of "Prison of Love."

I sat there, transfixed. I closed my eyes and pretended it was Lorna. I forced myself not to wonder how this pathetic no-talent dopester got hold of a song written exclusively for me. Maggie sang her way through all five verses, the material almost transforming her voice into something good. I was ripping off Lorna's snow-white gown and plunging myself into her when the music stopped and the lights went on.

And Maggie was ixnay, splitsville, off to Gone City. I tried her dressing room, the bar, the casino. I got her vehicle stats from the DMV and got nowhere with them. I slapped around a croupier with a junkie look, got Maggie's address, and found her dump cleaned out lock, stock, and barrel. I became a pistol-whipping, rabbit-punching, brass knuckle–wielding dervish then, tearing up the Gardena Strip. I got a half decent lead on a ginch Maggie used to whore with; the woman got me jacked on laudanum, picked my pocket, and left me in Gone City, ripe prey for a set of strong-arm bulls from the Gardena P.D. When I came off cloud ten in a puke-smelling drunk tank, Bill Malloy was standing over me with glad tidings: I'd been charged with six counts of aggravated assault, one count of felonious battery, and two counts of breaking and entering. Maggie Cordova was nowhere to be found; the other eyewitnesses were in protective custody. Bill himself was off the bank job, on temporary assignment to the Alien Squad, set to rustle Japs, the big cattle drive that wouldn't end until Uncle Sam gave Hirohito the big one where it hurt the most. My services were no longer required by the

D.A.'s office, and my night curfew waiver was revoked until somebody figured a way to chill out the nine felony charges accumulated against me . . .

I heard a knock at the door, looked out the window and saw a prowl car at the curb, red lights blinking. I took my time turning on lamps, wondering if it was warrants and handcuffs or maybe somebody who wanted to talk dealsky. More knocks—a familiar cadence. Bill Malloy at midnight.

I opened the door. Malloy was backstopped by a muscle cop who looked like a refugee from the wrong side of a Mississippi chain gang: big ears, blond flattop, pig eyes, and a too-small suitcoat framing the kind of body you expect to see on convicts who haul cotton bales all day. Bill said, "You want out of your grief, Hearns? I came to give you an out."

I pointed to the man-monster. "Expecting trouble you can't handle?"

"Policemen come in pairs. Easier to give trouble, easier to avoid it. Sergeant Jenks, Mr. Hearns."

The big man nodded; an Adam's apple the size of a baseball bobbed up and down. Bill Malloy stepped inside and said, "If you want those charges dropped and your curfew waiver back, raise your right hand."

I did it. Sergeant Jenks closed the door behind him and read from a little card he'd pulled from his pocket. "Do you, Spade Hearns, promise to uphold the laws of the United States Government pertaining to executive order number nine-oh-five-five and obey all other federal and municipal statutes while temporarily serving as an internment agent?"

I said "Yeah."

Bill handed me a fresh curfew pass and an LAPD rap sheet with a mugshot strip attached. "Robert no middle name Murikami. He's a lamster Jap, he's a youth gang member, he did a deuce for B and E and when last seen he was passing out anti-American leaflets. We've got his known associates on this sheet, last known address, the magilla. We're swamped and taking in semipros like you to help. Usually we pay fifteen dollars a day, but you're in no position to demand a salary."

I took the sheet and scanned the mugshots. Robert NMN Murikami was a stolid-looking youth—a samurai in a skivvy shirt and duck's ass haircut. I said, "If this kid's so wicked, why are you giving me the job?"

Jenks bored into me with his little pig eyes; Bill smiled. "I trust you not to make the same mistake twice."

I sighed. "What's the punch line?"

"The punch line is that this punk is pals with Maggie Cordova—we got complete paper on him, including his bail reports. The Cordova cooze put up the jack for Tojo's last juvie beef. Get him, Hearns. All will be forgiven and maybe you'll get to roll in the gutter with another second-rate saloon girl."

I settled in to read the junior kamikaze's rap sheet. There wasn't much: the names and addresses of a half dozen Jap cohorts—tough boys probably doing the Manzanar shuffle by now—carbons of the kid's arrest reports, and letters to the judge who presided over the B&E trial that netted Murikami his two-spot at Preston. If you read between the lines, you could see a metamorphosis: Little Tojo started out as a pad prowler out for cash and a few sniffs of ladies' undergarments and ended up a juvie gang honcho: zoot suits, chains and knives, boogie-woogie rituals with his fellow members of the "Rising Sons." At the bottom of the rap sheet there was a house key attached to the page with Scotch tape, an address printed beside it: 1746¼ North Avenue 46, Lincoln Heights. I pocketed the key and drove there, thinking of a Maggie-to-Lorna reunion parlay—cool silk sheets and a sleek tanned body soundtracked by the torch song supreme.

The address turned out to be a subdivided house on a terraced hillside overlooking the Lucky Lager Brewery. The drive over was eerie: Streetlights and traffic signals were the only illumination and Lorna was all but there with me in the car, murmuring what she'd give me if I took down slant Bobby. I parked at the curb and climbed up the front steps, counting numbers embossed on doorways: 1744, 1744½, 1746, 1746½. 1746¼ materialized; I fumbled the key toward the lock. Then I saw a narrow strip of light through the adjoining window—the unmistakable glint of a pen flash probing. I pulled my gun, *eased* the key in the hole, watched the light flutter back toward the rear of the pad, and opened the door slower than slow.

No movement inside, no light coming toward me. "Fuck, fuck, fuck," echoed from a back room; a switch dropped and big light took over. And there was my target: a tall, skinny man bending over a chest of drawers, a penflash clamped in his teeth.

I let him start rifling, then tiptoed over. When he had both hands braced on the dresser and his legs spread, I gave him the Big Fungoo.

I hooked his left leg back; Prowler collapsed on the dresser, pen flash cracking teeth as his head hit the wall. I swung him around, shot him a pistol butt blow to the gut, caught a flailing right hand, jammed the fingers into the top drawer space, slammed the drawer shut, and held it there with my knee until I heard fingers cracking. Prowler screamed; I found a pair of jockey shorts on the counter, shoved them in his mouth, and kept applying pressure with my knee. More bone crack; amputation coming up. I eased off and let the man collapse on his knees.

The shitbird was stone cold out. I kicked him in the face to keep him that way, turned on the wall light, and prowled myself.

It was just a crummy bedroom, but the interior decorating was *très outré*: Jap nationalist posters on the walls—racy shit that showed Jap Zeros buzz-bombing a girl's dormitory, buxom white gash in peignoirs running in terror. The one table held a stack of Maggie Cordova phonograph records—Maggie scantily attired on the jackets, stretch marks, flab, and chipped nail polish on display. I examined them up close—no record company was listed. They were obvious vanity jobs—fat Maggie preserving her own sad warbles.

Shitbird was stirring; I kicked him in the noggin again and trashed the place upside down. I got:

A stash of women's undies, no doubt Bad Bob's B&E booty; a stash of *his* clothes; assorted switchblades, dildoes, french ticklers, tracts explaining that a Jew-Communist conspiracy was out to destroy the world of true peace the German and Japanese brotherhood had sought to establish through peaceful means and—under the mattress—seventeen bankbooks: various banks, the accounts fat with cash, lots of juicy recent deposits.

It was time to make Shitbird sing. I gave him a waistband frisk, pulling out a .45 auto, handcuffs, and—mother dog!—an L.A. sheriff's badge and I.D. holder. Shitbird's real monicker was Deputy Walter T. Koenig, currently on loan to the County Alien Squad.

That got me thinking. I found the kitchen, grabbed a quart of beer from the icebox, came back and gave Deputy Bird an eye-opener—Lucky Lager on the *cabeza*. Koenig sputtered and spat out his gag; I squatted beside him and leveled my gun at his nose. "No dealsky, no tickee, no washee. Tell me about Murikami and the bankbooks or I'll kill you."

Koenig spat blood; his foggy eyes honed in on my roscoe. He licked beer off his lips; I could tell his foggy brain was trying to unfog an angle. I cocked my .38 for emphasis. "Talk, Shitbird."

"Zeck—zeck—order."

I spun the .38's cylinder—more emphasis. "You mean the executive order on the Japs?"

Koenig spat a few loose canines and some gum flaps. "Zat's right."

"Keep going. A snitch jacket looks good on you."

Shitbird held a stare on me; I threw him back some of his manhood to facilitate a speedy confession. "Look, you spill and I won't rat you. This is just a money gig for me."

His eyes told me he bought it. Koenig got out his first unslurred words. "I been doin' a grift with the Japs. The government's holdin' their bank dough till the internment ends. I was gonna cash out for Murikami and some others, for a cut. You know, bring 'em to the bank in bracelets, carry some official-lookin' papers. Japs are smart, I'll give 'em that. They know they're goin' bye-bye, and they want more than bank interest."

I didn't *quite* buy it; on reflex I gave Koenig's jacket pockets a toss. All I got was some women's pancake makeup—pad and bottle. The anomaly tweaked me; I pulled Koenig to his feet and cuffed him behind his back with his own bracelets. "Where's Murikami hiding out?"

"Fourteen-eleven Wabash, East L.A., apartment three-eleven. Bunch of Japs holing up there. What are you gonna—"

"I'm going to toss your car and cut you loose. It's *my* grift now, Walter."

Koenig nodded, trying not to look grateful; I unloaded his piece and stuck it in his holster, gave him back his badge kit, rounded up the bankbooks, and shoved him toward the front door, thinking of Lorna accompanied by Artie Shaw and Glenn Miller, the two of us enjoying Acapulco vacations financed by Axis cash. I pushed Koenig down the steps ahead of me; he nodded toward a Ford roadster parked across the street. "There, that's mine. But you ain't—"

Shots cut the air; Koenig pitched forward, backward, forward. I hit the pavement, not knowing which direction to fire. Koenig slumped into the gutter; a car sped by *sans* headlights. I squeezed off five shots and heard them ding metal; lights went on in windows—they gave me a perfect shot of a once-rogue cop with his face blasted away. I stumbled over to the Ford, used my pistol butt to smash in a window, popped the glove compartment, and tore through it. Odd papers, no bankbooks, my hands brushing a long piece of slimy rubber. I held it up and flicked on the dash light and saw a paste-on scar—*outré*—just like the one eyewitnesses at the bank job said one of the heisters had.

I heard sirens descending, blasting like portents of doomsday. I ran to my car and highballed it the fuck away.

My apartment was in the wrong direction—away from leads on Maggie into Lorna. I drove to 1411 Wabash, found it postmidnight still, blackout black—a six-story walk-up with every single window covered. The joint was stone quiet. I ditched my car in the alley, stood on the hood, jumped up, and caught the bottom rung of the fire escape.

The climb was tough going; mist made the handrails wet and slippery, and my shoes kept slipping. I made it to the third-floor landing, pushed the connecting door open, padded down the empty hallway to 311, put my ear to the door and listened.

Voices in Jap, voices in Jap-accented English, then pure Americanese, loud and clear. "You're paying me for a hideout, not chow at two-fucking-A.M. But I'll do it—*this time.*"

More voices; footsteps heading toward the hall. I pulled my gun, pinned myself to the wall, and let the door open in my face. I hid behind it for a split second; it was shut, and caucasian-san hotfooted it over to the elevator. On tippy-toes, I was right behind him.

I cold-cocked him clean—wham!—grabbed his pocket piece while he hit the carpet and dreamsville, stuffed my display handkerchief in his mouth, and dragged him over to a broom closet and locked him in. Two-gun armed, I walked back to the door of 311 and rapped gently.

"Yes?"—a Jap voice—from the other side. I said, "It's me," deliberately muffled. Mutters, the door opening, a jumbo Buddhahead filling the doorway. I kicked him in the balls, caught his belt mid-jacknife, pulled forward and smashed his head into the doorjamb. He sunk down gonesville; I waved the automatic I'd taken off the white punk at the rest of the room.

What a room.

A dozen slants staring at me with tiny black eyes like Jap Zero insignias, Bob Murikami smack in the middle. Arkansas toad stabbers drawn and pointed square at my middle. A Mexican standoff or the sequel to Pearl Harbor. Kamikaze was the only way to play it.

I smiled, ejected the chambered round from my pilfered piece, popped the clip, and tossed both at the far wall. Jumbo was stirring at my feet; I helped him up, one hand on his carotid artery in case he got uppity. With my free hand, I broke the cylinder on *my* gun, showing him the one bullet left from my shoot-out with Walter Koenig's killers. Jumbo nodded his head, getting the picture; I spun the chamber, put the muzzle to his forehead, and addressed the assembled Axis powers. "This is about bankbooks, Maggie Cordova, Alien Squad grifts, and that big heist at the Japtown B of A. Bob Murikami's the only guy I want to talk to. Yes or no."

Nobody moved a muscle or said a word. I pulled the trigger, clicked an empty chamber, and watched Jumbo shake head to toe—bad heebie-jeebies. I said, "Sayonara, Shitbird," and pulled the trigger again; another hollow click, Jumbo twitching like a hophead going into cold turkey overdrive.

Five to one down to three to one; I could see Lorna, nude, waving bye-bye Hearns, heading toward Stormin' Norman Killebrew, jazz trombone, rumored to have close to a hard half yard and the only man Lorna implied gave it to her better than me. I pulled the trigger twice—twin empties—shit stink taking over the room as Jumbo evacuated his bowels.

One to one, seven come eleven, the Japs looking uncharacteristically piqued. Now I saw my own funeral cortege, "Prison of Love" blasting as they lowered me into the grave.

"No! I'll talk!"

I had the trigger at half pull when Bob Murikami's voice registered. I let go of Jumbo and drew a bead on Bad Bob; he walked over and bowed, supplicant samurai style, at my gun muzzle. Jumbo collapsed; I waved the rest of the group into a tight little circle and said, "Kick the clip and the roscoe over."

A weasel-faced guy complied; I popped one into the chamber and tucked my Russki roulette piece in my belt. Murikami pointed to a side door; I followed him over, a straight-arm bead on the others.

The door opened into a small bedroom lined with cots—the Underground Railway, 1942 version. I sat down on the cleanest one available and pointed Murikami to a cot a few yards over, well within splatter range. I said,

"Spill. Put it together, slow and from the beginning, and don't leave anything out."

Bad Bob Murikami was silent, like he was mustering his thoughts and wondering how much horseshit he could feed me. His face was hard set; he looked tough beyond his years. I smelled musk in the room—a rare combo of blood and Lorna's "Cougar Woman" perfume. "You can't lie, Bob. And I won't hand you up to the Alien Squad."

Murikami snickered. "You won't?"

I snickered back. "You people mow a mean lawn and trim a mean shrub. When my ship comes in, I'll be needing a good gardener."

Murikami double-snickered—and a smile started to catch at the corners of his mouth. "What's your name?"

"Spade Hearns."

"What do you do for a living?"

"I'm a private investigator."

"I thought private eyes were sensitive guys with a code of honor."

"Only in the pulps."

"That's rich. If you don't have a code of honor, how do I know you won't cross me?"

"I'm in too deep now, Tojo. Crossing you's against my own best interest."

"Why?"

I pulled out a handful of bankbooks; Murikami's slant eyes bugged out until he almost looked like a fright-wig nigger. "I killed Walt Koenig for these, and you need a white man to tap the cash. I don't like witnesses and there's too many of you guys to kill, even though I'm hopped up on blood bad. Spiel me, papa-san. Make it an epic."

Murikami spieled for a straight hour. His story was the night train to Far Gonesville.

It started when three Japs, bank building maintenance workers pissed over their imminent internment, cooked up a plot with rogue cop Walt Koenig and a cop buddy of his—Murikami didn't know the guy's name. The plot was a straight bank robbery with a no-violence proviso—Koenig and pal taking down the B of A based on inside info, the Japs getting a percentage cut of the getaway loot for the young firebrands stupid enough to think they could hot-foot it to Mexico and stay free, plus Koenig's safeguarding of confiscated Jap property until the internment ended. But the caper went blood simple: guards snuffed, stray bullets flying. Mrs. Lena Sakimoto, the old dame shot on the street the next day, was the finger woman—she was in the bank pretending to be waiting in line, but her real errand was to pass the word to Koenig and buddy—the split second the vault cash was distributed to the tellers. *She* was rubbed out because the heisters figured her for a potential snitch.

Double-cross.

Bad Bob and *his* pals had been given the bank money to hold. Enraged over the deaths, they shoved it into Jap bank accounts, figured the two whiteys couldn't glom it, that the swag would accumulate interest until the internment was adios. Bob stashed the bankbooks at his crib and was soon to send the white boy fronting the getaway pad over to get them—but he got word a friend of his got greedy.

The friend's name was George Hayakawa, a vice-warlord in the Rising Sons. He went to Walt Koenig with a deal: He'd get the cash for a fifty-fifty cut. Koenig said no dealsky, tortured the location of the bankbooks and the address of the hideout out of Hayakawa, snuffed him, chopped off his dick, and sent it over in a pizza delivery box. A warning—don't fuck with the White Peril.

I pressed Murikami on Maggie Cordova—how did she fit in? The epic took on perv-o overtones.

Maggie was Bad Bob's sister's squeeze—the femme half of a dyke duo. She was the co-finger woman inside the bank; when Mrs. Lena Sakimoto got shot to sukiyaki, Maggie fled to Tijuana, fearing similar reprisals. Bob didn't know exactly where she was. I pressed, threatened, and damn near shot Murikami to get the answer I wanted most: where Maggie Cordova got "Prison of Love."

Bad Bob didn't know; I *had* to know. I made him a deal I knew I'd double-cross the second Lorna slinked into view. You come with me, we'll withdraw all the gelt, you take me to T.J. to find Maggie and the money's all yours. Murikami agreed; we sealed the bargain by toking a big bottle of laudanum laced with sake. I passed out on my cot with my gun in my hand and segued straight into the arms of Lorna.

It was a great hop dream.

Lorna was performing nude at the Hollywood Palladium, backed by an all-jigaboo orchestra—gigantic darkies in rhinestone-braided Uncle Sam outfits. She humped the air; she sprayed sweat; she sucked the microphone head. Roosevelt, Hitler, Stalin, and Hirohito were carried in on litters; they swooned at her feet as Lor belted "Someone to Watch Over Me." A war broke out on the bandstand: crazed jigs beating each other with trombone slides and clarinet shafts. It was obviously a diversion—Hitler jumped on stage and tried to carry Lorna over to a Nazi U-boat parked in the first row. I foiled Der Führer, picking him up by the mustache and hurling him out to Sunset Boulevard. Lorna was swooning into my arms when I felt a tugging and opened my eyes to see Bob Murikami standing over me, saying, "Rise and shine, shamus. We got banking to do."

We carried it out straight-faced, with appropriate props—handcuffs on Bad Bob, phony paperwork, a cereal box badge pinned to my lapel. Murikami impersonated over a dozen fellow Japs; we liquidated fourteen bank accounts to the tune of $81,000. I explained that I was Alien Squad brass, overseeing the confiscation of treasonous lucre; patriotic bank managers bought the story whole. At four we were heading south to T.J. and what might be my long-overdue reunion with the woman who'd scorched my soul long, long ago. Murikami and I talked easily, a temporary accord in Japanese-American relations—thanks to a healthy injection of long green.

"Why are you so interested in Maggie, Hearns?"

I took my eyes off the road—high cliffs dropping down to snow-white beaches packed with sunbathers on my right, tourist courts and greasy spoons on the left. Baby

Tojo was smiling. I hoped I didn't have to kill him. "She's a conduit, kid. A pipeline to *the* woman."

"*The* woman?"

"Right. The one I wasn't ready for a while back. The one I would have flushed it all down the toilet for."

"You think it will be different now?"

Eighty-one grand seed money; a wiser, more contemplative Hearns. Maybe I'd even dye a little gray in my hair. "Right. Once I clear up a little legal trouble I'm in, I'm going to suggest a long vacation in Acapulco, maybe a trip to Rio. She'll see the difference in me. She'll know."

I looked back at the highway, downshifted for a turn, and felt a tap on my shoulder. I turned to face Bad Bob and caught a big right hand studded with signet rings square in the face.

Blood blinded me; my foot hit the brake; the car jerked into a hillside and stalled out. I swung a haphazard left; another sucker shot caught me; through a sheet of crimson I saw Murikami grab the money and hotfoot it.

I wiped red out of my eyes and pursued. Murikami was heading for the bluffs and a path down to the beach; a car swerved in front of me and a large man jumped out, aimed, and fired at the running figure—once, twice, three times. A fourth shot sent Bob Murikami spiraling over the cliff, the money bag sailing, spilling greenbacks. I pulled my roscoe, shot the shooter in the back, and watched him go down in a clump of crabgrass.

Gun first, I walked over; I gave the shooter two good-measure shots, point blank to the back of the head. I kicked him over to his front side and from what little remained of his face identified him. Sergeant Jenks, Bill Malloy's buddy on the Alien Squad.

Deep shit without a depth gauge.

I hauled Jenks to his Plymouth, stuffed him in the front seat, stood back and shot the gas tank. The car exploded; the ex-cop sizzled like french-fried guacamole. I walked over the cliff and looked down. Bob Murikami was spread-eagled on the rocks and shitloads of sunbathers were scooping up cash, fighting each other for it, dancing jigs of greed and howling like hyenas.

* * *

I tailspinned down to Tijuana, found a flop and a bottle of drugstore hop, and went prowling for Maggie Cordova. A fat white lezbo songbird would stick out, even in a pus pocket like T.J.—and I knew the heart of T.J. lowlife was the place to start.

The hop edged down my nerves and gave me a *savoir faire* my three-day beard and raggedy-assed state needed. I hit the mule act strip and asked questions; I hit the whorehouse strip and the strip that featured live fuck shows twenty-four hours a day. Child beggars swarmed me; my feet got sore from kicking them away. I asked, asked, asked about Maggie Cordova, passing out bribe pesos up the wazoo. Then—right on the street—there she was, turning up a set of stairs adjoining a bottle liquor joint.

I watched her go up, a sudden jolt of nerves obliterating my dope edge. I watched a light go on above the bottle shop—and Lorna Kafesjian doing "Goody, Goody" wafted down at me.

Pursuing the dream, I walked up the stairs and knocked on the door.

Footsteps tapped toward me—and suddenly I felt naked, like a litany of everything I didn't have was underlining the sound of heels over wood.

No eighty-one-grand reunion stash.

No Sy Devore suits to make a suitably grand Hollywood entrance.

No curfew papers for late-night Hollywood spins.

No P.I. buzzer for *the* dramatic image of the twentieth century.

No world-weary, tough-on-the outside, tender-on-the-inside sensitive code of honor shtick to score backup pussy with in case Lorna shot me down.

The door opened; fat Maggie Cordova was standing there. She said, "Spade Hearns. Right?"

I stood there—dumbstruck beyond dumbstruck. "How did you know that?"

Maggie sighed—like I was old news barely warmed over. "Years ago I bought some tunes from Lorna Kafesjian. She needed a stake to buy her way out of a shack job with a corny guy who had a wicked bad case on her. She told me the guy was a sewer crawler, and since I was a sewer crawler performing her songs, I might run into him. Here's your ray of hope, Hearns. Lorna said she always wanted to see you one more time. Lor and I have kept in touch, so I've got a line on her. She said I should make you pay for the info. You want it? Then *give*."

Maggie ended her pitch by drawing a dollar sign in the air. I said, "You fingered the B of A heist. You're dead meat."

"Nix, gumshoe. You're all over the L.A. papers for the raps you brought down looking for me, and the Mexes won't extradite. *Givesky*."

I forked over all the cash in my wallet, holding back a five-spot for mad money. Maggie said, "Eight-eighty-one Calle Verdugo. Play it *pianissimo*, doll. Nice and slow."

I blew my last finnsky at a used clothing store, picking up a chalk-stripe suit like the one Bogart wore in *The Maltese Falcon*. The trousers were too short and the jacket was too tight, but overall the thing worked. I dry-shaved in a gas station men's room, spritzed some soap at my armpits, and robbed a kiddie flower vendor of the rest of his daffodils. Thus armed, I went to meet my lost love.

Knock, knock, knock on the door of a tidy little adobe hut; boom, boom, boom, as my overwrought heart drummed a big band beat. The door opened—and I almost screamed.

The four years since I'd seen Lorna had put forty thousand hard miles on her face. It was sun-soured—seams, pits, and scales; her laugh lines had changed to frown lines as deep as the San Andreas Fault. The body that was once voluptuous in white satin was now bloated in a Mex charwoman's serape. From the deep recesses of what we once had, I dredged a greeting.

"What's shakin', baby?"

Lorna smiled, exposing enough dental gold to front a revolution. "Aren't you going to ask me what happened, Spade?"

I stayed game. "What happened, baby?"

Lorna sighed. "Your interpretation first, Spade. I'm curious."

I smoothed my lapels. "You couldn't take a good thing. You couldn't take the dangerous life I led. You couldn't take the danger, romance, the heartache and vulnerability inherent in a mean-street-treading knight like me. Face it, baby: I was too much man for you."

Lorna smiled—more cracks appeared in the relief map of her face. She said, "Your theatrics exhausted me more than my own. I joined a Mexican nunnery, got a tan that went bad, started writing music again, and found myself a man of the earth—Pedro, my husband. I make tortillas, wash my clothes in a stream, and dry them on a rock. Sometimes, if Pedro and I need extra jack, I mix Margaritas and work the bar at the Blue Fox. It's a good, simple life."

I played my ace. "But Maggie said you wanted to see me—'one more time,' like—"

"Yeah, like in the movies. Well, Hearns, it's like this. I sold 'Prison of Love' to about three dozen bistro belters who passed it off as their own. It's ASCAP'd under at least thirty-five titles, and I've made a cool five grand on it. And, well, I wrote the song for you back in our salad days, and in the interest of what we had together for about two seconds, I'm offering you ten percent—you inspired the damn thing, after all."

I slumped into the doorway—exhausted by four years of torching, three days of mayhem and killing. "Hit me, baby."

Lorna walked to a cabinet and returned with a roll of Yankee greenbacks. I winked, pocketed the wad, and walked down the street to a cantina. The interior was dark and cool; Mex cuties danced nude on the bar top. I bought a bottle of tequila and slugged it straight, fed the jukebox nickels and pushed every button listing a female vocalist. When the booze kicked in and the music started, I sat down, watched the nudie gash gyrate, and tried to get obsessed.

Paul Engleman is a past winner of the PWA Shamus Award for best paperback P.I. novel of 1983 for his Mark Renzler novel Dead in Center Field. *There have been three more Renzler novels since then, the most recent being* Who Shot Longshot Sam? *Here Paul introduces a new P.I., a quick-fisted woman quite different from the medium-boiled Renzler.*

Death of a Fatcat

---

by Paul Engleman

I should have known better than to patronize the little shithole of a drugstore in my apartment building, but I needed a candy bar to tide me over until dinner. I was returning from the store with the makings for a marvelous feed—risotto primavera and veal limone. I wasn't the one making it. My neighbor Gino Principe was taking care of that. All I had to do was eat, which is one of my finer skills.

I used to be a regular at the drugstore, back when I smoked cigarettes and there was an entrance inside my building—no small convenience during a Chicago winter. It was dingy then, but there was a cute young pharmacist who'd fill my Ortho-Novum scrip well beyond expiration. Once when I lost a new dental filling he slipped me some Percodans to hold me until I could wring my dentist's neck.

Four years ago some new owners took over and named it Tru-Valu Drugs. Their first improvement was to lock the inside door. Then they expanded their product line until—with the exception of herpes creams and weight-loss pills—they had virtually forsaken medications in favor

146

of smut magazines, Twinkie knockoffs, and video rentals. They did do a thriving Medicaid business, but at a separate counter in back where the druggist sat behind a cage, probably balancing a Saturday night special on his lap. Once, I got into a shouting match with the assistant manager, a Brut-drenched baldo named Waldo, for the indiscretion of noting that he was still stocking Tylenol without safety caps. A batch at the Walgreen's three blocks down Clark Street had been laced with cyanide, and the stuff was supposed to have been recalled. I figured it was an honest mistake, but it turned out I was wrong. That was the last time I'd been in there. And the first time I'd phoned someone in anonymously to the state's attorney.

I was wavering between a Milky Way and an Almond Joy. I had plenty of time to decide. There were two lines, one of which stretched the entire length of the dirty magazine aisle. A hand-lettered sign said it was for lottery tickets only. I was in the shorter line, but that wasn't much of an advantage since neither one was moving. A dispute was raging up front regarding someone's lucky number.

I elected to buy both candy bars. The weight of the groceries made me decide I wasn't going to wait on any line. I stepped up to the counter and put down a dollar, recognizing the halfwit behind it as Waldo. Since our last encounter he'd started wearing a rug, but he was still marinating in the same cologne.

As I went out the door he shouted, "Hey, Fatso, come back here, six cents tax!" I was already on the sidewalk biting into my Milky Way when I realized it was me he was talking to. I almost gagged. I mean, how much does a goddamn candy bar cost these days? And this one was dried out and stale, like the ones you get from vending machines in the New York subway.

I would have gone back and paid him, but my favorite wino couple had divested me of all my change up the block near Banquet On A Bun and the smallest bill I had was a ten. And though I'd be the first to admit I could afford to lose a few pounds, I'm not fat by any means and I certainly didn't need some two-bit druggist who stocked his shelves with cyanide-laced Tylenol telling me that I was.

The next thing I knew he was outside next to me, pawing my arm with both hands and hollering for a cop. I was amazed that a guy who took a full minute to punch out a single lottery ticket could move so quickly; there's no telling how fast some people will react when six cents is at stake. Back inside they were probably looting the Lotto machine.

I'm not the touchy-feely type, never have been. Guys rub up against me on the El, I grind my heels into their feet. Waldo got the full treatment.

I dropped the groceries and did a two-step on his instep. That gave him something to think about and me a chance to pull away. Then I turned and cold-cocked the bastard.

One thing I've learned over the years: The instant someone threatens you, cold-cock him. These days you can't be too safe. You can't tell who's out there, who's not there, who's missing a page, who's missing a chapter. Nobody smokes anymore, nobody drinks. Not even in a bar. Everybody's working out. And for what? So they can annihilate the first person who gives them a reason to do it. My philosophy is, when in doubt, slug them. If it turns out you've overreacted, you can always apologize.

Waldo reeled backward. He would have gone over, but the window of the store held him up, framing him against the giant yellowing poster for a hand lotion called Gloves You Can't See. I figured I'd need extra time to get away with the groceries, so I gave him a good kick in the nuts. I picked up the Milky Way I'd dropped when he mauled my arm and tossed it at him, stifling the urge to tell him to shove it up his ass. I've got a bad temper, but I'm not one for public displays of vulgarity.

A guy standing at the bus stop applauded as I headed along Dickens Street to the Lincoln Park West side of the building. My adrenaline was gushing so hard when I pushed through the revolving doors that I went around twice. I felt a bit sheepish, but if you've never slugged somebody, let me tell you something: It feels pretty damn good.

On my way through the lobby Mitchell, our concierge,

said, "Mrs. Wotowicz was down here looking for you, Charley. She's got a problem again."

Mrs. Wotowicz is my elderly neighbor from across the hall. She's a sweetheart, but she always has a problem, and I'm always the person she chooses to solve it. She used to go to Mitchell but they had a falling out. I never got all the details and never asked for any of them.

"Is it Marsha?" I asked.

Mitchell nodded solemnly. He's very good at being solemn. "I'm afraid so."

Marsha is Mrs. Wotowicz's cat, a colossal lump of mushy white fur which had given her her full name, Marshmallow. She's about the same size as Mrs. Wotowicz and the same age in feline years. They bear a considerable resemblance to each other in both manner and temperament. They keep similar hours, each napping most of the day and staying up at night watching TV. They move at about the same speed, and both of them eat tuna directly from the can—Mrs. Wotowicz going for Chicken of the Sea and Marsha for Nine Lives. Marsha is in the habit of getting lost, and when she does, Mrs. Wotowicz comes to me.

I got off the elevator on the eighth floor as the Loud family from 801 was getting on. Their real name is Peters, but I call them the Louds because they yell more than anyone I've ever met. Mr. Loud is a chunky lawyer with a single furry eyebrow running the width of his forehead and a large mouth that never quite closes all the way. His wife is a mousy wisp of a woman with pursed lips and deep-set eyes who always looks on the verge of tears. But she can bellow with the best of them, which is to say she can hold her own with her husband. I've seen her chewing out their rotten kids across the street in the Lincoln Park Zoo on several occasions.

The Loud kids are both pudgy with orange coloring and splotchy freckles. There's a girl, Julie, about six, who has a habit of shrieking any time she doesn't get her way. Judging by the frequency of her shrieks, this is most of the time. I've never seen the boy, Jimmy, in anything that isn't festooned with the Chicago Cubs logo. He's about eight, and on summer evenings he and his father play catch in the park. I can hear dad giving instructions and the kid making excuses from half a mile away.

I should tell you that I don't like kids. A friend of mine who has three says it's a case of sour grapes, but I'll swear to my dying day that I've never wanted any. I babysit hers once in a while and we all get along fine, but after an hour of telling them stories and listening to theirs, I'm ready to tumble into Gracie's tavern up the street.

The Loud kids, however, are special. Them I truly despise. Not just because they're fat, loud, and ugly. There are other reasons, like the time I saw them throwing rocks at the wolves in the zoo or when I caught them coloring the mahogany elevator walls with crayons. But the worst was the time I asked Jimmy if the Cubs had won. I have no interest in baseball, don't know how the game is played, don't want to know, have never been to a game and don't ever want to go. I was asking merely to be cordial—why I thought I should be cordial, I don't know—and it turned out to be a costly mistake. The little shit kicked me on each leg. I was about to smack him, but instead looked to his mother for reaction and intervention. All she did was caution him in her normal tone, which is to say, yell, "Don't do that, Jimmy." Then at the same volume, she said to me, "You know how boys are. He always gets like this when the Cubs lose. Just like his father." I didn't ask to check her shins, I just got off the elevator at the next floor. Ever since I've taken great pleasure when the Cubs lose, because I know the Loud kid is miserable.

As the Louds pushed past me, I noticed that Mr. Loud had nicked his neck while shaving. Regrettably, he'd missed his vocal cords, so he was able to bellow quite freely about what a jerk the Cubs' manager was. Mrs. Loud looked her usual ravishing self in a wrinkled jogging suit, the only type of outfit I'd ever seen her in.

Mrs. Wotowicz was waiting for me outside my apartment, 812. Her head barely reached the sign halfway up the door that says CHARLEY DAVENPORT—PRIVATE INVESTIGATIONS. I've lived there ten years, the sign's been up two. It was a gift from my father, Charles Davenport, and it used to hang on his office down at Canal and Van Buren.

He always said he'd leave the business to me someday—after all, I was his only employee. Sadly, that day arrived sooner than anyone could have expected. I took over reluctantly, finishing off the paperwork he'd left behind. Since then it's been a part-time operation.

"Thank heavens you're back," she said. "I've been looking all over for you."

"Mitchell told me. Where do you think Marsha's hiding this time?"

"She's not hiding, Charley. I've looked *everywhere*. Somebody kidnapped her. I'm sure of it."

More likely Marsha was catnapping, but I knew not to differ with Mrs. Wotowicz. And I could see that she'd been crying. That wasn't part of the usual scenario.

"It's serious this time, Charley," she said as I put my key into the lock. "You know I don't have much money, but I'm willing to pay you anything." She held out a wrinkled five-dollar bill.

This also wasn't part of the usual scenario. Gino says Mrs. Wotowicz is so tight she could wring service for six out of a single teabag. "I'll bet it's those Japs in eight-oh-four," she said. "They say those people eat cat. I think you should confront them right away."

"Let me have a look around before we start accusing anyone. And by the way, I think they're Korean."

"Same difference."

Gino was already at work in the kitchen, banging around pots and pans. Gino is, as his last name means in Italian, a prince among men. He's strong, handsome, and stinking rich. He also has a terrific personality, the sort of guy who doesn't mind taking out the trash in the middle of the Super Bowl. But for one quirk in his personality, he'd be a prize catch for a woman in search of a husband. Sorry, gals, but Gino's into guys.

Aside from our sexual preferences, Gino and I have a lot in common, food in particular. He loves to cook it, I love to eat it. He moved next door six years ago, just after my divorce, and we soon worked out a nice little arrangement: I buy the groceries, he makes the dinner. He also washes the dishes.

I left him the groceries and half the Almond Joy, then went across the hall to look for Marsha. Finding her has always been my easiest assignment, but crawling around Mrs. Wotowicz's apartment—which hasn't been cleaned since John Paul II came to Chicago—can be mighty unpleasant. I started with the front closet, one of Marsha's favorite hiding places. I didn't find her, but I did manage to drop the candy bar into a tangle of cat hair, turning it into a mini-Marsha. That had been a dollar well spent.

I searched for half an hour, but there was no sign of the little beast. I even looked in the kitchen cabinets, the bureau drawers, the stove, and the refrigerator.

"See, what did I tell you? Somebody kidnapped her."

"Did you have the door open?"

"No, I never open the door. You know that."

I did, but somehow old slow Marsha had a pretty good record for slipping out. She usually sauntered to the stairwell near the trash chute, where the afternoon sun would provide warmth and also cook up anything that had spilled.

"Are you sure she didn't have a chance to get out?"

"Oh, now that I think about it, it was open when the drugstore man came. But only for a second. Do you know Waldo?"

I nodded. Oh yes, I knew Waldo all right.

"He's nice, don't you think?"

I didn't say. For a moment I wondered if Mrs. Wotowicz and Waldo had something going, but I figured I would have seen him, or at least smelled him.

She wanted me to talk to the Korean couple, but I put that off in favor of a search of the stairs. The trash chute was closed due to yet another breakdown of the compactor, and two garbage bags were propped against the fire escape door. Things were starting to smell a little fruity already.

Marsha wasn't on eight, and after checking on nine and ten, I decided to take the freight elevator to the top floor, fifteen, and work my way down. By the time I got to the basement, I had gained some insight into the eating habits of my fellow tenants—the Budget Gourmet was a very popular guy—but I hadn't turned up any trace of Marsha.

I spotted the lower half of Juan, our building engineer, sticking out of the trash compactor. He was cursing, and the words echoed inside the hollow metal heap and reverberated off the cement walls of the basement. Juan has a truly foul mouth, which he exercises at the slightest provocation, but on this occasion anything he said seemed justified to me. I wouldn't stick my head in the compactor for the entire national debt of Brazil. Juan also has a nice butt, and I tapped it to get his attention.

He banged his head as he extricated himself. Cussing wildly, he wheeled to confront whoever had added injury to insult. When he saw me, he quickly got control of himself. "Oh, it's you, Charley." That's the kind of respect a case of tequila every Christmas will buy you.

"On the blink again, I see," I said.

"Yeah, this thing never works." He rapped his wrench on the tube where the chute narrowed. "You tell people not to put big things down here, but the assholes, they never listen."

I nodded knowingly and asked if he had seen Marsha, whom he had helped me locate on previous occasions.

"No. I can't see nothing with my head up this fucking thing for the last fucking hour. But if I do, I let you know."

As I got back on the elevator, Juan called, "Hey, Charley, wait. I think I found out what's fucking up the compactor."

I didn't care what was wrong with it, at least I didn't think I did, but I waited while Juan walked toward me, carrying a jumbo Tru-Valu Drugs bag. He was shaking his head and as he got closer, I could see why. A limp white paw was hanging out of the bag.

"It's Marsha," Juan said. "I found her."

I don't especially like cats and I especially didn't like Marsha, but I could feel tears welling up in my eyes.

"God, it looks like someone strangled her," Juan said.

I nodded. That's always a logical conclusion when there's a cord tied tightly around the neck. "Why the hell would anybody want to kill a defenseless animal?" I said, more to myself than to Juan.

"Almost defenseless," he corrected. "She had pretty

sharp claws. I guess they must have been really mad about something."

"Who would do something so barbaric?"

"I don't know, Charley. There's a lot of weird people in this building."

I thought of one. "Do you know Waldo from the drugstore?"

Juan nodded. "He's one of the weirdest. I always see him in the stairwell looking through the stacks of magazines people throw away. He takes the dirty ones and sells them for a dollar."

I was willing to bet a dollar that Waldo had killed Marsha. I couldn't think of a motive. I just didn't like the asshole.

"How are we going to tell Mrs. Wotowicz?" Juan said.

"I'll take care of that." It wasn't going to be easy. "But first I'd like you to have a word with Waldo."

"Why me, Charley?"

"It's too complicated to explain, Juan." But I had to tell the whole sordid story before I convinced him to call Waldo to the backdoor while I waited around the corner and listened in on their conversation. Juan thought it was funny that I had punched Waldo out. He'd been wanting to do it himself but was afraid he'd get in trouble.

Waldo was still worked up about the abuse he'd suffered at my hands, and he recounted the incident in detail, inventing a bit to assuage his sprained ego. In his version, I had sprayed him with Mace and hit him with a lead pipe. But if he was lying when Juan asked if he'd seen Marsha, I couldn't tell from his tone. He freely admitted making a delivery to Mrs. Wotowicz but said he hadn't seen the cat. When Juan asked, as I'd instructed, if he'd made any other deliveries on the floor, he said, "Yeah, I dropped off some Kaopectate for that new gook couple in eight-oh-four." No wonder Mrs. Wotowicz liked Waldo.

We went up to my apartment, where Gino was stirring the risotto. Finding Marsha had killed my appetite, but one whiff of Cuoco Principe's work revived it. Gino reported that Mrs. Wotowicz had declined his offer to wait with him and had returned home. "You know how she is."

Indeed I did. Mrs. Wotowicz doesn't understand how I can speak to Gino, no less be his friend. She especially doesn't understand how I can eat the food he cooks. She once confided that she was afraid she'd catch AIDS from living across the hall from him.

I didn't know how to break the news about Marsha gracefully, so I did it in my customary graceless way. Mrs. Wotowicz grabbed the bag from me and clutched Marsha to her chest, bursting into tears and howling that she had nothing left to live for. Sobbing, she fell to the couch, tucked into a fetal position with the dead body of that fat cat pressed against her. It was as pathetic a sight as any I've seen.

Juan and I tried to comfort her, but she waved us away, moaning that she had no friends left in the world. We looked at each other, shrugged, then started to leave. At the door, I told her I'd be home all evening, to knock if she wanted anything.

"Yes, I do want something," she blurted, her tone suddenly a snarl. "I want you to find out who killed my Marshmallow. I *did* pay you five dollars."

I wasn't about to point out that I refused her money. I'd never do that. But I was startled by the sight of a sweet little lady turning so quickly into a sour old bitch. "I intend to, Mrs. Wotowicz," I said. "Right now."

"See, what did I tell you?" Juan asked when we got out in the hall. "There's lots of weird people in this building. And she's one of them."

Juan was right. This wasn't the first time I'd seen Mrs. Wotowicz turn ugly. But now I wondered just how weird she was. I thought about how mad she got with Marsha sometimes, talking as if the cat were her roommate. Every so often, she'd tell me she and Marsha weren't speaking to each other because of some slight the cat had committed. For a moment I wondered if Mrs. Wotowicz could have killed Marsha herself.

"What are you going to do now, Charley? Talk to the gooks?"

"Not you too, Juan."

"I'm sorry, I make a joke."

But that was exactly what I was going to do.

As I rang the buzzer to 804, I didn't know exactly what I was going to say. I had time to think of something, because it took a while for someone to answer the door.

While we were waiting Juan said, "That's too bad about the Cubs, isn't it, Charley?"

"What, they lost this afternoon?"

"Not just this afternoon, Charley. They lost for the whole *season*. Today's game clinched it. They choked again."

"Is that so?" The Cubs choked and someone choked a cat.

Just then, a slender Korean woman opened the door. "Can I help you?" She was smiling.

"I'm sorry," I said. "We've got the wrong apartment."

I headed down the hall with Juan at my heels. "Why did you say that, Charley? I thought you were going to ask about the cat."

I didn't bother to answer him. I went right to 801 and leaned on the buzzer.

Mrs. Loud answered the door. "What do you want?"

"I want to talk to that monster kid of yours about a dead cat."

"What? Jimmy?"

"How many monster kids do you have?"

I realized that was a dumb question when I spotted the adorable Julie jumping up and down on the couch. I realized it was an even dumber question when the biggest kid in the family appeared in the doorway next to his wife.

"What's going on here?" he demanded.

Mr. Loud was wearing a sleeveless white tee-shirt, the kind that used to be called an Italian dinner jacket in the Irish Catholic neighborhood where I grew up. I looked at the nicks on his neck where I thought he had cut himself shaving, then I noticed more nicks, lots of them, on his arms and chest. That fat old cat had put up one hell of a struggle.

"You killed a little old lady's cat over a goddamn baseball game! Buddy, you are one sick fuck."

"What? You're crazy, lady."

He started to close the door, but I pushed it open with my foot. Then I cold-cocked the bastard.

I hit him with everything I had, more than I thought I had, since I had unconsciously gripped my keys between my knuckles before letting him have it. Mrs. Loud let out a scream and, I swear, the whole building shook. Mr. Loud went down in a heap, down but not out. He still had the presence of mind to issue the threat that I'm sure was automatic, the threat that would make me lose about five seconds of sleep that night: "I'm going to sue you, lady."

"And I'm going to kick your nuts from here to Wrigley Field if you even think about trying to get up."

"I'm calling the police," Mrs. Loud said.

"Don't bother. I'll take care of that." I glared at her. "Sweetheart, you've got one sick fuck of a husband."

"Yeah, that's right," Juan said. "And he talks real loud all the time, too."

The neighbors began flocking into the hall to see what was going on. I walked right past them to my apartment, letting Juan take care of the recap. By the time I got washed up dinner was ready, but I didn't feel much like eating.

Loren D. Estleman has been one of the top writers in the private eye fold for ten years, since Motor City Blue, *the first Amos Walker novel, was cited as one of the notable mysteries of 1980 by the* New York Times. *Estleman has received Shamus Awards for his 1984 novel* Sugartown, *his 1985 short story "Eight Mile and Dequindre," and his 1988 short story "The Crooked Way." His most recent novels are 1989's* Silent Thunder *(featuring Walker) and* Peeper *(the debut of the bumbling, seedy Detroit P.I. Ralph Poteet).*

Estleman, we are delighted to say, has been featured in all four PWA anthologies.

Cigarette Stop

Loren D. Estleman

My pack ran out two miles north of the village of Peck. I crumpled it into the ashtray and started paying attention to signs.

I was an hour and a half out of Detroit, following State Highway 19 through Michigan's Thumb area on my way to Harbor Beach and my first job in more than a week. It was a warm night in late May and the sky was overcast, with here and there a tattered hole through which stars glittered like broken glass at the scene of an accident. My dashboard clock read 10:50.

Up there, miles inland from the resort towns along the Lake Huron coastline, there are no malls or fast-food strips or modern floodlit truck stops complete with showers and hookers to order; just squat brick post offices and stores with plank floors and the last full-service gas stations left in the western world. I pulled into a little stop-and-rob

on the outskirts of Watertown with two pumps out front
and bought a pack of Winstons from a bleach job on the
short side of fifty who had taken makeup lessons from the
Tasmanian Devil. The kid was standing by my car when I
came out.

He was a lean weed in dungarees, scuffed black oxfords,
and a navy peacoat, too heavy for the weather, that hung
on him the way they always do when you draw them from
a quartermaster. His short-chopped sandy hair and stiff
posture added to the military impression. Also the blue
duffel resting on the pavement next to him with ABS C. K.
SEATON stenciled on it in white.

"Lift, mister?"

I stripped the pack and speared a filter between my lips.
He looked safe enough, clear-eyed and pink where he
shaved. So had Richard Speck, Albert DeSalvo, and our
own John Norman Collins. "Where to?" I asked. "I'm
headed up to Harbor Beach."

"That'll do. My folks are in Port Austin."

"Why aren't you traveling up Twenty-five? That's the
coast highway."

"Why aren't you?"

"Seen one Big Boy, seen 'em all," I said.

"Me too."

"Hop in."

He threw his duffel into the back seat of the Mercury
and climbed into the passenger's seat in front. Under the
domelight he didn't look as fresh as I'd thought. His face
was drawn and pale as a clenched knuckle and he was
breathing hoarsely, as if he'd been running. Then I closed
my door and darkness clamped down over us both.

Back on the road, with the broken white line flaring and
fading in the headlamps, I made a comment or two about
the lack of traffic—where I came from, only two cars in
three miles meant nuclear war at the least—but he didn't
respond and I shut up. Well, in my own hitching days I'd
hoped for the company of drivers who didn't feel they had
to entertain me. Somewhere between Elmer and Snover
he slumped down in the seat with his knees up and his chin
on his chest. He didn't miss anything.

In Argyle I stopped for gas at a place that might have been the twin of the one in Watertown. While the attendant was filling the tank I used the men's room and bought a Coke from a machine to douse the nicotine burn in my throat. I bought another one, paid for the gas, and stuck the second can through the open window on the passenger's side. When the kid didn't reach for it I shook him gently by the shoulder. He fell over the rest of the way, and that's when I saw the blood shining in the light mounted over the pumps.

The attendant, a tall strip of sandpapery hide in baggy suitpants and a once-white shirt with *Norm* stitched in red script over the pocket, bobbed his Adam's apple twice when I showed him the dead body in my car, then went inside to use the telephone. Just for the hell of it I groped again for the big artery on the side of my passenger's neck. It wasn't any busier than it had been the first time I'd checked. I located the source of the blood in a ragged gash between two ribs on his right side under his shirt. He'd bled to death quietly while I was remarking on the thin traffic.

I went through his pockets. Nothing, not even a wallet. Straightening, I looked at the attendant through the window of the little store, gesticulating at the receiver in his left hand. I opened the rear door and inspected the duffel. I found sailor's blues rolled neatly to avoid wrinkles, cooking utensils and related camping equipment, and thick sheaves of some kind of newsprint, there presumably to keep the stuff from rattling as he carried it. The only identification Able Bodied Seaman C. K. Seaton had had with him was his name stenciled on his one piece of luggage. If it was his name.

Norm was hanging up the telephone. I carried the duffel behind the car, unlocked the trunk, threw it in, and slammed the lid just as he came out. I had no idea why. I didn't know why I did a lot of things I did, like picking up strange hitchhikers in downtown Nowhere.

"Raise anyone?" I asked Norm.

"State troopers. We ain't got no police in Argyle. You

reckon somebody croaked him?" He was gaping through the passenger's window with his chin in his lap.

"If he shot himself he ditched the gun. And you can lay off the dialect. I was born in a town not much bigger than this one. We wore shoes and everything."

"Shit." He dealt himself a Marlboro out of the bottom of a pack he kept in his shirt pocket and lit it with a throwaway lighter. "Thought you was one of them Detroiters come up here to the boonies to cheat us rustics out of our valuable antiques. Last month my boss sold a woman from Grosse Pointe a Coca-Cola sign he bought off a junkyard in Port Huron for ten bucks. She gave him fifty. It was the 'shucks' and 'you-alls' done it."

I consumed my Coke in place of the cigarette I really wanted; one of us lighting up that close to the pumps was plenty. "Where'd you graduate?" I asked him. "Jackson?"

His face squinched up. "Marquette. What gave me away?"

"You've got to start smoking them from the top of the pack if you don't want anyone to know you were inside. Out here we don't scramble for cigarettes when they fall out and scatter. Yet."

"You a cop?"

"Private." I showed him the ID.

"Amos Walker," he read. "I never heard of you."

"That doesn't make you special."

We were still going around like that a few minutes later when a blue-and-white pulled in off 19 and a blocky figure in a blue business suit climbed out the right side. "Christ, it's Torrance," Norm said. "Do me a favor, okay? Don't tell him about Marquette. Nobody knows about that around here."

"Nobody has to," I said. "What did they take you down for, anyway?"

"I stuck up a gas station."

Luther Torrance commanded the Cass City post of the Michigan State Police. He was square-built and shorter than they like them in that jurisdiction—which said something about what kind of cop he had to be to have made commander—with short brown hair and eyes that looked yellow in the harsh outdoor light, like a wolf's. The uniformed trooper who had driven him ran six-four and wore amber Polaroids. He stood around with his thumbs hooked inside his gun belt, in case Norm and I threw down a gum wrapper or something.

"Thirty-eight'd be my guess," said Torrance, stripping off a pair of rubber surgical gloves as he came away from the body in the Mercury. "Maybe nine-millimeter. It's still in there, so we won't be guessing long. You're the owner of the car?" He looked up at me.

I said I was and showed him the PI license. When he was through being impressed I told him what had happened, starting at the cigarette stop. He took it all down in a leather-bound notebook with a gold pencil.

"What's a private sleuth doing up here?" he asked.

"Does it matter?"

"Not if you're on vacation, which you aren't or you'd be a lot closer to the lake. Nobody comes through here unless he's lost or on his way someplace else. You don't look lost."

"Security job up in Harbor Beach."

"Judge Dunham's poker game." I must have reacted, because he showed me his bridgework. "Shoot, everybody in these parts knows about the judge's annual game. You don't shove a couple of hundred thousand back and forth across a table one weekend every spring and expect not to get talked about around here. That's why he needs security. Well, I'll check it out. This guy never introduced himself?"

I shook my head. "He said he had family in Port Austin."

"We'll send a man up there with a morgue shot. Any luggage?"

"No."

"Most hitchers have something. A backpack or something."

"This one didn't."

He tapped the gold pencil against his bridgework. Just then a county wagon pulled in and two attendants in uniform got out. He put away the pencil and notebook. "You heading straight up to Harbor Beach tonight?"

"Not this late. I thought I'd get a room and make a fresh jump in the morning. Any place you'd recommend?"

"The roaches all look alike up here. I got your address and number if we need you, or I can call the judge if we need you quick. We won't. I figure our boy got robbed and put up a fuss. Fact he didn't tell you he was wounded makes me think a dope deal went bad, something on that order. We get that, even here."

I said, "I guess there aren't any Mayberries anymore."

"There never were, except on television." He thanked me and walked back to take charge of the body. Norm, watching, was on his second pack of Marlboros. I noticed he'd opened this one on top.

The motel I fell into a mile up 19 was a concrete bunker built in a square U with the office in the base. The manager, fat and hairless except for a gray tuft coiling over the V in his Hawaiian shirt, took my cash and registration card and handed me a key wired to the anchor from the *Edmund Fitzgerald*. My room, second from the end in the north leg of the U, stood across from an ice machine illuminated like an icon under a twenty-watt bulb. I had a double bed, a TV, and a shower stall with a dispenser full of pink soap that smelled like Madame Ling's Secrets of the East Massage Parlor on Gratiot. The TV worked like my plans for the evening.

Back at the convenience store in Argyle I'd placed a call to Judge Dunham, whose round courtroom-trained voice came on the line after two rings. I said I had car trouble and was stuck for the night. I didn't say the trouble had to do with a stiff in the front seat.

"No sweat," he said. "Senator Sullivan won't be here till morning and I never start without my worst poker player. Just steam on in come sunup."

I pulled my overnight case out of the car, then as an afterthought grabbed Seaton's duffel and carried them both into the room. I was too keyed up to sleep. I broke my flat pint of J&B out of the case, stripped the cellophane off the plastic glass in the bathroom, and went out for ice. Under the lights in the parking lot the blood on my front seat looked black as I passed it. I wondered if I could charge the cleaning to the judge.

I was about to plunge my plastic ice bucket into the machine when someone came strolling along the sidewalk on the other side of the lot. Most of the rooms were vacant—mine was one of only three cars parked inside the U—so he was worth watching. He was built along the lanky lines of Norm, but younger, and made no sound at all on sneakered feet. He had on a dark jacket and pants, but I couldn't make out his features at that distance. He was carrying something.

He paused in front of the door to my room and stood for a moment as if listening. Apparently satisfied, he stepped off the sidewalk and approached my car. A hand came out of one of his jacket pockets with something in it.

A Slim Jim.

He was nobody's amateur. After casting a glance up and down the row of rooms, he tried the door on the driver's side, then slid the flat hooked device between the closed window and the outside door panel and yanked it up decisively. I heard the click.

My gun was in the overnight case in the room. I hardly ever needed it to get ice. I used the only other weapon I had.

"Hey!"

He was a pro down to the ground. The Slim Jim jangled to the pavement and he went into a crouch I knew too well. I let go of the ice bucket and wedged myself between the machine and the block wall. He fired twice, the shots so close together I saw the yellow flame as one continuous spurt. Much closer to home I heard a twang and a thud as the first bullet ricocheted off the concrete behind me and the second penetrated the ice machine's steel skin. Then he took off running, his lanky legs eating up pavement two yards at a bite, back in the direction he'd come. He hadn't waited to see if he'd hit anything. They never do, except in submarine pictures.

I pried myself loose from cover. On the other side of the building an engine started, wound up, and faded down Highway 19, gear-changes hiccoughing. A pair of red taillamps flicked past the edge of the motel and on into darkness. I waited, but no lights came on behind any of the dark windows and nobody came out to investigate. Gunshots late at night were nothing unusual there in raccoon country.

At my car I picked up the Slim Jim and wandered around with my head down until something tiny caught the light in a yellow glint. I picked it up and looked for its mate, but it must have rolled into the shadows. I didn't need it. I'd been pretty sure because of the close spacing of the shots that the weapon was an automatic and that I'd find at least one of the spent shells it kicked out. I had to take it into the room to make out what had been stamped into the flanged end: .38 SUPER.

I pocketed it, unpacked the Smith & Wesson in its form-fitted holster, checked the cylinder for cartridges, and clipped it to my belt. The fact that he'd come armed told me my visitor had been prepared to search the room if whatever he was after wasn't in my car—a room he had every reason to believe was occupied by me. That kind of determination usually meant a return engagement.

Why was another matter. I wasn't the most promising robbery target around. The Mercury was the oldest car in the lot and a hell of a long way from the most flashy. My clothes wouldn't get me past the door of the Detroit Yacht Club. My overnight case had been in my family since the last Kiwanis rummage sale. As far as I knew, the only person worth shooting in those parts was already dead. Shot with a .38.

I dumped the contents of C. K. Seaton's duffel out onto the bed and took inventory. One canteen, half full of something that smelled like water. Two cans of C rations. A knife and fork. One of those hinged camp pans divided into sections. Sailor's blues, unrolling into sailor's blues— nothing hidden there. And the crumpled sheaves of coarse paper to prevent the mess from banging around.

In the lamplight I liked the paper. I liked it a lot.

There were two bales, two feet by eighteen inches and two inches thick. I hefted one, rubbed individual sheets between thumb and forefinger. No newsprint. Rag paper.

I held a sheet up to the light and looked at the threads running through it.

I sat in the room's only chair and smoked a Winston down to the filter. The frayed end when I ground it out resembled my brain. I stood and put everything back into the duffel except the papers. Those I combined in one stack. From the shelf in the bottom of the telephone stand I removed the county directory and took it out of its heavy vinyl advertising cover. I doubled over the blank sheets, slid them inside the cover, and inspected the result. It looked bloated. I returned it to the shelf and put the heavy telephone book on top of it. Better.

There is no place in a motel room you can hide something where someone hasn't thought to look. But you can buy time.

I was dead in my shoes. If my friend came back for his burglar tool he would just have to wait until I woke up. I returned the camping equipment to the duffel, laid it lengthwise on the bed, drew the blanket over it, and stretched out in the chair with the lamp off and the revolver in my lap. Between the makeshift dummy and the time it would take my visitor's pupils to adjust from the lighted parking lot, I might have the opportunity to teach him a lesson in target shooting.

Three gentle raps on the door pulled me out of a dream in which Frank Sinatra, Gene Kelly, and another guy, dressed up in sailor suits in the big city, got themselves gunned down by someone with a .38 automatic. The third guy was me.

The luminous dial of my watch read 2:11. Well, he *might* bother to knock. I got up, straightening the kinks, drew back the hammer on the Smith & Wesson, crabwalked to the door, and used the peephole. The fisheye glass made an avian caricature of the man standing alone under the light mounted over the door. He was a middle-aged number going to gravity in a porkpie hat and a powder-blue sportcoat on top of a shirt with a spread collar. His hands were empty. I unlocked the door and opened it a foot and leveled the muzzle at his belly. His liquid brown eyes took in the weapon and gave nothing back. "Mr. Walker?"

"That's half of it," I said. "Let's have the rest."

"My name's Hugh Vennable. I have some fancy identification in my pocket if you'll let me take it out."

I sucked a cheek. "What time is it?"

He hesitated, then looked at his watch. "Two-fifteen, why?"

It was strapped to his right wrist. "Take out your ID," I said. "Use your right hand."

"How'd you know I'm a lefty? Oh." His smile was shallow. "Pretty slick." He fished out a leather folder and showed me his picture on a card bearing the seal of the United States Navy.

"You're with Naval Intelligence?"

He was still smiling. "I avoid saying it. Sounds like something you learn sitting around admiring your belly-button. Can I come in?"

I elevated the revolver's barrel and let down the hammer, stepping away from the door. "By the way, your watch is two minutes fast."

"I doubt it." He came in, a soft-looking heavy man, light on his feet. His hair was fair at the temples under a cocoa straw hat—his eyebrows were almost invisible against a light working tan—and he had a roll of fat under his chin. His quick graceful movements said it was all camouflage; I knew a street tiger when I saw one. He looked around the room and sat on the edge of the bed, exposing briefly the square checked butt of a 9-mm. Beretta in a speed holster on his belt.

I put away the Smith & Wesson. "I thought the navy issued .38 Supers."

"Phasing 'em out. Some prefer the old pieces, but I'm not one of them. Is that J and B?" He was looking at the pint bottle standing on top of the dresser.

"You're not on duty?"

"Sure, but I'm no fanatic."

I took the wrapper off another glass and poured two inches into it and the one I'd stripped earlier. I handed him one. "No ice, sorry. That trip's longer than you'd think."

"Never touch it." He made a silent toast and drank off the top inch. "The state police told me where to find you. You reported a dead man in Argyle?"

"Did you know him?"

"His name was Charles Seaton, USN. I've been tracking him since Cleveland."

"Tracking him for what?" I sipped Scotch.

"Federal robbery. You didn't tell the law about the duffel he was carrying."

"Was he?"

Vennable shook his head. "I'm not here to blow the whistle on you, son. I'd like a look in the bag."

"What would you expect to find?"

"A couple of reams of paper. Not just any paper. The kind they print currency on."

"What's a seaman doing with mint paper?"

"Not U.S. currency; navy scrip. Negotiable tender on any naval base in the world. We change the design and ink color from time to time to screw the counterfeiters, but never the paper. It's a special rag bond, can't be duplicated. The amount Seaton stole is worth maybe a couple of million on the European black market. Last week he and a partner ripped off an armored car on its way to Washington from the mill in Cleveland where the paper's made. Earlier tonight we pulled the partner out of Lake Huron near Lexington. I guess they both got their licks in."

"That's not far from where I picked him up." I replaced the liquor he'd drunk.

"Thank you kindly. I figure they shot it out over the booty and Seaton won, sort of. Which means he'd have had the paper with him when you linked up."

"He could've ditched it somewhere."

"He wouldn't throw it away and he was hurt too bad to waste time looking for a good hiding place. He's got people in Port Austin. He'd have gone that way for his doctoring."

"What about the third partner?"

A pair of transparent eyebrows got lifted. "Our scuttle-butt says he was twins. Not triplets."

"Someone tried breaking into my car a couple of hours ago. When I yelled he shot at me." I took the shell out of my pocket and handed it to him.

"Super." He sniffed at the open end and gave it back. "One of the stick-up men used a .38 auto. You get a look at him?"

"Not good enough for a court of law. But I'd know him."

"Another player? Well, maybe." He drained his glass and set it on the floor. "Where's the duffel?"

"Under the blanket."

He started, looked at the lump in the bed. "Thought you used pillows." He got up to pull back the covers and grope inside the sack. When he looked at me again I was pointing the Smith & Wesson at him.

"Hold on, son."

"That's just what I'm doing," I said. "You didn't find the paper because it isn't there. You killed Seaton rather than deal with him. Now you can deal with me."

He stood with his hands away from his body. "Son, you're shouting down the wrong vent."

"Yeah, yeah, Popeye," I said. "It was a good hand, but you overplayed it. The state police didn't tell you where to find me. They didn't know I'd be putting in at this motel. Neither did I when I left them. You had to have followed me, just like the guy you sent to break into my car."

"You saw my bona fides."

"I saw them. They might even be genuine. Who better to make off with Navy valuables than someone in Naval Intelligence? What happened, you get double-crossed by Seaton?"

"Seaton wouldn't know how to double-cross anyone. He was straighter than the Equator."

This was a new player. I'd inspected the bathroom window earlier and decided it was too narrow to admit anything human, but I hadn't reckoned on the skimpy proportions of the gent I thought of as Slim Jim, after his calling card. He'd shed his jacket, and his rucked-up shirt

told me it had been a snug fit, but here he was, walking out
of the bathroom with a nickel-plated .38 Super automatic
in his right hand. He had a yellow complexion and a
military buzz cut that helped his general resemblance to a
skull.

Vennable didn't look at him. "I didn't make up much,"
he told me, "just changed the names around. We stuck up
that armored car. Seaton was one of the couriers we locked
inside. He got out somehow, caught a ride, and jumped us
down the road. Nick here shot him when he was picking
up the paper we dropped. He lost his weapon, but he got
into the car with the paper and the driver took off. We
caught up with the car in Toledo. The driver said he'd
stopped and refused to go any farther, so Seaton left on
foot carrying the paper. That driver was full of talk when
Nick did the asking."

"So he hitched another ride north and you tailed him
and here you are," I said. "What about the dead man near
Lexington?"

"A little invention to explain Seaton's wound." Vennable
was smiling. "Shoot him, Nick. That paper's got to be in
this room."

I'd been through the Detroit Police training course, and
the situation's covered: Go for your primary target and
worry about the others later. The Navy must have had a
similar policy, because Vennable crouched and charged
me, clawing for the Beretta on his belt, and that's why I
shot him in the groin instead of the chest where I'd been
aiming. He reeled in front of Nick. Nick changed positions
to get a clear field. I shot him twice, once through his
partner. Somehow he was still standing when the door
splintered and Commander Torrance of the state police
put a third one in him before he knew about the first. I
don't know if he'd have fallen even then if he hadn't
tripped over Vennable. These wiry boys are hell for
stamina.

"This one's still flopping." Straightening, the blocky
commander jerked the Beretta from Vennable's holster
and leathered his own Police Special. Blood was pumping

between the Navy man's fingers where he lay moaning and clutching his crotch with both hands. The second bullet had passed through his left arm. "Tell 'em not to bother about any sirens for the other one."

I finished giving the information to the 911 operator and hung up. "What brought you, the shots in the parking lot?"

"Folks up here get involved; they make calls. When I heard the name of the motel I thought you might've checked in here. What's the skinny?"

Sliding the telephone book cover from under the directory, I opened it and held up the thick sheaf of paper. "This is what they killed my hitchhiker to get their hands on," I said.

"What the hell is it?"

"The dreams that stuff is made of." I told him the rest. By the time he had it all, the first ambulance had arrived. The room was full of state troopers and paramedics now.

Torrance's wolf eyes never left my face. "Why didn't you just turn the duffel over to me to begin with?"

"Old habit. When I pick someone up on the road I'm offering him protection, even if he was beyond it when I met him, and way beyond anyone's when we parted company. That included finding out who killed him and why."

"Boy, that's the worst lie I ever heard."

"I've told worse." I breathed some air. "Maybe I just wanted to see how this one ended. It was a long dull trip otherwise."

"Better. Was it worth it?"

"Put it this way. Before I leave here in the morning I'm buying a pack of cigarettes off the manager so I won't have to make any more stops. That's how I fell into this mess."

"Better make it a carton," Torrance said.

Jeremiah Healy's first John Francis Cuddy novel, Blunt
Darts, *was nominated for a Shamus Award for best first novel.*
The Staked Goat *won the Shamus for best novel. The three
subsequent Cuddy novels are* So Like Sleep, Swan Dive *(also a
Shamus nominee), and* Yesterday's News. *This is Healy's first
appearance in a PWA anthology—and it is long overdue.*

Someone to
Turn Out the Lights

by Jeremiah Healy

1

The O'Dell Law Offices were located in the old Pruden-
tial tower, abandoned by the insurer when it decided to
close a number of regional centers. I took the elevator to
the eleventh floor, then followed the corridor numbers
to the O'Dell office door. The common hallway reminded
me of the Empire Insurance building, where I had worked
as head of Boston claims investigation before becoming a
private investigator.

The wooden version of O'Dell's letterhead, which hung
next to the door frame, reflected what I'd expected: In
addition to the patriarch, Michael, who had called me,
there were two O'Dell males and one O'Dell female listed
as attorneys. Walking in, I was welcomed by a nondescript
receptionist and ushered immediately into Michael
O'Dell's office.

O'Dell stood awkwardly, though he appeared to be in
good physical condition for a man of sixty or so years. He
said, "John Francis Cuddy?" and I nodded. O'Dell shook

my hand, his palm wet, and asked me to be seated as a way of killing time until the receptionist exited, closing the door behind her.

His bushy gray eyebrows worked furiously as he opened a manila file on his desk and scanned it. He said, "This isn't going to be easy for me."

On the phone, he'd led me to believe some corporation needed my services. Now it seemed more personal.

"Maybe if you told me something about the client involved?"

O'Dell closed the folder, meshing his hands nervously on top of it. "You ever hear of the Cleary Carpet Cleaning Company?"

"I've seen photo ads. With their founder, right?"

"Right. Edward Cleary. Eddie and I go back to college together, Holy Cross."

"Me, too."

"I know. I found you through another alum who'd used you, vouched for your discretion."

"Cleary have a problem?"

"Yes, but he doesn't know it yet, and I'm damned if I know how to tell him."

"Can you tell me about it?"

"Eddie built the business himself, a truck at a time, eighty-, ninety-hour weeks. He and the business were my first clients out of law school, when I was operating over a deli in Brighton. Long before this place." He waved his hand around the tasteful office, and I got the impression the unspecified move to the Pru was the brainchild of one of his lawyerly relatives.

"Go on."

"Well, the Cleary Company's still privately held and one of the best in the area. Oh, they've taken it on the chin from some nationwide competitors, and they're not really geared up for some of the big, cover-your-overhead skyscrapers as customers, but it's a good organization with a loyal staff. And Eddie's damned proud of the fact that he's turned a profit every year since he opened. 'Never a year in the red, Mike,' and so on."

"And now his record's in danger?"

"I think so. Damn, I know so." O'Dell squared his shoulders. "Look, let me stop talking around this thing and give it to you straight, okay?"

"Fine."

O'Dell reopened the file. "Eddie's on vacation now. Takes a week every quarter. Fishing in the spring and summer, the Caribbean in the fall and winter. His wife died years ago, no kids, and the trips are the one extravagance he allows himself. So I don't like to disturb him, especially the way he's been looking lately. A little sickly, you know? But I needed some information for a tax matter I'm working on, and their bookkeeper was out, sprained his ankle getting off the bus, for God's sake. So I got the assistant bookkeeper to get me into the computer system, and I didn't believe what I saw."

"Somebody's been dipping?"

"That's what I figure it has to be, but I don't have any direct proof of it."

"Sounds like you want an audit, Mr. O'Dell. A CPA, not a private investigator."

O'Dell shook his head. "Let me show you what I've found out so far, and I think you'll see what I mean." He took a breath. "The company has a number of accounts in the fifty-thousand-dollar range. Eight to be exact. Well, I found a ninth I knew nothing about."

"Is that so unusual?"

"Eddie and I have dinner together once a week, maybe every two weeks. He talks business a lot, how great his employees are, and so on. He would have mentioned this outfit along with the others sometime."

"Could it be a new account?"

"No. The computer shows it being in-house for almost three years; thirteen thousand a quarter is the billing."

"And the money arrives while the founder is on his vacations."

"No," said O'Dell.

"No?"

"No, and that's what makes me even more suspicious. Eddie doesn't concentrate on the business like he used to, but his people bring him up to date as soon as he gets back on everything that happened the week he's gone. The money always arrives the Thursday before he takes off."

"So it's probably never part of his return summary."

"It's programmed not to be, seems to me."

"What's this outfit's name?"

"Plummer Industries."

"Never heard of them. They'd have to be pretty big to need fifty-two thousand of rug cleaning a year, wouldn't they?"

"Not as big as you'd think, though the way things are going, any one of the big accounts represents Cleary's technical profit margin for the year. But Plummer's relative size isn't the issue."

"What is the issue, then?"

"Except for a filing with the Secretary of State's office over on Beacon Hill, and a checking account with the Bank of New England, they don't exist. Period."

I thought about it. "Phony company pays money to Cleary for cleaning carpets they don't have? Doesn't make sense."

"That's what I mean. There's something wrong here, but before I tell Eddie Cleary that one of his people is diddling him, I want to have more proof than I've got. The problem is I can't get close enough to the three people it could be without tipping them that I'm suspicious. The whole thing is so screwy I want an investigator to look into it."

"Why only three people?"

"Because I know Eddie's internal setup well enough to eliminate everybody else." O'Dell handed me a paper. "Only these three have the kind of juice and access to pull off something like this."

The sheet had names, titles, and home addresses typed on it. I read aloud. "Manny Krebs, Director of Services."

"Manny's the guy who actually oversees the carpet cleaning operations. He's the nervous kind, but he could conceivably submit an invoice for work that never got done, then somehow use the trucks for other work that paid him under the table."

I didn't quite see that, but I went on. "Anita Singer, Director of Sales."

"Anita basically brings in new business. It's tough in this line for a woman, but Eddie was impressed by the way she worked her way through school. She's done pretty well, based on the customers I do recognize as new ones, but she'd also be in the best position to create a phony one."

"George Bates, Director of Accounting."

"That's the guy who turned his ankle. George isn't really an accountant in the education sense, but he's been there twenty years. Eddie met him driving somewhere. There's never been a hint of trouble before, but he's obviously in the best position to cook the books."

"You said you checked Plummer's corporate filings. Did you pick up its officers, directors, that sort of thing?"

"Yes. Here."

He handed me a photocopy of the cover sheet for the Plummer Industries incorporation. Three men filled all positions: incorporators, officers, even shareholders. The names were James Meeney, Ronald J. Roche, and Derwood Robinson. The company's principal place of business was an address in Somerville past Lechmere Sales. The men's addresses were scattered all over Boston.

I said, "Any of these names mean anything to you?"

"No. I checked the phone book on the company and all three of them. Nothing listed. I even drove by Plummer's given address. Empty lot."

We resolved retainer and billing, and I stood to go.

O'Dell sighed, a glacier shifting. "Can you help me here?"

"I can try."

2

"Homicide, Murphy speaking."

"The switchboard warned me I was being recorded. Do you keep the machine going when they transfer my—"

"Cuddy, I don't have time for this jive. You want something, say it straight, all right?"

"All right." I pictured him: a stolid black Buddha crushing the receiver in his hand. "I'd like you to run some names for me."

"This got anything to do with something I should know about?"

"Just a simple corporate security check, Lieutenant."

"All right, let's have 'em."

I gave him Edward Cleary, the three company employees, and the three principals of Plummer Industries. Then I threw in Michael O'Dell for good measure. Murphy said he'd leave any information on my tape machine.

Manny Krebs lived in a wooden three-decker in East Boston within deafening range of Logan Airport's runways. That evening I watched him dash out of his house, shirttails flapping, and climb into a three-year-old Cadillac in the driveway. He took the most direct route possible to the Wonderland greyhound track, me trailing in my Prelude.

I'm not much of a gambler, but I prefer the horses to the dogs. Krebs loved the puppies enough to jog through traffic from the parking lot to the admissions gate. Staying behind Krebs by three people in line, I saw an older man approach him. The man grabbed Krebs genially by the arm and mouthed, "Manny, how you doing?" before Krebs urgently broke the grasp and trotted toward a betting window, tout sheet in hand.

I went up to the elderly gent. "That Manny, he's always in a rush to lose his money."

The man chuckled. "Yeah. The guy's here every night. You'd think he'd learn to bet better or walk slower, make his dough last."

"I don't know. I don't do that well myself."

"Pal, you gotta do better than Manny there. I tell him, 'Manny, you might as well throw the money into the street, all the talent you got for picking the fast ones.'"

I smiled and moved after Manny. Lounging against the rail, I watched him agonize over the failure of his softly chanted "number six, number six" to beat the other anorexic hounds pursuing Swifty, the mechanical rabbit.

Krebs had a long, sorrowful face, with deep-set brown eyes and thinning brown hair.

I moved closer, interrupting his comparison of the entries in the next race. "Don't feel bad. I thought six'd finish in the money, too."

"Yeah," he said, not looking up, circling numbers on his sheet with a red felt-tip pen.

"Hey, aren't you Mr. Krebs?"

He looked up at me, then at my extended hand. He shook absently. "Yeah, Manny. Manny Krebs. Who are you?"

"John Francis. I'm a friend of Jim Meeney over at Plummer Industries. I think your company does their carpets."

Nothing flashed over his expression. "I don't think so. Where's their offices at?"

"Somerville. Just past Lechmere Sales."

Krebs seemed apologetic. "Jeez, we got a lotta accounts over that way, but I never heard of these Plummer people. Maybe you saw me somewheres else?"

"Maybe. I visit a lot of the operations, over there."

Krebs darted his eyes to the toteboard, then back again to his selections. "Look, buddy, I don't mean to be rude or nothing, but I got some picks to make here. Be seeing you."

He hurried off toward the pari-mutuels. Gambling and embezzling often go hand in hand, but I think Krebs had forgotten about Plummer and me by the time he took out his wallet.

The next morning I laid the roses across the least green part of the sod, hoping to mask what the sunshine had burned due to the cemetery's erratic watering system.

It's like trying to cover the hole in a sweater, John. Everything you do just makes it more obvious.

"I know." Rising, I looked past Beth's headstone to the harbor below us. A couple of sailboats were tacking across each other's bows, violating what I thought were the right of way rules on the water. "I wish this case were a little more obvious."

What's the trouble with it?
I told her.
Wouldn't there be easier ways of embezzling?
"Probably. But employees who tap the kitty generally think the more complicated it is, the less likely they'll be caught."
Are they right?
"Not usually."

3

"Thank you, Mr. Francis, but I can't imagine we'd switch from our present system of forms to another, even if you had your samples with you."

"I understand, Ms. Singer."

She put a sympathetic smile on her pretty, thirtyish face, framed by blond Doris Day hair. "I know it's tough to be turned down cold in sales, but if only you'd called first, I could have saved you the trip."

"That's okay. I was in the area anyway, so I thought I'd give it a try. Ron Roche over at Plummer suggested I see you."

"Ron Roche?"

"Yes."

She pursed her lips, thoughtful, then wagged her head. "I don't think I know him. At Plummer, you said?"

"Plummer Industries. Over past Lechmere Sales. I thought you were the one who signed them up for Cleary here."

Singer shrugged. "Not me. I thought I'd canvassed just about every prospect we didn't already have in-house when I started, but I guess I must have missed that one." She picked up a pen and moved a post-it pad into place. "Is this Mr. Roche the one I should see?"

"Yes. If he's not in, try Derwood Robinson. Or even James Meeney."

She took them down, asking reasonably for correct spellings and underlining the company name. "Thanks for the tip. I'll try to reciprocate sometime, but right now I've got a lunch date."

I said I could find my own way out and did, waiting in the Prelude in the parking lot. Singer appeared shortly and hopped into a Toyota Celica. I followed her to the Mass Pike, then west till we got to Wellesley, a tony suburb. She twisted and turned for a while before pulling into a driveway that angled up to a massive, pillared colonial. Singer left the car and walked to the broad entryway, pushing the buzzer. I parked down the road a hundred feet and came back in time to see an attractive, fortyish woman open the front door. Hugging each other, they moved inside.

Five minutes later, the window curtains to an upstairs bedroom were drawn against the cruel afternoon sun and potentially prying eyes. Feeling vaguely disoriented, I returned to my car.

George Bates hobbled out his front door on crutches. The house was a modest two-family in Arlington, a solid suburb north and west of the city. Five-foot-four and portly, he wore his sandy hair long and slicked back, fifties style. I expected a dedicated employee like Bates to put in a half day's work. Instead he took the Arlington Heights number 77 bus down Massachusetts Avenue into the bowels of the Harvard Square station. I parked illegally and raced down the pedestrian entrance to the subway, just managing to spot him and sprint the twenty yards to the rear door of the Red Line car he'd chosen. A college kid graciously yielded her seat to him, and he got off four stops later at Park Street, in downtown Boston.

Above ground, Bates lurched his way down Tremont Street, resting every block or so. He finally turned harborside and struggled through a revolving door into the gallery offices of a national stock brokerage house. He went up to a man about my age sitting behind a desk. They greeted each other like old friends and then hunched over some documents, smiling and pointing like two codgers admiring photos of their grandchildren.

A heavy woman in a business skirt and blouse swept by me with a file in her hand. I said, "Excuse me?"

She turned. "Oh, sorry."

"No harm done, but I was just wondering. Do you work here?"

"Yes, yes I do. Can I help you with something?" Her manner indicated she hoped not.

I gestured toward Bates and the broker. "The younger fellow talking with the man on crutches. He's a dead ringer for a classmate of mine at Harvard, and I was wondering, is his name Cabot Lithgow? We called him 'Skipper' at school."

She restrained her impatience beautifully. "No, no I'm afraid not. That's Jared Kane. He did go to Harvard, though."

"Oh, thank you. I'm so glad I asked now. You've saved me a bushel of embarrassment."

"Don't mention it," she said, bustling away.

I waited till Bates left Mr. Kane, then found a pay phone and called the brokerage house.

"Jared Kane here."

"Mr. Kane, this is John Francis calling. George Bates referred me to you. In fact, he mentioned he was seeing you today. I hope I'm not disturbing anything?"

"Not at all, Mr. Francis. In fact, you just missed George."

Kane seemed too polite to mention that Bates hadn't said a thing about me to him. "Oh, that's too bad. How did he seem on the ankle, by the way?"

"Oh, he tottered a bit, but he's too tough a sort to let it slow him down. How can I help you?"

"Well, George and I were talking about investments, and as I told him, with my aunt passing on and all, I have about as much as he does in relatively liquid assets . . ."

"And?"

I could almost hear Mr. Kane salivating on the other end of the line. "And George has been so pleased by how well you've done by him, he said you were the man to talk to."

"Ah, Mr. Francis—"

"Oh, please, call me John."

"Thank you. And call me Jared. Well, we've certainly done our best for George, but I must confess, he does so much of the research and weighing himself, I daresay he should be the broker and I the client."

We both had a good laugh over that one, and I made an appointment with him the next week that I had no intention of keeping.

The message on my tape machine was simple and direct. Or directive. "Call me at home tonight."

When I reached Murphy, he said, "Ran your names. What's going on here?"

The statute that licenses private investigators says you give information only to your client. The reality is you tell the police what they want to know or they stop telling you what you need to know. I gave him the abridged edition.

"You do get into some weird trashcans, boy."

"What do you have?"

"On Edward Cleary, Michael O'Dell, Manny Krebs, and Anita Singer, nothing. On brothers Meeney, Roche, and Robinson, plenty. About all you need, though, is their current and permanent address."

"Walpole."

"Commissioner wants us to call it Cedar Junction now, but the bars be as strong and the walls as thick."

"How long?"

"Dinosaurs. Meeney been in the longest, since sixty-two. Roche I got from sixty-three, Robinson sixty-six. All lifers, no possibility of parole."

"What about George Bates?"

"That's the cute one. He's an alum. Did himself a dime for armed robbery."

"When did he hit the streets?"

"Sixty-eight. If the paperwork's righteous, he been clean as a baby's conscience ever since. Help you out?"

"Good question."

4

George Bates was at work early the next day. His office was an interior one, a fluorescent light shining overhead and a brass gooseneck lamp with a green glass shade arching incongruously next to the computer terminal

Michael O'Dell had described to me two days earlier. Bates swiveled around in his chair as I entered. He bade me sit and asked how he could help me.

"I'd like to talk about Plummer Industries."

"Plummer."

"Yes, and your classmates, too. Meeney, Roche, and Robinson, Esquires."

Bates leaned back in his chair, pulling on his nose with the fingers of his left hand. "You wouldn't by any chance be John Francis, too, would you?"

"My first and middle names."

"I thought Jared Kane was nuts when he called to thank me for the referral, but I played along. Have you talked with anybody else about Plummer?"

"Anita Singer and Manny Krebs."

"They don't know anything about it."

"I know. When I mentioned Plummer and the boys to them, neither even flinched."

"You talk with anybody besides Anita and Manny?"

He seemed an innocuous little guy, but he'd spent at least ten years learning bad habits from badder folks, so I resettled myself in the chair, right leg tensed for traction and motion. "Just the police."

"Oh." Bates chewed on his lower lip. "Oh, that's a relief."

"A relief?"

He looked at me, amused. "Yes, Mr. Cuddy. I'm long past violating parole, though I don't see what I've been doing as criminal anyway. I'm just relieved you haven't talked with Mr. Cleary. Who was it sicced you on me, anyway? Let me guess: Mike O'Dell?"

"That's confidential."

"That makes it O'Dell all right. He came in here needing something the day I was in the hospital, and he stumbled across the Plummer account, right?"

"Why don't you tell me about it?"

"I guess I'll have to. O'Dell tell you how Mr. Cleary and I met?"

"Like I said, you tell me."

"So very careful, are you? Good, I like that. Makes me willing to trust you on this. I met Edward Cleary twenty years, six months, and twelve days ago. Know how I can remember that so well?"

"Probably the day they let you out."

A hardening seeped into his voice. "You're a comer, you are. I was trying to hitch a ride. In the rain. New suit, cardboard suitcase just a little stiffer than the suit, black Corfam shoes. Nobody picked up hitchers along there."

"Except Cleary."

"Right. He was a helluva guy then, my friend. Knew I was fresh out, could see it without me having to tell him, but he gave me a lift and asked what I could do. I told him I studied accounting inside, but I couldn't really see anybody taking a chance on me outside. He said he would, and I started here two days later."

"And?"

"And for seventeen years everything was rosy. Oh, we had some tough times, but Mr. Cleary was a helluva businessman, too, and we weathered them. Everybody pulled together, and we cleared a profit every quarter."

"Until three years ago."

"Right. Until then, when the nationals started cutting us out of the big, new jobs. Oh, the old customers stayed loyal just like the staff here, but we stopped getting the new business you need to stay up there."

"Enter Plummer Industries."

"Yeah. I'd been saving the whole time I was here. Never took more than three days off at a time in twenty years, and I rode the market just right. Got into two-families in Arlington there and rolled some over into twelve-unit brick buildings. Then I got lucky with some commercial land out by 495 that I bought before anybody thought of high tech pushing that far west."

"You're Plummer Industries."

"In a manner of speaking. I borrowed the names for the formal staff, because I knew Jimmy, Ron, and Der weren't likely to be wheeling and dealing much themselves. I set up the corporate shell, established a bank account, and salted it from time to time with my capital gains and whatnot from the other deals."

"But why?"

"Why?"

"Yeah. Why set up Plummer to pay money to Cleary for work Cleary never did?"

Bates picked up a pencil, pointing it at me like a gun barrel. "Because Edward Cleary picked up a con on a crummy day outside Walpole when he didn't have to, then offered the con a job that meant something and trusted the con to do it right. Then said Mr. Cleary started to lose his grip just enough at the wrong time competitionwise, and now Cleary Carpet Cleaning just can't catch up. We can't get back there to profitability no matter how much Anita hustles or Manny scrubs, get me?"

"And thanks to Plummer, Cleary's still never had a year in the red."

"You've got it."

"A hell of a thing to do."

"What?"

"Squandering your own retirement money on a business you know is going down."

Bates snorted. "It's nothing. Weren't for Mr. Cleary, I'd be washing dishes somewhere, not sitting on enough to see me through whatever time's left. Which is more than Mr. Cleary's got, from the look he's had lately."

Bates softened a bit. "No, I'll just limp along for a while, long enough to see Mr. Cleary safe in the ground with his record intact. Besides, after he's gone, they'll need me here for a while to wind things down. Somebody's got to turn out the lights, right?"

I just nodded at Bates.

He said, "So, what do you do now?"

"Not me. We. We go see lawyer O'Dell and you tell him what you told me."

I stood while Bates shrugged into his coat and onto his crutches. I reached for the switch on the wall.

"Please," he said, smiling slightly, "let me get that."

John Lutz is a past Shamus Award winner and Edgar Award nominee in the short story category, and he is a past president of PWA. His short story collection, **Better Mousetraps,** *was published in 1988 by St. Martin's Press. He has two active P.I. series, one featuring Alo Nudger, the other featuring Fred Carver. His Carver novel* Kiss *won the PWA Shamus Award for best P.I. novel of 1988. He is one of the four people who have appeared in every PWA anthology to date. This is the first Carver short story.*

Someone Else

by John Lutz

This Wayne Garnett was Carver's first client in the new office on Magellan Avenue in downtown Del Moray, Florida, or maybe the whole mess wouldn't have happened.

Carver had decided to separate his business from Edwina as much as possible; some hairy situations had evolved that hadn't needed to include her. So Carver had stopped working out of her house by the sea, where he lived with her. Edwina told him it wasn't necessary, that she didn't mind him using the house for an office. But she was in real estate, and when Carver insisted, she got him a deal on a year's lease on the office on Magellan, in a fairly new cream-stucco building that also housed an insurance brokerage and a car rental agency and was across the street from the Art Deco courthouse and jail.

So there Carver found himself, sitting behind his gleaming new executive desk and staring at his new beige filing cabinets, and in walked Garnett out of the glaring afternoon heat and said, "The lettering on the door says this is a detective agency. You follow wayward wives?"

"I have," Carver said.

Which opened up a lot of possible clever remarks by Garnett, only he was a serious type and sat down and let out a long breath and didn't smile.

"Your wife?" Carver asked, meeting serious with serious.

Garnett nodded. He was a big man, about six feet tall and going to fat in a hurry. Maybe forty-five, fifty years old. He was wearing tan dress slacks, gray suede shoes, and a white polo shirt that had brown horizontal stripes that accentuated his paunch. He'd been handsome, but now his regular-featured face was fleshy and blotched, and his straight dark hair was thinning. Another five years and he'd be as bald on top as Carver. "Gloria's her name. Gloria Garnett. I'm Wayne Garnett. I own a car dealership over on West Palm Drive. Maybe you've seen it. Maybe you've seen our television commercial, where I show how you can afford payments on a new Volkswagen just by cutting back on smoking and junk food."

Enough about you, Carver thought. He said, "Tell me about Gloria."

And without asking about Carver's rates, Garnett began describing his problems with his wife. That should have been a warning to Carver, but he was the new boy on the block and eager to make good, and right now any client looked like luck.

"Gloria's younger than me," Garnett said. "Only twenty-eight years old." He fished his wallet from a hip pocket and drew out a color snapshot, which he tossed on the desk.

Carver bent forward and saw an attractive, dark-haired woman with dramatic Latin features. She was smiling into the camera, squinting a little in bright sunlight, and there was a teasing kind of fire in her dark eyes. A vivacious woman even in two dimensions. The word "spitfire" came to mind.

"Nice-looking," Carver said. "Why do you want her followed?"

"The reason you might guess. I think she's secretly

seeing someone else. Things have changed between us—she's gotten colder toward me. I phone her from the office and she's hardly ever home. Her car's logging a lot of mileage she can't explain. Thing is, Carver, she's hiding something from me—I can tell! That gnaws on me, goddammit! I gotta know what it is! *Who* it is!"

"What if you don't like what I find out?"

"That won't concern you. I'll pay you in advance." He tilted sideways in his chair to raise one wide buttock and got out his wallet again. Pulled a wad of bills from it and peeled off ten hundreds and fanned them out on Carver's bare new desk. "Refund what you don't use, and tell me if and when you need more."

Carver got up and limped with his cane over to the shiny file cabinets. Garnett noticed the stiff left knee and the cane and looked for a moment as if he might have some misgivings, as if he doubted Carver could keep up with the wayward Gloria. Then he seemed to consider that the sign on the door had said Private Investigator and that meant Carver could do the job, otherwise he'd be in some other line of work.

"I'll type up a standard contract for you to sign," Carver said, pulling open the top drawer on its smooth nylon casters.

"I don't wanna sign anything," Garnett said. "That's why I'm paying in cash. I don't want Gloria to ever be able to say I hired somebody to follow her, that I didn't trust her or I harassed her."

Carver figured that Garnett was already thinking ahead to possible divorce proceedings, as if his wife's infidelity could be taken for granted.

"If you're looking for absolute proof of adultery—" Carver began.

Garnett interrupted him. "I don't need absolute *proof*, Carver—I just wanna know! You understand?"

Carver understood enough to take the job. Wished later that he'd understood enough to turn it down.

The Garnetts lived on Verde Avenue, a palm tree–lined street in an old but fashionable part of town. Theirs was

one of the few newer homes, an expensive brick ranch
house set well back from the street and surrounded by a
jungle of lush foliage.

Carver parked his ancient and rusting Oldsmobile convertible down the street where he could see the Garnetts'
driveway. The car's canvas top was up to shade the interior
from the fierce Florida sun, though it was only eight A.M.,
ten minutes before Wayne Garnett was due to leave for
work at his car dealership.

Right on time, Garnett pulled out of the driveway in a
black Volkswagen GT with tinted windows. He turned left,
away from Carver, and the little car putt-putted smoothly
around a gentle curve in the sun-dappled street and
disappeared.

Gloria wasted little time. Carver had drunk only half the
coffee he'd stopped to get at a McDonald's drive-through
when a white VW convertible bounced out of the Garnett
driveway. The little car's top was down and it passed
Carver going fast and still accelerating. The pretty dark-
haired woman in the photograph was driving.

Carver started the Olds and drove around the block in a
hurry so he could catch up.

Gloria Garnett headed east, then turned north on
Beachside Drive. She was driving slower now. Carver, in
the Olds, hung far back. He could afford the distance
between them; Beachside was wide and straight here,
bordering the whitecaps rolling in on the pale stretch of
sand. The fetid, rotting scent of the sea was pushed ashore
by a soft breeze off the ocean. A low-flying gull with
flashing white wings kept pace with the car for a while,
then screamed as if in alarm and arced seaward, soaring
on the breeze. Gloria drove as if she knew where she was
going, her long black hair whipping in the whirl of wind in
the little convertible.

She surprised Carver. Suddenly the car slowed, then
made a right turn onto a deserted parking lot that over-
looked a stretch of public beach.

Gloria stopped the convertible with its snub nose pointing toward the sea. Carver drove past the gravel lot and

parked on the road shoulder where he could see what
went on in the lot without being obvious.

He watched Gloria get out of her car and stride toward
a wooden bench that was facing the ocean. She was
wearing a loose-fitting blue blouse and a darker blue long
skirt that billowed in the wind and occasionally afforded a
glimpse of tanned, shapely legs. There was the same snap
in her walk that he'd noticed in her eyes. When she
reached the beach her sandals began flapping and tossing
sand up behind her heels. She was carrying a book in one
hand, a large straw purse in the other.

Carver drove onto the lot and parked at the other end,
away from the VW convertible. He got out of the Olds and
limped to an iron rail, the tip of his cane dragging in the
gravel. He leaned casually on the warm rail and gazed at
the sun-hazed horizon, as if studying the undulating,
sparkling ocean.

The bench was at the edge of a concrete walkway that
ran parallel with the sea. A few people were walking the
beach barefoot, either in swimming trunks or suits or with
their cuffs rolled up. Now and then someone fully dressed
strolled past on the sidewalk that led to a cluster of
condominiums farther down the beach. Gloria didn't seem
to notice anyone. She'd sat down on the bench, put on a
pair of sunglasses, and, facing the ocean, was engrossed in
reading her book.

Gloria didn't glance up at the people who infrequently
walked past the bench. After about half an hour, a blond
woman in a white uniform—maybe a nurse's uniform—
who was pushing an elderly white-haired man in a wheelchair, stopped near the bench. Carver figured they'd come
from the condos up the beach. The old guy was hunched
forward and had a blanket or shawl over him despite the
warm morning. Probably a private nurse with her patient.

The woman sat down next to Gloria on the bench, and
Gloria's head jerked up and back as if she hadn't been
reading at all but had been dozing and was suddenly
awakened. Then she sat with her head bowed, maybe
reading again. The nurse said something to her, smiled,

and got up and pushed the old man in the wheelchair back toward the condominium towers glimmering in the sun.

Gloria sat reading a while longer, not even glancing up when some teenage boys ran past yelling at each other. A few other passersby glanced over at her, then continued on their way.

After about twenty minutes, it struck Carver that she hadn't moved. Hadn't turned a page or looked up at a low-flying pelican flapping past. Asleep again?

Feeling uneasy, he took the three wooden steps to the beach, set his cane tentatively in the soft sand, and limped toward the bench.

When he was twenty feet away he noticed the dark stains spotting the sand beneath the bench. When he was ten feet away he knew the stains were blood.

When he limped around in front of the bench he saw that there were dark stains on the open book in Gloria Garnett's lap, that she was dead.

Lieutenant William McGregor was seated at his desk and adding powdered cream to his coffee. He stirred. Sipped. Smiled. He hadn't offered Carver any coffee.

McGregor was a towering blond man who looked more Swedish than Scottish. He had narrow shoulders and a lanky, loose-jointed frame, an obscene smile, and a wide gap between his front teeth that he often prodded with the pink tip of his tongue. He also had the most sour breath ever aimed at Carver. One of McGregor's friends might have told him about the breath, only McGregor had no friends and didn't deserve any. He liked it that way.

His office in Del Moray police headquarters was spacious and modern and had a window with a peek-a-boo view of the ocean several blocks away. He'd recently been promoted to Homicide, which was why he was interested in Gloria Garnett's death.

He picked up the packet he'd torn open and whose contents he'd sprinkled in his coffee and said, "They call this stuff nondairy whitener. Know why? 'Cause if you read the label close you find out there ain't a drop of cream or milk in it." He tossed the crumpled packet aside. "Kinda shit oughta be against the law."

"You called me here to talk about Gloria Garnett," Carver said. "Her murder *is* against the law."

"The M.E.'s still working on her," McGregor said, "but she was killed by a .38 bullet through the heart. That much we do know. What we don't know is what you were doing at the scene."

Carver told him. Everything. This was a homicide and nothing to get cute over.

McGregor leaned back and laced his fingers behind his long neck. He studied Carver with his creepy little close-set eyes. He said, "So you figure this nurse pushing the old fucker in the wheelchair did this Gloria with a silencer, hey?"

"I didn't say that."

"You implied it."

"I told you her head snapped back and then forward when the nurse sat down next to her on the bench. I thought then maybe she'd been dozing and had awakened suddenly. Now I'm telling you that might be when she was shot."

"By the nurse?"

"More likely by the old guy in the wheelchair. Had a gun with a silencer concealed beneath his shawl. The nurse probably sat down to prop up Gloria in case she started to fall and draw attention to what had happened."

"Don't make sense. Sounds about as real as the cream in this coffee."

"Find the nurse and the old guy, maybe it will make sense."

"There is no nurse and old guy. Not so far."

"What about Garnett? You talked to him yet?"

"Told him his wife was dead. He acted upset. Who wouldn't be? She was a fine-looking piece. Great bazooms. Younger than him, too, by about fifteen years."

Carver had forgotten how much he disliked McGregor; now it was coming back. "Why don't you get your sick mind working on finding out if he has any idea about who might have killed her?"

"He might have killed her himself," McGregor said. "In fact, he probably did. He's being questioned now."

Carver didn't understand this. "You can't have enough on him for a murder charge. You must know that."

"So right you are. We'll eventually have to let him walk." McGregor leaned back in his chair, gazed down his nose at Carver. "Something *you* oughta know. Garnett owns this car dealership out on West Palm, sells a couple of foreign makes. Maybe you seen him on TV lying his ass off about how you can give up cigarettes and Twinkies and afford a new car. Anyway, Narcotics got tipped a while back that he was also into the drug game in a big way. Know who tipped the narcs? Mrs. Garnett."

"She informed on her husband?" Carver didn't like where McGregor might be going with this. "Why would she do that?"

"Good question. But, hey, I got a good answer. Garnett was seeing a woman on the side, according to Gloria. He'd deny it whenever she'd ask him about it, and they'd have a big brawl. The neighbors could tell you all about it. Hubby beat her up about a month ago. She says he tried to choke her with her gold neck chain. The Garnetts didn't get along, it seems."

"Guess not."

"Interesting thing is," McGregor said, "she was having second thoughts about testifying against him. She really loved him, for all the twisted reasons women love scumbags like Garnett. When it came right down to it, I don't think she'd really have given us anything on him in court."

"Something we'll never find out," Carver said.

"That was the object of her murder," McGregor said. "Though if Garnett hadn't killed her, one of his associates would have eventually done it. The drug business is nasty. She was probably dead the moment she talked to us. Only so many ways to protect a witness, and none of 'em perfect."

Carver knew that was true.

"But we come now to a little lesson in international trade," McGregor said, "so listen close. Volkswagens are built in Mexico, some of them, and some of those are shipped to Garnett's dealership. In certain cars, somebody at the other end of the supply line in Mexico would replace the insulation above the headliners with cocaine, which Garnett would remove and wholesale here in the States. Gloria knew about it, had some trouble with hubby, and came to us. She was scared of him as well as in love with him, mixed-up cunt that she was. And she was supposed to give us her deposition against him after his arrest, which was going to take place when the next coke shipment arrived at his dealership. But without the wife's testimony, Narcotics has got no case. Nothing. They're over at the car dealership now searching for evidence, but they won't find any. It's all been removed."

"So Garnett found out his wife was going to rat on him and had her killed."

McGregor sat forward and said, "Almost right, Carver. He's got an airtight alibi for the time of her death—says he was with some friends. They'll swear to it. Drug buddies. They're lying, all of them. Know why?"

Carver knew why.

"That's right," McGregor said. "Garnett was the man in the wheelchair, the old guy with the gray wig and the shawl. And the gun equipped with a silencer."

Carver felt a seething rage boil up in his stomach, move through his body. He was squeezing the crook of his walnut cane so hard his knuckles were bloodless and ached. "And the nurse pushing him was his other woman."

"Hey, that's awful astute of you," McGregor said, "but too late. Gloria was in the habit of driving to the beach every morning and reading, and Garnett took advantage of that. And of you. Don't you get it, shit-for-brains? Garnett hired you so you could witness Gloria's murder by an old man in a wheelchair. So you could tell us it wasn't Garnett who killed his wife."

"But we know damned well it *was* him!"

McGregor's eyes got tiny and cold. "Do we? Does a judge? A jury? You saw a nurse and an old man in a wheelchair near Gloria . . . *maybe* at the time she was shot. Ever heard of reasonable doubt?"

Carver planted the tip of his cane and levered himself to

his feet. If he hadn't had the bad leg he would have paced angrily, maybe punched a wall.

McGregor gave him a mean smile. "You're the reason for the reasonable doubt."

Carver didn't at all like furnishing a killer with an alibi. Bad for business. Bad for the soul.

Garnett would be occupied at police headquarters for a while longer. Carver figured if he was going to be an accessory to a perfect murder, a little breaking and entering was nothing to cause concern. Maybe there'd be something in Garnett's house on Verde Avenue that would provide a way to nail him for murdering his wife.

After parking down the block, Carver limped to Garnett's address and up the long and winding concrete driveway. Palm trees and azalea bushes lined the drive, making most of it, and the house, invisible from the street. A million cicadas ratcheted noisily in the bushes, but that was the only sound. A guy like Garnett, with a lot to hide, must like it here.

Carver rang the bell and waited a long time to make sure no one was home. Then he tried the knob. The front door was locked, but it had a window in it and he didn't see any alarm wiring on the glass.

After a glance around, he used his cane to break out the glass, then he reached in and released a deadbolt lock. He tried the door again, and it opened.

The inside of the house was cool and more luxurious than he'd expected. Modern furniture, all smoked glass and sharp angles. Peach-colored carpet and drapes. He could see through the kitchen and out sliding glass doors to a screened-in pool behind the house. The water in the pool was rippling gently, holding captive the sunlight that had filtered through the screen.

He roamed about, saw a desk in Garnett's office. The drawers yielded nothing other than the usual household correspondence and a few innocuous business letters. The bookshelf behind the desk contained automotive manuals and a stack of paperback western novels. On the desk's corner was a small empty brass picture frame; probably it had contained the photo of Gloria Garnett that her husband had shown to Carver when he'd hired him and made him an unwitting accomplice in murder.

The master bedroom was vast. It smelled strongly of rose-scented perfume, as if some had been spilled and would pervade the room forever. One wall was entirely mirror, and the bed was round and covered with a blue quilted spread. Carver set the tip of his cane in the soft carpet and limped over to one of the dressers.

It was Gloria's. The drawers contained expensive lingerie, sweaters, and blouses, yet they were only half full. The top drawer held a jewelry box, empty.

Garnett's dresser revealed that he wore silk underwear. Carver wasn't surprised. He opened other drawers and searched through socks and neatly folded sportshirts and denims. All expensive labels. In the bottom drawer, beneath some folded beachwear, lay half a dozen empty picture frames of various sizes.

Carver walked over to the closet and rolled open the tall sliding doors. There were a few dresses on one side of the closet, and the other side was stuffed with men's clothing. He looked at the empty wire hangers dangling between the dresses, wondering what it all meant.

He limped out of the bedroom and into the kitchen. The refrigerator was well stocked. There was a bottle of red wine chilling in a special temperature-controlled compartment. On top of the refrigerator was a wooden wine rack that held half a dozen more bottles, tilted forward so their contents would keep the corks from drying out.

A door from the kitchen led to the garage. Carver stood on the single step and looked at a silver-blue Mercedes convertible, the only vehicle in the three-car garage other than a ten-speed Schwinn bike and a red riding mower that looked like an expensive kid's toy. Somewhere in the garage a wasp droned like a miniature and continuous alarm buzzer. There was something about the way the Mercedes was parked, with its sleek nose almost touching the front wall of the garage, as if to leave maximum room behind the car.

Carver stood thinking about the empty picture frames,

the depleted dresser drawers and closet in the master bedroom. He went back into Garnett's office and searched through some keys he'd noticed in one of the drawers.

It took him only a few seconds to find the spare keys to the Mercedes. He limped back out into the garage and opened the car's trunk.

It held three suitcases and a garment bag. He unzipped the bag part way and saw a silky dress. Worked the latches on one of the suitcases and opened it far enough to reveal a gauzy nightgown, a travel clock, and a small electric hair-dryer. The smallest suitcase, a blue nylon carry-on, contained stacks of ten- and twenty-dollar bills, fastened neatly with rubber bands. Hell of a lot of money.

Carver closed the trunk lid and leaned on it. The garage was warmer than the rest of the house and he was perspiring, but he hardly noticed. Gloria had been having second thoughts about testifying against her husband, McGregor had said. Maybe Wayne Garnett had also had second thoughts about his future.

Hot as it was in the garage, Carver felt ice on the back of his neck.

He was about to limp into the kitchen when he heard a car stop outside in the driveway. Quickly he made his way to the garage's overhead door and peered through one of its narrow dusty windows.

A cab had stopped in the driveway, far enough up so that whoever got out wouldn't be visible from the street.

Carver watched the cab back out and drive away, its exhaust fumes wavering in the heat. Watched the woman who had climbed out stride in her high heels up the sun-bleached driveway toward the house.

He reached over and punched the button that started the electric garage door opener.

The opener growled to life. The wide door jerked, then laboriously and noisily began to roll itself up section-by-section to flatten out again along the garage ceiling.

The woman standing surprised in the driveway wore a terrified expression. She was dainty and attractive, with strong Latin features and long dark hair too thick and wavy to tame. Her skin-tight blue skirt was short; so were her legs, but they were shapely and she had nice knees and ankles and could get by with any skirt she wanted to wear.

Carver could understand why, when she'd had second thoughts, so had Wayne Garnett. Why they'd chosen the ugly but only way out for both of them. She looked something like the woman in the photograph Garnett had shown Carver in the office. Put a blond wig on her and she'd look more like the nurse pushing the wheelchair on the beach—the one who'd watched while the woman Wayne Garnett had hired to carry a purse and a book, and drive to a bench by the sea and read—and whose corpse he'd later identified as that of his wife—died of a bullet to the heart.

Who had the victim been? One of life's untraceables, no doubt, without friends or relatives. Probably an illegal alien, or maybe a prostitute up from Miami. She'd been someone who didn't matter to Wayne Garnett. Or to his wayward wife.

Carver limped out onto the sun-washed driveway toward the woman. The cicadas were ratcheting again. Screaming their timeless, desperate mating call. Love making the world go round.

He said, "Hello, Gloria."

She backed a wobbly step and started to shake her pretty head in denial.

Then she shrugged, smiled sadly, and said hello back. Said it a certain way.

God, she was beautiful!

But not worth it.

Marcia Muller's Sharon McCone is probably the oldest contemporary American female P.I.—in terms of service, that is. No other active female P.I. has been appearing for as long as Sharon, who first surfaced in Edwin of the Iron Shoes *(1977) and who appeared most recently in* The Shape of Dread *(1989). Here, Marcia and Sharon appear in a PWA anthology for the second time, the first time since the first anthology.*

Final Resting Place

by Marcia Muller

The voices of the well-dressed lunch crowd reverberated off the chromium and formica of Max's Diner. Busy waiters made their way through the room, trays laden with meatloaf, mashed potatoes with gravy, and hot turkey sandwiches. The booths and tables and counter seats of the trendy restaurant—one of the forerunners of San Francisco's fifties revival—were all taken, and a sizable crowd awaited their turn in the bar. What I waited for was Max's famous onion rings, along with the basket of sliders—little burgers—I'd just ordered.

I was seated in one of the window booths overlooking Third Street with Diana Richards, an old friend from college. Back in the seventies, Diana and I had shared a dilapidated old house a few blocks from the U.C. Berkeley campus with a fluctuating group of anywhere from five to ten other semi-indigent students, but nowadays we didn't see much of each other. We had followed very different paths since graduation: She'd become a media buyer with the city's top ad agency, drove a new Mercedes, and lived graciously in one of the new condominium complexes near the financial district; I'd become a private investigator with a law cooperative, drove a beat-up MG, and lived chaotically in an old cottage that was constantly in the throes of renovation. I still liked Diana, though—enough that when she'd called that morning and asked to meet with me to discuss a problem, I'd dropped everything and driven downtown to Max's.

Milkshakes—the genuine article—arrived. I poured a generous dollop into my glass from the metal shaker. Diana just sat there, staring out at the passersby on the sidewalk. We'd exchanged the usual small talk while waiting for a table and scanning the menu ("Have you heard from any of the old gang?" "Do you still like your job?" "Any interesting men in your life?"), but then she'd grown uncharacteristically silent. Now I sipped and waited for her to speak.

After a moment she sighed and turned her yellow eyes toward me. I've never known anyone with eyes so much like a cat's; their color always startles me when we meet to renew our friendship. And they are her best feature, lending her heart-shaped face an exotic aura and perfectly complementing her wavy light brown hair.

She said, "As I told you on the phone, Sharon, I have a problem."

"A serious one?"

"Not serious, so much as . . . nagging."

"I see. Are you consulting me on a personal or a professional basis?"

"Professional, if you can take on something for someone who's not an All Souls client." All Souls is the legal cooperative where I work; our clients purchase memberships, much as they would in a health plan, and pay fees that are scaled to their incomes.

"Then you actually want to hire me?"

"I'd pay whatever the going rate is."

I considered. At the moment my regular caseload was exceptionally light. And I could certainly use some extra money; I was in the middle of a home-repair crisis that threatened to drain my checking account long before payday. "I think I can fit it in. Why don't you tell me about the problem."

Diana waited while our food was delivered, then began: "Did you know that my mother died two months ago?"

"No, I didn't. I'm sorry."

"Thanks. Mom died in Cabo San Lucas, at this second home she and my father have down there. Dad had the cause of death hushed up; she'd been drinking a lot and passed out and drowned in the hot tub."

"God."

"Yes." Diana's mouth pulled down grimly. "It was a horrible way to go. And so unlike my mother. Dad naturally wanted to keep it from getting into the papers, so it wouldn't damage his precious reputation."

The bitterness and thinly veiled anger in her voice brought me a vivid memory of Carl Richards: a severe, controlling man, chief executive with a major insurance company. When we'd been in college, he and his wife, Teresa, had crossed the Bay Bridge from San Francisco once a month to take Diana and a few of her friends to dinner. The evenings were not great successes; the restaurants the Richardses chose were too elegant for our preferred jeans and tee-shirts, the conversations stilted to the point of strangulation. Carl Richards made no pretense of liking any of us; he used the dinners as a forum for airing his disapproval of the liberal political climate at Berkeley, and boasted that he had refused to pay more than Diana's basic expenses because she'd insisted on enrolling there. Teresa Richards tried hard, but her ineffectual social flutterings reminded me of a bird trapped in a confined space. Her husband often mocked what she said, and it was obvious she was completely dominated by him. Even with the nonwisdom of nineteen, I sensed they were a couple who had grown apart, as the man made his way in the world and the woman tended the home fires.

Diana plucked a piece of fried chicken from the basket in front of her, eyed it with distaste, then put it back. I reached for an onion ring.

"Do you know what the San Francisco Memorial Columbarium is?" she asked.

I nodded. The Columbarium was the old Odd Fellows mausoleum for cremated remains, in the Inner Richmond district. Several years ago it had been bought and restored by the Neptune Society—a sort of All Souls of the funeral industry, specializing in low-cost cremations and interments, as well as burials at sea.

"Well, Mom's ashes are interred there, in a niche on the second floor. Once a week, on Tuesdays, I have to consult with a major client in South San Francisco, and on the way back I stop in over the noon hour and . . . visit. I always take flowers—carnations, they were her favorite. There's a little vaselike thing attached to the wall next to the niche where you can put them. There were never any other flowers in it until three weeks ago. But then carnations, always white ones with a dusting of red, started to appear."

I finished the onion ring and started in on the little hamburgers. When she didn't go on, I said, "Maybe your father left them."

"That's what I thought. It pleased me, because it meant he missed her and had belatedly come to appreciate her. But I had my monthly dinner with him last weekend." She paused, her mouth twisting ruefully. "Old habits die hard. I suppose I do it to keep up the illusion we're a family. Anyway, at dinner I mentioned how glad I was he'd taken to visiting the Columbarium, and he said he hadn't been back there since the interment."

The man certainly didn't trouble with sentiment, I thought. "Well, what about another relative? Or a friend?"

"None of our relatives live in the area, and I don't know of any close friend Mom might have had. Social friends, yes. The wives of other executives at Dad's company, the neighbors on Russian Hill, the ladies she played bridge with at her club. But no one who would have cared enough to leave flowers."

"So you want me to find out who is leaving them."

"Yes."

"Why?"

"Because since they've started appearing it's occurred to me that I never really knew my mother. I loved her, but in my own way I dismissed her almost as much as my father did. If Mom had that good a friend, I want to talk with her. I want to see my mother through the eyes of someone who *did* know her. Can you understand that?"

"Yes, I can," I said, thinking of my own mother. I would never dismiss Ma—wouldn't *dare* dismiss the hundred-and-five-pound dynamo who warms and energizes the McCone homestead in San Diego—but at the same time I didn't really know much about her life, except as it related to Pa and us kids.

"What about the staff at the Columbarium?" I asked. "Could they tell you anything?"

"The staff occupy a separate building. There's hardly ever anyone in the mausoleum, except for occasional visitors, or when they hold a memorial service."

"And you've always gone on Tuesday at noon?"

"Yes."

"Are the flowers you find there fresh?"

"Yes. And that means they'd have to be left that morning, since the Columbarium's not open to visitors on Monday."

"Then it means this friend goes there before noon on Tuesdays."

"Yes. Sometime after nine, when it opens."

"Why don't you just spend a Tuesday morning there and wait for her?"

"As I said, I have regular meetings with a major client then. Besides, I'd feel strange, just approaching her and asking to talk about Mom. It would be better if I knew something about her first. That's why I thought of you. You could follow her, find out where she lives and something about her. Knowing a few details would make it easier for me."

I thought for a moment. It was an odd request, something she really didn't need a professional investigator for, and not at all the kind of job I'd normally take on. But Diana was a friend, so for old times' sake . . .

"Okay," I finally said. "Today's Monday. I'll go to the Columbarium at nine tomorrow morning and check it out."

* * *

Tuesday dawned gray, with a slowly drifting fog that provided the perfect backdrop for a visit to the dead. Foghorns moaned a lament as I walked along Loraine Court, a single block of pleasant stucco homes that dead-ended at the gates of the park surrounding the Columbarium. The massive neoclassical building loomed ahead of me, a poignant reminder of the days when the Richmond district was mostly sand dunes stretching toward the sea, when San Franciscans were still laid to rest in the city's soil. That was before greed gripped the real-estate market in the early decades of the century, and developers decided the limited acreage was too valuable to be wasted on cemeteries. First cremation was outlawed within the city, then burials, and by the late 1930s the last bodies were moved south to the necropolis of Colma. Only the Columbarium remained, protected from destruction by the Homestead Act.

When I'd first moved to the city I'd often wondered about the verdigrised copper dome that could be glimpsed when driving along Geary Boulevard, and once I'd detoured to investigate the structure it topped. What I'd found was a decaying rotunda with four small wings jutting off. Cracks and water stains marred its facade; weeds grew high around it; one stained-glass window had buckled with age. The neglect it had suffered since the Odd Fellows had sold it to an absentee owner some forty years before had taken its full toll.

But now I saw the building sported a fresh coat of paint: A medley of lavender, beige, and subdued green highlighted its ornate architectural details. The lawn was clipped, the surrounding fir trees pruned, the names and dates on the exterior niches newly lettered and easily readable. The dome still had a green patina, but somehow it seemed more appropriate than shiny copper.

As I followed the graveled path toward the entrance, I began to feel as if I were suspended in a shadow world between the past and the present. A block away Geary was clogged with cars and trucks and buses, but here their sounds were muted. When I looked to my left I could see the side wall of the Coronet Theater, splattered with garish, chaotic graffiti; but when I turned to the right, my gaze was drawn to the rich colors and harmonious composition of a stained-glass window. The modern-day city seemed to recede, leaving me not unhappily marooned on this small island in time.

The great iron doors to the building stood open, inviting visitors. I crossed a small entry and stepped into the rotunda itself. Tapestry-cushioned straight chairs were arranged in rows there, and large floral offerings stood next to a lectern, probably for a memorial service. I glanced briefly at them and then allowed my attention to be drawn upward, toward the magnificent round stained-glass window at the top of the dome. All around me soft, prismatic light fell from it and the other windows.

The second and third floors of the building were galleries—circular mezzanines below the dome. The interior was fully as ornate as the exterior and also freshly painted, in restful blues and white and tans and gilt that highlighted the bas relief flowers and birds and medallions. As I turned and walked toward an enclosed staircase to my left, my heels clicked on the mosaic marble floor; the sound echoed all around me. Otherwise the rotunda was hushed and chill; as near as I could tell, I was the only person there.

Diana had told me I would find her mother's niche on the second floor, in the wing called Kepheus—named, as the others were, after one of the four Greek winds. I climbed the curving staircase and began moving along the gallery. The view of the rotunda floor, through railed archways that were banked with philodendrons, was dizzying from this height; the wall opposite the arches was honeycombed with niches. Some of them were covered with plaques engraved with people's names and dates of birth and death; others were glass-fronted and afforded a view of the funerary urns. Still others were vacant, a number marked with red tags—meaning, I assumed, that the niche had been sold.

I found the name Kepheus in sculpted relief above an archway several yards from the entrance to the staircase.

Inside was a smallish room—no more than twelve by
sixteen feet—containing perhaps a hundred niches. At its
front were two marble pillars and steps leading up to a
large niche containing a coffin-shaped box; the ones on
the walls to either side of it were backed with stained-glass
windows. Most of the other niches were smaller and
contained urns of all types—gold, silver, brass, ceramics.
Quickly I located Teresa Richards': at eye level near the
entry, containing a simple jar of handthrown blue pottery.
There were no flowers in the metal holder attached to it.

Now what? I thought, shivering from the sharp chill and
glancing around the room. The reason for the cold was
evident: Part of the leaded-glass skylight was missing.
Water stains were prominent on the vaulted ceiling and
walls; the pillars were chipped and cracked. Diana had
mentioned that the restoration work was being done
piecemeal, because the Neptune Society—a profitmaking
organization—was not eligible for funding usually available to those undertaking projects of historical signifi-
cance. While I could appreciate the necessity of starting on
the ground floor and working upward, I wasn't sure I
would want my final resting place to be in a structure
that—up here, at least—reminded me of Dracula's castle.

And then I thought, just listen to yourself. It isn't as if
you'd be peering through the glass of your niche at your
surroundings! And just think of being here with all the
great San Franciscans—Adolph Sutro, A. P. Hotaling, the
Stanfords and Folgers and Magnins. Of course, it isn't as if
you'd be creeping out of your niche at night to hold long,
fascinating conversations with them, either . . .

I laughed aloud. The sound seemed to be sucked from
the room and whirled in an inverted vortex toward the
dome. Quickly I sobered and considered how to proceed.
I couldn't just be standing here when Teresa Richards'
friend paid her call—*if* she paid her call. Better to move
about on the gallery, pretending to be a history buff
studying the niches out there.

I left the Kepheus room and walked around the gallery,
glancing at the names, admiring the more ornate or
interesting urns, peering through archways. Other than

the tapping of my own heels on the marble, I heard nothing. When I leaned out and looked down at the rotunda floor, then up at the gallery above me, I saw no one. I passed a second staircase, wandered along, glanced to my left, and saw familiar marble pillars . . .

What is this? I wondered. How far have I walked? Surely I'm not already back where I started.

But I was. I stopped, puzzled, studying what I could discern of the Columbarium's layout.

It was a large building, but by virtue of its imposing architecture it seemed even larger. I'd had the impression I'd only traveled partway around the gallery, when in reality I'd made the full circle.

I ducked into the Kepheus room to make sure no flowers had been placed in the holder at Teresa Richard's niche during my absence. Disoriented as I'd been, it wouldn't have surprised me to find that someone had come and gone. But the little vase was still empty.

Moving about, I decided, was a bad idea in this place of illusion and filtered light. Better to wait in the Kepheus room, appearing to pay my respects to one of the other persons whose ashes were interred there.

I went inside, chose a niche belonging to someone who had died the previous year, and stood in front of it. The remains were those of an Asian man–one of the things I'd noticed was the ethnic diversity of the people who had chosen the Columbarium as their resting place—and his urn was of white porcelain, painted with one perfect, windblown tree. I stared at it, trying to imagine what the man's life had been, its happiness and sorrows. And all the time I listened for a footfall.

After a while I heard voices, down on the rotunda floor. They boomed for a moment, then there were sounds as if the tapestried chairs were being rearranged. Finally all fell as silent as before. Fifteen minutes passed. Footsteps came up the staircase, slow and halting. They moved along the gallery and went by. Shortly after that there were more voices, women's, that came close and then faded.

Was it always this deserted? I wondered. Didn't anyone visit the dead who rested all alone?

More sounds again, down below. I glanced at my watch, was surprised to see it was ten-thirty.

Footsteps came along the gallery—muted and squeaky this time, as if the feet were shod in rubber soles. Light, so light I hadn't heard them on the staircase. And close, coming through the archway now.

I stared at the windbent tree on the urn, trying to appear reverent, oblivious to my surroundings.

The footsteps stopped. According to my calculations, the person who had made them was now in front of Teresa Richards' niche.

For a moment there was no sound at all. Then a sigh. Then noises as if someone was fitting flowers into the little holder. Another sigh. And more silence.

After a moment I shifted my body ever so slightly. Turned my head. Strained my peripheral vision.

A figure stood before the niche, head bowed as if in prayer. A bunch of carnations blossomed in the holder— white, with a dusting as red as blood. The figure was clad in a dark blue windbreaker, faded jeans, and worn athletic shoes. Its hands were clasped behind its back.

It wasn't the woman Diana had expected I would find. It was a man, slender and tall, with thinning gray hair. And he looked very much like a grieving lover.

At first I was astonished, but then I had to control the urge to laugh at Diana's and my joint naïveté. A friend of mine has coined a phrase for that kind of childlike thinking: "teddy bears in the brain." Even the most cynical of us occasionally falls prey to it, especially when it comes to relinquishing the illusion that our parents—while they may be flawed—are basically infallible. Almost everyone seems to have difficulty setting that idea aside, probably because we fear that acknowledging their human frailty will bring with it a terrible and final disappointment. And that, I supposed, was what my discovery would do to Diana.

But maybe not. After all, didn't this mean that someone had not only failed to dismiss Teresa Richards, but actually loved her? Shouldn't Diana be able to take comfort from that?

Either way, now was not the time to speculate. My job was to find out something about this man. Had it been the woman I'd expected, I might have felt free to strike up a conversation with her, mention that Mrs. Richards had been an acquaintance. But with this man, the situation was different: He might be reluctant to talk with a stranger, might not want his association with the dead woman known. I would have to follow him, use indirect means to glean my information.

I looked to the side again; he stood in the same place, staring silently at the blue pottery urn. His posture gave me no clue as to how long he would remain there. As near as I could tell, he'd given me no more than a cursory glance upon entering, but if I departed at the same time he did, he might become curious. Finally I decided to leave the room and wait on the opposite side of the gallery. When he left, I'd take the other staircase and tail him at a safe distance.

I went out and walked halfway around the rotunda, smiling politely at two old ladies who had just arrived laden with flowers. They stopped at one of the niches in the wall near the Kepheus room and began arguing about how to arrange the blooms in the vase, in voices loud enough to raise the niche's occupant. Relieved that they were paying no attention to me, I slipped behind a philodendron on the railing and trained my eyes on the opposite archway. It was ten minutes or more before the man came through it and walked toward the staircase.

I straightened and looked for the staircase on this side. I didn't see one.

That can't be! I thought, then realized I was still a victim of my earlier delusion. While I'd gotten it straight as to the distance around the rotunda and the number of small wings jutting off it, I hadn't corrected my false assumption that there were two staircases instead of one.

I hurried around the gallery as fast as I could without making a racket. By the time I reached the other side and peered over the railing, the man was crossing toward the door. I ran down the stairs after him.

Another pair of elderly women were entering. The man

was nowhere in sight. I rushed toward the entry, and one of the old ladies glared at me. As I went out, I made mental apologies to her for offending her sense of decorum.

There was no one near the door, except a gardener digging in a bed of odd, white-leafed plants. I turned left toward the gates to Loraine Court. The man was just passing through them. He walked unhurriedly, his head bent, hands shoved in the pockets of his windbreaker.

I adapted my pace to his, went through the gates, and started along the opposite sidewalk. He passed the place where I'd left my MG and turned right on Anza Street. He might have parked his car there, or he could be planning to catch a bus or continue on foot. I hurried to the corner, slowed, and went around it.

The man was unlocking the door of a yellow VW bug three spaces down. When I passed, he looked at me with that blank, I'm-not-really-seeing-you expression that we city dwellers adopt as protective coloration. His face was thin and pale, as if he didn't spend a great deal of time outdoors; he wore a small beard and mustache, both liberally shot with gray. I returned the blank look, then glanced at his license plate and consigned its number to memory.

"It's a man who's been leaving the flowers," I said to Diana. "Gordon DeRosier, associate professor of art at S.F. State. Fifty-three years old. He owns a home on Ninth Avenue, up the hill from the park in the area near Golden Gate Heights. Lives alone; one marriage, ended in divorce eight years ago, no children. Drives a 1979 VW bug, has a good driving record. His credit's also good—he pays his bills in full, on time. A friend of mine who teaches photography at State says he's a likable enough guy, but hard to get to know. Shy, doesn't socialize. My friend hasn't heard of any romantic attachments."

Diana slumped in her chair, biting her lower lip, her yellow eyes troubled. We were in my office at All Souls—a big room at the front of the second floor, with a bay window that overlooks the flat Outer Mission district. It had taken me all afternoon and used up quite a few favors to run the check on Gordon DeRosier; at five Diana had called wanting to know if I'd found out anything, and I'd asked her to come there so I could report my findings in person.

Finally she said, "You, of course, are thinking what I am. Otherwise you wouldn't have asked your friend about this DeRosier's romantic attachments."

I nodded, keeping my expression noncommittal.

"It's pretty obvious, isn't it?" she added. "A man wouldn't bring a woman's favorite flowers to her grave three weeks running if he hadn't felt strongly about her."

"That's true."

She frowned. "But why did he start doing it now? Why not right after her death?"

"I think I know the reason for that: He's probably done it all along, but on a different day. State's summer class schedule just began; DeRosier is probably free at different times than he was in the spring."

"Of course." She was silent a moment, then muttered, "So that's what it came to."

"What do you mean?"

"My father's neglect. It forced her to turn to another man." Her eyes clouded even more, and a flush began to stain her cheeks. When she continued, her voice shook with anger. "He left her alone most of the time, and when he was there he ignored or ridiculed her. She'd try so hard—at being a good conversationalist, a good hostess, an interesting person—and then he'd just laugh at her efforts. The bastard!"

"Are you planning to talk with Gordon DeRosier?" I asked, hoping to quell the rage I sensed building inside her.

"God, Sharon, I can't. You know how uncomfortable I felt about approaching a woman friend of Mom's. This . . . the *implications* of this make it impossible for me."

"Forget it, then. Content yourself with the fact that someone loved her."

"I can't do that, either. This DeRosier could tell me so much about her."

"Then call him up and ask to talk."

"I don't think . . . Sharon, would you—"

"Absolutely not."

"But you know how to approach him tactfully, so he won't resent the intrusion. You're so good at things like that. Besides, I'd pay you a bonus."

Her voice had taken on a wheedling, pleading tone that I remembered from the old days. I recalled one time when she'd convinced me that I really *wanted* to get out of bed and drive her to Baskin-Robbins at midnight for a gallon of pistachio ice cream. And I don't even like ice cream much, especially pistachio.

"Diana—"

"It would mean so much to me."

"Dammit—"

"*Please.*"

I sighed. "All right. But if he's willing to talk with you, you'd better follow up on it."

"I will, I promise."

Promises, I thought. I knew all about promises. . . .

"We met when she took an art class from me at State," Gordon DeRosier said. "An oil painting class. She wasn't very good. Afterwards we laughed about that. She said she was always taking classes in things she wasn't good at, trying to measure up to her husband's expectations."

"When was that?"

"Two years ago last April."

Then it hadn't been a casual affair, I thought.

We were seated in the living room of DeRosier's small stucco house on Ninth Avenue. The house was situated at the bottom of a dip in the road, and the evening fog gathered there; the branches of an overgrown plane tree shifted in a strong wind and tapped at the front window. Inside, however, all was warm and cozy. A fire burned on the hearth, and DeRosier's paintings—abstracts done in reds and blues and golds—enhanced the comfortable feeling. He'd been quite pleasant when I'd shown up on his doorstep, although a little puzzled because he remembered seeing me at the Columbarium that morning. When I'd explained my mission, he'd agreed to talk with me and graciously offered me a glass of an excellent zinfandel.

I asked, "You saw her often after that?"

"Several times a week. Her husband seldom paid any attention to her comings and goings, and when he did, she merely said she was pursuing her art studies."

"You must have cared a great deal about her."

"I loved her," he said simply.

"Then you won't mind talking with her daughter?"

"Of course not. Teresa spoke of Diana often. Knowing her will be a link to Teresa—something more tangible than that urn I visit every week."

I found myself liking Gordon DeRosier. In spite of his ordinary appearance, there was an impressive dignity about the man, as well as a warmth and genuineness. Perhaps he could become a friend to Diana, someone who would make up in part for losing her mother before she really knew her.

He seemed to be thinking along the same lines, because he said, "It'll be good to finally meet Diana. All the time Teresa and I were together I'd wanted to, but she was afraid Diana wouldn't accept the situation. And then at the end, when she'd decided to divorce Carl, we both felt it was better to wait until everything was settled."

"She was planning to leave Carl?"

He nodded. "She was going to tell him that weekend, in Cabo San Lucas, and move in here the first of the week. I expected her to call on Sunday night, but she didn't. And she didn't come over as she'd promised she would on Monday. On Tuesday I opened the paper and found her obituary."

"How awful for you!"

"It was pretty bad. And I felt so . . . shut out. I couldn't even go to her memorial service—it was private. I didn't even know how she had died—the obituary merely said 'suddenly.'"

"Why didn't you ask someone? A mutual friend? Or Diana?"

"We didn't have any mutual friends. Perhaps that was the bond between us; neither of us made friends easily. And Diana . . . I didn't see any reason for her ever to know about her mother and me. It might have caused her pain, colored her memories of Teresa."

"That was extremely caring of you."

He dismissed the compliment with a shrug and asked, "Do you know how she died? Will you tell me, please?"

I related the circumstances. As I spoke DeRosier shook his head as if in stunned denial.

When I finished, he said, "That's impossible."

"Diana said something similar—how unlike her mother it was. I gather Teresa didn't drink much—"

"No, that's not what I mean." He rose and began to pace, extremely agitated now. "Teresa did drink too much. It started during all those years when Carl alternately abused her and left her alone. She was learning to control it, but sometimes it would still control her."

"Then I imagine that's what happened that weekend down in Cabo. It would have been a particularly stressful time, what with having to tell Carl she was getting a divorce, and it's understandable that she might—"

"That much is understandable, yes. But Teresa would *not* have gotten into that hot tub—not willingly."

I felt a prickly sense of foreboding. "Why not?"

"Teresa had eczema, a severe case, lesions on her wrists and knees and elbows. She'd suffered from it for years, but shortly before her death it had spread and become seriously aggravated. Water treated with chemicals, as it is in hot tubs and swimming pools, makes eczema worse and causes extreme pain."

"I wonder why Diana didn't mention that."

"I doubt she knew about it. Teresa was peculiar about illness—it stemmed from having been raised a Christian Scientist. Although she wasn't religious anymore, she felt physical imperfection was shameful and wouldn't talk about it."

"I see. Well, about her getting into the hot tub—don't you think since she was drunk, she might have anyway?"

"No. We had a discussion about hot tubs once, because I

was thinking of installing one here. She told me not to expect her to use it, that she had tried the one in Cabo just once. Not only had it aggravated her skin condition, but it had given her heart palpitations, made her feel she was suffocating. She hated that tub. If she really did drown in it, she was put in against her will. Or after she passed out from too much alcohol."

"If that was the case, I'd think the police would have caught on and investigated."

DeRosier laughed bitterly. "In Mexico? When the victim is the wife of a wealthy foreigner with plenty of money to spread around, and plenty of influence?" He sat back down, pressed his hands over his face, as if to force back tears. "When I think of her there, all alone with him, at his mercy . . . I never should have let her go. But she said the weekend was planned, that after all the years she owed it to Carl to break the news gently." His fist hit the arm of the chair. "*Why* didn't I stop her?"

"You couldn't know." I hesitated, trying to find a flaw in his logic. "Mr. DeRosier, why would Carl Richards kill his wife? I know he's a proud man, and conscious of his position in the business and social communities, but divorce really doesn't carry any stigma these days."

"But a divorce would have denied him the use of Teresa's money. Carl had done well in business, and they lived comfortably. But the month before she died, Teresa inherited a substantial fortune from an uncle. The inheritance was what made her finally decide to leave Carl; she didn't want him to get his hands on it. And, as she told me in legalese, she hadn't commingled it with what she and Carl held jointly. If she divorced him immediately, it wouldn't fall under the community property laws."

I was silent, reviewing what I knew about community property and inheritances. What Teresa had told him was valid—and it gave Carl Richards a motive for murder.

DeRosier was watching me. "We could go to the police. Have them investigate."

I shook my head. "It happened on foreign soil; the police down there aren't going to admit they were bribed, or screwed up, or whatever happened. Besides, there's no hard evidence."

"What about Teresa's doctor? He could substantiate that she had severe eczema and wouldn't have gotten into that tub voluntarily."

"That's not enough. She was drunk; drunks do irrational things."

"Teresa wasn't an irrational woman, drunk or sober. Anyone who knew her would agree with me."

"I'm sure they would. But that's the point: You knew her; the police didn't."

DeRosier leaned back, deflated and frustrated. "There's got to be some way to get the bastard."

"Perhaps there is," I said, "through some avenue other than the law."

"How do you mean?"

"Well, consider Carl Richards: He's very conscious of his social position, his business connections. He's big on control. What if all of that fell apart—either because he came under suspicion of murder or if he began losing control because of psychological pressure?"

DeRosier nodded slowly. "He *is* big on control. He dominated Teresa for years, until she met me."

"And he tried to dominate Diana. With her it didn't work so well."

"Diana . . ." DeRosier half-rose from his chair. "What about her?"

"Shouldn't we tell her what we suspect? Surely she'd want to avenge her mother somehow. And she knows her father and his weak points far better than you or I."

I hesitated, thinking of the rage Diana often displayed toward Carl Richards. And wondering if we wouldn't be playing a dangerous game by telling her. Would her reaction to our suspicions be a rational one? Or would she strike out at her father, do something crazy? Did she really need to know any of this? Or did she have a right to the knowledge? I was ambivalent: On the one hand, I wanted to see Carl Richards punished in some way; on the other, I wanted to protect my friend from possible ruinous consequences.

DeRosier's feelings were anything but ambivalent, however; he waited, staring at me with hard, glittering eyes. I knew he would embark on some campaign of vengeance, and there was nothing to stop him from contacting Diana if I refused to help. Together their rage at Richards might flare out of control, but if I exerted some sort of leavening influence . . .

After a moment I said, "All right, I'll call Diana and ask her to come over here. But let me handle how we tell her."

It was midnight when I shut the door of my little brown-shingled cottage and leaned against it, sighing deeply. When I'd left Gordon DeRosier's house, Diana and he still hadn't decided what course of action to pursue in regard to Carl Richards, but I felt certain it would be a sane and rational one.

A big chance, I thought. That's what you took tonight. Did you really have a right to gamble with your friend's life that way? What if it had turned out the other way?

But then I pictured Diana and Gordon standing in the doorway of his house when I'd left. Already I sensed a bond between them, knew that they'd forged a united front against a probable killer. Old Carl would get his, one way or the other.

Maybe their avenging Teresa's death wouldn't help her rest more easily in her niche at the Columbarium, but it would certainly salve the pain of the two people who remembered and loved her.

T. D. Stash has appeared in three novels by W. R. Philbrick. The second book in the series, The Crystal Blue Persuasion, *was nominated for a Shamus Award as best paperback P.I. novel of 1988. This is Stash's first short story appearance, and Philbrick's first appearance in a PWA anthology.*

Bad to the Bone

by W. R. Philbrick

1

The man was good at what he did. So good it killed him.

I was taking it easy in the bait shack, watching the way light played off the brass-green waters of the inner harbor, when Mutt came in with the news.

"They found *Fidelity*," he said. "Drifting off Crawfish Key. Empty."

Fidelity was Ray Florio's guide boat, a glass skimmer like my own, built for stalking gamefish through shallow turtlegrass flats. Ray was the best bonefish guide in the business, bar none. When it came to spotting the gray ghosts of the flats, the man was uncanny. I like to think I have a good eye for bones, but I'd seen Ray Florio cast a white-feather fly at a spot of clear, empty water and come up with a twelve-pound specimen that ran like an Olympic sprinter on methedrine. The man was a great fishing guide. No argument there.

"One of them tour boats spotted her," Mutt said. "The Coast Guard towed her in."

"Any sign of Ray?"

Mutt shook his bald, sun-mottled head. "Nope," he said.

"He'll turn up," I said, putting my feet up on a crab trap.

218

It was hot, the air was still, the prospect of an afternoon nap beckoned.

Mutt frowned, creasing his leathery jowls. Reminding me of a hairless hound dog with a dangerous glint in his eye. "Ray Florio's a no 'count son of a bitch," he said. "I grant you that. But all the same he's a fellow waterman. Now git off yer lazy butt and help me find 'im."

Shame did it. That and the fact that Mutt contrived to pull the trap out from under my feet.

On the way out of the basin I swung the skiff around and made a pass by the wharf where the Coast Guard had parked *Fidelity*. What I saw there lightened my heart.

"Hell," I told Mutt. "His push pole is missing."

Mutt brightened some. He knew what I was getting at. A guide will use a long fiberglass pole to push his boat through the shallow waters. The pole also functions as a kind of anchor. You jam it down into a soft spot in the bottom and lash a line from the forked end of the pole to a cleat on the boat. Then, if you're stalking a wary bonefish, it's more than likely that at some point you'll get out of the boat and wade through the ankle-to-knee-deep waters, waiting for the perfect moment to make your cast.

Probably Ray had gotten absorbed in the hunt and returned to find that *Fidelity* had slipped her leash. Chances were he was still out there on the flats cursing the sun and the rising tide—and his client, if he happened to have one along. Or he might have been solo, checking out feeding patterns, bringing his charts up to date.

"The poor insufferable bastard!" I shouted, gunning the outboard as we cleared the jetty. "He'll be plenty wet and mean by the time we find 'im!"

Cussing out Ray Florio was pure jealousy on my part. Partly it was his unrivaled facility for finding fish. Partly it was because he'd stolen a girl from me once, back when we were boys. The girl was named Cindy Louise, and still is, although her last name has changed a few times since. The first time was to Florio, but that didn't take, not with the way Ray treated her. He'd left their honeymoon bed to chase a little blond stewardess from Sarasota and then had the meanness of spirit to check into the same motel with her, two doors down from Cindy Louise.

That was the other thing Ray was good at. Getting a woman into his bed and then humiliating her. All done with a handsome, flashing smile that made the hurt deeper. To Ray, love was just another four-letter word, a useful lure.

"Hell, it's only talk," he used to brag to his pals at the Laughing Gull. "Can I help it if they believe me? What's the big deal anyhow?"

I think he truly didn't know what the big deal was. For Ray Florio a beautiful woman was like a prize gamefish— something to be chased, caught, and then released. He never understood the anguish his indifference caused. He simply didn't care.

We cruised the shallow waters west of the harbor. Saw turtles in the turtlegrass, a few barracuda feeding on frenzied needlefish. Didn't see bonefish. Didn't see any sign of Ray Florio or the push pole that had come loose from his skiff.

After a while Mutt put away the binoculars and said, "Seems to me Ray favored the flats off Boca Chica, ocean side."

"True," I said. "Damn few bones over here. Mostly permit in these waters. Or tarpon on the right tides."

"Ray's a bonefish man, right? So why'd he be all the way over here by Crawfish Key?"

It was an excellent question. When we found the answer we found Ray Florio. Which raised a lot of other questions.

There was a half moon rising and it spilled enough light over the glittering water to put the low mangrove islands off Boca Chica Key in distinct relief. Navigating by seat of the pants and memory, I managed to get through the narrow channels without putting *Bushwhacked* aground or fouling the prop.

The night air was thick with the stench of mangroves. Off-islanders, getting their first whiff of the saltwater swamps, complain of pollution and sewage, but the stink is as old as the sea. It has to do with the myriad creatures who live and die in the network of underwater roots. Most of the creatures who fetch up on the mangroves are bird or fish or crustacean, but not all.

Not all.

It was Mutt who first spotted the slim silhouette of the missing push pole.

"That 'un ain't got no branches," he said.

I squinted against the darkness and shook my head. I'd been scanning the broad shallows that were Ray's favorite fishing grounds, expecting to see the distinctive forks on the upper end of the pole. The push pole Mutt spotted was buried forks down only a few yards from a low, densely packed jungle of mangrove bushes.

Not something Ray would have done. Maybe that explained my deep sense of uneasiness as I maneuvered the skiff close-in and took hold of the abandoned pole.

"Give me a hand," I said to Mutt.

It took both of us to wrench the pole loose from the mud. And even then it was heavy. Way too heavy. Dead weight heavy. We pulled until something loosed itself from the bottom and thumped quietly up against the side of the skiff.

Mutt shone a flashlight over the edge. "The poor sum bitch," he sighed. "How'd he get himself all tangled up like that?"

There was a length of rope lashed to the forks. I'd been expecting that. I hadn't been expecting to find the other end of the rope coiled around Ray Florio's neck.

2

Lieutenant Detective Nelson Kerry, my friend in the Key West Police Department, was up in Miami attending a crime-stoppers' convention. By luck of the draw I got Mitchell Porter. His attitude left something to be desired.

"I 'member you all," he said, puffing on a short fat cigar. "You a troublemaker, boy. Why'd you want to go and drown a man like Ray Florio?"

"Now hold on, Sergeant. Don't—"

Whereupon he poked me with the wet end of the cigar and said, "Don't say 'don't' to me, boy. Jes' answer the question."

So I answered that particular question and a lot of other questions and by the time Porter gave up, dawn was breaking. I wandered home feeling like something that had been blown ashore in a storm. Despite Porter's aggressive bluster he seemed inclined to agree with my theory that Ray's death had been accidental. Drowning in shallow water is easier than you might think. All you have to do is slip and bump your head. The tidal currents would do the rest, tangling the body in the line, carrying Ray's skiff around to Crawfish Key. Case solved. No mystery, no murder.

The session with Detective Sergeant Porter was bad, but finding Mutt Durgin asleep in my hammock was more than I could bear. Mutt owns a bait shack and the smell of it follows him everywhere.

"Up," I said, shaking him awake. "Don't slam the screen door on your way out."

"Have a little respect," he said.

"Sorry," I yawned. "Fresh out. Used all I had on the cops and got a wet cigar butt in the ear for my efforts."

"The dumb bastard."

"My sentiments exactly," I said.

"No," Mutt replied, holding up a small, leather-bound appointment book. "I mean the guy who killed Ray Florio. He left this behind."

The coffee helped. I drank most of the pot while Mutt told me about breaking into Florio's place. Actually, he didn't have to break in. Someone had already done so. All Mutt had to do was walk through the broken slider and poke around to his heart's content.

"Made an awful mess," he said. "Him that was there first, not me."

"What makes you think Ray was murdered?"

Mutt shrugged, stirring the coffee with his finger. "Stands to reason, don't it? Must be a hundred folks wanted to kill the bastard at one time or another. Including you."

"Years ago," I said.

"Also me," Mutt said.

"You?"

"That purty little barmaid at the Half Shell," he said.

"I had no idea."

Mutt sighed, not meeting my eyes. "Just as well, I guess. She wanted me to sell off the business and move up to Orlando. Get a real job, you know?" He shuddered at the recollection. "But it'll sure enough put ugly notions in your head when a man like Ray Florio tricks a woman into breaking your heart. What I figure, somebody finally got to 'im."

With me being interrogated, Mutt had decided to pay the visit to Florio's home on Stock Island.

"Weren't no home, really," he explained. "Ray got this doubled-up trailer fitted out as a love nest. Built-in bar, king-size waterbed, mirrors on the walls, ceiling, everywhere. Even got hisself a hot tub off the back porch."

I asked Mutt what he had expected to find there.

"Knowin' Ray, I figured there might be a woman waitin'. Thought she might know somethin'. Weren't no woman, though. Time I got there the place had been busted up. Torn apart like somebody was lookin' for somethin'." He grinned and held up the leather-bound appointment book in which Ray Florio had marked down his clients. "This, maybe."

"How come you found it and they didn't?" I asked.

"'Cause it weren't at his place," Mutt said, licking his thumb as he flipped through the pages. "Were in the dash of his pickup truck, right where Ray always parked it. Behind my bait shack."

If Nel Kerry had been on duty, I'd have turned the appointment book over to him. I was not so inclined to cooperate with Mitchell Porter, not after he'd mashed a wet cigar butt in my ear. So what I did, I photocopied the pages in the appointment book and put it back in Ray's truck. If Porter happened to find it, he happened to find it. Meantime I could check out the names and numbers and see if any of them connected with a killer.

It was a long list. Ray, being a genius at landing the most elusive and prized of the sports fish, had plenty of clients. He was booked through most of the year. Mostly repeat business. The notations indicated that he turned down almost as many requests as he honored. That burned me a little—he'd never tried to pass any of his excess business on to any of the other fish guides. Men he'd worked alongside for years.

The last entry was to reserve a full day for a Dr. Eliot, of New Rochelle, New York. Ray had listed two numbers beside the name. I tried the first and found myself speaking to a Puerto Rican housemaid.

"The doctor at the hospital," she informed me. "Can't nobody call him there, though. Never get through."

"This is Ray Florio," I drawled. "The doc left a couple of personal items down here in Key West the other day. Just wanted to know if I should drop them in the mail."

The maid swore in Spanish. She was more than a little surprised when I understood.

"Why do you call me a stupid white snake?" I asked.

"Because you lie. Dr. Eliot never go to Key West the other day. Trip get canceled."

She hung up before I could get any more pointers in Spanish maledictions. I dialed the other number and got Eliot's office. I tried pleading a medical emergency, but his secretary was unimpressed. She would take a message.

"Look, I know he's got a beeper," I said. "Can't you beep him?"

"Can I have your name please?" the frosty voice asked. "If you're a patient of Dr. Eliot's, we'll have you on the computer."

I sighed. "That was a fib. My name is Ray Florio. I'm Dr. Eliot's fishing guide. He's been coming down here to Key West for years. He'll want to hear from me, I guarantee it."

The secretary grudgingly agreed to pass the request along. I gave her my number and waited. I had time to water the plants and feed the fish. For that matter, I had time to give the weathered stucco a coat of whitewash, but didn't. Someday. Eventually I settled down in the hammock and, sure enough, that worked. The phone rang.

"Ray?"

"This is not Ray Florio speaking, Dr. Eliot. This is Detective Mitchell Porter of the Key West Police."

"But my secretary said—"

"I needed to have you return the call, doctor. Figured the prospect of bonefishing might work."

The doctor and I had a fairly long conversation, considering that he was due back in surgery. "Let 'em bleed" seemed to be his philosophy. It was fun being Detective Porter over the phone. (In real life I'd sooner be a wharf rat; they're smaller, cleaner, and smarter.) I didn't let on that Ray Florio was dead, just that his boat had been found and that he was missing.

"Odd," the doctor responded. "Very odd. I had a spot open on my schedule and called Ray only last week. We were supposed to be all set. I had flight reservations confirmed, my reels packed, everything. Then he calls me back and cancels."

"Does that often happen?" I asked.

"Never. Been out with Ray two, three times a year for a long time now. Always there at the dock waiting. Always found me good fish. Hell, *great* fish."

"He tell you why he canceled?"

The doctor chuckled. "Said he'd hurt his back. I assumed he was just making an excuse. Of course I didn't say that."

"Why not?" I said.

"Ray's the best. Figure I'm lucky to have him."

I put down the phone and shook my head. Amazing. I couldn't get an appointment with my own dentist. Ray Florio made doctors wait and they loved him for it.

3

The appointment book was a dead end. Ray Florio had canceled a day-trip with an important client. Knowing Ray, he'd have done that for only one reason—because he had a new client who was willing to pay more money. A last-minute deal. If the deal had a name or a number, Ray hadn't bothered to write it down in his book.

I wondered if whoever trashed Ray's love nest knew that. It might be an interesting angle, but I wasn't quite sure how to play it. An ad in the papers? Too risky, might alert Detective Porter. And if I had a name, I wouldn't need to advertise, or so the killer might reason.

I decided the best way to circulate the information was to shoot off my big, boozy mouth. By way of preparation I located an old bottle of schnapps and daubed it on like aftershave. They'd be able to smell me coming. As to a convincing stagger, the secret is to walk like you're under low gravity conditions. The moon, say, or Mars. Pick a planet. And don't overdue it: A drunk has plenty of practice making his stagger subtle. Ditto for slurring the words.

The most likely place to find an appreciative audience for my drunk act was the Laughing Gull, Ray Florio's hangout. I snagged the leather notebook from his truck and entered the tiki bar with a song on my lips. Take my word for it, "The Wild Colonial Boy" isn't often heard at the Laughing Gull. Not my rendition anyway. Molly, the bar manager, poured me a double schnapps and a beer chaser.

"Must be your birthday, huh?" she asked, patting my cheek. "Have a blast, handsome."

I sipped the beer and managed to lose the schnapps in a potted palm. Then I ordered drinks all around. The local juiceheads at the tiki bar suddenly became attentive. As a ploy for more free drinks I was encouraged to sing another verse of "The Wild Colonial Boy." Since the first verse had exhausted my knowledge I obliged with "Wake Up Darling Corey," figuring a moonshine song couldn't miss in an outdoor bar. Wrong. Some tin-eared sneak turned on the jukebox, so I gave up on the sodden troubadour routine and started bragging about my recent good fortune.

"I'm in the money, honey," I confided to Molly. "Pour us another, hokay? An' for all my friends."

Molly obliged. It occurred to me that she had not been immune to Ray Florio's reputed charm.

"Damn shame," I said. "Ain't it a shame about poor Ray?"

"I sincerely hope he's burning in Hell," she said.

"That's as may be," I said, lowering my voice to a whisper that could have been overheard in Havana. "What matters to me, I've got a line on his rich clients. All I gotta do, reel 'em in, take their money."

The Laughing Gull has a mixed clientele of tourists, conchs, and the occasional fishing guide. My claim to Florio's client list excited some interest among the latter.

"What'd Ray do, leave it to you in his will?"

I shrugged, tucking the book back in my shirt pocket. "Let's just say I got lucky."

"Thought you was a tarpon man, Stash."

"Sure," I said. "Any fool can catch a tarpon. Bonefish is where the real money's at. So I'm switchin' over."

Somebody laughed. It sounded ugly. "Catchin' Ray Florio's clients is one thing. Catchin' them bones is another."

The bantering went on and on. When I knew my message had been read loud and clear I moved my act to Zach's Bar, and from there to Captain Tony's. I got pretty adept at ditching shots of schnapps. After a while I could almost feel the local grapevine humming with the news that T. D. Stash, the laziest fishing guide in the Florida Keys, had his mitts on Ray Florio's little leather-bound notebook.

Something was bound to happen. Trouble was, it happened sooner than I expected. After exiting Captain Tony's I proceeded west on Greene Street, intending to cut along the waterfront. Tired and full of beer and wishing I'd had the sense to bring my bike, or call a cab. I was turning south on Grinnel, steering for home, when something large and dark moved out of a doorway.

Whatever it was, it went for my head with an object that felt like a Louisville Slugger. I tried to duck. Almost made it.

* * *

Nel Kerry got back from the crime-busters' convention two days later. By that time I felt strong enough to walk over to the station house. Dizzy and weak in the knees, but pretty fair considering the thirteen stitches above my right ear and a minor concussion that made it hard to hold down breakfast.

"Lemme talk to the lieutenant," I asked the desk sergeant.

"Who's asking?"

"Tell him Che Guevara."

"Who?"

"Just a guy in the wrong place at the wrong time. Like me."

Nel Kerry didn't look happy to see me. He was staring at a framed picture on his desk when I lowered myself into the hard wooden chair he keeps for interviewing miscreants. Nel and I go way back. Once upon a time we were best friends, in the way only ten-year-olds can be best friends. Then Nel grew up to be a cop and I grew up to be an unlicensed troublemaker, and it's never been quite the same.

"'Lo, Nel. Solve a lot of crime up there in Miami?"

He looked up, winced at what he saw, then looked away. "Not one," he said laconically.

"See this pumpkin on my shoulders? Pal of yours tried to hit it out of the park."

That got his attention.

"This pal of yours," I continued, "he's untidy, know what I mean?"

Nel shrugged, waiting for me to go on.

"I passed out for a while. Passed out several times, in fact, until old Mrs. Sawyer came out for her milk and found me loitering under her rhododendrons. Lucky for me she called an ambulance instead of the cops."

Nel said, "What's that supposed to mean?"

"Means that before I passed out the second time I crawled to the doorway where my assailant was hiding. I found this."

I reached into my shirt pocket and put the contents on his desk. One short, moist cigar butt.

"Mitchell Porter have himself a pretty wife?" I asked. "Assuming he does, you've got motive."

Nel stared glumly at the cigar butt. "Sorry?" he said.

"Ray Florio. Half the town preferred him dead. Porter got to him first, that's all. One of his stool pigeons must have told him I had Ray's appointment book. Porter's name wasn't in there, but he didn't know that. So he came after me."

Nel stared at me, then at the desk. "That's your evidence, a cigar butt?"

I stroked the swatch of bandage on the side of my head. "I figure you can do better. There may be physical evidence on Ray's boat or in his trailer. I'm assuming Porter trashed the place, looking for anything that would tie him to Florio. And if Porter's as dumb as I think he is, he'll still have that notebook in his possession."

Nel sighed and opened his desk drawer. "He's not," he said.

"What?"

"Mitchell Porter. He's not as dumb as you think he is." Nel removed Ray Florio's notebook from the drawer and placed it on his desk, adjacent to the cigar butt. "He turned it over to me."

"He *gave* you that notebook?" I said, blinking at the damned thing. "He tell you how he got it?"

The lieutenant nodded, studying me. It was an uncomfortable feeling. So was the silence that ensued. Nel leaned back in his chair. The creaking sound made my head hurt more.

"You're not going to let this go, are you?" he said.

"No," I said.

"You'll keep poking until you turn up something."

"That's the way I do it, pretty much."

"You'll pursue Ray Florio's killer even though you hated Ray?"

I nodded. "I feel I'm obliged to," I said.

More silence. Nel picked up the framed picture and

studied it. He put it down gently and said, "Let's discuss this hypothetically, shall we?"

"Sure," I said, staring at the picture and the notebook. "Why not?"

Nel took his time. I could almost feel him searching for the words to make it right.

"For the purpose of this discussion, let's call the killer X," he said, his voice quiet and gentle. "Let's assume X has a teenage daughter. Thirteen. Looks older, acts younger."

"Ray was seducing a thirteen-year-old girl?"

"This is hypothetical, remember?" Nel said, giving me a hard look. "Okay, suppose X wants to get Florio alone. Not to kill him, you understand. Just to threaten a little. Make an impression somehow. Beg the son-of-a-bitch to leave his little girl alone. So X calls Florio and gives him a phony name, hires him for the day. X even manages to catch a bonefish, his very first. But he doesn't forget why he's there and when he gets the chance he confronts Florio. Who doesn't like it, not one bit. You know Ray, I guess. Big smile, bad temper. Mean. So he takes a swing at X. And X takes a swing right back. And knocks Florio out of the boat, where the miserable bastard has the audacity to drown in two feet of water. Just like that."

"Just like that?" I said. Whispering.

"Hypothetically," Nel said. "What could X do? It would look like cold-blooded murder, right? Death penalty murder. So he panics. Leaves Ray where he'll be found, drives the boat a good distance away, and wades ashore."

I closed my eyes. A little man was inside my head, trying to beat his way out. "How does Porter fit in?" I asked.

"Let's assume Porter had a suspect in custody. And X, not wanting to get an innocent man in trouble, confessed to Porter. Who decided to help X."

It was more than my poor head could take. Also the cigar butt was bothering me. Disgusting thing. I flicked it from the desk to the trash can and stood up.

"I better go home and think about this," I said. "Hypothetically."

Nel Kerry nodded. As I left he handed me Ray Florio's notebook. The leather made me itch. I dropped it in the water not far from Mutt's bait shack and waited just long enough to make sure the ink would bleed. Then I headed home.

The hammock was like a cool cocoon. I lay inside it, aware of the sea-laden air whispering through the screens, and thought about beautiful bonefish and beautiful young girls and the particular beautiful girl in the silver frame on Nel Kerry's desk. I thought about friends and enemies, love and hate, good and bad. About doing the right thing. I wanted to think about it for a long, long time.

Forever, maybe.

Bill Pronzini is a past president of PWA, a multiple Shamus Award winner, a multiple Edgar nominee, and a past recipient of PWA's Life Achievement Award. He is also the fourth of the four writers who have appeared in every PWA anthology. In 1988 he published his tour de force *"Nameless Detective" novel,* Shackles; *the most recent title in the series is* Jackpot (1990). *"Stakeout" is his latest "Nameless" short story.*

Stakeout

by Bill Pronzini

Four o'clock in the morning. And I was sitting huddled and ass-numb in my car in a freezing rainstorm, waiting for a guy I had never seen in person to get out of a nice warm bed and drive off in his Mercedes, thus enabling me to follow him so I could find out where he lived.

Thrilling work if you can get it. The kind that makes any self-respecting detective wonder why he didn't become a plumber instead.

Rain hammered against the car's metal surfaces, sluiced so thickly down the windshield that it transformed the glass into an opaque screen; all I could see were smeary blobs of light that marked the streetlamps along this block of 47th Avenue. Wind buffeted the car in forty-mile-an-hour gusts off the ocean nearby. Condensation had formed again on the driver's-door window, even though I had rolled it down half an inch; I rubbed some of the mist away and took another bleary-eyed look across the street.

This was one of San Francisco's older middle-class

residential neighborhoods, desirable—as long as you didn't mind fog-belt living—because Sutro Heights Park was just a block away and you were also within walking distance of Ocean Beach, the Cliff House, and Land's End. Most of the houses had been built in the thirties and stood shoulder-to-shoulder with their neighbors, but they seemed to have more individuality than the bland row-houses dominating the avenues farther inland; out here, California Spanish was the dominant style. Asians had bought up much of the city's west side housing in recent years, but fewer of those close to the ocean than anywhere else. A lot of homes in pockets such as this were still owned by older-generation, blue-collar San Franciscans.

The house I had under surveillance, number 9279, was one of the Spanish stucco jobs, painted white with a red tile roof. Yucca palms, one large and three small, dominated its tiny front yard. The three-year-old Mercedes with the Washington state license plates was still parked, illegally, across the driveway. Above it, the house's front windows remained dark. If anybody was up yet I couldn't tell it from where I was sitting.

I shifted position for the hundredth time, wincing as my stiffened joints protested with creaks and twinges. I had been here four and a half hours now, with nothing to do except to sit and wait and try not to fall asleep; to listen to the rain and the rattle and stutter of my thoughts. I was weary and irritable and I wanted some hot coffee and my own warm bed. It would be well past dawn, I thought bleakly, before I got either one.

Stakeouts . . . God, how I hated them. The passive waiting, the boredom, the slow, slow passage of dead time. How many did this make over the past thirty-odd years? How many empty, wasted, lost hours? Too damn many, whatever the actual figure. The physical discomfort was also becoming less tolerable, especially on nights like this, when not even a heavy overcoat and gloves kept the chill from penetrating bone-deep. I had lived fifty-eight years; fifty-eight is too old to sit all-night stakeouts on the best of cases, much less on a lousy split-fee skip-trace.

I was starting to hate Randolph Hixley, too, sight unseen. He was the owner of the Mercedes across the street and my reason for being here. To his various and sundry employers, past and no doubt present, he was a highly paid freelance computer consultant. To his ex-wife and two kids, he was a probable deadbeat who currently owed some $14,000 in back alimony and child support. To me and Puget Sound Investigations of Seattle, he was what should have been a small but adequate fee for routine work. Instead, he had developed into a minor pain in the ass. Mine.

Hixley had quit Seattle for parts unknown some four months ago, shortly after his wife divorced him for what she referred to as "sexual misconduct," and had yet to make a single alimony or child support payment. For reasons of her own, the wife had let the first two barren months go by without doing anything about it. On the occasion of the third due date, she had received a brief letter from Hixley informing her in tear-jerk language that he was so despondent over the breakup of their marriage he hadn't worked since leaving Seattle and was on the verge of becoming one of the homeless. He had every intention of fulfilling his obligations, though, the letter said; he would send money as soon as he got back on his feet. So would she bear with him for a while and please not sic the law on him? The letter was postmarked San Francisco, but with no return address.

The ex-wife, who was no dummy, smelled a rat. But because she still harbored some feelings for him, she had gone to Puget Sound Investigations rather than to the authorities, the object being to locate Hixley and deter-mine if he really was broke and despondent. If so, then she would show the poor dear compassion and understanding. If not, then she would obtain a judgment against the son-of-a-bitch and force him to pay up or get thrown in the slammer.

Puget Sound had taken the job, done some preliminary work, and then called a San Francisco detective—me—and farmed out the tough part for half the fee. That kind of cooperative thing is done all the time when the client isn't wealthy enough and the fee isn't large enough for the primary agency to send one of its own operatives to another state. No private detective likes to split fees, particularly when he's the one doing most of the work, but ours is sometimes a back-scratching business. Puget Sound had done a favor for me once; now it was my turn.

Skip-tracing can be easy or it can be difficult, depending on the individual you're trying to find. At first I figured Randolph Hixley, broke or not, might be one of the difficult ones. He had no known relatives or friends in the Bay Area. He had stopped using his credit cards after the divorce, and had not applied for new ones, which meant that if he was working and had money, he was paying his bills in cash. In Seattle he'd provided consultancy services to a variety of different companies, large and small, doing most of the work at home by computer link. If he'd hired out to one or more outfits in the Bay Area, Puget Sound had not been able to turn up a lead as to which they might be, so I probably wouldn't be able to either. There is no easy way to track down that information, not without some kind of insider pull with the IRS.

And yet despite all of that, I got lucky right away—so lucky I revised my thinking and decided, prematurely and falsely, that Hixley was going to be one of the easy traces after all. The third call I made was to a contact in the San Francisco City Clerk's office, and it netted me the information that the 1987 Mercedes 280 XL registered in Hixley's name had received two parking tickets on successive Thursday mornings, the most recent of which was the previous week. The tickets were for identical violations: illegal parking across a private driveway and illegal parking during posted street-cleaning hours. Both citations had been issued between seven and seven-thirty A.M. And in both instances, the address was the same: 9279 47th Avenue.

I looked up the address in my copy of the reverse city directory. 9279 47th Avenue was a private house occupied by one Anne Carswell, a commercial artist, and two other

Carswells, Bonnie and Margo, whose ages were given as eighteen and nineteen, respectively, and who I presumed were her daughters. The Carswells didn't own the house; they had been renting it for a little over two years.

Since there had been no change of registration on the Mercedes—I checked on that with the DMV—I assumed that the car still belonged to Randolph Hixley. And I figured things this way: Hixley, who was no more broke and despondent than I was, had met and established a relationship with Anne Carswell, and taken to spending Wednesday nights at her house. Why only Wednesdays? For all I knew, once a week was as much passion as Randy and Anne could muster up. Or it could be the two daughters slept elsewhere that night. In any case, Wednesday was Hixley's night to howl.

So the next Wednesday evening I drove out there, looking for his Mercedes. No Mercedes. I made my last check at midnight, went home to bed, got up at six A.M., and drove back to 47th Avenue for another look. Still no Mercedes.

Well, I thought, they skipped a week. Or for some reason they'd altered their routine. I went back on Thursday night. And Friday night and Saturday night. I made spot checks during the day. On one occasion I saw a tall, willowy redhead in her late thirties—Anne Carswell, no doubt—driving out of the garage. On another occasion I saw the two daughters, one blond, one brunette, both attractive, having a conversation with a couple of sly college types. But that was all I saw. Still no Mercedes, still no Randolph Hixley.

I considered bracing one of the Carswell women on a ruse, trying to find out that way where Hixley was living. But I didn't do it. He might have put them wise to his background and the money he owed, and asked them to keep mum if anyone ever approached them. Or I might slip somehow in my questioning and make her suspicious enough to call Hixley. I did not want to take the chance of warning him off.

Last Wednesday had been another bust. So had early Thursday—I drove out there at five A.M. that time. And so had the rest of the week. I was wasting time and gas and sleep, but it was the only lead I had. All the other skip-trace avenues I'd explored had led me nowhere near my elusive quarry.

Patience and perseverance are a detective's best assets; hang in there long enough and as often as not you find what you're looking for. Tonight I'd finally found Hixley and his Mercedes, back at the Carswell house after a two-week absence.

The car hadn't been there the first two times I drove by, but when I made what would have been my last pass, at twenty of twelve, there it was, once again illegally parked across the driveway. Maybe he didn't give a damn about parking tickets because he had no intention of paying them. Or maybe he disliked walking fifty feet or so, which was how far away the nearest legal curb space was. Or, hell, maybe he was just an arrogant bastard who thumbed his nose at the law any time it inconvenienced him. Whatever his reason for blocking Anne Carswell's driveway, it was a dumb mistake.

The only choice I had, spotting his car so late, was to stake it out and wait for him to show. I would have liked to go home and catch a couple of hours sleep, but for all I knew he wouldn't spend the entire night this time. If I left and came back and he was gone, I'd have to go through this whole rigmarole yet again.

So I parked and settled in. The lights in the Carswell house had gone off at twelve-fifteen and hadn't come back on since. It had rained off and on all evening, but the first hard rain started a little past one. The storm had steadily worsened until, now, it was a full-fledged howling, ripping blow. And still I sat and still I waited . . .

A blurred set of headlights came boring up 47th toward Geary, the first car to pass in close to an hour. When it went swishing by I held my watch up close to my eyes: 4:07. Suppose he stays in there until eight or nine? I thought. Four or five more hours of this and I'd be too stiff to move. It was meat-locker cold in the car. I couldn't start the engine and put the heater on because the exhaust, if not the idle, would call attention to my presence. I'd wrapped my legs and feet in the car blanket, which provided some relief; even so, I could no longer feel my toes when I tried to wiggle them.

The hard drumming beat of the rain seemed to be easing a little. Not the wind, though; a pair of back-to-back gusts shook the car as if it were a toy in the hands of a destructive child. I shifted position again, pulled the blanket more tightly around my ankles.

A light went on in the Carswell house.

I scrubbed mist off the driver's-door window, peered through the wet glass. The big front window was alight over there, behind drawn curtains. That was a good sign: People don't usually put their living room lights on at four A.M. unless somebody plans to be leaving soon.

Five minutes passed, while I sat chafing my gloved hands together and moving my feet up and down to improve circulation. Then another light went on—the front porch light this time. And a few seconds after that, the door opened and somebody came out onto the stoop.

It wasn't Randolph Hixley; it was a young blond woman wearing a trenchcoat over what looked to be a lacy nightgown. One of the Carswell daughters. She stood still for a moment, looking out over the empty street. Then she drew the trenchcoat collar up around her throat and ran down the stairs and over to Hixley's Mercedes.

For a few seconds she stood hunched on the sidewalk on the passenger side, apparently unlocking the front door with a set of keys. She pulled the door open, as if making sure it was unlocked, then slammed it shut again. She turned and ran back up the stairs and vanished into the house.

I thought: Now what was that all about?

The porch light stayed on. So did the light in the front room. Another three minutes dribbled away. The rain slackened a little more, so that it was no longer sheeting; the wind continued to wail and moan. And then things got even stranger over there.

First the porch light went off. Then the door opened and somebody exited onto the stoop, followed a few seconds later by a cluster of shadow-shapes moving in an awkward, confused fashion. I couldn't identify them or tell what they were doing while they were all grouped on the porch; the tallest yucca palm cast too much shadow and I was too far away. But when they started down the stairs, there was just enough extension of light from the front window to individuate the shapes for me.

There were four of them, by God—three in an uneven line on the same step, the fourth backing down in front of them as though guiding the way. Three women, one man. The man—several inches taller, wearing an overcoat and hat, head lolling forward as if he were drunk or unconscious—was being supported by two of the women.

They all managed to make it down the slippery stairs without any of them suffering a misstep. When they reached the sidewalk, the one who had been guiding ran ahead to the Mercedes and dragged the front passenger door open. In the faint outspill from the dome light, I watched the other two women, with the third one's help, push and prod the man inside. Once they had the door shut again, they didn't waste any time catching their breaths. Two of them went running back to the house; the third hurried around to the driver's door, bent to unlock it. She was the only one of the three, I realized then, who was fully dressed: raincoat, rainhat, slacks, boots. When she slid in under the wheel I had a dome-lit glimpse of reddish hair and a white, late-thirties face under the rainhat. Anne Carswell.

She fired up the Mercedes, let the engine warm up for all of five seconds, switched on the headlights, and eased away from the curb at a crawl, the way you'd drive over a surface of broken glass. The two daughters were already back inside the house, with the door shut behind them. I had long since unwrapped the blanket from around my legs; I didn't hesitate in starting my car. Or in trying to start it: The engine was cold and it took three whirring tries before it caught and held. If Anne Carswell had been driving fast, I might have lost her. As it was, with her creeping along, she was only halfway along the next block behind me when I swung out into a tight U-turn.

I ran dark through the rain until she completed a slow

turn west on Point Lobos and passed out of sight. Then I put on my lights and accelerated across Geary to the Point Lobos intersection. I got there in time to pick up the Mercedes' taillights as it went through the flashing yellow traffic signal at 48th Avenue. I let it travel another fifty yards downhill before I turned onto Point Lobos in pursuit.

Five seconds later, Anne Carswell had another surprise for me.

I expected her to continue down past the Cliff House and around onto the Great Highway; there is no other through direction once you pass 48th. But she seemed not to be leaving the general area after all. The Mercedes' brake lights came on and she slow-turned into the Merrie Way parking area above the ruins of the old Sutro Baths. The combination lot and overlook had only the one entrance/exit; it was surrounded on its other three sides by cliffs and clusters of wind-shaped cypress trees and a rocky nature trail that led out beyond the ruins of Land's End.

Without slowing, I drove on past. She was crawling straight down the center of the unpaved, potholed lot, toward the trees at the far end. Except for the Mercedes, the rain-drenched expanse appeared deserted.

Below Merrie Way, on the other side of Point Lobos, there is a newer, paved parking area carved out of Sutro Heights park, for sightseers and patrons of Louis' Restaurant opposite and the Cliff House bars and eateries farther down. It, too, was deserted at this hour. From the overlook above, you can't see this curving downhill section of Point Lobos; I swung across into the paved lot, cut my lights, looped around to where I had a clear view of the Merrie Way entrance. Then I parked, shut off the engine, and waited.

For a few seconds I could see a haze of slowly moving light up there, but not the Mercedes itself. Then the light winked out and there was nothing to see except wind-whipped rain and dark. Five minutes went by. Still nothing to see. She must have parked, I thought—but to do what?

Six minutes, seven. At seven and a half, a shape materialized out of the gloom above the entrance—

somebody on foot, walking fast, bent against the lashing wind. Anne Carswell. She was moving at an uphill angle out of the overlook, climbing to 48th Avenue.

When she reached the sidewalk, a car came through the flashing yellow at the intersection and its headlight beams swept over her; she turned away from them, as if to make sure her face wasn't seen. The car swished down past where I was, disappeared beyond the Cliff House. I watched Anne Carswell cross Point Lobos and hurry into 48th at the upper edge of the park.

Going home, I thought. Abandoned Hixley and his Mercedes on the overlook and now she's hoofing it back to her daughters.

What the hell?

I started the car and drove up to 48th and turned there. Anne Carswell was now on the opposite side of the street, near where Geary dead-ends at the park; when my lights caught her she turned her head away as she had a couple of minutes ago. I drove two blocks, circled around onto 47th, came back a block and then parked and shut down again within fifty yards of the Carswell house. Its porch light was back on, which indicated that the daughters were anticipating her imminent return. Two minutes later she came fast-walking out of Geary onto 47th. One minute after that, she climbed the stairs to her house and let herself in. The porch light went out immediately, followed fifteen seconds later by the light in the front room.

I got the car moving again and made my way back down to the Merrie Way overlook.

The Mercedes was still the only vehicle on the lot, parked at an angle just beyond the long terraced staircase that leads down the cliffside to the pitlike bottom of the ruins. I pulled in alongside, snuffed my lights. Before I got out, I armed myself with the flashlight I keep clipped under the dash.

Icy wind and rain slashed at me as I crossed to the Mercedes. Even above the racket made by the storm, I could hear the barking of sea lions on the offshore rocks beyond the Cliff House. Surf boiled frothing over those rocks, up along the cliffs and among the concrete foundations that are all that's left of the old bathhouse. Nasty night, and a nasty business here to go with it. I was sure of that now.

I put the flashlight up against the Mercedes' passenger window, flicked it on briefly. He was in there, all right; she'd shoved him over so that he lay half sprawled under the wheel, his head tipped back against the driver's door. The passenger door was unlocked. I opened it and got in and shut the door again to extinguish the dome light. I put the flash beam on his face, shielding it with my hand.

Randolph Hixley, no doubt of that; the photograph Puget Sound Investigations had sent me was a good one. No doubt, either, that he was dead. I checked his pulse, just to make sure. Then I moved the light over him, slowly, to see if I could find out what had killed him.

There weren't any discernible wounds or bruises or other marks on his body; no holes or tears or bloodstains on his damp clothing. Poison? Not that, either. Most any deadly poison produces convulsions, vomiting, rictus; his facial muscles were smooth and when I sniffed at his mouth I smelled nothing except Listerine.

Natural causes, then? Heart attack, stroke, aneurysm? Sure, maybe. But if he'd died of natural causes, why would Anne Carswell and her daughters have gone to all the trouble of moving his body and car down here? Why not just call Emergency Services?

On impulse I probed Hixley's clothing and found his wallet. It was empty—no cash, no credit cards, nothing except some old photos. Odd. He'd quit using credit cards after his divorce; he should have been carrying at least a few dollars. I took a close look at his hands and wrists. He was wearing a watch, a fairly new and fairly expensive one. No rings or other jewelry—but there was a white mark on his otherwise tanned left pinkie, as if a ring had been recently removed.

They rolled him, I thought. All the cash in his wallet and a ring off his finger. Not the watch because it isn't made of gold or platinum and you can't get much for a watch, anyway, these days.

But why? Why would they kill a man for a few hundred bucks? Or rob a dead man and then try to dump the body? In either case, the actions of those three women made no damn sense . . .

Or did they?

I was beginning to get a notion.

I backed out of the Mercedes and went to sit and think in my own car. I remembered some things, and added them together with some other things, and did a little speculating, and the notion wasn't a notion anymore—it was the answer.

Hell, I thought then, I'm getting old. Old and slow on the uptake. I should have seen this part of it as soon as they brought the body out. And I should have tumbled to the other part a week ago, if not sooner.

I sat there for another minute, feeling my age and a little sorry for myself because it was going to be quite a while yet before I got any sleep. Then, dutifully, I hauled up my mobile phone and called in the law.

They arrested the three women a few minutes past seven A.M. at the house on 47th Avenue. I was present for identification purposes. Anne Carswell put up a blustery protest of innocence until the inspector in charge, a veteran named Ginzberg, tossed the words "foul play" into the conversation; then the two girls broke down simultaneously and soon there were loud squawks of denial from all three: "We didn't hurt him! He had a heart attack, he died of a heart attack!" The girls, it turned out, were not named Carswell and were not Anne Carswell's daughters. The blonde was Bonnie Harper; the brunette was Margo LaFond. They were both former runaways from southern California.

The charges against the trio included failure to report a death, unlawful removal of a corpse, and felony theft. But the main charge was something else entirely.

The main charge was operating a house of prostitution.

* * *

Later that day, after I had gone home for a few hours' sleep, I laid the whole thing out for my partner, Eberhardt.

"I should have known they were hookers and Hixley was a customer," I said. "There were enough signs. His wife divorced him for 'sexual misconduct'; that was one. Another was how unalike those three women were—different hair colors, which isn't typical in a mother and her daughters. Then there were those sly young guys I saw with the two girls. They weren't boyfriends, they were customers too."

"Hixley really did die of a heart attack?" Eberhardt asked.

"Yeah. Carswell couldn't risk notifying Emergency Services; she didn't know much about Hixley and she was afraid somebody would come around asking questions. She had a nice discreet operation going there, with a small but high-paying clientele, and she didn't want a dead man to rock the boat. So she and the girls dressed the corpse and hustled it out of there. First, though, they emptied Hixley's wallet and she stripped a valuable garnet ring off his pinkie. She figured it was safe to do that; if anybody questioned the empty wallet and missing ring, it would look like the body had been rolled on the Merrie Way overlook, after he'd driven in there himself and had his fatal heart attack. As far as she knew, there was nothing to tie Hixley to her and her girls—no direct link, anyhow. He hadn't told her about the two parking tickets."

"Uh-huh. And he was in bed with all three of them when he croaked?"

"So they said. Right in the middle of a round of fun and games. That was what he paid them for each of the times he went there—seven hundred and fifty bucks for all three, all night."

"Jeez, three women at one time." Eberhardt paused, thinking about it. Then he shook his head. "*How?*" he said.

I shrugged. "Where there's a will, there's a way."

"Kinky sex—I never did understand it. I guess I'm old-fashioned."

"Me too. But Hixley's brand is pretty tame, really, compared to some of the things that go on nowadays."

"Seems like the whole damn world gets a little kinkier every day," Eberhardt said, "A little crazier every day, too. You know what I mean?"

"Yeah," I said, "I know what you mean."

Julie Smith has created three sleuths—lawyer Rebecca Schwartz, sometime-P.I. Paul McDonald (who also writes mysteries), and Officer Skip Langdon of the New Orleans Police Department. Attorney Schwartz appears in Death Turns a Trick, The Sourdough Wars, *and* Tourist Trap, *McDonald in* True-Life Adventure *and* Huckleberry Fiend. *Officer Langdon solves her first case in Smith's latest book,* New Orleans Mourning. *This is Smith's first appearance in a PWA anthology.*

Montezuma's Other Revenge

by Julie Smith

"McDonald, meet me at Perry's in an hour, okay?"

I stared at my computer, unable to imagine what was going to fill up the next three chapters of my current masterwork—I already had two chases and a brawl. And as my answering machine burbled on, I found myself also unable to imagine the arrogance of someone who expected me to drop this wildly important project at the snap of his larcenous fingers.

"I've got a job for you—same as last time, fifty-five dollars an hour."

Sixty, I thought, on account of the short notice.

"I've been burgled."

Suddenly the disembodied voice had my full attention. This was like a man biting a dog. Or kidding a kidder, maybe. The speaker was Booker Kessler, my very good friend—the burglar from the right side of the tracks who planned to stop burgling as soon as his psychoanalysis started kicking in. Booker could probably have gotten into Fort Knox if he put his mind to it. He was the quintessential second-story man, the pro of pros, the consummate criminal. If he'd been burgled, I could be at Perry's in forty-five minutes. This was one story I wanted to hear.

And then, of course, there was the matter of the money. Though I am a mystery writer by trade, the popular acclaim I deserve continues to elude me and so, therefore, do the bucks I need. I'm a former reporter ("investigative" is redundant, said my grizzled old city editor), and besides that I once had a great job writing client reports for a private detective. So every now and then someone asks me to do a little dicking around, which is no phrase of mine, but which tickles my girl friend, Sardis Kincannon, to death.

I was on the Bay Bridge heading for San Francisco in twenty minutes. By the time I hit Perry's it was almost exactly five o'clock. In minutes, the joint would be jumping with horny young professionals and flashy clerical help. I couldn't think why Booker had chosen it, except that he was Booker. A skinny runt in his mid-twenties, he had more women than a computer has bytes and he was always on the make for more.

He was there already, elegant in a sort of untailored jacket that looked like something of Sardis's, sipping a Perrier. A woman with hair like a lion's mane towered over him, peeling him a grape, most probably. He waved me over. "McDonald! This is Angie. Angie, Paul. Angie, Paul and I are going to talk business, okay?"

Without a word, Angie went slinking away, obedient as one of the Stepford wives.

"So who'd burgle a burglar?" said I, followed by, "I'll have a gin and tonic, please."

"Well, actually, I just said that to get you interested."

"You mean you weren't burgled? I'm going to pick up my toys and go home."

"Well, I think I was. Technically. I mean, I'm not sure. But it wasn't breaking and entering. I let the thief in of my own free will, and spent the afternoon pleasing and delighting her beyond all human imagining."

"Ungrateful bitch." I tried not to laugh, but apparently not hard enough. I ended up spewing gin all over the bar.

"It's not funny, McDonald. She came sixteen times."

That did it. By now, I had slipped off the bar stool and was rolling about on the floor in a manner that was starting to make people think I was weird. The nurses in the crowd were discussing ways to keep me from biting my tongue. But I couldn't help it. The goddamn peanut was so goddamn arrogant about his thrice-weekly conquests. It was about time he got his comeuppance. So to speak.

"I met her at the Billboard Cafe," he said.

I stared down at the bar and shook my head. Only Booker would pick up someone at the Billboard Cafe. It had good food, an arty crowd mixed in with a lot of suits, and it stood on the worst corner in San Francisco. Every day at noon, the line for lunch stretched around the block. A different kind of breadline for that particular corner, though the neighborhood in general—especially at night—was more or less the hottest ticket in town.

The Billboard was part of the chic SoMa—South of Market—scene. So were galleries, nightclubs, lofts, restaurants, artists, nightcrawlers, Armani-clad Iranians, everyone else on the cutting edge, and the preppies and yuppies who popped down now and then to get a gander at the action. Since everyone in town went to the Billboard for lunch, theoretically there was no reason you couldn't meet someone there, except that how would there be time with a new crowd always pressing to get in? And who ever meets anyone at lunch, anyway?

"She just walked up to my table," said Booker. "I was with another woman, too. She said she'd seen me around and always wanted to meet me and thought she'd introduce herself. So I asked her to join us. And then Kristi had to go back to work—"

"Hold it. She just walked up to your table? Weren't you a tiny bit suspicious?"

He shrugged. "Hell, no. They do that all the time."

. She introduced herself. What's

CeeCee what?"

, not succeeding even slightly in
most nonchalant guy on Union
, McDonald. There wasn't any reason

"Jesus, Booker. For your sake, I hope you practice safe
sex."

"Jealous?"

"Okay. So you and CeeCee ended up at your place—"

"Where she admired the artwork. One in particular—
and after she left I realized it was missing."

"Oh, no!" For the first time I was genuinely sympathetic.
Booker has spent his ill-gotten gains on a truly fabulous art
collection—mostly paintings, but some sculpture—of
which he's justly proud.

"Actually, it wasn't anything that special. I mean, it's a
pretty good piece, but I'd only had it a day or two and
hadn't fallen in love yet."

"What was it?"

"A sculpture—a ceramic piece, actually—by a Central
American artist who signs his work 'Miguel.' He's just
starting to catch on in this country. I know this sounds
weird, but he works in a sort of pre-Columbian style."

"You're right. It sounds weird."

"Well, he doesn't copy the pieces, but he's inspired by
them—he takes off from them, combines designs, sort of.
The piece I lost was kind of a little squatting toad that also
looked a little like a crocodile. About so high." He held his
hands six inches apart. "And CeeCee had one of those
oversized purses."

"What color is the sculpture?"

"Plain terra cotta."

"And what does CeeCee look like?"

"Oh, about five-four, a hundred and five pounds. Last
seen wearing black leather mini. Hair black for the first
couple of inches—at the roots, that is—and white for the

next eight or ten. Sticks out about a foot. B
lips. And a lot of black stuff on the eyes."

"Bleeagh."

"Cutest little ass you ever saw."

"Every second female south of Market answers
description."

"That's why I need a very good dick to find her."

I could have made a dick joke, but it didn't seem
appropriate. I said, more or less sarcastically, "Where do
you think I should look? Just hit the nightclubs till dawn?"

"Unless you figure out how to dress in the next few
hours, you wouldn't get into any of them."

"Where, then?"

"As it happens, I do know something about her. She
works at the Clay Gallery—where I purchased the sculpture."

There was no point asking him why he'd rather hire me
than just walk over to the gallery and sit down until
CeeCee gave him back his sculpture. I already knew.
Paranoia. The gallery owner might call the cops, or
CeeCee might say he'd given it to her and *she* might call the
cops, or a cop might just happen to drop in to buy a work
of art. And Booker was allergic to cops till his analysis
started working.

And so at noon the next day—galleries never seem to
open before lunchtime—I sauntered into the Clay Gallery
(which wasn't on Clay Street, but south of Market) and
asked to see CeeCee, which is hard to say. CeeCee, it
seemed, had taken the day off to pack.

"Pack?" said I, wondering if she were skipping town, and
if she were, how many hours work I could get out of a
cross-country chase.

"She got a one-woman show in L.A."

"Ah. She's an artist, too."

The person I was talking to could have been CeeCee
herself except that her hair was blue instead of white and
hung to her right shoulder, yet grew only half an inch long
above her left ear, which was pierced six times and
harbored six earrings. Dawn, her name was.

"She's a ceramicist," said Dawn, indicating a multicolored amoeba-like object about half my height and at least my weight. And I am not considered a small man.

"That's hers? I mean, she had a lot of those to pack?"

"She may take the whole week off," said Dawn.

I leaned closer, aping a smitten collector. A tiny placard said the artist was Cynthia C. Hollander. It was a start.

There was a C. C. Hollander on a small Potrero Hill street, and I figured that had to be my woman—or close enough. If she wasn't the right CeeCee, this one probably got enough of her calls to know where to find her. I headed over there.

Hers was a downstairs apartment, up a short flight of steps to a little porch. On the porch were some shards—as if a ceramicist, in her haste to get ready for her big one-woman show, had dropped a piece of her work. And yet these were plain terra cotta, not glazed as CeeCee's other piece had been. There was mail in the mailbox. No one answered the bell. I couldn't see in from the porch, but there was a big uncurtained window that looked out on the street.

So of course I climbed down, found a few bricks to stand on, held onto the windowsill, and risked arrest by hoisting myself up high enough to see in. The place had been tossed, and thoroughly. The kind of tossed where they rip the upholstery to shreds.

I tried the door, which didn't open at first, but Booker had taught me the credit card trick. In ten minutes— Booker could have done it in ten seconds—I had the door open. And by the stink I knew someone was dead.

CeeCee was under the sofa cushions, still wearing the black leather mini. Her throat had been slit.

In my reporting days I saw a lot of bodies, but I'd never seen this particular brand of mutilation and I felt my gorge rising in a manner unbecoming even to a part-time dick. That wasn't all. Sweat broke out on my forehead and my head felt light and swimmy.

I'm not the sort who faints—the job description precludes it—but if I were I couldn't have done it in peace because of the hideous noise that suddenly assailed my ears. I realized the burglar alarm had gone off with me standing over a body in a place which I had just broken into and entered. I heard sirens, too. Or I thought I did until I shook my head once or twice to clear it.

At about that time, the telephone—which wasn't a burglar alarm at all—stopped ringing and a voice that said it was CeeCee's spoke to the caller. And then another female voice said, "Hi, CeeCee, it's just Mom calling. Good news, I think. Dad double-checked and it turns out we *could* cash out a bond and lend you the money for the packing and shipping charges. At least I think it'll cover them. It might help anyway. Give me a call when you get in."

As CeeCee's mom talked to her ex-daughter, I took great gulps of air, nor caring what it smelled like, just needing to get it into my lungs. On some weird kind of automatic pilot, not knowing why, I followed the voice to its origin, an answering machine in a bedroom in roughly the same condition as the living room.

I took a minute there to pull myself together and then I went over the whole place. Apparently, there was another occupant—a female roommate who had the second bedroom. Her room hadn't been spared either. Nor had the bathroom and kitchen. And that was it—no studio, so I gathered CeeCee had one elsewhere.

I went back to her room to call the cops, and on a whim played back her messages. There were others from her mother, one from Dawn at the gallery, a couple from a wimpy-sounding guy named Jeremy, and two that caught my attention.

"It's Rico, baby," said a whispery, nasty, smug, self-satisfied voice. "We've got Sabina. She'd make a real nice sacrifice, and it just happens we could use one right now. Or maybe if you return my property we could find a cat or a chicken."

The second was also from Rico. It came after one Jeremy and two Moms, so probably a reasonable amount of time had gone by in the interim. "Hi, babe. We're getting Sabina ready now. The Aztecs may have used virgins, but we do the opposite. We sacrifice our maidens several different kinds of ways, if you take my meaning.

She's on the altar now, and so is one of our high priests. I've already had my turn with her—"

CeeCee picked up the phone at this point, sounding out of breath, "Rico? Rico, I just got in. And guess what, I made a big discovery. I dropped the sculpture, asshole. So now I'll set the terms, okay? Bring Sabina home now! And also bring five thousand dollars—" Here, the machine clicked off, having recorded for as long as it was programmed to record.

But I got the idea. Dropping the statue had given CeeCee a whole new outlook on things—apparently because it contained information she could use for blackmail.

CeeCee had probably kept her Rolodex on the table by her bed, along with her telephone, but nothing was where it should have been. I found it on the floor under some pieces of what had once been a mattress.

There was only one Rico—Rico Rainey—and I was pretty sure he was the right one because his address was a place called the Hall of Montezuma. It was on Minna Street, which is more of an alley than otherwise, so it couldn't be too hall-like, but I could understand the temptation Rico had been faced with if he had an Aztec theme on his hands.

I phoned Booker and quickly filled him in. When he was breathing regularly again, I said, "Listen, I'm calling Blick now. If I stay and tell him all this, it'll be at least a half hour, maybe an hour and a half, before the cops make a move.

"Sabina must be the roommate. Maybe she's dead already and maybe she's not, but I've been in a house with a corpse and her mother's voice and some other stuff for twenty minutes, and I don't feel like waiting for Blick to get off his ass and find out. You want to meet me at the Hall of Montezuma, whatever the fuck that is, in ten minutes?"

"Yeah." I could barely hear Booker's voice. I knew he was feeling bad because he had made love to CeeCee and now she was dead. Kind of a king-sized postcoital *tristesse*. But I don't mean to make fun—Booker may be a criminal, but is otherwise a person of sterling character and deep sensitivity. He also hates violence—and since we were bound to encounter some at the Hall of Montezuma, he must have been good and stirred up by CeeCee's death. He wouldn't bring a gun, I knew. He didn't believe in the things.

And then I called my least favorite cop, Homicide Inspector Howard Blick. "I want to report a homicide—"

"Who is this?"

"Jean-Paul Sartre. That's J-e- . . ."

"Spell it!"

"I'm trying to. J-e- . . ."

"G-e-what?"

Too late I realized it was going to take the whole ten minutes I had just to get the name spelled properly. If Blick had become a tubewinder instead of a cop, the San Francisco Police Department would have been better served.

"Forget it," I said, and gave the address.

"McDonald, is that you, goddammit? It better not be you, you douchebag!"

I should have kept my mouth shut, but Blick pushes my buttons. "Up yours, dicknose," I remarked sweetly, and then I got the hell out.

Back in the light of day, everything seemed very vivid, very bright, and somewhat larger than life, which I felt damned glad to be living at the moment. Details caught my eye: a single rose blooming in CeeCee's tiny front yard, or front flower bed—actually, just a strip of dirt—a ticket on a car parked illegally across the street; Ceecee's handwriting on a letter in her mailbox . . .

I investigated. Yes, the same writing as on the Rolodex cards, and the return address was none other than her own—she'd sent herself a letter. I pulled it out and felt it. Heavy. I ripped it open—a locker key to God knew where. I put it in my pocket.

Booker was waiting for me, in jeans and a black leather jacket that had probably cost slightly less than I'd get for the book I was working on. His car was parked in front of the Hall, as unprepossessing a place as everything else on Minna Street. You found it by its label next to the second floor hall. The door was

e go in?"

ne asks, we'll say we took a
ie shores of Tripoli."

much more hall-like space
... A couple of torches burned on
...ning Rico must have meant when he
...ie altar—though no maiden was currently being
...ped on it. In fact, there was a caged chicken on it. The
odor of incense hung thick in the air.

The place had no windows, but the walls were white,
newly painted, and hung with pre-Columbian masks that
showed up well in the torchlight. Statues—also pre-
Columbian, or maybe fakes or Miguels—stood on pedes-
tals that lined the walls. A bunch of them had been massed
around the altar.

On the floor were small rugs, and some kind of weird
music was playing. The whole effect wasn't so much eerie
as trying way too hard for eerie and ending up bogus.

The thing that most spoiled the effect, to tell you the
truth, was the table at the top of the stairs with a box
marked "Donations" on it. Not to mention the woman who
sat behind it, her short, spiky magenta hairdo looking as if
it would be wrecked beyond repair by an Aztec headdress.

"Hi," she said. "I'm Sabina."

Booker and I looked at each other, then quickly cased
the Hall. Empty—or so it seemed, anyhow. I turned back
to Sabina, put my face close to hers, smiled, and spoke very
low. "Hi," I said. "CeeCee's dead."

Her eyes were blue, I noticed, as they expanded to
resemble blue Frisbees, full of fear. Her jaw went slack and
I thought for a minute she was going to scream. She didn't
but she glanced around, terrified, as if she were surrounded. If it was an act, it was a good one.

I took her wrist. "Come on. We'll get you out of here."

She didn't even stop to grab her purse. She wasn't the
soul of discretion, either. She had on those black, lace-up
old-lady shoes that hip young ladies love so much and that
have little heels on them that sound like a parade. She set

her legs going like two blades of an eggbeat
pursued by demons on uncarpeted stairs, and th
a thing we could do to stop her. We simply tore a
and once outside, slammed ourselves into Booke
peeling out like characters in an Eddie Murphy mov

She was sitting on my lap in the front seat, since no o
had time for the back, and she was crying now. Suddenl
she caught on that she had leaped extremely precipitately
into the arms of strangers. "Omigod!" she wailed. "Who
are you?"

I didn't know where to start, but Booker said, "Are you
CeeCee's roommate?"

She nodded.

"I'm the guy that bought the sculpture."

That seemed to satisfy her.

"We went looking for it," I said, "and found her."

I was all for leaving SoMa altogether, but Booker was a
fan of Hamburger Mary's, so we went there after making
a deal with Sabina—our half of the story for her half.

Bucked up by a few beers, into which she would have
been crying if such a thing were possible without making a
spectacle of oneself, she explained first about the Hall of
Montezuma.

"It's a cult, I guess you'd call it. I mean, Rico says it's a
revival of the Aztec religion—they have all these weird
rituals and chicken sacrifices. I don't know—they get a
pretty good crowd some nights. Students go in for that
sort of thing, you know, and some from the Art Institute
went a few times and word got out about the artworks."

She paused for a minute, looking puzzled. "They aren't
Aztec, is the only thing—and a lot of them aren't really
pre-Columbian. But anyhow, most of them are pretty
good. So people started going just to see them like it was a
gallery. The rituals were like this added attraction or
something. Anyhow, that's how CeeCee and I found the
place."

"So who's Rico?"

"Rico? He's—uh—the priest, I guess you'd call it. He's—
um—really handsome and kind of scary, like when he slits
the chickens' throats, you know what I mean?"

We nodded.

"I don't know—that turns some people on, I guess. I mean, he has these women all over him all the time. CeeCee was one of them. He came around our place a lot." She lowered her gaze, for a moment actually affording the tears a beer target. "He started coming on to me and, I don't know, I guess I was just competitive with CeeCee. I started seeing him over at the Hall. And then I kind of got hooked on him." She looked up again, the hard part over.

"What happened was, CeeCee got this big opportunity down in L.A.—I mean, it really is a big deal—it could make her a lot of money. But have you seen that elephantine stuff of hers? It was going to cost a fortune to get it there. So she asked Rico to lend her some money and he wouldn't do it. She asked him, see, because she knew how much goes into that Hall—it costs fifteen bucks to come to a ritual, and then they always collect more money once you're there and everything. I mean, it really is a cult, although—" She stopped, as if trying to collect her thoughts.

"Although what?" I prompted.

"Something about Rico—he founded the thing and he's the high priest and everything, but he doesn't really talk about it when he's, like, off duty. Anyway, a lot of money comes through there, but the bastard wouldn't lend her any. He said it belonged to the church and he couldn't.

"Well, that pissed CeeCee off, and I guess she was a little desperate, anyhow, so she took one of the statues. It wasn't hard because she sometimes worked the desk, like I was doing today, and I guess she thought he wouldn't notice. Anyway, she knew perfectly well what she could get for a Miguel at the gallery where she worked. To tell you the truth, she also knew they wouldn't ask a lot of questions about where she got it. Everything's on consignment, of course, but if someone bought it, she'd get just about enough to cover her expenses. And they have a list of preferred customers who'd been looking for something of the sort. They'd just arrange a private sale, the customer would never know the statue was stolen, and everybody'd be happy."

"Call me Mr. Preferred," said Booker.

Sabina nodded. "So it was sold almost the minute she stole it. But meanwhile I didn't know anything about any of this. I mean, I knew he hadn't lent her the money, but I didn't know she'd stolen something from him. So the way he told it, it got me all outraged—like how dare she! And he asked me to stay at the hall a day or two and pretend to be kidnapped." She shrugged.

"So I said okay. Look, I was jealous. I'm an artist, too, and she was the one with the big break and everything—" Booker waved a hand, explaining that she didn't have to explain.

"Anyway, that was the last I heard. I didn't know she'd gotten it back—he didn't tell me—all's he said was he hadn't heard from her." Her eyes got big again. "And then he started talking about how that statue had a curse on it. I mean, it's not even *old*. And he said he was worried about her and all—"

I said, "You were getting suspicious, weren't you?"

She nodded, miserable. When she spoke, her voice was tiny. "I was really getting scared."

"With good reason. When she tried to blackmail him, he apparently didn't waste any time."

She turned Frisbee eyes on me. "Would he have killed me, too?"

"Maybe." Actually, I didn't think he would have, because he hadn't yet, but I needed her help and I wanted her mad as hell.

The plan we proceeded to put together was simple, and the first part went beautifully. That was the part where Sabina phoned Rico, said she had what was in the sculpture, or anyway, the key to it, that she'd be glad to give it to him for a small finder's fee—say a thousand or so—and would he meet her later?

The next part went okay, too. That was the part where we got Sabina some handcuffs and a gun—actually, one of those really realistic-looking squirt guns.

The third part was the actual confrontation, due to occur at seven P.M. in a very narrow alley near China Basin. We'd blocked one end with my car and the other with Booker's, so no one could drive in. If Rico came alone, we could take him; if he didn't, Sabina would have to get away in one of the cars.

At seven sharp she stood between the cars, more or less in front of two one-story buildings across from each other. Booker was on top of one building, I was on top of the other. A man entered the alley—alone.

"Rico?" called Sabina.

"Yeah."

He kept coming till he'd passed Booker's car, had gotten about ten feet away from her. She was holding the gun with two hands, like the cops do on TV. It looked pretty real.

Sabina shouted, "Don't come any closer."

Rico stopped.

"Empty your pockets."

This was the perfect time to jump him, but we'd agreed we wouldn't do it till we were sure he wasn't armed. He threw a packet of bills at Sabina. She threw the locker key at him.

Cautiously, Rico knelt to pick it up. The moment had arrived. The plan was for me, being far the larger, to jump him and subdue him, Sabina helping with firearm threats. If there was real trouble, Booker would further surprise Rico by jumping on his head. Otherwise, he'd stay put till Sabina had produced the cuffs, and then he'd come down and cuff Rico while I sat on him or something.

The only problem was, I slipped as I was starting to jump. I regained my balance, but Rico had caught on by this time, and he moved quickly. So did Sabina. And so, alas, did Booker. He meant to jump on Rico to take up the slack, but unfortunately, he landed on Sabina. She hollered, they both went down, it was general bedlam, and Rico took off running.

I jumped now, landing more or less safely—at any rate not breaking anything—and took off after him. He ran another block down our alley, then turned down a main street, and then into another alley. I wasn't even close to catching him, but eventually he had to run out of steam. Or I did. In this neighborhood—industrial by day, deserted at night—we could probably trot about for hours unmolested. It was just a question of endurance. And I was panting like a husky in hell.

I ran on, following the far distant footsteps, vaguely aware of some noise far behind me, blood pounding in my ears. And suddenly I realized Rico's footsteps had stopped. But too late. "Slow down, bro'," said a voice.

I not only slowed, I stopped. Two guys who looked burnt out—one white, one Chicano—had headed Rico off and captured him. That would have been great except that they didn't seem to be planning to turn him over to me. One was holding him by his collar, a knife at his throat. The other also had a knife. He took a step toward me.

And then I became better aware of the clatter behind me. About a millisecond later a female voice said, "Police. Freeze or I'll blow your heads off."

We all froze. The burnouts dropped their knives. And then Rico shouted, "Sabina!" and unfroze. He headed toward me, trying to get past. Now I really did jump him.

And a male voice said, "Police. Freeze or I'll blow your heads off."

It was one of the goddamn muggers. Both of them were cops on some kind of surveillance job involving drugs, but we found out that part quite a bit later.

You'd think Blick would have been so grateful he'd have practically kissed my hand, but instead he made us stay at the Hall all night (Hall of Justice, not Montezuma), telling and retelling our stories, and not giving us anything back in return.

It all came out later, though. We had unwittingly, it seemed, cracked a major gang of art thieves. That is, CeeCee had. The key opened a locker in the Greyhound terminal that held a small pre-Columbian gold pendant. CeeCee had apparently dropped the Miguel and realized when it cracked open what Rico was up to, which was buying legitimate artworks and bringing them through customs filled with much more valuable stolen ones—part of a cache taken from a museum a few years ago. She'd stashed the pendant in the locker and mailed the key to herself, in case Rico tried to get tough—but she'd under-estimated how tough he was going to get.

The pieces were being brought in slowly, one by one, through customs stations that didn't tend to X-ray. They were sold to well-heeled buyers out of Rico's pseudo-Aztec storefront cult, which made a nice cover. He didn't really need it, though. He just liked the drama, power, women, and extra bucks he got out of it. He had a record as long as a fishing line.

Incidentally, there was a reward involved—from the museum that lost the loot. Booker wasn't eligible, having melted into the shadows during the alley confrontation in which the "P" word was mentioned, but Sabina and I would have happily split it. That is, we would have if Blick hadn't explained about the nineteen or twenty things he would charge us with if we tried to claim it.

He and the two undercover gorillas got it, a turn of events I blame on the ghost of a certain well-known Aztec emperor. After all, Booker and Sabina and I were the second bunch of gringos to come along and demolish the Aztec religion.

Dick Stodghill introduced P.I. Henry Paige in the second PWA anthology, Mean Streets. *He has had many short stories published in magazines, and is a semi-regular in the pages of* Alfred Hitchcock's Mystery Magazine. *Here he and Henry put in a second appearance in one of our anthologies.*

Bypass for Murder

by Dick Stodghill

For the third time in less than an hour Henry Paige turned to look out the window of his office high above Main Street. There was no window. He mumbled a blunt, descriptive word, one he never used in mixed company, then began whistling tunelessly through his teeth.

Ron Blades stood at the open door, drumming his knuckles against the frame. "Anything wrong, Henry?"

Paige gave him a cold look, then an even more frigid smile. "Nothing that a little fresh air and sunshine wouldn't cure. Even the patter of rain against the window if it's raining outside. In here who knows?"

Blades looked around the cubbyhole of an office. "It isn't much of a place to work, Henry. Makeshift. Not at all cheerful. I'm going to see if we can't come up with something better for you."

"I don't care if it's better, just so it has a window."

"I'll work on it, Henry. In the meantime, would you do a little checking on this for me?" He dropped a file folder on the desk. "It's no big deal, but anything you can dig up that might help me defend the insurance company's position would be appreciated. As of now I have nothing."

262

pened the folder. "Anything I need to know
___ ___at's in here?" He looked up quickly, cocking an
eyebrow. "Ron, there *isn't* anything in here."

"Not much. That's what I mean, Henry. A woman was
electrocuted, but Michiana Life is contending its double
indemnity clause for accidental death doesn't apply because the insured's negligence was responsible. The victim's husband filed suit last week and Michiana retained us
to represent them. Look it over, see what you can dig up.
Don't push too hard, I'm not really expecting anything."

Paige riffled the few sheets of paper in the folder. "This
husband, he didn't waste any time, did he? It only happened two months and two days ago."

Blades smiled a laconic smile. "He probably figures he
could do twice as much with fifty thousand as with
twenty-five, and he wants to do it now."

"Give me a hint, Ron. What kind of stuff are you hoping
I'll come up with?"

"I don't know, Henry. Anything at all, I guess. Maybe
something to show the woman was habitually reckless. You
know, accident-prone through her own carelessness."

"For starters, keeping a radio next to a washing machine
in the basement wasn't too prudent."

Blades laughed while turning to leave. "You're dating
yourself, Henry. Nobody calls them washing machines
anymore. They're just washers today."

"Yeah," Paige said under his breath, "and I'll bet you
don't call your refrigerator an ice box."

As usual, Jack McKelvey was on the end stool at the
tavern on Chestnut Boulevard just off Fourth Street. Paige
went over, shaking his head more in admiration than
disapproval. "Have you moved from here since last night,
Mac?"

McKelvey gave him a stony glance. "You've been mean-
er'n a three-legged dog with fleas since you closed up the
agency and went to work for that bunch of ambulance
chasers downtown. It emasculated you, Henry. You've lost
your self-respect."

"Smoking another cigar, huh, Mac? I thought the doctor

told you to give them up. Besides, don't you know people around you don't like cigars?"

"To hell with the doctor. To hell with people, too."

"Come on, Mac. You can't go through life saying to hell with people."

"I can't? Well, I sure wish somebody had thought to tell me that before my seventy-fifth birthday."

"So do I." Paige eased onto a stool, stifling a yawn. "Maybe you're right about closing my agency. I'm bored, Mac. Working for somebody else, it's no way to live. I wish something exciting would come along."

"Me too," said McKelvey. "Some young chick about fifty-five that knows how to have a good time."

"Very funny. I'm talking about work."

"That's all you ever talk about. Girls are more fun."

"Oh, can it, Mac. Do you remember a woman getting electrocuted up on Eighteenth Street a couple of months back?"

"Nope."

"By a radio in her basement."

"I said I don't remember. What about her?"

"Nothing much. The insurance company doesn't want to pay double indemnity."

McKelvey laughed sourly. "Name me one time, Paige, when an insurance company ever wanted to pay anything. So you're gonna help 'em not pay it, right?"

"I'm going to check it out, if that's what you mean. I can't see that the company has a prayer, though. Guess I'll run a neighborhood check in the morning, then talk to the bereaved husband. For what it's worth, he filed suit before the grass had time to come up on his late wife's grave."

"Want some help? I could run the check for you."

Paige thought back to the time McKelvey had taught him the business. Right after the war when McKelvey Investigations was the biggest agency in town. "You haven't worked in ten years, Mac. You've hardly moved from that stool in ten years. Maybe you should check yourself into a nursing home."

"Maybe I should flatten your nose."

"Maybe you can do some checking around the husband's office out in west Akron for me."

"Maybe."

"Good morning," said Paige. The beefy woman who had answered his knock eyed him suspiciously. He smiled and continued, "I'm running a routine credit check on one of your neighbors"—he pretended to read from the form in his hand—"Karl Schmall. Are you acquainted with him?"

The woman resisted his charm. "What's this about?"

Paige gave her another reassuring smile. "Just routine. I imagine he's buying a new car or something like that. As far as you know, is he a man of good character?"

"As far as I know. I've never had much contact with the man. We don't socialize with the neighbors, you know."

"Sometimes that's smart. But to your knowledge he doesn't come home drunk every night?" Again Paige smiled, hoping it was an endearing one. "Doesn't beat his wife or anything like that?"

The woman frowned. "His wife is dead. Doesn't your form say that?"

Paige glanced down at the empty spaces on the sheet of paper, shaking his head. "For goodness sake, imagine that. Did she die recently?"

"A few months ago. She was electrocuted. A terrible thing, just terrible. Very upsetting to the neighborhood."

"I can imagine. How did it happen?"

"She was doing the laundry and the basement floor was wet. She reached over to turn on a radio and . . ."

Paige went on shaking his head. "Tchk, tchk! That wasn't a smart thing to do. Not smart at all. Was she a careless person that way?"

"Not at all. She was a quiet, thoughtful young woman. Very pleasant and courteous. Of course, I didn't know her more than just to say hello. Now, if that's all . . ."

"Yes, and thanks for your help." Some help, Paige was thinking as he went down the front steps and on to the next house. Like most in the neighborhood of tall trees north of Broad Boulevard, the immaculate two-story dated to the mid-1920s, the time when Cuyahoga Falls was losing its identity and becoming a bedroom community for Akron. As he looked over the familiar surroundings, Paige found it startling that he could remember when the subdivision was only a decade old and many of the trees were saplings.

The answers he received at the second house were similar to those at the first. He went on to the third. The woman who came to the door was even older than Paige, raw-boned and crafty-eyed. After listening to him repeat his pretext she opened the screen door. "Come inside," she ordered. "I don't like to stand out here talking for all the neighbors to see."

Paige glanced around but saw no sign of prying eyes. He followed the woman to a musty living room crowded with furniture dating to the time when the house was new and the woman had been a young girl. While waving him to a chair she said, "So that lowlife across the street is out spending the blood money, eh?"

"Lowlife? Blood money?"

"Well, maybe not blood money. I'm not implying he killed her or anything, understand. But, mister, if you think he was sorry to see her go, you've got another think coming."

"Why do you say that?"

"Because—now I don't nib, understand—anybody could see how he treated her. Why, she hadn't been under the ground a week when Myrt . . . well, no need to mention names. Anyway, he was seen having dinner at The Glens with a blond hussy. Laughing and carrying on, disgusting it was. At least that's what I've been told."

"Just unwinding, perhaps? You know, putting it out of his mind."

"Too bad he didn't put his next-door neighbor out of his mind. It was shameful the way he carried on right under his wife's nose, and Nina being such a sweet person and all. It broke up the Dooleys' marriage, and it served the little strumpet right. Now Karl Schmall doesn't give Molly Dooley the time of day and it's exactly what she deserves, the harlot."

Paige coughed. "None of the other neighbors mentioned any of this. You, uh, seem to know the people better."

"I have eyes and a brain. And I hear things. Not that I pry or listen to gossip, understand, but a person sees and hears things. After all, Karl Schmall and Molly Dooley were the talk of the town."

"Guess I missed hearing it, but I've been out of touch. Nina Schmall's accident, it must have been upsetting to everyone."

"Of course it was. She was such a sweet thing and all. If it had happened any other way, I'll tell you there would have been some suspicious people around. As it was, well . . ."

"But you're not saying it wasn't an accident?"

"I'm saying it certainly was convenient for some people, that's all. Now, what did you say that no-account is buying before his wife is cold in her grave?"

While ringing Molly Dooley's doorbell Paige decided to abandon his pretext. He was surprised when she came to the door wearing a wrinkled dress with a seam ripped open on one side. She was in her forties, older than he had expected, and twenty pounds overweight. Her mousy hair, angular features, and untidy appearance didn't fit the image of the femme fatale that had taken shape in his mind. He would have to remember to tell McKelvey that Molly Dooley was dowdy.

He said, "I'm Henry Paige, Mrs. Dooley. My firm represents the company that insured Nina Schmall. I wonder if you'd be kind enough to help me a moment?"

"How?"

"Just a few routine questions. There was a double indemnity clause in the policy on her life, you know. When that's the case, there sometimes are things that have to be cleared up."

"Well . . . oh, what the hell, come on in. I doubt if I can help you but come ahead. I don't really know much about any of it." She led him to the kitchen, waved him to a chair, and said, "Coffee?"

"Thanks. Just black." He sat down beside a cluttered

table. When she joined him, steaming cups in hand, he said, "I suppose you were shocked by what happened. Was Nina Schmall a reckless person? I mean, did she make a habit of doing things like keeping a radio in a wet basement?"

"Not at all. She was a wimpy little thing, afraid of her own shadow. And her basement wasn't wet. At least it wasn't when I used to go over."

"Used to? Haven't you been there lately?"

"Not in months. We hadn't gotten along recently."

Paige decided to play all his cards. "Because of the affair you were having with her husband?"

Molly Dooley blinked, then gave a terse laugh. "Now, where did you hear that? Wait, don't tell me. Old lady Hunnicutt across the street, right?"

"It, uh, well, seems to be common knowledge."

"Common is right. Okay, so there's no point in denying it. Sure, Karl played me for a sucker and I was dumb enough to fall for his line. He turned out to be a louse, but he's always had what you'd call charm." She paused, cheeks flushing. "Even with statuesque blondes."

"I heard about that, too. Do you know her name?"

"I can't see what any of this has to do with Nina's insurance. But sure, I know her name. Monica Hunter and she's—if you can believe it—a basketball coach at some high school around here." Molly Dooley gave a contemptuous snort, then repeated, "A basketball coach!"

"Girls' basketball is a big thing," said Paige. "They draw some real crowds for the tournament. Your, uh, relationship with Karl Schmall broke up your marriage, didn't it?"

"Has the FBI got a dossier on me or what? Since you already know, why ask?"

Paige cleared his throat. "Just confirming. Was the divorce your husband's idea?"

"No, mine. I was led to believe that . . . well, that it wouldn't be the only one. David, my husband, didn't even know what was going on, but then he always did live off in a world of his own. He fought against the divorce and still hasn't accepted it. He'd come back in a minute if I'd have him."

"What does he do? Work, I mean."

"He's what they call a computer technician. It's the only thing he cares about except having someone provide the comforts of life so he can spend all his time playing with his toys."

"When did you find out about Monica Hunter, Mrs. Dooley?"

"A month or so ago. Look, are you going to ask me any questions about Nina Schmall or not?"

"Was her death an accident?"

Molly Dooley's eyes narrowed. "You don't know that by now? You mean that's why you're nosing around?"

After settling on the stool next to McKelvey, Paige gave a dispirited sigh. "I met some beautiful people today, Mac. Before I came over I stopped by the apartment and took a shower, but I still can smell my day. Now I've got to go back out tonight and talk to Karl Schmall. I'm not supposed to, but I am."

"What do you mean you're not supposed to?"

"Because he's the plaintiff in a suit my firm is defending. I shouldn't talk to him without his lawyer's permission."

"You know, Paige, you used to be a pretty good private eye, with pride and resourcefulness. Now look at you. A Milquetoast who sold his soul to a pack of jackals for thirty pieces of silver every Friday afternoon."

"I said I'm going out to see Schmall, didn't I?"

McKelvey laughed. "Yes, and you'll find him a real piece of work. From what I picked up around his office, he's Greater Akron's premier womanizer. I mean, I like the girls as well as the next guy, but this Schmall doesn't even recognize them as such. 'Scores,' I think that's the term he would use. Spoils it for the rest of us, know what I mean? I've never laid eyes on the guy, but already I know enough about him to relish the thought of seeing him boiled in oil. Could it be arranged, do you think?"

"His latest is a basketball coach."

"So I heard. My God, Henry, remember the good old

days when we used to date secretaries and waitresses and registered nurses? Can you imagine telling somebody, 'This is my girl the basketball coach'? But that isn't why he's putting the moves on her."

"What's that supposed to mean?"

"She's a *rich* basketball coach, Henry. A suntanned, outdoor All-American girl whose father happens to hold controlling interest in one of the bigger polymer firms in town."

"You're just surmising that's the reason."

"Sure. And I'm surmising the sun will set in the west about an hour from now. They say she's a real looker, but that isn't the cause of Schmall's interest. Bet on it, pal."

Paige sighed again. "The detective who went out when Nina Schmall was electrocuted said the concrete floor was wet from a leaky hose on the washer. It had a hole in it, but he said there was no reason to suspect foul play."

McKelvey grunted disdainfully. "The Indians blew another one today. Three errors in the bottom of the ninth. Do you suppose this cop would rule out foul play?"

Paige ran words through his mind, searching for one that would best describe Karl Schmall. He settled on oily. Schmall's gray suit was a little too stylish, his razor-cut hair a little too neat, his smile a little too perpetual. Paige pictured him trying to claw his way out of a manure vat.

Schmall was saying, "Be my guest if you want to look around the basement. I haven't been down there since the day it happened."

"Just routine," Paige murmured as he followed Schmall to a door opening off the kitchen. He went down the rickety steps alone.

The concrete floor was dry. He examined a plastic hose that was disconnected and draped over a stationary tub. It looked to him like the hole had been made with an ice pick. He dropped the hose and picked up a table model radio dating to the 1950s. He turned it over, read a label taped to the bottom, decided the radio was pretty much like any other from that period. After wrapping the cord around the white plastic cabinet, he carried it back upstairs.

Schmall was waiting in the kitchen. Paige patted the radio while saying, "No reason you'd object to my taking this for a few days?"

Schmall hesitated, then said, "Be my guest."

"I saw your sticker on the cabinet, Walt," Paige said to the sandy-haired man his own age standing behind the counter. "Can you tell me how long ago you worked on it?"

Walt studied the radio a moment, frowning, then went to a file drawer and came back holding a card. "Five months ago," he said. "Did the work myself."

"I didn't realize you made any repairs these days. You've always told me you're nothing but a bookkeeper since transistors and printed circuits came along."

"Except when an old-timer like this comes in. I grab every one of these babies for myself. The young guys don't like 'em, but I'd be happy if we got ten a day like it. We don't see many, though, and as often as not the owner decides to junk those we do get when he finds out what it'll cost. My God, Henry, do you know the price of tubes today for these old sets? A crime, that's what it is, a damn crime. That's why I have every used tube I can lay hands on stored in the back room to sell at half price."

"I guess you know what happened with this set?"

"Sure I know. I was expecting someone to come around about it, but no one did 'til now."

"Why were you expecting it?"

"Been watching too much TV, I guess. Figured the police would want it checked out by an expert. Or if they handled it themselves, that they'd at least want to talk to me about it, since it carried my sticker."

"Everybody accepted it as an accident, Walt. They let it go at that. Can you give it the once-over for me?"

Walt pulled off the tuning and volume control knobs, then used a nutdriver to remove four chassis bolts. As he slid the chassis from the cabinet he said, "I've already checked one thing, Henry. Let me check one more."

He went to a workbench and returned with a small

multimeter. After switching a knob to a new setting, he held the two probes together, made an adjustment, then placed the probes on opposite sides of a small part. The needle on the meter flopped over to zero.

Walt set the meter aside and looked at Paige. "Shorted line-bypass condenser. The young guys call them capacitors, but they were just plain old condensers in my day."

"You say it's shorted? What exactly does that mean?"

"It means this set is a potential killer under the right conditions. It's an *AC-DC* model with a hot chassis, Henry. If this condensor shorts out, one side of the line voltage goes right to it."

"Then that's what caused the accident?"

Walt shook his head. "Under normal conditions the user wouldn't suspect anything was wrong, because shorting out the line-bypass condenser has no effect on operation. And when you're wet, even just your feet, the body's natural resistance drops to practically nothing. But even then someone standing on a concrete floor, which would make them part of the circuit to ground, would have one final protection—plastic knobs. That's all they'd touch."

Paige picked up one of the knobs, then gave Walt a questioning look. "This seems like metal to me, Walt."

"It is metal. Both of them are. That's what I meant when I said I'd checked one thing even before I pulled the chassis."

"Let me make sure I understand," said Paige. "With wet feet on a concrete basement floor and a shorted line-bypass condenser and a metal knob you have . . ."

"You have the one-ten line voltage hitting a body that's grounded and without its natural resistance. In this case, Henry, I'd say you have murder."

"Murder? How do you figure that?"

"Dammit, Henry, I've been fooling around with radios for better than half a century, and I've survived in a competitive business for nearly forty years now. Do you think I could have done it using cheap discount-house parts and letting an AC-DC set go out of the shop with metal knobs?"

"Cheap parts?"

Walt pointed to the one in question. "Look at this thing. An old paper condenser, and a cheap one at that. I don't know where you'd even go to find one like it today. You know why it's in here? Because you can short one out deliberately if you have a reason." He held out the card he'd gotten from a drawer. "And look here. Two years ago I replaced the line-bypass condenser. But not with this one. And when this set left the shop four months ago, you'd better believe it didn't go out the door with metal knobs on it."

Jack McKelvey finished his beer, then banged the green Rolling Rock bottle on the bar for another. When it was in front of him he faced Paige. "So now what? Going to turn it back over to the cops?"

"Before long. First I want to talk to Schmall again. And Molly Dooley, too. To tie up the loose ends for my report, I think I'll talk to her ex-husband and the other woman—what's her name, Monica Hunter?"

"But obviously Schmall's the guilty party?"

"I'm not sure, Mac. Except for the insurance money, I don't see a motive."

McKelvey made a snorting sound. "How many motives do you normally require, Paige? Fifty thousand smackers or even twenty-five would go a long way toward roping in a shapely blonde with access to really big bucks. That's not motive enough to satisfy you?"

Monica Hunter was everything they had said she would be. Even so, Paige decided she wasn't for him. There was a hardness about her that he didn't care for. Not that it mattered anyway, of course. Still he was a little disappointed.

"For some reason," he said, "I had the impression you knew Karl Schmall before his wife's death."

"As I told you, we met at the funeral home. Nina and I went to school together, so I stopped during calling hours."

"I hate calling hours. Funerals, too, for that matter."

"So do I, but I wanted to pay my respects."

On his way out Paige was thinking how thrilled Nina would have been over the way Monica Hunter went about it.

"You have it figured all wrong," David Dooley told Paige. "Schmall was nuts about his wife. What happened really hurt him. Hurt him bad."

Paige studied the gangly, thin-lipped man of forty or so. His words had taken Paige by surprise. He said, "How about, uh, him and your wife? I mean that doesn't look like he was so crazy about his own does it?"

Dooley gave a humorless laugh. "Molly didn't mean anything to Schmall. Just another woman, that's all. Somebody like him plays the field, but it doesn't mean he isn't satisfied with what he's got at home. What happened to his wife, it tore him all apart inside."

"Maybe you're right," said Paige. He covered a yawn with his hand, then stood up to leave. In passing he nodded toward a partially disassembled computer Dooley had been working on when he arrived. "Never could figure those things out. Not even how to use the one down at the office."

Dooley was sneering. "A lot of old people like you are that way. Learning is the easiest thing in the world, but not if you're scared."

Paige, halting when his hand was on the doorknob, turned to look back at Dooley. "But your wife, she didn't take what was going on with Schmall as casually as he did, right?"

Dooley angrily shook his head. "He had her buffaloed all the way. A guy like that takes another man's woman away from him and has his fun, then forgets her. His type doesn't give a damn about what happens afterwards, and they never figure the same thing can happen to them. Then when it does, like with Schmall, it rips them all apart."

Paige sipped at the cup of coffee Molly Dooley had given him, finding it too weak for his taste. For a moment he tapped the fingers of his free hand on her kitchen table, then put the cup back on its saucer and pushed it aside, shaking his head. "This whole business really has me confused. People seem to think Karl Schmall was in love with his wife. I've heard he . . . uh, well, might fool around on the side, but really loved her very much."

Molly Dooley laughed. "Who told you that nonsense? Deep down Karl never in his whole life gave a damn about anybody but himself. Love Nina? He was bored out of his mind with her."

"When did you decide he never cared about anyone but himself? I mean, you couldn't have believed that all along."

"Of course I believed it all along," she said. "I was just stupid enough to think it would be different with me. I should have known men are all alike."

"All alike? You're not saying your ex-husband ran around, too?"

"I don't mean alike that way. I mean selfish, only caring about themselves. Looking out for number one. Dogs in the manger, all of them."

Paige chuckled quietly. "Maybe I should have had that coffee tested before I drank it."

She shook her head, smiling a little. "I didn't mean you. Maybe at one time, but now you're too, uh . . ."

"Old? I have a friend you should meet. He's seventy-five, but he'd be chasing you around the table."

"Actually I didn't mean *all* men. It's just an expression, something you say. You know what I mean." She glanced at a clock over the sink. "Do you always work this late?"

"Not when I can help it. Do you happen to have a key to the Schmall house?"

"Don't tell me you're planning to sneak in there?"

"You never can tell. Do you?"

"As a matter of fact, yes. That's it on the nail by the door. We exchanged them not long after they moved in so we could check on things when one or the other was on vacation, stuff like that. We never got around to giving them back after . . . oh, you know."

It was early afternoon when Paige eased his dark blue Chrysler Fifth Avenue into the space reserved for him in the parking deck behind the two buildings connected by the Orangerie Mall in downtown Akron. He used a handkerchief to wipe away a spot of something greasy on the chrome grillwork. Satisfied, he went to the elevator and on to the law offices of Layne, Roth, Blades and Hanley. For months he had been the investigator for the firm but still regretted giving up his private detective agency just so he could go on eating.

Lou Roth was standing in the doorway of Ron Blades' private office. As usual when Paige came in any time after nine A.M. Roth looked at him, then checked his watch. Paige, as usual, didn't bother telling him he had worked late the past two nights and even after taking the morning off would clock well over forty hours for the week.

Blades smiled from the chair behind his mahogany desk. "Hello, Henry. Finding anything I can use on that Schmall case?"

"There's one more thing to do on it this evening. I think I've got it figured out."

"That isn't what he asked you," Roth said peevishly. "He wants to know if you have anything he can use."

Paige looked past him to Blades. "I'll give you my report in the morning, Ron."

He went back to the elevator and down to the ground floor. A band was playing so he followed the sound to the brick plaza in front of the building. Sirens blared as policemen on motorcycles escorted a car north on Main Street, then turned onto Mill and stopped at the curb. A girl of twelve or thirteen stepped out of the car, smiling self-consciously as a public address announcer introduced her as the Soap Box Derby champion from Anderson, Indiana. The crowd applauded.

Paige watched for a moment, then turned away. Girls in the Soap Box Derby, think of that. How times have changed. And now they assembled the cars from kits so it was hard to tell one from another. He thought back to some of the homemade clunkers that had run the long course at Derby Downs the first year he had entered the city race in Akron. If there had been a resemblance between any two of them it wasn't by intention. No, it wasn't much like 1937 anymore, but he decided he would go out to the track at the airport even so. It just wouldn't seem right, sitting alone in the apartment on All-American Soap Box Derby weekend.

Corinne had always wanted to go. The parade and the pageantry, the celebrities, the excitement of the race, she had enjoyed it all. Paige went back inside and on to the parking deck. There was nothing important to do until evening. He decided to drive out to the cemetery.

David Dooley was scowling. "Back again, huh? What is it this time?"

Paige waited until they were inside before saying, "I finally have all the pieces put together. It reminds me of a book I read a long time ago. This fellow was out for revenge, but instead of killing the people he was after he killed the ones they loved the most. He figured that would hurt them more than dying. But maybe you were wrong about Schmall."

"What are you talking about?"

"Maybe Karl Schmall didn't really love his wife the way you thought he did. It could be you did him a favor by killing her. I have an idea you were dead wrong thinking it would break him all up the way you told me it did. Did you know he found a replacement for her before her body even left the funeral home? Fixing up that radio was no problem for somebody with your knowledge of electronics, and getting in the house whenever you wanted was easy enough for you, but you were wasting your time. Mr. Dooley, you murdered an innocent woman and didn't accomplish a thing by it."

"Do you get a bonus for something like this?" McKelvey asked.

Paige shook his head. "Why should I? The insurance company has decided to go ahead and pay off since it wasn't an act of God, it didn't happen in war, and the victim wasn't really negligent. So now the firm won't make much money on it. Nothing like it would have if the case had gone to trial."

"So aside from solving a murder no one realized *was* a murder, or even much cared, what did you accomplish except costing the people you work for a lot of dough?"

Paige smiled. "That's what one of the partners said. Lou Roth, he said all I've done since they hired me is cost them money. He thinks they should fire me."

"Maybe he's right. I mean if you do this kind of thing all the time, you could break up a thriving law practice."

"Maybe you should get together with Lou Roth."

"Maybe I should. Let's have dinner first, though. On me. That fifty bucks you gave me for helping out is burning a hole in my pocket."

"I'm surprised you haven't spent it already on one of your lady friends."

"Truth is I had a date lined up for tonight. She came down with the vapors so I'm taking you to dinner instead."

"Okay, if that's what you want. But it has to be a place with windows. Mac, have you ever noticed how many rooms don't have windows these days?"